D0005758

THE ORACLE

VALERIO MASSIMO MANFREDI is professor of classical archaeology at the Luigi Bocconi University in Milan. He has carried out
a number of expeditions and excavations in many sites throughout the Mediterranean, and has taught in Italian and international
universities. He has published numerous articles and academic
books, mainly on military and trade routes and exploration in the
ancient world.

He has published nine works of fiction, including the 'Alexander'
trilogy, translated into twenty-seven languages in forty-two countries.

He has written and hosted documentaries on the ancient world
transmitted by the main television networks, and has written fiction
for cinema and television as well.

He lives with his family in the countryside near Bologna, Italy.

Also by Valerio Massimo Manfredi

ALEXANDER: CHILD OF A DREAM

ALEXANDER: THE SANDS OF AMMON

ALEXANDER: THE ENDS OF THE EARTH

SPARTAN

THE LAST LEGION

THE TALISMAN OF TROY

THE TYRANT

VALERIO MASSIMO MANFREDI

THE ORACLE

Translated from the Italian by Christine Feddersen-Manfredi

PAN BOOKS

First published 2005 by Pan Books
an imprint of Pan Macmillan Ltd
Pan Macmillan, 20 New Wharf Road, London N1 9RR
Basingstoke and Oxford
Associated companies throughout the world
www.panmacmillan.com

ISBN 0 330 43792 5

First published in Italian 1990 as *L'Oracolo* by
Arnoldo Mondadori Editore S.p.A., Milano

1 3 5 7 9 8 6 4 2

A CIP catalogue record for this book is available from
the British Library.

Typeset by SetSystems Ltd, Saffron Walden, Essex
Printed and bound in Great Britain by
Mackays of Chatham plc, Chatham, Kent

For Christos and Alexandra Mitropoulos

My name is Nobody: mother, father and friends, everyone calls me Nobody.

Homer, *Odyssey* IX, 366–7

1

Ephira, north-western Greece, 16 November 1973, 8 p.m.

THE TIPS OF the fir trees trembled suddenly. The dry oak and plane leaves shuddered, but there was no wind and the distant sea was as cold and still as a slab of slate.

It seemed to the old scholar as if everything around him had suddenly been silenced – the chirping of the birds and the barking of the dogs and even the voice of the river, as if the water were lapping the banks and the stones on its bed without touching them. As if the earth had been shaken by a dim, deep tremor.

He ran his hand through his white hair, thin as silk. He touched his forehead and tried to find within himself the courage to face – after thirty years of obstinate, tireless research – the vision he had sought.

No one was there to share the moment with him. His workers, Yorgo the drunk and Stathis the grumbler, had already left after having put away their tools, their hands deep in their pockets and their collars turned up. Their footsteps on the gravelly road were the only sound to be heard.

Anguish gripped the old man. 'Ari!' he shouted. 'Ari, are you still there?'

The foreman rushed over: 'I'm right here, Professor. What is it?'

But it was just a moment's weakness: 'Ari, I've decided to stay a little longer. You go on to town. It's dinner time, you must be hungry.'

The foreman looked him over with a mixture of affection and protectiveness: 'Come with me, Professor. You need to eat something and to rest. It's getting cold, you'll catch your death out here.'

'No, I'll just be a little while, Ari. You go on ahead.'

The foreman walked off reluctantly, got into the service car and headed down the road to town. Professor Harvatis watched the car's lights slash the hillside. He then went into the little tool shed, resolutely took a shovel from its hook on the wall, lit a gas lamp and started towards the entrance to the building which housed the ancient Necromantion: the Oracle of the Dead.

At the end of the long central corridor were the steps that he had unearthed over the last week. He started down, going much deeper than the sacrifice chamber, and ended up in a room still cluttered by the dirt and stones that hadn't been cleared away. He looked around, sizing up the small space that surrounded him, and then took a few steps towards the western wall until he was in the centre of the room. His shovel scraped away the layer of dirt covering the floor until the tip of the tool hit a hard surface. The old man pushed aside the dirt, uncovering a stone slab. It was engraved with the figure of a serpent, the cold symbol of the other world.

He took the trowel from his jacket pocket and scraped all around the slab to loosen it. He stuck the tip of the trowel into a crack and prised up the slab by a few centimetres, then flipped it back. An odour of mould and moist earth invaded the small chamber.

A black hole was open before him, a cold, dark recess never before explored. By anyone. This was the *adyton*: the chamber of the secret oracle. The place in which only a very few initiates had ever been admitted, with one purpose. To call up the pale larvae of the dead.

He lowered his lamp and saw yet more stairs. He felt his life quivering within him like the flame of a candle just before it goes out.

By night
our ship ran onward towards the Ocean's bourne,
the realm and region of the Men of Winter,
hidden in mist and cloud. Never the flaming
eye of Helios lights on those men
at morning, when he climbs the sky of stars,
nor in descending earthward out of heaven;
ruinous night being rove over those wretches.

He recited Homer's verses under his breath like a prayer: they were the words of the Nekya, the eleventh book of the *Odyssey*, recounting Odysseus's journey to the realm of the shades.

The old man descended to the second underground chamber and raised his lamp to see the walls. His brow wrinkled and beaded up with sweat: the lamplight danced all around him guided by his trembling hand, revealing the scenes of an ancient, terrible rite – the sacrifice of a black ram, blood dripping from his gashed neck into a pit. He stared at the faded figures, eaten away by the damp. He stumbled closer and saw that there were names, people's names, cut into the wall. Some he recognized, great persons from the distant past, but many were incomprehensible, carved in letters unknown to him. He stepped back and the lamplight returned to the scene of the sacrifice. More words escaped his lips:

With my drawn blade
I spaded up the votive pit, and poured
libations round to it the unnumbered dead:
sweet milk and honey, then sweet wine, and last
clear water; and I scattered barley down.
Then I addressed the blurred and breathless dead . . .

He walked to the centre of the chamber, knelt down and began to dig with his bare hands. The earth was cold and his fingers numb. He stopped to warm his stiffened hands under his armpits; his breath was fogging up his eyeglass lenses and he had to take them off to dry them. He began digging again, and his fingers found a surface as smooth and cold as a piece of ice; he pulled them back as if he had been bitten by a snake nesting in the mud. His eyes jerked to the wall in front of him; he had the sensation that it was moving. He took a deep breath. He was tired, he hadn't eaten all day: an illusion, certainly.

He plunged his hands back into the mud and felt that same surface again. Smooth, perfectly smooth. His fingers ran over it, all around it, clearing off the mud as best he could. He brought the lamp close. Under the brown earth, the cold, pale glitter of gold.

He dug with fresh energy, and the rim of a vase soon appeared. A Greek crater, incredibly beautiful and minutely crafted, was buried in the dirt at the exact centre of the room.

His hands moved quickly and expertly and, under the feverish digging of his long, lean fingers, the fabulous vase seemed to emerge from the earth as if animated by an invisible energy. It was very, very ancient, entirely decorated with parallel bands. A large medallion at the centre was engraved with a scene in relief.

The old man felt tears come to his eyes and emotion overwhelm him: was this the treasure he'd been searching for his whole life? Was this the very core of the world? The hub of the eternal wheel, the centre of the known and the unknown, the repository of light and darkness, gold and blood?

He put down the lamp and stretched his trembling hands towards the large glittering vase. He closed his hands around it and lifted it up to his face, and his eyes filled with even greater stupor: the medallion at the centre depicted a man on foot armed with a sword, with something raised to his shoulder: a long handle . . . or an oar. Facing him was another man, dressed as a wayfarer, who lifted his hand as if to question him. Between them, an altar, and next to it three animals: a bull, a ram and a boar.

Great God in heaven! The prophecy of Tiresias engraved in gold before his eyes, the prophecy which announced Odysseus's last voyage . . . The voyage that no one had ever described, the story that had never been told. A journey over dry land, an odyssey through mud and dust towards a forgotten land, at a great distance from the sea. To a place where people had never heard of salt, or of ships, where no one would recognize an oar, and could mistake it for a winnow, a fan used for separating the chaff from the grain.

He turned the great vase over in his hands and saw other scenes; they leapt to life, animated by the lamplight dancing on their surface. Odysseus's last adventure, cruel and bloody, in fulfilment of a fate he could not escape . . . forced to travel so far from the sea, only to return to the sea . . . to die.

Periklis Harvatis held the vase against his chest and raised his eyes to the northern wall of the *adyton*.

It was open.

Dumbfounded, he found himself facing a narrow opening, an impossible, absurd gap in the inert stone. It must have always been there, he reasoned, perhaps he just hadn't noticed it in the wavering light of the lamp. But deep inside, he realized with merciless certainty that he had somehow forced open that dim, threatening aperture. He took a few steps forward, still holding the vase, and picked up a little stone. He threw it into the opening. The stone was swallowed up without making a sound, neither when he hurled it nor after.

Was the abyss without end?

He moved forward to put an end to these dark imaginings. 'No!' he roared out, with everything he had in him. But his voice did not sound at all. It imploded within him, obliterating every scrap of strength. He felt his legs collapsing as he was invaded by intense cold, overwhelmed by crushing pressure. That hole was stronger than anyone and anything, it would suck up and devour any living energy.

But how could he turn back now? What meaning would his life have? Hadn't he been pursuing, for years and years, the proof for his theories, so often ridiculed? He was still in the real world, after all. He would go forward. He held out the lamp with one hand and gripped his treasure to his chest with the other.

He stepped forward, willing himself to believe that his hand would meet the wall, but he was wrong. His thin fingers stretched into nothingness, the lamplight shrank into a tiny point. That point revealed all that he had vaguely sensed for years and years. And this flash of understanding drained the very life from his veins.

He shrank back, horrified and weeping, and fumbled for the opening to the tunnel that had brought him to the threshold of the abyss. He dragged himself towards the stairs. The vase had become intolerably heavy but he couldn't let go. He would rather die clutching it to his chest, go out in glory, have the last laugh.

He backed up again and stumbled; the wall dissolved in the halo cast by the lamp. As he made his way in its feeble light, he felt his heartbeat weakening, becoming slower and slower. He finally found the bottom step and pulled himself, gasping, to the upper chamber. With immense effort, he pushed the slab back over the opening and covered it with dirt. He picked up the vase and hobbled to the tool shed.

He couldn't stand the sight of it an instant longer. He covered it convulsively with a blanket from the cot. Struggling, he found a sheet of paper and a pen and began to write. He put the letter into an envelope, wrote an address and sealed it. He knew he was dying.

ARI SLOWLY SIPPED his Turkish coffee and smoked a cigarette, tipping the ashes into the remains of his meal still in the dish in front of him. He glanced at the road with each drag. The last diners had gone, and the tavern owner was busy cleaning up. Every now and then he'd walk over to the window and say, 'Looks like rain tonight.' He turned the chairs over on to the tables and wiped the floor with a wet rag. The telephone rang, and he set down the broom and picked up the receiver. He paled and gasped with the phone still in his hand, glancing over at Ari, who was smoking. He stuttered: 'Ari, come quickly . . . O my Lord, O most Holy Virgin . . . get over here, it's for you.'

Ari jumped to his feet and picked up the phone: a death

wheeze on the other end, pleading interrupted by sobs, the voice
– nearly unrecognizable – of Professor Harvatis. He flicked away
the cigarette butt burning his fingers and ran to the car. He
raced back up towards the excavation tool shed, where he could
still see a light on. Wheels skidding as he entered the courtyard,
he jumped out, leaving the engine running. He grabbed an axe
from the trunk of the car and approached the half-open door,
poised to defend himself. He kicked it open and found the
professor: curled up in a corner of the room, near the telephone
table, with the receiver still swinging next to his head.

His face was deathly pale and carved by deep wrinkles, his
body was shaking uncontrollably. His legs were stretched out on
the floor as if paralysed and his hands clutched a shapeless bundle
to his chest. His eyes, veiled with tears, flickered back and forth,
as if his mind, invaded by panic, could no longer control their
movements.

Ari dropped the axe and knelt down next to him: 'My God,
what has happened? Who did this to you?' He reached out
towards the bundle. 'Here, let go, give it to me . . . I'm taking
you to the hospital in Preveza.'

But Harvatis clutched the bundle even tighter. 'No. No.'

'But you've been hurt, dear Mother in heaven, come on, in
the name of God . . .'

Harvatis half closed his eyes: 'Ari, listen, do as I say . . . you
have to do as I say, understand? Take me to Athens, right away,
now.'

'To Athens? Not over my dead body . . . you should see
yourself! Here, let me help you.'

The old professor's stare turned suddenly hard, sharp, his
voice peremptory: 'Ari, you must absolutely do as I say. There's
a letter on the table. You must take me to Athens, to the address
that's on the envelope. Ari, I've got no one left to me. No family
and no friends. What I found under there is killing me. And
maybe many others will die this very night, understand? There's
someone I have to see; I must tell him what I've discovered. To
ask him for help . . . if it's possible . . . if we're still in time.'

Ari looked at him, completely disconcerted: 'Good God, Professor, what on earth are you saying? . . .'

'Ari, don't betray me. For whatever in life is dearest to you, Ari, do as I say . . . do as I say.' The foreman lowered his head, nodding. 'If I should . . . die before we get there, you deliver the letter.'

Ari nodded again. 'Give me that bundle at least, let me put it in the car.' He shook his head. 'What is it, anyway?'

'Take it to the storeroom in the basement of the National Museum. The key's in my jacket pocket.'

'Whatever you say, Professor, don't worry, I'll do what you want me to do. Here, let me help you.' He picked the old man up like a child and eased him on to the back seat of the car. He took a last look before closing the door: the old man would never make it to Athens. He had seen death in the face. A goner if he'd ever seen one.

He went back to the tool shed, hung up the phone, picked up the letter and took a quick look around. Everything was perfectly in place – there was no hint that anyone had broken in; a familiar smell of onion and olive oil permeated the air. Had the old guy just suddenly gone crazy? And where had he found that thing he wouldn't let go of? He would have liked to check out the excavation area, but the professor was dying out there in the back seat of his car. He closed the door behind him and went back outside.

'Let's go, Professor. We're going to Athens. Try to rest . . . lie down . . . sleep, if you can.' He put the car into gear. The old man didn't answer, but Ari could hear his laboured, faltering breathing. And feel his desire to keep an impossible appointment, in Athens.

The car sped down the deserted streets of the town, and the tavern owner, from behind the dirty windows of his place, saw it shoot by in a cloud of dust down the road to Missolungi. The next day he'd have a strange story to tell his first customer.

Athens, 16 November, 8.30 p.m.

'Claudio, it's late. I'm out of here ... What about you? We could get something to drink at the Plaka before we call it a night. There are these girls we met ...'

'No thanks, Michel, I'm not leaving yet. I have to finish up on these files. I've got to get this work out of the way.'

'You don't know what you're missing. Norman and I picked up a couple of Dutch dolls on a tour. We're going to take them for a drink at Nikos's and then maybe go to Norman's place in Kifissìa.'

'Not bad. So how do I fit in anyway – the odd man out?'

'Okay, okay, you're too much in love to think about having a little fun. What's up for tomorrow?'

'Oh right, Michel – I've heard that tomorrow there's something going on at the Polytechnic, something big. There's going to be a huge protest demonstration against the government and the police. The students' committee is talking about a lock-in. They say that the situation in the university has become impossible. Police infiltration, spies ... people disappearing and you never find out what happens to them.'

'Who told you, Heleni?'

'Yeah, it was her. But it's stuff that everyone knows. Why?'

'Nothing. So what are you going to do, go to the Polytechnic yourself?'

'No. Why should I? We don't have anything to do with it. It's their thing. But I'm going to hang out here at the Institute tonight anyway. You know Heleni; she won't let them start anything without her ...'

'Okay. Well, see you here tomorrow, then. 'Night, Claudio.'

'Goodnight, Michel. Say hi to Norman.'

His friend left and he could soon hear the sound of his Deux-Chevaux as it coughed its way into motion.

Claudio Setti returned to the epigraphy files he had been working on. He stood up and walked over to the shelves to check a volume; as he was pulling it out a smaller booklet fell to his feet. He bent down to pick it up and gave it a look. The heading on the title page was:

PERIKLIS HARVATIS
Hypothesis on the necromantic rite in the *Odyssey*, Book XI

He started to read the first pages with growing interest, forgetting the files he was working on for his thesis, while a strange uneasiness crept up on him, a sense of confusion and solitude.

The phone rang. He stared at it at length before putting down the book and picking up the receiver.

'Claudio?'

'Heleni, honey, is that you?'

'*Agapimou*, you're still studying! Have you had dinner?'

'I thought I'd grab a sandwich and keep working.'

'I need to see you. I'm going back to the University tonight.'

'Heleni, please . . . don't go.'

'Can't you meet me here? I'm not far, at the Tò Vounò tavern. Please?'

'All right. I'll come. Have them fix me something to eat.'

He gathered up his notes to put them into his backpack. As he was about to close it, his gaze fell on the little book he'd left on the table. Too bad he couldn't finish it. He put it back on the shelf, switched off the lights and left, throwing his military-style jacket with the fake fur lining over his shoulders.

The streets were nearly deserted. He passed alongside the agora, where the ancient marble gleamed unnaturally white in the moonlight, and slipped down one of the roads in the intricate maze of the Plaka district. Every now and then, between the rooftops and terraces, the Parthenon loomed on his right, like a vessel of the gods shipwrecked on a cliff between the sky and the houses of men. He reached the old Wind Tower square where the tavern was.

He could see Heleni's black hair through the misty window. She was sitting alone with her elbows on the table and seemed to be watching the thin thread of smoke rising from her cigarette as it sat in the ashtray.

He walked in behind her and put his hand on her hair. Without turning, she took his hand and kissed it. 'I really wanted you to come.'

'You know I want to see you. It's just that I have to get this work done. I want to get my degree. I'm serious about that.'

'I know you're serious. They have *dolmades* tonight. I've told them to heat some up. Is that okay?'

'Sure, *dolmades* are fine.'

The girl nodded and a waiter brought two plates and a pan with the stuffed grape leaves.

'It's about tomorrow.'

'Heleni, what do you mean, it's about tomorrow? What's that supposed to mean?'

'We're going to make a proclamation on the University radio asking for a general strike. This government will have to drop their mask and show who they really are. Students at the universities of Salonika and Patras are going to rise up with us. We'll make such a racket that they'll hear us all over Europe!'

'Oh, Christ. Now she wants a revolution. "Darling, there's a revolution tomorrow." What time? Have you decided what time it's going to be?'

'Stop that. You're Italian, you're going to finish your thesis and go back home. You'll find a job. It's hell here. Those pigs are strangling this country. They're selling it piece by piece, they're prostituting it. You know how many of my friends have suddenly dropped out of circulation because they took part in a protest or because they signed up for a political party—'

'Heleni, love, it'll never work, there's no hope. It's like South America here; the US don't want to run any risks, so they back the military and squash the left. There's no way out. It's useless, believe me.'

'Probably. Anyway, it's been decided. At least we can say we tried.'

'I suppose that the revolution can't do without you.'

'Claudio, what's wrong with you? Where have all your fine speeches about freedom and democracy gone? The inheritance of the ancient Greeks, Socrates and Pericles and all that other shit? You sound like you're on the state payroll, for God's sake!' She was excited. Claudio looked at her for a moment without speaking: God, she was as beautiful as Helen of Troy, scornful and proud. Small, slender hands and eyes as deep and black as the night sky, her T-shirt draped on her breasts like a sculpture by Phidias. He'd rather take her prisoner than let her be exposed to any danger.

'Heleni, what would I do if something happened to you? You know . . . you know I feel the same way you do . . . but I can't stand the thought of you risking your life in there. You've been occupying the University for three days now; the prime minister won't be able to keep the military out of it for much longer, even if he wanted to. They're going to strike hard, and fast, and the people won't be backing you up. They're too afraid, they have jobs and families to worry about, a long past and not much of a future . . .'

The girl smiled: 'Come on. There's nothing they can do to us. It's not like they're animals; they're not going to tear us to pieces! I told you, it's going to be a peaceful demonstration. No one will be carrying weapons.'

A street musician entered just then and started to play his bouzouki. Some of the regulars joined in to sing 'Aspra, kòchina, kìtrina . . .', a melody that Claudio and Heleni had sung many times with their friends and which seemed very touching to them just then. Heleni's eyes glistened: 'How often we've sung this one! It's still lovely, isn't it?'

'Heleni, listen, come away with me. We'll leave everything behind and go to Italy. We'll get married, find work, anything will do . . .'

The girl shook her head and her hair shaded her eyes, tossed lightly on her cheeks and neck. 'I've got a more exciting idea. Let's go to my house. Maria's at the movies with her boyfriend, they won't be back till after midnight. Let's make love, Claudio, and then you'll take me to the University. I can't miss tomorrow. It will be a great day, all the young people of this country rising up together. And I know our people are behind us; I haven't lost hope.'

They walked out on to the street and Heleni raised her eyes to the starry sky: 'It's going to be a beautiful day tomorrow.'

SHE STRIPPED IN front of him without hesitation and with none of the innate modesty she'd always shown. She let him look at her and desire her, proud of her beauty and her courage, sitting on the edge of the bed, illuminated by the soft light of the table lamp. Claudio knelt, nude and trembling, at her feet. He kissed her knees and lay his head on her lap as he caressed her hips. He leaned her back on to the bed and wrapped his arms around her, covered her with his broad chest and wide shoulders as if he wanted to make her part of his own body. But he felt the darkness of the night weighing on his back, crushing as a boulder, cold as a knife.

And he heard a distant sound like thunder, and the pealing of a bell.

His heart felt as though it would burst, and Heleni's heart beat against his, between her superb breasts, beautiful Heleni, amazing and gentle, more precious to him than life and as warm as the sun. No one could dissolve their embrace, no one could hurt her. She would always be his, no matter what happened.

They dressed sitting on opposite sides of the bed and then embraced again as if they could not bear to leave one another.

'Now take me,' said the girl. She had already prepared a bag with some clothes and a little food. Claudio helped her on with her jacket.

THE ENORMOUS VEHICLE surged forward, tracks biting into the asphalt, spewing out a dense cloud of black smoke from its exhaust pipes. It headed off roaring and clattering down the dark streets. From the wide gate of the barracks other tanks followed the first, turrets bristling with machine guns. They were dark and gleaming and they reflected the street lights. Behind the tanks were trucks loaded with soldiers in fighting order. They hunched silently on the benches, their helmets down over their eyes and guns on their laps. The officers wore taut expressions as they mutely inspected their soldiers' uniforms and equipment, eyes on their watches. Orders crackled over the radio, to be answered in monosyllables. They were setting out for a mission without glory.

They passed Eleusis and Piraeus and headed towards the city in two groups: one would arrive from the south, from Odòs Pirèos and Omonia Square, the other from the north, turning down Leofòros Patissìon at full speed and passing in front of the National Museum. A gust of wind blew the pages of a newspaper over the white stairs, between the tall Doric columns.

The last tank hauled up sideways at the Leofòros Alexandras intersection to block off traffic. The tank commander opened the turret and stretched out to take stock of the situation. His radio headset hung around his neck and his hands were stuck in his belt. Suddenly a car sped around the corner, headlights high and blinding. He pulled out his handgun in a split second and took aim. The car stopped just a few steps from the tank and a man got out, unshaven and haggard. He looked around, bewildered.

'Stop! Go no further!' shouted the officer. 'The centre of the city is blocked off. Turn back immediately.'

The man held his ground. 'Please,' he shouted back, 'let us pass. I have a very sick man in the car, I have to take him to the hospital.'

'Not this way. Take him to Abelokipi or Kifissìa.'

'But what's happening? What are you doing here?'

'I told you to get out of here. Don't make me repeat it,' the officer shouted irritably.

The man went back to his car and opened the back door: 'Professor . . . Professor, we can't get by. Soldiers are blocking off the whole area. Professor Harvatis, can you hear me? Answer me, please.'

Periklis Harvatis was lying on the back seat, his face half hidden by the collar of his jacket. He seemed to be in a deep sleep. Ari took his hand: it was icy cold.

'Professor, we can't go any further. It's all been useless. Oh my God . . . I'll take you to the hospital.'

He got back into the car and set off towards Kifissìa at full speed. He pulled up in front of the hospital there and ran over to the night-duty attendant's station. 'Hurry, hurry! For the love of God, there's a man in my car who is sick, very sick. Hurry, please, he may be dying.'

Two nurses followed him with a stretcher and they loaded the apparently lifeless professor on to it.

'It was no use coming to Athens,' Ari muttered disconsolately. 'Why did I listen to you?' But the old man could no longer hear him.

Ari went back to the car, took the letter out of his pocket and read the address: it was inside the area blocked off by the military, but he suddenly knew he couldn't hold on to it another minute. His watch said 2 a.m.; he was worn out with exhaustion and devastated by the futility of their journey through the night. But he had to see this through to the end.

He turned down Acharnòn Street in an attempt to proceed parallel to Patissìon Street where the tank garrison was. He had to get as close as possible without getting noticed. He parked in a little square and continued on foot, hiding in a doorway or behind the corner of a house when he saw a search patrol approaching. He couldn't understand what was happening. He finally got to the address written on the letter: 17 Dionysìou Street. It was an old building with chipped plaster and green blinds, but there didn't seem to be a living soul there. The shutter was completely lowered and padlocked at the bottom. The name of a print shop was displayed on the sign above. He felt like he was dreaming.

'Are you looking for someone?' A deep, hoarse voice behind him made him jump. He spun around and found a man of about fifty in a grey coat with a felt hat worn low over his eyes. He tried to make out the man's features, but the halo of a street light behind him made that impossible.

'I'm . . . looking for a man named Stàvros Kouras. I have to give him a letter. I thought he lived here, but all I can see is this closed shutter . . . it seems to be a print shop. Maybe you know . . .'

The man watched him silently, hands deep in his pockets. Ari felt his blood run cold.

'Stàvros Kouras doesn't exist, sir.' He took his right hand from his pocket and stretched it out. 'If you like, you can give me that letter.'

Ari backed up and banged against the shutter, shaking his head, then started to run as fast as he could, without once looking back. He reached his car and jumped in, switching on the ignition, but the car wouldn't start. He turned around to look at the street he'd come from but it was empty. He tried the key again and flooded the engine. The smell of gasoline was strong; he'd have to let it evaporate. He waited a couple of minutes and tried again. On his third try the engine finally spurted to life. He took a look at the rear-view mirror as he was backing up to turn into the street: just at that moment, far off down the road, the stranger he had spoken to turned the corner. He was walking slowly, his hands in his pockets.

CLAUDIO HUGGED HELENI again, then stepped back and looked her in the eye: 'There's nothing I can say to change your mind, is there? I have no influence over you at all.'

Heleni smiled and her eyes seemed to light up the night: 'Silly, you're the only one I care about.'

'And the revolution.'

'We've already discussed this whole thing and I've demonstrated that your objections don't hold water. Go home, honey, and go to sleep. Don't worry about me. If everything goes well, I'll come out again tomorrow night and we'll have an ouzo together at Nikos's.'

Claudio scowled: 'And what if things don't go well?'

'I'll find you, don't worry. You'll never be able to get away from me, for the rest of your days . . . you know that a Greek girl from a good family only gives herself to the man of her life.'

'I've made a decision. I'm coming in with you.'

'Claudio, stop that! Tomorrow you've got to turn in your paper. And this isn't your place anyway – you're not enrolled in this university, and you're not even Greek. Really, you should go now. I promise you that nothing will happen. I'll be careful. I won't do anything foolish. We'll have security people posted at the gates. I'll be inside with the committee working on our proclamation for the press.'

'Swear to me that you'll take care of yourself and that tomorrow night you'll be at Nikos's.'

'Promise. I swear.' She gave him a last kiss.

'And listen, I'll be at the Institute, right near the phone. Call me once in a while, if you can.'

'If they don't cut us off.'

'Right.'

'Ghià sou, krisèmou.'

'Ciao, my love.'

Heleni ran towards the University gates. Two boys and a girl were on guard duty near a little bivouac. They opened the gates to let her in. Heleni turned to wave and the fire lit up her excited face. She looked as if she were going to a party.

Claudio pulled up the collar of his jacket to ward off the cold wind blowing light and sharp from the north, and walked straight down Patissìon Street. The sky was clear and full of stars and it was already Saturday morning. Heleni was right: what could happen on such a beautiful night, just a day before Sunday?

He didn't feel like sleeping, and thought he'd walk over to Omonia Square where there was always a café open. Find a freshly printed newspaper and drink a good cup of Turkish coffee. Maybe he'd even find an Italian newspaper, like La Stampa – they'd been covering the student uprising on the front page, while Il Corriere hadn't even made mention of it yet.

He took a new pack of Rigas from his pocket and stopped

behind a street lamp to light a cigarette. When he raised his eyes, the quiet night air was suddenly rent by a roar, and a monstrous tank erupted rumbling from a side street, blinding him with its headlights. It made a complete turn, digging at the asphalt with its heavy tracks, and headed off roaring towards the University, followed by two trucks. Another tank was advancing fast from the other direction; a minute later it stopped in front of the Polytechnic, revolving the gun on its turret towards the colonnade of the atrium.

Claudio fell against the lamp-post, beating his fist against the icy metal, again and again until it hurt. Heleni was their prisoner.

He started running until his heart was close to bursting, racing down the maze of streets at the foot of Mount Licavittòs. He stopped, gasping for breath, and then started running again, aimlessly, until he found himself in the huge deserted space of Sintàgmatos Square. The Greek parliament: two *evzones* guards marched back and forth before the tomb of the unknown soldier. The gold and black of their jackets shone in the night and their white skirts fluttered in the wind. From this distance they seemed like puppets, like the toys crowding the tourist stalls in the Plaka. Behind them, the great marble warrior slept, naked, the sleep of death, and the words of a great man from the past engraved on the stone above him seemed blasphemous on that wretched night.

2

'I'M THE DOCTOR on duty. Who is it that you're looking for?'

'My name's Aristotelis Malidis. I'd like to know how the man I brought in an hour ago is doing. His name is Periklis Harvatis.'

The doctor picked up the phone and called up to the ward. 'I'm sorry,' he told him a short time later, 'the patient has passed away.'

Ari bowed his head and made the triple sign of the cross in the Greek Orthodox manner. 'May I speak with the doctor who admitted him? The professor had no relatives; I'm his assistant. He didn't have anyone else in the world.'

The doctor called up again. 'Yes, go on up. Ask for Dr Psarros, second floor.'

Ari took the elevator. He glanced at himself in the mirror inside: the bright light of the bulb rained on him from above, deeply carving his tired face and making him look very much older than he was. The door opened on to a long, neon-lit corridor. Two nurses were playing cards in a smoke-filled glass room, in front of an ashtray overflowing with butts. Ari asked for Dr Psarros and was brought to his office. On the doctor's desk was a radio playing classical music.

'My name is Malidis. I was the one who brought Professor Harvatis here an hour ago. I know he's . . . dead.'

'We did everything we could. But it was too late, he was too far gone. Why didn't you bring him sooner?'

Ari hesitated. 'What did he die of?'

'Cardiac arrest. Probably a heart attack.'

'Why do you say "probably"? Weren't the symptoms clear?'

'The cause of death was not entirely clear, no. Perhaps you can help us. Tell me how it happened.'

'I'll tell you what I know. Can I see him first?'

'Yes, certainly. The body is still in room number nine.'

'Thank you.'

Professor Harvatis was lying on a little bed with a sheet pulled up over him. Ari uncovered his face and could not hold back his tears – the signs of his ordeal still showed in his sunken temples, the black circles around his eyes, the tightness of his jaw. Ari dropped to his knees, pressing his forehead against the bed: 'I didn't find anyone at that address, Professor. You were mad to send me there, and perhaps I've gone mad as well. Oh God, my God, if only I hadn't listened to you, you'd still be alive now . . .' Ari got up, gently touched the professor's forehead and covered it again with the sheet. He looked up: Harvatis's clothes were folded on a chair and his jacket was hanging from a coat hook.

'There's something else I still have to do for you, Professor . . .' He glanced towards the door and then took down the jacket and started going through the pockets. He pulled out a small set of keys with plastic tags. He left the room and went towards Dr Psarros's office, but as he approached, he realized that the doctor was speaking on the phone.

'A man of about sixty who says his name is . . . Malidis, I think. Yes, all right, I'll try to keep him here on some pretext, but you get here as fast as you can. There's something unconvincing about all this. Yes, that's right, the second floor. I'll wait here, but hurry, please.'

Ari pulled back, looked towards the nurses' room, then walked softly towards the elevator. He took it down to the lobby, nodded at the front desk nurse and a few minutes later was back in his car, driving towards the centre.

The main entrance of the National Museum was on Leofòros Patissìon Street, now garrisoned by tanks. But he could still get

in through the service entrance on Tositsa Street. Incredibly, he
managed to park quite easily, near the door. He took the bundle
from the back seat, opened the service door using Professor
Harvatis's key, and went into the museum. He walked straight
towards the security booth and disconnected the alarm.

The total darkness of the rooms and corridors was pierced
here and there by the little safety lights on the switches. He
could faintly hear the echo of excited voices coming from
outside, over the background noise of the trucks and tanks
patrolling the area surrounding the University. He went into the
basement, found the storeroom and let himself in with the key.
The room was completely isolated, without an external window
or even a vent.

He switched on the light and placed the object that a man
had perhaps died for on the table. He removed the blanket
it was wrapped in, and the vase towered majestically in the
airless atmosphere of the underground room. Ari stared at it,
frozen with amazement: it was the most beautiful and the most
terrible thing he had ever seen, as disturbing as the frowning
mask of Agamemnon at Mycenae, as splendid as the golden
cups of Vafio, as lovely as the blue ships of Thera. It was absolutely perfect, as if its creator had just finished crafting it, with
just the slightest traces of dried mud and dust in its sculptured
relief.

'Would a man die for this?' He lay his hand on the embossed
surface, reading that unknown story with the tips of his fingers.
He didn't understand, and yet felt mesmerized by its power.
Then he wrapped the edges of the blanket around it again and
hid it.

He was deathly weary and griefstruck, confused and bewildered, and desired nothing but oblivion. Sleep, if only for a short
time. He found a corner of the room free of antique ceramic
fragments and tools, pulled over a bag of sawdust used for
cleaning, and collapsed on to it. The light flickered and went out
and he closed his eyes, but the great vase continued to gleam
behind his eyelids with blinding force.

THE GIRL GOT up, half naked, looking for the bathroom. She opened the medicine cabinet and popped an Alka-Seltzer in a glass of water. She watched the bubbles fizzing in the glass as the phone started to ring. She walked into the hall and picked up the receiver with one hand, her drink in the other: 'Hello?'

'Who the hell are you? Damn it, what are you doing there? Michel, Norman! Call them right away! Call them now, do you understand me?'

The girl was about to hang the phone up, annoyed, but Michel had awakened and was standing in front of her: 'Who is it?'

The girl shrugged and handed him the receiver, beginning to drink her hangover potion.

'Who is it?'

'Michel, for the love of God, get over here . . .'

'Claudio, is that you? What time is it? Where are you?'

'Michel, the army, tanks, they're attacking the Polytechnic! Please come right away, Heleni is in there, there's not a minute to lose!'

'All right, Claudio. Tell me exactly where you are.'

'In the telephone booth at Syntagmatos Square.'

'Okay. Don't move. We'll be there.'

'No, wait. Patissìon is blocked off, you won't get through. Take Hippokratous Street and try to go down Tositsa. I'll wait for you there, in the staff parking lot at the museum. But hurry, for God's sake, get here as fast as you can!'

'Okay, Claudio, we're coming right away.'

He dropped the receiver, ran to the hall and opened the door to the other bedroom. He turned on the light: Norman Shields and the girl he was sleeping with sat up in bed, rubbing their eyes. Michel grabbed Norman's clothes from a chair and threw them at him.

'The army is attacking the Polytechnic. Claudio's there, and he needs our help. We have to get over there now. I'll start up the car.'

The girl was following him around without understanding a

thing, glass still in hand: 'Would someone please tell me . . .' But Michel didn't even hear her. He pulled on some jeans and a sweater, stuck his bare feet into a pair of gym shoes, stuffed some socks into his pockets, grabbed his jacket and raced down the stairs, searching through all his pockets for his car keys.

The little Citroën started up without any trouble for once, and as he was backing out through the gate, Norman opened the passenger door and got in, still half dressed: 'Is it that bad? What did he say exactly?'

'The army is attacking the Polytechnic. They're using tanks.'

'But have they attacked or are they just blocking off the University? Maybe they just want to intimidate them.'

'I don't know. Claudio is out of his mind. We have to get over there.'

He took a curve at full speed, tilting the car dangerously and nearly toppling over Norman, who was tying his shoes. Norman muttered: 'Damn French cars. They make you seasick!'

Michel pressed down harder on the accelerator. 'They've got soft suspensions. There are lots of cobblestone roads in France. Listen, there should be some Gauloises in the glove compartment. Light one up for me, will you? My stomach hurts.'

THE OFFICER WALKED to the middle of the road and began to talk into a battery-run megaphone. His voice was fuzzy and nasal: 'You have fifteen minutes to clear the premises. I repeat, exit immediately and abandon the University. If these orders are not obeyed, we shall be obliged to take the building by force!'

The students were crowded into the courtyard behind the gate, bewildered and uncertain, watching the tanks and troops in battle gear. There was a moment of silence, in which only the threatening rumble of the M47s' engines could be heard.

Somebody rekindled the fire and a swarm of sparks rose upwards towards the sky. A youth with curly hair and just a shadow of a beard walked resolutely towards the gate and shouted at the officer: '*Molòn lavè!*' It was the phrase in ancient Greek that Leonidas had shouted proudly at the Persians twenty-five centuries before at Thermopylae, two words as dry and hard as bullets: 'Come and get us!'

Another drew up alongside and echoed him: '*Molòn lavè!*', then another and another still. They climbed up the bars of the gate and raised their fists rhythmically, and their cry became a chorus, a single voice vibrating with passion, with disdain, with determination. And the officer trembled at that voice and at those words that he had heard as a child at his school desk – the cry of Hellas against the barbarian invader penetrated into his chest like the stab of a knife. He looked at his watch and his men jerked their arms into position, ready to attack at his order.

He shouted again into the megaphone: 'This is your last warning. Disband immediately and clear out of the University buildings.' But the cry of the students was stronger and more powerful, and nothing could subdue them. Suddenly, from a nearby church, a bell pealed, solemn, persistent, grievous. Ringing out in alarm. Another bell answered from another bell tower, and that sound infused the youths with new energy and gave new vigour to their cry.

The fifteen minutes passed and their shouted words continued to afflict him, like fire raining down from the sky, mixing with the bronze thunder of the bells.

He looked again at his watch and at his men, undecided. Another officer, higher in rank, advanced and stood next to him. 'What are you waiting for? Go ahead, give the order.'

'But, Colonel, they're all over the gates.'

'They were warned. Their time is up. Proceed!'

The tank advanced towards the gate, but the students didn't move. The tank commander in the turret turned towards the colonel, who urged him on with a gesture of his hand. 'Forward, I said! Forward!'

The tank started up again and drove straight into the gate, which fell inward on impact. The students dropped to the ground in bunches and were crushed under the gate. The troops surged forward while still more youths flooded out of the building, attempting to put up opposition. The soldiers opened fire, aiming to kill, and the courtyard sounded with cries, moans and confused yelling as the frantic students searched for their friends, tried to assist the wounded. The boy with the curly hair lay on the ground in a pool of blood. Many raced, shouting, up the stairs, followed by their attackers who knocked them out with the butts of their rifles, stabbed them with their bayonets. Some sought shelter behind closed doors, but the soldiers broke through and rushed down the halls and into the classrooms, shooting wildly. Splinters of wood and chunks of plaster flew left and right. Flakes of plaster rained down from the walls and ceilings.

Michel's car was just arriving at the designated spot, but Claudio was nowhere to be seen.

'What do we do now?' asked Norman.

'Wait here. This is where we were supposed to meet. He must have gone in. If he comes out with Heleni, he'll need us and the car. We'll keep the engine running and stay ready. This is the only way he can come out.'

Claudio was inside the University, running from room to room in search of Heleni. He shouted her name down the halls, up the staircases. He saw her suddenly come out on a landing with a group of her comrades. A squad of soldiers appeared at that moment at the end of the corridor and their leader shouted: 'Stop! You're under arrest!' The youths ran towards a window, trying to drop down from it and get out that way. The officer shouted again, 'Stop!', and let go with a burst of machine-gun fire. Claudio saw Heleni stand motionless for an instant against the wall before a red stain spread over her chest, her legs crumpled and her eyes fluttered shut.

He raced up the stairs, indifferent to the shots, the shouts, the thick dust. He reached the girl an instant before she hit the floor. He lifted her up. The officer at the bottom of the stairs had pulled out his pistol and was aiming it at him. Claudio turned desperately to the left, to the right. He saw the door of an elevator and threw himself against it, hitting the call button with his elbow. The lift was right there and the door opened.

He dived in and closed the door just an instant before the butt of a rifle could block it. He pressed the ground floor button and the elevator jerked into service as numerous shots rang against the door. He dropped to the floor with Heleni in his arms while two, three bullet holes opened in the sheet metal and the sharp odour of gunpowder invaded the chamber. The elevator started to descend. As soon as the door opened on to the ground floor, Claudio ran out, carrying Heleni, unconscious and pale as death. She was covered with blood. The stairs resounded with the stamping of his pursuers' boots. He found himself in front of an open classroom and hid with the girl under the professor's desk. The soldiers entered, took a long look around, then ran off down the hall.

Claudio left the room and made his way towards the building's rear wing where he found the staff door unlocked. He ran out into the courtyard on Tositsa Street, flattened himself against the wall and waited until the street was clear.

He could hear more shooting, crying, howls of protest and rage, the roar of engines, vehicles burning rubber down Patission Street, harshly delivered orders. The revolt had been put down. Only the pealing of the bells continued to rip through the darkness of the night, obsessive and despairing.

He lay Heleni on the ground and ran towards the little gate that led on to the street. He opened it, turned back to get her and raced through the courtyard as fast as he could, nearly running into Norman and Michel. Claudio was unrecognizable. His eyes were red, his face burnt black and his clothing shredded. He held Heleni's motionless body in his arms and his shirt and jeans were soaked with her blood. When he saw his friends, he collapsed to his knees and managed to blurt out amidst his tears: 'It's me. Help me, please.'

ARI JERKED AWAKE at the tolling of the bells and the noise of the shooting, but he was so tired that he couldn't snap out of his slumber. It seemed like another one of the countless nightmares that had tormented his brief sleep. A stitch in his side woke him up fully and he got to his feet, rubbing the painful area. The woeful alarm sounded by the church bells was muffled in that underground chamber, making it even more unreal and ominous. He switched on the light and looked back towards the wall: the edges of the blanket had fallen off the vase and it gleamed brightly in front of him as cries of rage and pain and gunshots echoed outside. He covered it, knotting the corners well, and hid it hurriedly under a table, then headed towards the service exit. He heard a noise at the door. Someone was banging at it, trying to get it open. 'Who's there?' he asked. 'What do you want?'

'Open up, for the love of God, we're students. One of us is wounded.' Ari opened the door and several youths tumbled in: three boys, one of them carrying a girl who was unconscious and seemed seriously wounded.

'Ari, is that you?' said Michel. 'What luck. I thought you were at Parga with Harvatis.'

'Michel? I was in Parga, I just . . . I just arrived. But why have you come here? This girl has to be brought to the hospital immediately.'

Claudio approached him, clutching Heleni to his chest. She seemed to have regained consciousness; a low moan came from her mouth. 'She's been shot. If we take her to a hospital we'll all be arrested. You have to help us find a doctor . . . or a clinic that we can trust.'

Ari led them forward: 'Follow me, quickly.' They crossed the room with the Cycladic sculptures, reached the service stairs and descended into the basement. He opened the door of the storeroom. 'No one will come to look for you here,' he said. 'Wait for me, I'll be back as soon as I can. Try to stop the bleeding, if you can. She mustn't lose any more blood.' He left, pulling the iron door shut behind him.

'We should stretch her out,' said Claudio. They rearranged Ari's sawdust bed and lay Heleni down gently. Claudio carefully took off her jacket and unbuttoned her blouse, baring her shoulder.

Michel was close by: 'The wound is very high, the bullet may not have hit any vital organs. We have to staunch it.'

Claudio pulled a handkerchief from his pocket. 'This is clean; we can use this.'

Norman looked around. 'This is a restoration lab. There must be some alcohol somewhere.' He went through the cabinets and shelves, opening bottles of solvent and sniffing at them: 'Here, this is alcohol.'

Claudio soaked the handkerchief and cleaned the wound carefully. The girl trembled and cried out in pain. She opened her eyes and looked around bewildered: 'Claudio . . . Claudio . . . where are we?'

'We're safe, my love. Stay calm, you must be still. You've been wounded. We're going to take care of you. Now stay calm, try to rest.' Heleni closed her eyes.

Claudio ripped his shirt into strips and bandaged the wound as best he could. It had stopped bleeding.

'We have to keep her warm. We need a blanket.'

Michel started to take off his down jacket.

'Wait, there's a blanket,' said Norman, pointing to a large bundle under a table. He untied the corners and backed up in shock. 'My God! Look at this!' Claudio and Michel turned and saw the embossed golden vase, the figure of a warrior with an oar on his shoulder, the ram and the bull and the boar with its long tusks. The last bell of the revolt tolled its dying peal into the sky of Athens, full of stars and desperation.

Michel seemed stunned by the vision of the vase. He had stood up and was staring at the wonder which had so suddenly appeared out of nowhere. 'What is that? My God, I can't believe it. Claudio, what is it?'

Claudio was bent over Heleni and was holding her hand as if he could pass his warmth and his vigour into her still body. He turned slightly and saw the vase. For long moments, everything else seemed to fade away. The little book that had fallen at his feet at the archaeological school library flashed into his mind:

'Hypothesis on the necromantic rite in the *Odyssey*, Book XI.' He turned immediately back to Heleni.

'A fake if I ever saw one. Inspired by some verses from the *Odyssey*, maybe; the Nekya, the journey into the land of the dead . . .'

'But it's made of gold!' Michel stuttered.

'Good fakes are always made of the best materials . . . makes them more credible. It looks like an imitation of the Ugarit cups, same style. It can't be authentic. Give me the blanket.'

Norman lifted the vase and Michel slipped off the blanket, handing it to Claudio who arranged it around Heleni.

'What do we do with this?' asked Norman, setting the vase back on the table.

'Hide it,' said Claudio. 'It was hidden when we found it.'

'Yeah,' said Norman. 'Strange, isn't it? Looks like it was just unearthed. There are still traces of dust and mud on it.'

Michel ran his finger over the surface of the vase, rubbing a little of the sediment between his thumb and index finger.

'Blood.'

Norman started: 'What are you saying, Michel?'

'It's not mud. It's blood. Centuries old. Millennia old, maybe. It's so old it's turned to humus. I've seen it before in a sacrificial trench in the Plutonium of Hierapolis in Turkey. This vase was immersed in the blood of a great number of victims. It certainly comes from one of the great sanctuaries.'

Claudio shivered. 'Hide it,' he said, without taking his eyes off Heleni's face. Norman and Michel obeyed. They put it into an old cabinet in the corner of the room.

Ari came in shortly thereafter. 'You were right,' he said. 'The police are checking all the hospitals. Anyone going in with wounds or bruises is being arrested.'

Claudio turned towards him: 'Heleni needs help right away,' he said. 'I've staunched the wound, but she's feverish. She needs blood, and antibiotics. The bullet is probably still in her body.'

'In five minutes a taxi will come to the rear entrance; it will take you to a surgeon's office. He's a friend, he won't ask questions. But he'll need some medicine and supplies for the transfusion. Michel, you take your car and go buy the things on this list at the night pharmacy in Dimitriou Square, and bring them to the address I've written at the bottom. Does anyone know what blood type the girl is?'

'A-positive,' said Claudio. 'She's wearing a blood-donor medal.'

'Like me,' said Norman. 'I'll give her my blood.'

'Good. Let's not waste any more time. Come on, let's bring her outside.' He noticed the blanket that Heleni was wrapped in, looked under the table where the vase had been and then back at the boys.

'We couldn't find anything else,' blurted Michel.

Ari hesitated a moment, then said, 'You did the right thing. What did you do with it?'

Michel nodded towards the cabinet.

'Please don't speak with anyone about this. Please. It was discovered by Professor Harvatis. It was his . . . last discovery. He's dead now. Swear to me that you won't mention it to anyone.'

The boys all nodded.

'Let's go now,' said Ari, 'we have to take care of your friend.'

Norman and Claudio crossed their hands to form a makeshift seat and carried her to the taxi, which was already waiting with its engine running. Ari murmured the address to the taxi driver and the car sped off. Norman sat in front and Claudio, huddled into a corner of the back seat, held Heleni's head on his lap. He touched her forehead: it was ice cold.

Michel in the meantime was speeding in his little Deux-Chevaux down streets that were beginning to fill up with early morning traffic.

It seemed as if the pharmacist were expecting him: they gave him the things he asked for without a word. Michel paid and took off again immediately. He was careful to avoid the streets in the centre and not draw attention to himself. When he was sure he was out of danger he stepped on the accelerator. The address was not far now.

Just as he was about to turn left, a police car emerged unexpectedly from a side street, siren on and lights flashing. Michel thought he would die. The car passed him and signalled for him to pull over to the right. Michel did so and tried to stay calm.

The policeman took a look at the vehicle's French plates and approached the driver's side with his hand to the peak of his cap.

'Tò diavatirio, parakalò.'

Michel took out his driver's licence and passport.

'Oh, so you know Greek,' said the policeman.

'Yes,' said Michel. 'I speak your language a little. I'm at the French archaeological school in Athens.'

'A student, then. Well, well. Don't you know there is a fifty-kilometre speed limit here?'

'Oh, I'm sorry. I was going to pick up my professor at the station and I'm late. I didn't hear the alarm clock go off.'

The other policeman, the patrol car's driver, had got out and was walking around the Deux-Chevaux, looking inside. He suddenly approached his partner and whispered something into his ear. Michel was sweating, but tried to maintain a nonchalant air.

'Get out, please,' said the officer, suddenly quite serious.

'Listen, give me a break, I'm really late.' He put his hand on his wallet. 'If you can tell me how much I owe you for the fine ... See, if my professor gets here and he doesn't see me I'll be in a lot of trouble ...'

'Please. Get out.'

Michel got out of the car and stood in the middle of the street, wallet in hand.

One of the policemen took out a flashlight and started to search the car interior. He directed the beam of light at the back seat. A large bloodstain. Heleni's blood. Then he opened the pharmacy bag: bandages, a transfusion needle, xylocain, catgut, antibiotics.

'I'm afraid your professor will have to get a taxi,' he said with a sneer. 'You'll have to explain a few things to us, Mr Charrier.'

They took him to a large grey building nearby and led him down into the basement, locking him into an empty room. He waited, trying to make sense of what was going on, the muffled shouts, moaning, footsteps, doors slamming, comings and goings. When a man came to interrogate him, he told him that he would not say a word unless a representative of the French consulate were present.

But he did speak, almost immediately. Very few withstand the *falanga*. When the first blows hit the bare soles of his feet, he gritted his teeth, drawing on all the courage he had and all his affection for his friends, but the pain penetrated cruelly all the way to his brain, severing his will.

He shouted, he cried and he swore, and then wept disconsolately. The cramps that tore through every fibre of his being and every centimetre of his skin did not prevent him from realizing what he had done. He was conscious that he had already broken down, had already betrayed. And this knowledge was even more painful than the torture.

His persecutor struck calmly and precisely, as if he heard nothing. It seemed a job like any other, and he continued for a while, even after Michel had told everything he knew . . . everything. He seemed to want to punish him for allowing him to finish up so quickly.

The interrogator wiped his forehead, and then his hairy, sweaty chest, with a handkerchief. He said something into an intercom hanging from the ceiling and a plain-clothes policeman came to accompany Michel to an adjacent room. He stood at the threshold for a moment while they brought another young boy in, handcuffed, his face bruised, mouth full of blood and eyes terrified.

Michel tried to get up, but as soon as his feet touched the floor he collapsed, screaming with pain. Two policemen tied the other boy to the torture bed and removed his shoes and socks. They then picked Michel up bodily and took him out.

The door closed behind them with a sharp click. As Michel was dragged down the hall behind an officer, he could hear prolonged, suffocated moans, almost animal-like, coming from behind the closed door. He lowered his eyes as he stumbled and tripped to his destiny. They threw him on to an iron chair.

'Well,' said the officer, whose name tag identified him as 'Capt. Karamanlis'. 'Suppose you tell me all over again: who were you transporting in your car and where were you taking the medical supplies you had?'

'A friend of mine who was wounded at the Polytechnic last night. We were trying to help her.'

The man shook his head: 'How stupid of you. You should have brought her to a hospital. Or were you trying to hide something?'

'We had nothing to hide. We didn't want her to have to suffer what you just did to me. Or to that poor boy back there.'

'They are subversives; they deserve no compassion. They are the ruin of our country. You're a foreigner. You shouldn't have got mixed up in this. Now. You tell me everything you know, and we'll pretend we never saw you. No one will ever know who was here tonight. No report will be made. What was that girl's name?'

'Her name's . . . Heleni Kaloudis.'

'Kaloudis, you said? All right. And now tell me where she is. Come on, I give you my word as an officer that no harm will be done to her. We'll take care of her. Then we'll see. When she's better, she'll have to answer some questions, naturally, but believe me, we don't hurt women. I'm a man of honour.'

Michel told him and the officer's face lit up in satisfaction. 'Finally, finally: the voice on the radio. That damned voice on the radio. Good boy, good work, you have no idea how helpful you've been. The girl you were trying to help is a dangerous criminal, a threat to the security of the nation. Naturally, you're a foreigner, you couldn't imagine . . .'

Michel's eyes widened: 'What are you saying? What are you saying, God damn it? What's this business about the radio? What dangerous criminal? I don't believe a word of what you've said. You bastard!'

Karamanlis chuckled. 'Throw him into a cell,' he said to his men. 'We don't need him any more.' He left the room and disappeared up the stairs. Michel was dragged out into the hall. The man with the hairy chest was leaning against the door jamb of the interrogation room, smoking a cigarette. No sound came from the room, not even a whimper.

'I've done everything I can,' said the doctor. 'I've put her on a drip to raise her blood pressure and I've stopped the haemorrhage, but this girl needs a transfusion and your friend is nowhere to be seen. Something must have happened to him.'

Claudio twisted his hands: 'I don't understand, I just can't figure it out . . .'

Norman got to his feet: 'Claudio, this situation could turn critical from one moment to the next. If there had been some minor snag, Michel would have called, he would have got word to us somehow. Something very serious must have happened. Why don't you call Heleni's parents? You're taking too much responsibility upon yourself.'

'They live in Komotini, there's nothing they can do from way up there. It would just worry them to death. But what could have happened to Michel?'

'I can't imagine. Even calculating for traffic jams, roadblocks, whatever, he should have been here more than an hour ago.'

'Maybe he's in an area that's been sealed off by the military and he can't get out.'

'Well why hasn't he called us, then?'

'Maybe they've cut the phone lines, what do I know?'

Heleni, lying on a bed, opened her eyes. 'Claudio,' she said, 'we can't stay here. We're even putting the doctor at risk. I can't go to the hospital; they'd arrest me immediately. Listen, I feel better, I really do. Call a taxi and take me to my apartment. Then you can go and look for the medicines and things that Michel was supposed to bring. The doctor could come by tonight and finish up. He said the bullet went right through me. I'm going to be okay. Michel will show up sooner or later, but now we have to get out of here, please . . .'

'Heleni's right, Claudio,' said Norman.

'Yeah, maybe it's the only thing to do.' He turned to the doctor: 'What do you think?'

'Maybe . . . She's young, and she's not losing blood any more. There are nutrients in the drip. But she mustn't do anything, just lie still, and sleep if she can. My office is open until seven; I'll come after I close. Where's her house?'

They told him.

'I'll be there at eight o'clock. The curfew doesn't apply to doctors. Norman, you be there for the transfusion.'

'When can we move her from there?'

'Not before a week's time. Absolutely not, for any reason.'

'Of course. And I'll tell her parents right away.'

'Go now. I'll call a taxi for you.'

Claudio dressed her and Norman went down to the street to check that it was clear. The taxi driver rang the doorbell twice, and Claudio and the doctor came down supporting Heleni, who was pale and unsteady.

'How do you feel?' Claudio asked.

Heleni tried to reassure him: 'I feel better, really. You'll see, everything will be okay. If we get to my place, we'll be fine.'

They got into the cab and Norman closed the door. Claudio lowered the window and gestured for him to come close: 'Norman?'

'Yes?'

'We're not going to Heleni's house. The police might be on to us. I'll bring her to my room at the Plaka.'

'You're right, that's a much better solution. I wanted to suggest it myself. I'll see you there tonight.'

Claudio took his hand: 'Swear to me that you won't say anything to anyone, for the love of God. Except for the doctor, of course. Tell him right away about the change of address for tonight.'

'Don't worry, I won't let you down.' He smiled: 'But I'm warning you, Heleni will never be the same with a pint of Welsh blood in her veins. You'll be no match for her. Go now.'

Claudio gave the driver his address and the taxi took off immediately.

'Why did you give him your address?' whispered Heleni.

'The police will have interrogated dozens of people by now: they've arrested hundreds of students. So many people knew you . . . someone might have talked.'

'There are no traitors among us,' said Heleni, and the colour seemed to flare up in her pale face for an instant.

'I know, but it's better not to take risks. There were two thousand of you in there. In any case, no one knows me. We'll call your parents from the booth near my house. Take it easy now. Lean on me.'

Heleni rested her head on his shoulder and closed her eyes. The taxi driver glanced at them now and then in his rear-view mirror: they had been in a doctor's office and she looked so pale, with those dark circles around her eyes. The boy was so big and so scared looking. That whore must have just had an abortion, and he was to blame, the worm. Young people had no morals nowadays, and no shame. They should be whipped. Give them an inch and they get into all kinds of trouble. Like those others at the University. Give them a finger and they'll take your whole arm . . . what they needed was a good whipping, university my ass . . .

The taxi took the long way round to the Plaka, behind the Olimpieion, and finally stopped in front of a little whitewashed house. A grapevine curled over the enclosure wall and a couple of cats were rummaging through the uncollected garbage bags. Claudio leaned forward and paid the driver. Heleni, who seemed to have dozed off, sat up.

'We're here,' Claudio whispered in her ear. 'Do you think you can walk? We don't want anyone noticing us.' Heleni nodded. Claudio got out and opened the door for her. He took her hand and walked her slowly towards the external staircase that led up to his little one-roomer. The taxi disappeared into the maze of streets in the old city and Claudio put his arm around Heleni to hold her up. He let her in and had her lie down on the bed, covering her with a blanket.

'I have some meat in the fridge. I'll make you some nice strong broth. You have to drink a lot and rest. Don't worry, you'll be safe here. Nobody knows me.' He double-locked the door.

Heleni followed him with her eyes. 'Do you know what the inhabitants of Plaka are called?'

Claudio opened the refrigerator door and took out the meat. 'No, I don't. What are they called?'

'Gàngari. It means "bolts".'

'That's a funny name.'

'It's in memory of the resistance of Plaka against the Turks during the siege of Athens in 1925. They bolted the gates to the city and bolted the doors to every house in the Plaka, determined to defend themselves house by house if necessary.' She caressed him with a long melancholy gaze. 'Now you are a gangaros, and it's my fault.'

'You got it: you're worse than the Turks, you are. Now be quiet and sleep. I'll wake you when the broth is ready.'

He put the meat in a big soup pot, and added water, vegetables and lots of salt. 'This'll help raise your blood pressure . . . until Norman and the doctor get here to top you up, darling. But what in God's name could have happened to Michel, why didn't he call? . . .' He lit the burner under the pot and fell back on to a chair. He watched the blue flame lick the pot for a while, but was overcome by fatigue. His head soon dropped forwards and he fell fast asleep.

3

THE DESK CLERK at the embassy put down the receiver and dutifully filled out the visitor's pass: 'Mr Norman Shields for Mr James Henry Shields, diplomatic affairs'.

Norman impatiently pulled it out of his hand: 'George, do you really have to go through all this red tape to let me see my father? Can't you see I'm in a hurry, dammit? The air of Athens must be going to your head.'

'It's the rules, sir. And it's a very bad day today.'

'Come on, George, even the cleaning ladies here know me. You're right, George, it's a horrible day, and now can I see my father?'

The clerk nodded and Norman slipped into the elevator and went up to the second floor. He reached his father's office as he was dictating a letter to his secretary.

'Dad, I need to speak to you urgently about something very important.'

'Just let me finish this letter and I'll be with you . . . "and given the traditional spirit of friendship that joins our two countries, I sincerely hope that this operation will be concluded successfully and to our mutual benefit. Allow me to express our deepest esteem, as I look forward to a note from your embassy which will permit us to proceed with our project. Sincerely yours, etcetera, etcetera . . ." Well, what is it this time, Norman? Have you lost at cards or got a girl in trouble?'

Norman waited until the secretary had left, then sat down

and put both hands on the table. 'Dad, it's dead serious this time. I need your help.'

James Shields looked at him more attentively: 'Jesus, Norman, look at you! Have you been in a fight?'

'No! Christ, Dad, I didn't sleep all night. I was out with Michel and with Claudio Setti, an Italian friend of mine – his girlfriend was inside the Polytechnic. Her name is Heleni Kaloudis, maybe you've heard of her. She was wounded; those pigs put a bullet right through her. We brought her to a doctor to try to get a transfusion but it didn't work out. She refused to go to the hospital; the police would have thrown her right into prison. Michel went to get some medicine, but he never came back, I'm afraid the police have got him and . . .'

James Shields scowled. 'Calm down,' he said, 'and get a hold of yourself. Start from the beginning and tell me exactly what happened. I'll help you if you want, but you have to tell me the whole story.'

Norman pulled his hands off the table and squeezed them between his knees. 'Oh Christ. We may not even be in time any more. Okay, Michel and I were in Kifissìa with a couple of girls. Claudio called suddenly in the middle of the night and told us to meet him right away at the Polytechnic . . .'

He told his father everything, from start to finish, continually glancing at the pendulum clock on the wall and at his own wristwatch, carrying on a single-handed battle against time. His father listened carefully, taking a few notes on a small pad.

'Do you think anyone might have seen you? Anyone from the police, that is?'

'I don't know; I can't say they didn't, it was such a mess around the Polytechnic. What I'm afraid of is that they've got Michel . . . there's no other explanation. Heleni is terribly weak, and she's not getting the treatment she needs. She can't go to the hospital. The police will be looking for her; I'm afraid she's been on the radio all the time lately. Dad, what I'm asking you is to send an embassy car to pick her up and take her to the British hospital. She needs a blood transfusion immediately.'

'It's not so simple, Norman. As you said, the Greek police will certainly be looking for her. What you've proposed would be undue interference in the internal affairs of our host country and—'

'Christ, Dad!' shouted Norman. 'I'm asking you to save the life of a twenty-year-old girl who's risking death just because she was trying to make her country a better place, and you're giving me this diplomatic crap!' He got up abruptly, toppling over his chair: 'Fine, just forget about it. I'll take care of everything myself.'

He turned to leave, but his father stood between him and the door. 'Don't be an idiot. Pick up that chair and sit down. I'll see what I can do. Give me a few minutes.'

He dialled an internal extension and exchanged a few words with a colleague in another office. He picked up his notepad from the table and left the room. Norman started pacing back and forth in the small space.

His relationship with his father had been cold for some time, if not downright hostile. He hadn't wanted to ask him for help; he didn't want to give him the satisfaction of knowing he was in trouble. But now that he'd spoken to him, he was sorry he hadn't done so right away. Everything would have been resolved by now. He should have thought of it himself, dammit. Both Claudio and Michel knew about the situation and would never have dared to ask him to contact his father. God damn it. Lord knew what kind of trouble Michel was in, or if Heleni would pull through. How stupid he'd been. What an idiot. All this bullshit about independence. If he was going to run home crying like a kid, at least he should have done it straight away.

It was no use blaming himself now; what was important was getting things accomplished quickly. Every minute was important.

His father came back into the room, smiling: 'Where are your friends? We've got a car ready to go; they'll be safe in less than an hour.'

His voice trembled: 'Dad, I don't know how . . . my Italian

friend lives in a one-room apartment in the Plaka, thirty-two Aristomenis Street, second floor; there's a little external staircase. I could go with the driver.'

'Absolutely not. We'll send an operative who's done things like this in the past. But he has to work alone. I'm sure you understand why.'

'Yes, of course I do. But please hurry.'

'Thirty-two Aristomenis Street, you said?'

'That's it.'

'I'll go and give him instructions.' He started down the hall.

'Dad?'

'Yes?'

'Thanks.'

Norman returned to the office and went to the window. He saw his father go into the courtyard, say something to the driver of a car waiting with its engine running. The car shot off immediately, headed towards the Plaka. There was so much traffic, it would take time . . . time . . .

'THIRTY-TWO ARISTOMENIS STREET. They got here by cab and are in the second-floor apartment. She's with a young man. They've been there for about half an hour.'

The *astynomia* officer picked up the microphone: 'This is Captain Karamanlis. Can you see if the apartment has a phone line?'

'No, no phone. The apartment is isolated.'

'Are you sure they didn't meet anyone before going to the apartment?'

'Absolutely. The taxi brought them here directly without a stop. The only person they spoke to was a friend of theirs who walked them down from the doctor's office.'

'And where is he now?'

'He left on foot, but he's being followed by Roussos and Karagheorghis, car number twenty-six.'

'All right. Don't move an inch and don't lose sight of them. I'm holding you responsible.'

'Got you.' The policeman turned off the radio and lit a cigarette. The window at second-floor level was still closed and there were no signs of life. He couldn't figure out why he was tailing these two kids. They sure seemed innocent enough. His partner at the steering wheel leaned back, pulling his cap over his eyes.

The radio crackled to life again a few minutes later: 'Captain Karamanlis here, are you listening?'

'Yes, Captain. Go ahead.'

'Proceed to arrest them, immediately.'

'But nothing's happened.'

'I've spoken with car twenty-six. The boy they were following entered the British embassy, and shortly thereafter a car with a plain-clothes agent was seen leaving the embassy. He's headed in your direction. They may interfere, it's happened before. I don't want problems. Arrest them and bring them here.'

'Will do. Over.'

They entered the courtyard, went up the external staircase and banged at the door.

'Open up. Police.'

Claudio jerked awake and Heleni shook out of her slumber as well. The pot was boiling on the stove and the room was filled with the delicious smell of broth. The two young people looked at each other with an expression of agonized panic.

'Someone told them where we are!' gasped Claudio. 'Fast, outside the bathroom window. There's a terrace: from there you can get into the attic apartment; it's empty.'

He turned towards the door: 'Just a minute! I'm coming!' He helped Heleni get up and urged her towards the bathroom, trying to help her up on a chair so she could get out the window.

'I can't do this!' she cried. 'I'll never make it, Claudio. Let them take me.'

'Open this door or we'll knock it down!' the policemen were yelling from outside.

'I'll distract them. You do what I told you to do. Leave the attic apartment through the back door and cross the street;

there's a little church right there, Aghios Dimitrios. Hide there and wait for me.' He closed the bathroom door and went towards the main door, which was already swaying under the blows of the police outside.

'Where's the girl?' they shouted, pointing their pistols at him.

'She left with her parents an hour ago.'

The officer slapped him hard: 'Where is she?' Claudio didn't answer. The other went to open the bathroom door, but Claudio lunged after him and landed a punch to the nape of his neck, knocking him out cold. The first officer tried to hit Claudio with the butt of his pistol, but Claudio saw it coming out of the corner of his eye, slipped to the side and tripped him. The man fell down hard on to the floor but managed to spin round, and jumped up, pointing his gun straight at Claudio.

'I'll blow your brains on to the wall if you make a move.'

Claudio put his hands up, backing off. The policeman struck him in the stomach, again and again, until he doubled over in pain, then drove a knee up into his face, splitting his lip. Claudio collapsed to the ground, mouth and nose bleeding. The other man had got up and now kicked open the bathroom door. He saw the chair near the window and looked out. Heleni was dragging herself weakly across the terrace, towards the attic. He pointed his gun at her: 'Come back this way, baby, we have to talk.'

The car from the British embassy arrived a few minutes later. The driver parked and began to get out, but then ducked back in quickly, lowering his head: two men were coming down the side stairs. One was holding a girl under his arm: she was pale, with black-rimmed eyes, stumbling at every step. The other dragged a semi-conscious boy, his face and clothing covered with blood. They got into a car parked on the other side of the street and took off. The British agent turned on his radio: 'Hello?'

'James Shields here. Well?'

'Sorry, too late. The police were just accompanying them out as I pulled up. What should I do?' asked the agent.

Silence on the other end.

'Sir, if you send me a couple of guys from special services, we could head them off before they get to destination.'

'No. Come right back. There's nothing more we can do.'

Shields turned to Norman: 'I'm sorry, son. They were arrested by the Greek police just before our operative got there. I'm very, very sorry.'

Norman covered his eyes: 'Oh my God!' he said. 'Oh my God.'

THE CAR ENTERED police headquarters. The officer at the wheel got out and opened the back door. Others came and took Heleni away. Claudio tried to stop them, but was dragged forcefully to another entrance. When the door opened, he caught a glimpse of Michel sitting between two policemen in an adjacent room.

Their eyes crossed for a moment but Michel seemed not to recognize him. Claudio's face was all swollen up, his eyes reduced to two slits, his lips puffy and bloody, his dirty hair plastered to his forehead.

Michel couldn't comprehend how everything could have happened so quickly. Twenty-four hours ago, he was just a boy, lively and full of enthusiasm. Now he was broken and humiliated, deprived of all sentiment and feeling. They carried him out and put him in a car headed towards Faliron.

'Where are you taking me?'

'To the airport. You've been released. You're going back to France.'

'But I have a house in Athens, all my things, my clothes. I can't just leave.'

'Yes you can. Your things will be shipped to you. Your plane is leaving in a little over an hour. We've even bought you a ticket.'

At the airport, a ground hostess met them with a wheelchair.

'He's just been operated on,' said the policeman. 'He won't be able to walk for a week. He'll need help at his arrival in France as well.'

'Certainly,' said the hostess. 'We've already been notified.' She pushed Michel in the wheelchair past the metal detector and parked him at the gate. He was carried to his seat near the window.

The plane took off and flew low over the city and port before beginning its ascent. A steward started to illustrate emergency procedures and show the passengers how to use the life jackets under their seats if they were forced to make an emergency landing, but Michel wasn't listening. He looked down at the Acropolis, and from this height it seemed desolate. A field of chalky skeletons.

There was the agora, the archaeological school, emerging from the low houses of the Plaka. He would never see Athens again. Never.

And his memories? Would he ever be able to rid himself of them? His friends: Claudio, Norman. He'd met them two years before, on a mule track between Metsovon and Ioannina. They were hitch-hiking and he brought them to Parga in his Deux-Chevaux. Friends at first sight. An exclusive, fierce, crazy friendship, they had raced through life together, always the best, plotting adventures, studying, arguing, discussing the destiny of the world at the local dives, drinking retsina at the tavern, hitting on girls . . . Heleni, what a beauty. A knock-out. And Heleni had chosen Claudio. He had tried with her as well, but then forgot her, what the hell, your best friend's girlfriend . . . She had become part of them. Heleni, so beautiful and so sweet, courageous and proud. He had turned her in. He had been unforgivably weak, a coward. That was the thought that tortured him, made him bleed inside. How could he ever forget what he'd done?

What kind of life was left to him? How could he ever find the strength to do anything again? Oh, Athens, Athens. He'd never see her again. Never again.

The stewardess repeated her question: 'Would you like something to drink, sir?'

Michel didn't turn but his voice was firm and polite. 'No thank you. I don't want anything.'

CLAUDIO WAS LEFT for hours in total isolation in a freezing, windowless cell, without a cot, just an iron door and a single chair, iron as well. They had taken his belt and shoestrings with his wallet and watch. He had no way of calculating how much time had passed.

The light bulb spread a flat, harsh light. The walls didn't let through any sound and his own footsteps rang out as if he were pacing back and forth in a tin can.

His soul had never been filled with such anguish. He was tormented by his despair and the physical pain that racked his eyes, his mouth, his ribs. It was intolerable. Not a fibre of his being was free of pain. When he heard footsteps outside his cell and the door swung open, he was ready for murder. He wanted nothing more than to strike the man in the doorway with a killing blow, to crush him, to mangle him. He gripped the back of the iron chair as if it were his shield.

The man was of average height, freshly shaven, impeccable in his *astynomia* uniform. His hair was streaked with white and his moustache was neatly trimmed. He was calm and nearly reassuring. He came closer and his aftershave smelled cool, even pleasant.

'Sit down,' he said in Italian. 'Police Captain Karamanlis. I'm here to help you.'

'I'm an Italian citizen. I have the right to call my consulate. You have to release me. I'll have you put on trial.'

The officer smiled: 'My friend. I could eliminate you whenever I like. Your corpse would disappear and never ever be found. And I would collaborate with the utmost zeal to help your consulate, providing them with false information that would close the case for ever.'

He took out a pack of cigarettes and offered one to Claudio, who accepted it, taking a long drag. 'And now that your situation is clear to you, I want you to know that what I've just suggested is the last thing I want to do. I studied in Italy, I admire your country greatly and I'm quite fond of your people.'

Right, thought Claudio. Now he'll give me that old proverb: Italians and Greeks, same face, same race.

'And then,' said the officer, 'you know how the old saying goes: Italian and Greek, same face, same race. Right?' Claudio didn't answer. 'Now, listen well to what I have to say. There's only one way you can save yourself and save the girl. You don't want anything to happen to her, do you?'

'Have her taken to the hospital, immediately. She's been wounded, she's in danger of dying . . .'

'We know. And the longer you wait, the greater the danger becomes. It all depends on you. We want to know everything about Heleni Kaloudis: who her friends were, her accomplices. Who is behind her. What were their plans, what were they plotting? Who were their contacts in the Communist party, and what about foreign agents? Bulgarians? Russians?'

Claudio lost hope. That man already had a story worked out, and all he wanted was to hear it confirmed. Nothing would convince him otherwise.

'Listen, I'll be sincere because the only thing I want to do in this world is save Heleni. There is not a grain of truth in what you're thinking. Heleni's just part of the students' movement, like thousands of others at the University. But if you want I'll confess to everything: plots, foreign agents, orders from above, as long as I see her in a hospital bed being treated by capable doctors.'

Karamanlis looked at him with a mixture of condescension and satisfaction: 'I'm glad that you've decided to collaborate, although I understand your desire to exculpate your girlfriend. I must tell you that your . . . confession will be compared word by word with what the girl has told us.'

Claudio backed up towards the wall, gripping the chair: 'You can't interrogate her in her condition! You can't do that, you can't!'

'We have to; we have a duty to do so, Mr Setti, and when

we have compared your two statements and found them in agreement, you'll be released and the girl will be treated so that she'll be capable of facing trial . . .'

'No, I'm sorry, Captain, you weren't listening to me. I'll collaborate only if I see that the girl is being treated, otherwise you can forget it. Forget it! You can cut me to pieces, cut off my balls, tear off my fingernails . . . what else is on the torture agenda? I will not say one word, not one, you got that? Do you understand? The girl has to be brought immediately to the hospital, not interrogated, is that clear?' Claudio shouted. His eyes were bulging, veins stood out in his neck and temples. He looked crazy.

The captain backed up towards the door, which was opened behind him in an instant. An officer approached him: 'She didn't say a word,' he whispered. Karamanlis's face twitched in a strange smirk, in grotesque contrast with his smooth, respectable countenance.

'How is she?' he asked.

'Weak. If we force our hand, she'll buy it.'

'None of my concern. Make her talk. We'll get this one talking too. Has the Englishman arrived?'

'Yes, but there's not much to tell him yet.'

Claudio had come a step closer and was trying to figure out what was happening. Karamanlis took pleasure in his anguished expression. 'Your friend's not talking,' he said, 'if that's what you're wondering. But she will, I can guarantee it. I've called in just the right person to make your girlfriend talk . . . and you too. Sergeant Vlassos.' The officer gave a little giggle. 'Sergeant Vlassos is a charmer, especially with the ladies. You know what his colleagues call him? They call him *O Chiros*, the pig.'

Claudio started screaming and seized the chair, hurling it forward, but the door had already closed behind Captain Karamanlis and the chair crashed loudly against the iron.

ARI ENDED HIS shift at the museum at 2 p.m. He had gone to the director that morning to report the sudden death of Professor

Harvatis and to turn in his keys. The director hadn't asked any questions because Harvatis had been on the staff at Antiquities and wasn't his direct responsibility. Ari had for years had a state transfer to the Ephira excavation site for a couple of months every summer, after which he'd return to his regular custodian's job at the museum. It was all perfectly normal. But Ari didn't breathe a word about the gold vase hidden in the basement or the letter he had in his pocket.

He went into a tavern and ordered something to eat. As he was waiting, he tried to think things through, to decide what to do next. Who should he contact? Who could he ask for advice? What should he do with the letter? He took it from his inside jacket pocket and turned it over in his hands. The waiter brought a little carafe of the house retsina and Ari sipped at his glass without taking his eyes off the wrinkled envelope on the table. He picked up a knife to slit it open and see what the letter said, but then thought better of it: he'd promised the old professor before he died that he'd deliver it to the address written on the envelope.

He'd have to go back to Dionysìou Street, to that printer's. He'd surely find someone there. He was foolish to have let that man frighten him; it could have been anyone, one of those derelicts who wander around all night with nothing better to do. Everything looks different during the day, but at night an encounter like that would have scared the wits out of anyone.

The waiter brought some chicken and rice and a plate of salad with cheese and Ari started to eat hungrily: he hadn't eaten anything for at least twelve hours. He thought of the boys hiding in the museum, and of the girl. Had they managed to save her?

The waiter returned with another little carafe of wine.

'I didn't order any more wine,' protested Ari.

The waiter put the carafe down and pointed to a man sitting near the door: 'It's on him.'

Ari turned slowly and felt his blood run cold: it was him, no doubt about it, the man who had spoken to him on Dionysìou

Street. He couldn't see his face, but he had on the same dark coat and the same wide-brimmed hat worn low over his eyes.

He was smoking and had a glass of wine on the table in front of him.

Ari put the letter in his pocket, picked up the carafe with one hand and his glass with the other and went to the stranger's table. He put them down.

'I can't accept anything from someone I don't know. How did you find me? What do you want from me?'

The man lifted his head and held out his hand.

'The letter. The letter addressed to Stàvros Kouras.'

His eyes were light-coloured, a soft blue, darker at the edges, like ice on a chilly winter's morning. His black hair and beard were streaked with white, his dark skin furrowed by deep wrinkles. He looked to be about fifty, more or less.

'But you aren't Stàvros Kouras,' said Ari uncertainly.

'Sit down,' said the man, as if giving an order which could not be disobeyed. Ari did, and the man took a long drag on his cigarette.

'Now listen,' he said. 'There's no time to waste. Stàvros Kouras doesn't exist; it's only a name. That letter was written by Periklis Harvatis, wasn't it?'

Ari felt a knot in his throat. 'Periklis Harvatis is dead,' he said.

The man fell silent for a few moments, without betraying any emotion.

'Was he your friend? Did you know him?' insisted Ari.

The man lowered his gaze: 'We were working on a project together . . . an important project. That's why you absolutely have to give me that letter. I must read it.'

Ari took it out of his pocket and looked deeply into the stranger's eyes. 'But who are you?' It was difficult to meet his gaze for any length of time.

'I'm the man that letter is meant for. If that weren't the case, why would you have found me at that address, at that very moment? And how would I know who had written it? Give it to me. It's the one thing you have left to do.' He spoke as if saying obvious, unquestionable truths. Ari held it out. The man took it, practically tearing it from him. He opened it, ripping the envelope, and read it rapidly. Ari watched his forehead under the brim of the hat. Not a quiver. No emotion, smooth as stone.

'Harvatis brought something with him. You know what I'm speaking about. Where is it?'

'Locked up, in the basement of the National Archaeological Museum.'

'Did you . . . see it?'

'Yes.'

'No one else?'

Ari felt embarrassed, as if he had to justify his actions to this man whose name he didn't even know.

'A few young people saw it . . . university students who . . .' The man stiffened, and a flash of rage darkened his features. 'Oh, mother of God, you know what happened last night, don't you? You were out, I saw you. They were students escaping from the Polytechnic. There was a girl, she was wounded . . . I know them, nearly all of them. They're students from the foreign archaeology schools. What else could I do? The storehouse in the basement was the only safe place. Then what happened was that . . .'

'Where are they now?'

'I don't know. I gave them an address of a doctor who was willing to treat the girl without reporting her to the police. I don't know anything else, I haven't heard from them.'

'Then the police have them. They've surely been caught.' He got up, leaving a twenty-drachma coin on the table. 'Who are they? Tell me who they are.'

'Why, what do you want to do?'

'If you don't tell me who they are, they have no hope.'

'The one I know best is Michel Charrier, a boy studying at the French school of archaeology. The other two are called Claudio Setti and Norman . . . something. The wounded girl's name is Heleni Kaloudis. That's all I know.'

The man nodded and walked towards the exit.

'Wait, tell me your name at least, how can I get in touch with you again? . . .' Ari followed him, pushing at the glass door that had already closed behind him, and walked out onto the pavement. The trucks passing were full of soldiers and screaming sirens tore through every corner of the city.

The man had disappeared.

4

SERGEANT VLASSOS WALKED up the hall with short, rapid steps, sticking the toe of his foot forward and moving his small, fat hands rhythmically over his hips. He was heavy and thickset and his shirt looked as if it was about to tear over the huge, hard belly which protruded well over his belt. He wore his hair very short to disguise his incipient baldness, but he always had a two-day-old beard, black and stiff on his milk-white skin. His eyes were light in colour and watery, pacific, the eyes of a clerk. Ferocious and cowardly at the same time, faithful as a dog and deferential to his superiors, he was capable of savage atrocity as long as he was guaranteed impunity.

There was this little whore who'd had a good time with the boys at the University for days on end. Now she didn't want to collaborate. That little bitch on the radio who spat out all kinds of poison and insults against the police. And now she was refusing to answer the questions they were putting to her.

'This is a job for you,' the chief had said. 'Vlassos, you take care of it: this baby is all for you, do whatever you want with her. Got my message, old friend? Anything you have to . . .' and the chief had smiled in that way that meant, 'You know what I mean, don't you, buddy?'

And Vlassos had answered: 'You can count on me, Chief, I know how to handle these things.'

'That's what I wanted to hear. We'll see if your . . . bedside manner is sufficient to get her to see things our way. Otherwise we'll just have to repeat the treatment until she becomes more reasonable. It's not a problem for you to repeat the treatment if necessary . . .'

And Vlassos snickered: 'Oh, no, no, not a problem for me . . .'

HELENI WAS LYING on an iron bed, drowsy with weakness and exhausted by her anaemia, but she lifted her head and tried to get up on her elbows when the door opened and Sergeant Vlassos's corpulent figure filled the doorway.

'Now I'll get you to talk, you little whore, I'll get you talking . . .'

Heleni begged him through her tears: 'For the love of God . . .' she said with a faint voice, 'please . . . don't hurt me.'

'Shut up!' yelled Vlassos. 'I know what I have to do.' He lifted his hand and slapped her face with all his might. Behind the door, Karamanlis was watching everything through a one-way window: behind him a man with a taut face, evidently upset, drew back into the shadows of the corridor so as not to see.

'We'll find out everything we want to know now,' Karamanlis said without turning around. 'And if she doesn't talk, he will, I can guarantee it, mister.'

'Your methods are disgraceful and you are a sod, Karamanlis,' said the foreigner. 'I wish you'd drop dead.'

'Don't be a hypocrite. Your friends are as interested as I am in knowing what's behind this story, who's manoeuvring these fools. We're lucky to have caught so many of them, and they'll give us all the information we need. You just let me work and don't break my balls.'

Claudio arrived at that moment, dragged down the hall by a policeman. Karamanlis made a gesture and the man pushed Claudio against the door with his face up against the window. Claudio saw Vlassos violently slapping Heleni's face again. He turned, screaming, towards Karamanlis, but the man holding him twisted his arm to the point of breaking it. Claudio fell to his knees but never stopped shouting and insulting the officer:

'Coward, bastard, your mother fucked a Turk! Goddamned fucking murderer!'

Karamanlis paled, took him by the shoulders and lifted him back up to window level, smashing his face against the glass. 'See, look at that, you'll talk now, you'll tell us everything you know, won't you? You'll quit playing the smart guy, won't you?'

Claudio was paralysed with horror: Heleni lay there motionless, unconscious. But hitting the girl had obviously excited Vlassos, and he was unzipping his pants, displaying the hairy obscenity of his groin. He lifted Heleni's skirt, tore off her underwear and mounted her, sweat-soaked, panting and groaning.

Claudio felt something break inside him, shatter like a sheet of ice smashed by a hammer. 'There's nothing to say!' he yelled. 'There's nothing to tell! Stop him, for God's sake, stop him! Stop him!' He twisted free, swiftly pulled his arm back and dealt a lightning-quick blow to the cop who had been holding him, devastating his face. The man fell back, moaning, covering his smashed nose and broken jaw with his hands. Claudio pounded against the door like a battering ram and would have crushed himself against the armour-plating had another two policemen not lunged at him and blanketed his face and body with wild, violent blows, immobilizing him on the ground. One of them pinned his knee on Claudio's chest and held both hands around his neck.

Karamanlis, white as a rag, ordered them to get him back up and make him watch, but the man behind him intervened: 'Stop that animal, Karamanlis. Stop him, for God's sake, can't you see that she's dead? Christ, he's killed her, that damned bastard. Stop him or you'll have hell to pay for this.'

Heleni's body shook under his last thrusts like the disjointed body of a rag doll; her eyes rolled up whitely.

Karamanlis opened his mouth and called Vlassos, to no effect. It took two men to pull him off Heleni's corpse.

The man standing in the shadows could no longer hold back and approached Karamanlis: 'Idiot, now you'll have to kill the boy too, after what he's seen. Great results, you idiot, you piece of shit. And yet you're a citizen of an allied country, you goddamned imbecile.'

Claudio was about to lose his senses; his left eye a mere slit in his swollen cheek. It was winking with tiny, dry movements, seemingly automatic, but each time he blinked, his eye captured a face and branded it in his memory: Captain Karamanlis, officers Roussos and Karagheorghis, the man with the English accent illuminated by the fluorescent tube on the ceiling . . . and Vlassos. He never saw him leave the room, but as his mind sank into unconsciousness, his nostrils were filled with the sharp, nauseating odour of rape.

Karamanlis, who had been tense but impassive, suddenly seemed exhausted. His face was lumpy and wrinkled, his fore-head beaded with sweat. 'Take him away,' he ordered. 'As soon as it's dark, take him out of the city and get rid of him. Don't leave a trace, or you'll be in the worst trouble you've ever imagined. You can bury her in the same place,' he added, indicating Heleni's body, which had been repositioned on the bed.

An hour later, Karamanlis passed near the door of the cell where Claudio was being held and he stopped, astonished. A strange sound was coming from within, a song, he would say, although he couldn't understand the words. A gentle, pain-filled melody that rose higher and sweeter, a disturbing, desolate rhapsody. The officer felt a sense of annoying discomfort – the absurd song rang out like an intolerable challenge. He beat his fist against the door, shouting hysterically: 'That's enough! Stop that, damn you! Cut it out with this whining!'

The voice fell away and the long hall was plunged back into silence.

THE LARGE BLUE car came to an abrupt stop in front of the police barracks guardhouse. The light blue flag with its three gold stars on the left bumper indicated that a highly ranked officer was aboard. The driver got out and opened the rear door, snapping to attention before his superior. The man was dressed in the elegant uniform of the Greek navy. He smoothed his jacket and adjusted the gloves over his long, sturdy fingers. The sentry looked over distractedly and then, struck by the man's steely gaze, stiffened into the present-arms position.

The penetrating intensity of his stare, the dark cast of his skin and the deep wrinkles that creased his brow suggested that his stripes had been earned in long years at sea, amidst wind and fire.

He entered with a strong stride, briefly touching his hand to his peaked cap, and walked straight to the front desk.

'I'm Admiral Bogdanos,' said the officer, showing an ID card that he rapidly returned to his inside jacket pocket. 'I must speak immediately with the chief of police.'

'Just a moment, Admiral. I'll call him immediately.' The sergeant lifted the telephone receiver and dialled an internal extension.

Sitting on the other side of Karamanlis's desk were Roussos and Karagheorghis, charged with making Heleni Kaloudis and Claudio Setti disappear as though they had never existed. At the telephone's ring the captain interrupted his careful instructions and answered with an annoyed tone: 'What is it? I said I wasn't to be disturbed.'

'Captain, there's a certain Admiral Bogdanos here, and he says he must speak with you immediately.'

'I can't now. Tell him to wait.'

He had spoken so loudly that the navy officer, standing right in front of the sergeant, heard him. His eyes flashed with anger: 'Tell him to report to me within one minute if he doesn't want to end up court-martialled. Remind him that a state of emergency is in effect.'

Karamanlis got to his feet. 'It'll be dark soon,' he was saying to his men. 'Carry on exactly as I told you.' He took his cap from the coat rack and went to the entrance. He strode down the corridor leading to the front desk, opened the glass door, and found the navy officer standing in front of him, legs wide, arms crossed behind his back.

His eyes dropped to the cap sitting on a chair. He was probably a member of the joint chiefs of staff, or the Junta itself. Karamanlis attempted to put on a tough demeanour nonetheless.

'May I know, Admiral, why you have interrupted my work at such a delicate moment? And may I see your identification and your credentials?'

The officer gestured peremptorily with his gloved hand and turned away, walking to a corner of the room reserved for the officer on duty. Karamanlis followed him, abashed.

'You are a fool,' hissed the admiral, turning abruptly. 'How could you think of holding foreign citizens prisoner? Citizens from two of our most important allies? Haven't you seen what the foreign press is writing about us? We stand accused of infamy; important loans to our National Bank have been suspended. All we needed was for you to create a diplomatic incident! The French boy, Charrier, and the Italian, Claudio Setti, what the hell have you done with them?'

Karamanlis felt his knees buckle: he had to be a secret-service agent to know so much!

'Well? I'm waiting for an answer.'

Karamanlis tried bluffing: 'Your information is incorrect, Admiral. We are holding no foreigners here.'

The officer froze him with a stare: 'Don't make your situation any worse than it is, Captain. Anyone can make a mistake, and I can understand how, due to an excess of zeal, you may have taken certain initiatives. But if you don't collaborate, you're risking much more than your career. My superiors have entrusted me with correcting this damned business immediately, before it gets out of hand. Now talk, for God's sake.'

Karamanlis gave up: 'Charrier was interrogated until he revealed the names of his accomplices. We sent him to France with a travel order. He left on the 4 p.m. Air France flight yesterday.'

Bogdanos reacted angrily, nervously punching his left hand: 'Damn it! This will set off a scandal. The French government will be up in arms; we'll never hear the end of it.'

'The boy won't say a thing. He's the first to want this story buried.'

'What about the Italian?'

'He's . . . dying.'

'An interrogation, I presume?'

Karamanlis nodded.

'I imagined as much. Turn him over to me now. If he dies, we have to simulate an accident and invent an explanation for his relatives and the Italian press.'

'I'm taking care of it, Admiral.'

'Goddamn you, do as I say or you'll have to explain all this to a military court, I swear it. I don't trust you. I'll take care of this matter personally.'

Karamanlis hesitated a moment: 'Follow me, then,' he said, walking towards the hall. They went out of a side door which led on to a little courtyard at the back of headquarters. A car with two officers aboard was just about to go through the gate.

'Stop!' shouted Karamanlis. The car jerked to a halt. He took the keys from the man at the wheel and opened the trunk. A tangle of bloody bodies appeared: a young man and a young woman.

'So this is Heleni Kaloudis,' said Bogdanos. Karamanlis was startled. He never would have imagined that the secret services were keeping him under such strict surveillance.

'She was already half dead when she got here. She had been wounded at the Polytechnic. I tried to get her to tell us what she knew. She was already nearly dead . . .'

They suddenly heard a moan from something moving in the trunk.

'Christ, he's still alive. I'm holding you accountable for this, Captain. I should have you arrested. Don't leave the station, and wait for orders from the Military Staff Office.' The admiral turned to one of the policemen: 'Go to the front courtyard and have my car brought round to the back, immediately.'

The officer looked at Karamanlis for approval.

'Do as he says.'

The admiral had Claudio Setti, still unconscious, transferred to the back seat of the vehicle.

'Bury that body,' he ordered, indicating Heleni's corpse curled up in the trunk, and staring at Karamanlis with disgust. 'This whole story has been handled horribly. The army should never have dirtied their hands with it; that's what the police are for.'

It had become dark. The car with Heleni's body in it took off fast heading north, and the blue car holding Admiral Bogdanos followed it through traffic, taking the opposite direction at the first roundabout.

CLAUDIO WAS RACKED with pain as he regained consciousness; coloured lights whirled above him and he heard a deep, hoarse voice. How long would it be before they finished him off? He prayed it would be soon. He couldn't imagine living with the memory of what he had seen.

'Now turn right,' said the voice, 'and pull over under those trees.' The driver did so and turned off the engine. 'Flash your headlights twice, then switch them off.'

Claudio realized that he was inside a car, lying on the back seat, arms and legs free of constraints. There was an officer wearing a navy uniform in the front passenger's seat. He pulled himself up slowly until he could see out of the bottom of the window. A man was approaching the car, walking quickly in the shadows of the tree-lined street. He stopped a few metres away and the street lamp lit his face. It was Ari! The custodian at the National Museum who had let them into the basement and then sent them to the doctor. Was it he who had betrayed them?

The man sitting in front opened the door and Ari came closer. Ari's eyes filled with astonishment as he recognized him: 'You? Holy Mother in heaven! But . . . the uniform . . .'

'Don't ask questions, there's no time. The police could be here at any second. The Italian boy is safe: he's here in the car, but he's been beaten to a pulp . . . inside and out. See if you can do something for him. His French friend was sent back to his country, expelled. Probably with a travel order. The girl's dead,

I'm afraid. I got there too late.' He gestured to the driver, who opened the back door and helped Claudio out.

'You brought a car, I hope.'

Ari roused himself from the state of shock that had nearly paralysed him: 'Yes . . . yes, there's my car, it's parked next to those trees.'

Claudio was transferred to the old Peugeot that had brought Periklis Harvatis to Athens just two days earlier, and lay down like a dog. He didn't have the strength even to speak.

'What do I have to do?' asked Ari. 'How can I find you if I need help?'

'Take him far enough away that no one will recognize him.'

'What about Professor Harvatis? The mission he entrusted me with?'

A gust of cold wind swept through the trees, strewing the ground with dead leaves. The man took a long breath and turned back towards the street as an old bus rattled by, jolting at each pothole and threatening to fall to pieces at any minute.

'The . . . vase,' he said, looking Ari in the eye again. 'Is it still in the museum basement?'

'Yes.'

'And you haven't said anything to anyone?'

'No, I haven't.'

'Take it away from there, now, tonight, and hide it. I'll come to you when it is time. Now go.'

'But please . . . tell me at least—'

'Go, I said.'

'But how will you find me? I don't even know myself where I'm going.'

'I'll find you, don't worry. It isn't easy to escape me.'

Ari turned and walked towards his car. He started it up and took off.

'Where are you bringing me?' asked Claudio's voice behind him.

'Where no one can find you. And now lie back and sleep, if you can, my son.'

'Let me die. You can't imagine what I've seen . . . what I've suffered.'

'You'll resign yourself and you'll go on living . . . to see that justice is done. Your time has not yet come, my boy, because you've been pulled alive from the maw of hell.' Ari slowed down so he could turn off on to the road for Piraeus.

'Wait,' said Claudio. 'Stop just a moment, please.' Ari pulled over to the pavement and Claudio struggled to pull himself up into a sitting position. He lowered the window and leaned out to look back. Admiral Bogdanos's blue car had vanished. At the edge of the street was a man, wearing a hat low over his eyes and wrapped in a dark coat, who was lifting his hand in the direction of the centre of the road. The old bus stopped, moaning and squeaking, to let him on. It left again, spitting out a great cloud of black dust that was instantly dispersed by the wind, now stronger and colder. Claudio rolled up the window and saw that Ari was looking back as well.

'Who was that man who brought me here? Why did he do it?'

'I don't know,' said Ari, turning the key again to start up the car. 'I swear to you that I do not know, but I'm sure that we'll see him again. Lie down now, we've got a long road ahead of us.'

Claudio curled up on the seat, pressing his knees against his cramp-ridden stomach. He suffocated his desperation and rage, his inconsolable pain, his infinite solitude, hands stuffed hard against his mouth.

An hour or two passed, or maybe just a few minutes, he couldn't say: the car stopped and Ari came round to open the door and help him out.

'We're here, son. Come on, lean on me.'

THE RING OF the telephone interrupted the dark thoughts of Captain Karamanlis, who was sitting in his office in front of a barely nibbled sandwich and a glass of water. He lifted the receiver: 'Central police headquarters, who is this?'

'This is Dr Psarros from the municipal hospital of Kifissìa. I have a suspicious case to report.'

'Captain Karamanlis here. Go ahead.'

'Saturday night, a dying man was brought in. Periklis Harvatis, inspector of the Central Antiquities and Fine Arts Service, according to the ID in his pocket. He didn't pull through, despite our efforts; time of death approximately one hour after admittance. The man who brought him into the hospital came back some time later and asked to see him. He was acting so strangely that I notified the district police, but by the time an officer got to the hospital he had disappeared without a trace. We were unable to ascertain under what circumstances the patient was reduced to such a precarious state.'

'The man who brought him in – do you know who he was?'

'The name he left at the front desk was Aristotelis Malidis, but it may have been a cover.'

'Were you able to certify the cause of death?'

'Cardiac arrest. We've asked for permission to perform an autopsy, but given the current situation, the medical examiner has been busy elsewhere.'

Karamanlis wrote down the name in a notebook. 'Malidis, you said. I'll see what I can find out about him. I'll call you back if I need more information. But why not the Kifissìa district police?'

'I don't imagine they'll be able to take the case. The chief of police is being investigated for his position regarding the . . . evacuation of the Polytechnic. That's why I've called you.'

'You did the right thing, Doctor. Thank you. Goodnight.'

'Goodnight to you, Captain.'

Karamanlis buzzed the switchboard immediately. 'Get me the Head of the Antiquities and Fine Arts Service. It's at Kleomenis Ikonomou.'

'Captain, the offices will have closed hours ago.'

'Then look for him at home, dammit! Get his name from the Minister of Education. Do I have to tell you how to blow your nose?'

'But there won't be anyone left at the Ministry of Education except for custodians.'

'Get the director-general out of bed, dammit, and see what he knows about an inspector named Harvatis. Yeah, that's right, Periklis Harvatis. And a guy named Aristotelis Malidis. No, I have no idea whether he worked for them. That's it, good boy. Call me back when you've found out something.'

Karamanlis grabbed his sandwich and started chewing again in no better a mood, downing it with a little mineral water. He felt somehow that this weird story might get him out of some trouble. Goddamned meddler, that Bogdanos, and dangerous to boot. He wanted to find out more about him, discreetly, as soon as this mess blew over. He had some friends at the Ministry of Defence. The telephone rang again: 'Well, what did you find out?'

'No, nothing yet, Captain. I'm calling about something else. There's a young man here, a foreigner, who insists in speaking with the headquarters chief. He says it's urgent and extremely important.'

'What's his name?'

'He says it's Norman Shields.'

'Shields, you said? S-H-I-E-L-D-S?'

'That's it.'

'Let him through. I'll see him immediately.'

'FOLLOW ME, MR SHIELDS. Colonel Norton is waiting for you in his office.' The official led him down the deserted halls of the United States embassy until they reached a door marked 'Cultural Attaché'. He knocked.

'Come in!' said a voice from inside.

'Mr James Henry Shields for you, Colonel.'

'Come right in, Shields, sit down. I've been looking forward to seeing you again. So, how did things go?'

'Goddamn it, Colonel, this was not our agreement! You've cornered me into a horrible position. I won't have it. There's a limit to everything – certain principles must be respected, blast it. We are not criminals. How could you ever have thought of working with that swine Karamanlis!'

Colonel Norton abruptly changed the cordial expression with which he had welcomed his guest. 'Shields. Careful what you say or I'll have my men throw you out of here, no questions asked. You agreed to collaborate with us, and we needed certain information. If you have that information, you can give it to me and get the fuck out of here. I'm sick of your whining. If you don't like this job, go join the boy scouts and stop exasperating me.'

Shields regained his customary composure: 'Fine, Colonel, then you'd like to know how things went? First of all, Karamanlis got absolutely nowhere and knows as much now as he did before. In return, he committed such a monstrosity that if it leaks we are all fucked to hell, you and me included. And now I hope you have the balls to listen to what happened, because I threw up my guts before coming here to make this report.'

Norton lowered his gaze, embarrassed and at a loss to imagine what had so disturbed a man like James Henry Shields, former SAS officer and British Intelligence agent, detached to Greece during the civil war and later to Vietnam and Cambodia during the worst years of guerrilla warfare.

'I'M CAPTAIN KARAMANLIS. Please sit down. What can I do for you?'

Norman Shields's eyes were puffy and rimmed with black circles, as if he hadn't slept in days. The shirt he was wearing was filthy at the collar and cuffs and his trousers were crumpled and baggy at the knees. He had a hard time talking, as if his search for just the right words was a hopeless endeavour.

'Captain, sir,' he said, 'listen to me well, because I'm offering you the chance to become fabulously rich in just one hour's time.'

Karamanlis glanced up with a quizzical expression, as though he doubted that the person he had before him was in his right mind. Norman read his thoughts.

'I can prove what I'm about to say. You can check on it while I wait here.'

'And what have I done to deserve such a magnificent opportunity?'

Norman continued his speech as though he'd rehearsed it, paying no attention to Karamanlis. 'Saturday night a priceless Mycenaean vase of pure gold was hidden in a secret place here in Athens. The object does not appear in any publication, and no one knows of its existence. It was certainly unearthed during a recent excavation, but that's all I can say.'

Karamanlis was suddenly intent: 'Continue. I'm listening.'

'Free my friends – Claudio Setti, Heleni Kaloudis and Michel Charrier as well, if he's here – and I'll tell you where you can find it. You can remove it easily from where it is, and I'll arrange to get it to Sotheby's in London for you. You can make a million dollars. Seems like a fair exchange.'

Karamanlis started at the mention of such a sum, but assumed his best expression of honest civil servant, although his unshaven beard and bristly moustache must have hinted at his unsettled state of mind. 'I will ignore the implications of what you have just said, for the moment. What does interest me is turning this archaeological treasure which belongs to the past of our country over to the Antiquities and Fine Arts Service. As far as your friends are concerned, I do not have the power to liberate anyone, especially anyone who still has to account to the law, but if I remember well,' he continued, pretending to consult a file, 'they were brought in for a simple check, and I'm sure they'll be released quite soon.'

'I want them out now or I won't tell you a thing.'

'Watch what you say; I could have you arrested.'

'Just you try. The British embassy knows I'm here,' Norman lied. 'My father is in charge of diplomatic affairs.'

'The only thing I can guarantee is that we will cut through the red tape and have them out by, let's say, tomorrow.

Naturally, if you refuse to give me the information you are in possession of, I may be forced to prolong the term of precautionary imprisonment . . .'

'You're mistaken if you think I'll give you any information without precise guarantees.'

'I'm sorry, but you'll just have to trust me. You tell me where that object is and tomorrow morning you'll see your friends. I can guarantee it.'

'Tomorrow morning?'

'That's right.'

'The vase is at the National Archaeological Museum.'

'What a good hiding place. You see, in this case your problems are solved. The museum is protected by an alarm system and no one can get in until tomorrow morning. If you don't see your friends by then, you can advise the director and have him take the vase, if you have qualms about me.'

'Then I'll tell you where it is tomorrow morning.'

'Impossible. I'll be leaving the city for several days. You have to tell me now.'

'All right. But don't you dare try to screw me, or I'll find a way to make you pay for it.'

Karamanlis didn't reply to his provocation.

'The vase is hidden in the corner cabinet of the storehouse, the second door on the left of the basement corridor. It's in a drum of sawdust. Remember, Karamanlis, that if you don't keep up your end of the deal, you'll be sorry.' He got up and went to the door.

'I don't believe a word of your intentions to turn it over to the Fine Arts,' he said before leaving. 'In any case, I'll keep my promise. If you let my friends out I'll arrange for you to sell the piece and make the amount I've mentioned. If you want to handle it yourself, I have nothing against that. I'll be around for a few days; you can find me at the British school of archaeology. After that I'm leaving, and I'll never set foot in this wretched country again.'

He raced out to the street, stopped the first taxi he saw and jumped in.

'Where to?' asked the driver. Norman gave him his address and, as the cab took off, looked back towards police headquarters. He imagined his friends being held prisoner in some dark corner of that gloomy building. If he'd played his cards right, their suffering would soon be over. And yet a doubt began to take seed, becoming more of a conviction with each passing hour. How could the police have got wind of Claudio's apartment in the Plaka, when no one but he knew they were there? And what had happened to Michel? There was only one explanation for his disappearance. The police had arrested him and forced him to talk. Poor Michel.

Ten minutes later, Karamanlis left the building as well and got into a patrol car headed towards Omonia Square. The director of Antiquities had been found in a restaurant in the centre and was waiting for Karamanlis to join him for coffee.

5

THE ENIGMATIC SPLENDOUR of the Mycenaean kings glowed in the torch beam, their austere faces eternal captives of the gleaming gold. The silent chambers of the great museum rang with the slow footsteps of the chief custodian, Kostas Tsountas, doing his rounds, just like every night, in the faint light of the safety switches. The same walk, every night, from the Mycenaeans to the kouroi to the Cycladic art and then, last, through the room with the ceramics and frescoes of Santorini.

The beam of light caressed the lovely marble shapes and the custodian felt perfectly at home in the atmosphere, in a dimension quite unreal yet somehow close and familiar.

He had spent his whole life amidst these creatures of stone, of gold and of bronze, and he felt he could nearly hear them breathing in the solitude of the night. He captured them in the darkness, one by one, with his torch. During the day, they were nothing but inanimate objects, offering themselves up to the hurried consideration of organized tour groups trotting behind their guides in a hum of different languages. But they came alive for him at night.

His routine took him up to the second floor and the enormous vase of Dipylon with the funeral procession that stretched around its belly, figures frozen in geometric grief. Kostas Tsountas was at an age when he had begun to ask himself who would weep for him when his time came. He checked his watch before returning to his guard station. Twenty to twelve; at midnight his shift would be over.

He heard the telephone ring: a huge, sudden noise that made him startle. Who could it be at this hour? He hurried towards the entrance and managed to pick up the receiver before the ringing stopped. 'Hello?' he said, catching his breath.

'This is Ari Malidis, who am I speaking with?'

'Ari? What do you want at this time of night? It's me, Kostas.'

'Kostas, I'm so sorry to bother you, but I have a problem.'

'What is it? It had better not be too complicated; I'm off in fifteen minutes.'

'Listen, I've been going through the inventory for the dig and I've realized that there's an important piece missing. If the director checks up on me tomorrow morning I'm in big trouble. You know how finicky he is. The fact is that poor Professor Harvatis didn't have a chance to put things in order; you know he died suddenly, and I'm trying to fix things. Please, Kostas, let me in so I can put a piece back in the storeroom.'

'You're crazy, Ari. After the museum's closed no one can come in.'

'Kostas, for the love of God, it's a jewel, very small and very precious. It's been in my house for three days; if the director finds out there'll be hell to pay. Please, it won't take me long. Do me this favour. Just two minutes; enough time to put it back with the other finds from the dig.'

Tsountas fell into a perplexed silence. 'All right,' he said. 'I'll let you in this time, but if it should ever happen again, it's your problem. I don't want trouble.'

'Thanks, Kostas. I'll be there in fifteen minutes.'

'Sooner. If not you'll have to convince the guy on the second shift, who's new on the job. He won't open up even if you cry.'

'I'll be there right away. I'll knock three times on the back door.'

'All right, but get moving.'

He put down the receiver and took a bunch of keys to

disconnect the alarm in the eastern section of the museum. 'Some people just don't have any common sense,' he grumbled to himself. 'How could he ask me for such a favour? I could lose my job, dammit.' On the other hand, Ari wasn't a bad guy, he was an honest man, and had seemed really worried.

He waited ten minutes, then crossed the Cycladic room and went towards the offices. He disconnected the alarm and soon heard the three knocks at the door and a voice, 'It's Ari, let me in, please.'

'Get in here, and hurry. I have to turn the alarm back on in five minutes. Try to be out of here by then.'

'Just give me time to go down and come back up,' promised Ari, slipping through the half-opened door and hurrying down the basement stairs.

Kostas closed the door, muttering under his breath, when the telephone began to ring again. 'Oh Lord,' said the old man, accelerating his pace, 'who could it be this time? Thirty years and nothing ever happens, and now, in just ten minutes . . . Oh, good heavens, good heavens. What if . . .'

'National Archaeological Museum,' he answered, lifting the receiver and trying to conceal his agitation.

'The general director of Fine Arts and Antiquities speaking. Who is this?'

'The chief custodian, Kostas Tsountas. What is it, sir?'

'I'm calling from a police car. We'll be at the front door in five minutes. We have to search the premises.'

The old man thought he would die, but tried to gain time: 'I'm not authorized to open up for anyone at this time of night. If you really are the general director, you know that we're subject to checks and that we have orders to refuse any request. I can't obey a voice on the telephone.'

'You are perfectly right, Mr Tsountas,' said the voice. 'I'll be providing an order written on the Ministry letterhead, along with my personal identification card. I'm with Captain Karamanlis of the Athens police. I congratulate you on your diligence.'

Tsountas found the strength to answer: 'I'll look at the documents, sir, and decide whether the door should be opened.' He hung up and fell back on to the chair.

Ari! He had to get him out of there before they came to inspect the place. Maybe someone had seen him going in and called the police; what else could have happened? He got up and ran towards the basement stairs. He yelled: 'Ari! Ari! Get out of there on the double, the police are on their way for an inspection!' There was no answer. He went down two steps at a time, nearly breaking a leg, and rushed to the storeroom door: 'Ari! Get out of here, the police are coming, they'll be here any minute!' His words echoed between the bare brick walls of the basement and died, leaving the building in total silence once again.

He grabbed the handle of the door: it was locked. Thank goodness, Ari had already left. He searched his bunch of keys feverishly to find the one that would open the storeroom so he could check that everything was in order. He opened the door, switched on the light and gave the room a once-over. Everything looked fine. He locked it again and went back up to the main floor. His heart was in his throat: his weight, his age and all this excitement had taken their toll. He heard the bell ringing at the entrance and then a roar of thunder that seemed to shake the whole building. Someone was beating down the front door with a weapon of some kind; the noise was resounding all through the museum's rooms and halls.

At the front entrance, he adjusted his uniform, dried the sweat that was dripping down his brow, then called out as steadily as he could: 'Who is it? What do you want?'

'It's the general director, Tsountas. I'm with police Captain Karamanlis. I called five minutes ago. I'm about to pass a written order on official letterhead under the door, as I said I would, along with my ID card and that of Captain Karamanlis. Check everything and then open the door immediately. Any resistance will be considered insubordination, with all due consequences.'

Tsountas checked the documents to see that everything was

in order, then opened the door, relieved that Ari had left after putting that piece in the storeroom.

'Come in, sir,' he said, removing his cap. 'Please excuse me, but I'm sure you realize that I'm responsible . . .'

'Do you have a map of the museum?' asked Karamanlis immediately. 'I have to inspect the premises.'

'What in goodness' name has happened?' asked Tsountas, taking a folded tourist map from the souvenir counter and handing it to the officer.

'It seems that a group of subversives used the museum as their base during the occupation of the Polytechnic,' explained the director. 'Most likely with the complicity of a museum employee, without whom they wouldn't have been able to enter. The captain wants to search the museum before any evidence disappears . . . I'm sure you understand.'

Tsountas didn't feel so sure any more, and suddenly remembered Ari Malidis's strange request to enter the basement in the middle of the night . . . could he be the accomplice they were talking about? No, impossible. Ari had never got mixed up in politics, in all the thirty years he'd known him.

ARI WAS IN a panic: he had looked everywhere after thoroughly going through the corner cabinet where the boys had said they'd hidden the vase. When he'd heard Kostas Tsountas's footsteps and his key turning in the lock, he'd flattened himself behind some shelves, where the brooms were kept, but as soon as Tsountas had left, he'd begun searching again. It was simply nowhere to be found. He was crushed.

Professor Harvatis had died for nothing . . . the treasure which had cost him his life had disappeared, perhaps into the hands of someone who could not understand its value and its meaning. What would he say to that man when he came back for the vase? Because he'd be back, could be back at any moment, to ask for what was his.

The room wasn't very big and there weren't many places where such an object could be hidden, but his anguish drove him to rummage everywhere without any plan in mind, and then to search the same places once again in the conviction he hadn't looked well enough.

That man would be back, holy Mother of God, he'd be back with that iron stare and that voice capable of making anyone obey him. How could he tell him that he'd lost it . . . lost it for ever?

A footstep sounded in the hall and Ari slipped back into his hiding place. Someone was putting the key in the lock, opening the door, heading straight for the corner cabinet.

Captain Karamanlis knew what he was looking for. He took the bucket of sawdust out of the cabinet, dipped his hands in and lifted the embossed vase up towards the ceiling to observe it in the lamplight. The reflection of the gold on his face made him look deathly pale and more than a little bit crazy, but his gaze was eloquent: that marvel had instantly invaded his mind. He seemed lightning-struck, and the astonished, avid look in his eyes betrayed tumultuous feeling.

Ari realized that he had no choice. He slipped behind the other man, and when Karamanlis put the vase down he hit him hard with his torch between the nape of his neck and shoulders. He collapsed without a cry.

Tsountas and the nightwatchman who had just arrived to take over his shift found him ten minutes later, stretched out on the floor, groaning. They helped him up.

'Captain, Captain, what happened? Do you feel ill?'

Karamanlis got to his feet, leaning against the wall for a few seconds. He passed his hand over his eyes and looked slowly around, eyes coming to rest on the empty surface of the table in front of him. He said in a calm voice: 'I must have passed out. I haven't slept for two nights, maybe it's the stuffy air down here . . . there aren't any windows. Let's get out of here, I need a breath of fresh air.' They went back up to the main floor.

'The captain passed out,' said Tsountas.

'It's nothing. I just felt a little dizzy, that's all. I'm just tired.'

'Did you find what you were looking for?' asked the director.

Karamanlis sneered as he massaged the back of his neck. 'Yes,' he said. 'I did. And someone will pay for it sooner or later, you can be sure of that.' They walked out of the front entrance together. Karamanlis stopped a taxi to have the director taken home.

'Aristotelis Malidis – does that name mean anything to you?'

The director shook his head.

'He works for the Service. I'd like to know everything possible about him. Send me his personal file, please. Today if you can. I'll be waiting for it.'

'Of course, Captain. Do you have evidence against him?'

'Nothing certain. Just . . . a suspicion. But it's best to check things out.'

'Naturally.'

'Goodnight, director, and thank you for your collaboration.'

'Goodnight, Captain. Always at your disposal.'

Karamanlis watched as the taxi sped off into the night, and walked to his own car. It was time for him to go to sleep, even though the day had been a bad one, unsatisfactory in every way. With a fresh mind tomorrow morning, he'd decide what to do.

KOSTAS TSOUNTAS HAD finished his shift and was planning on going to bed as well. He jumped on his bicycle and started to pedal steadily. He couldn't wait to get home, although he was afraid he wouldn't sleep. His headlight cast a little beam on to the dark street, sometimes intense and sometimes weak, depending on the incline. In front of his house, he pulled out the key for the little garage, raised the shutter and put his bike inside. It was as shiny now as when he'd bought it twenty years ago. He closed the shutter carefully, trying not to make a noise, and knelt down with difficulty to close the padlock, although he knew well there was nothing worth stealing in there.

A hand touched his shoulder as he was getting up: his legs crumbled beneath him and he fell back down on his knees, trembling with fear.

'It's me, Kostas, it's Ari.'

The old man struggled to get up, leaning against the shutter. 'You? Now what do you want? Don't you think you've fooled me enough for one night? I'm sure that you didn't put anything back in that storeroom. You came to wipe away the traces of some nasty business of yours, didn't you? Don't you care anything about the honour and reputation of an old colleague?'

'It's true,' said Ari, his head low. 'I did come to erase something, and I was the one who let the subversives into the museum. Three terrified kids, they were, trying to help a girl who was wounded; those butchers put a bullet right through her, the poor child. I tried to save them, while many others just like them were falling under fire, being mangled by their tanks. Poor kids . . .' His voice trembled with indignation and sorrow. 'They were our children, Kostas, oh holy Mother of God.' His eyes welled up. 'They were our children . . .'

'You did the right thing,' said the old man. 'By God, you did the right thing. I couldn't imagine.' He sat down on the front steps. 'Sit down here with me for a moment,' he said, 'just for a moment.'

OFFICERS PETROS ROUSSOS and Yorgo Karagheorghis were travelling on the state road for Marathon and were entering the wooded area on the Pentelikos heights. They weren't far from the appointed spot: the big hydroelectric basin fed by the Mornos river. A little road led off the state highway, following the shoreline in a north-westerly direction and ending up in a densely forested area. A small boat was waiting for them, tied to a stake on the shore.

They loaded up Heleni's body and some weights. Karagheorghis left the car's headlights on and got into the boat behind his companion, who was sitting at the rudder. Roussos started up the little diesel engine at the stern and directed the boat towards the middle where the water was deepest. It was totally dark, and his only point of reference was the light in the dam's control cabin which was blinking on and off about half a mile in front of him. Roussos, sitting at the stern with the rudder in hand, was thinking of how he would spend the bonus the chief would give him for carrying out this mission. Karagheorghis had planned everything out carefully: the body was all strapped up with nylon cord and the weights would take her right to the bottom.

They'd reached the spot, near a little peninsula on the left side of the lake. Karagheorghis switched on a light on board to tighten the straps, then threw the body overboard, followed by the weights which would drag it to the bottom.

In the dim light, Heleni's white forehead and long hair remained visible for an instant, like a tuft of black algae floating in the Stygian swamp.

Then Roussos switched off the light, accelerated and veered towards the shore, towards the car's headlights; those little white staring eyes guided him safely back through the night, back to the land of the living.

IT WAS POURING with rain, a dirty rain that sullied the windscreen on the squad car with black streaks. All Karamanlis had in his stomach was a cup of coffee, although he'd already smoked a couple of cigarettes. Roussos and Karagheorghis must have completed their mission; he'd seen the 'okay' signal, a string of *komboloi* beads hanging from the rear bumper of his car, which he always left parked in front of the house. There was another problem, however: the Italian boy. What was Bogdanos going to do with him? If the kid talked, it might get him into real trouble; he didn't know what to expect from a guy like Bogdanos.

He had to find out first of all who was giving him his orders, and how he could get back in control of the situation. There must be something in the guy's reserved file, some way he could blackmail him. He turned on the radio to listen to the morning news. What he heard gave him a real start: 'There has been a terrorist attack in the immediate vicinity of police headquarters. A car loaded with explosives has blown up with two people aboard: a man and a woman. A wing of the building has been damaged.'

Karamanlis switched on his service radio and picked up the microphone: 'This is Captain Karamanlis. What the hell were you waiting for to inform me? I heard the news over the radio.'

'We were trying to call you, Captain. The radio station must have intercepted the message, they're right nearby.'

'All right. Keep everyone away from the scene. I'll be there in two minutes. Over.'

'We'll wait. What should we do with all these reporters?'

'Don't let them get close, and don't make any statements until I get there. Has anyone showed up from the district attorney's office yet?'

'Not yet, but the coroner has been notified and he should be here in twenty minutes. Over.'

'Okay. I repeat, keep everyone away. I'll be right there. Over and out.'

He took a blinker from his glove compartment and set it on the roof of the car, turned on the siren and rushed at top speed through the already chaotic city traffic. When he arrived, he saw a cordon of police keeping a group of onlookers away. Behind them the wreckage of a car covered the asphalt over a wide area; what was left of the chassis was enveloped in a cloud of steam and extinguisher foam. There was blood everywhere, and shreds of human body parts covered by sheets of plastic.

An officer approached him: 'It fully appears that they were planning to bomb the station, but the explosives went off before they could park the car: real amateurs.'

'Any possibility of identifying the bodies?'

'None. There was so much explosive aboard that they practically disintegrated. If you'd like to come in, we're preparing a report for the district attorney's office.'

'All right. You continue collecting all the evidence, I'll be back in a few minutes. If the coroner arrives, let me know immediately.'

He went into the office and checked the report, skimming it rapidly. The telephone rang: 'Police headquarters: Captain Karamanlis speaking.'

An unmistakable voice answered: 'It's Bogdanos.' Karamanlis loosened his tie and nervously lit another cigarette.

'I'm listening,' he said.

'Is it true that there were a man and a woman aboard that car?'

'Yes, that's right.'

'Are the bodies identifiable?'

'The biggest piece is like a pack of cigarettes.'

'Good. We have the solution to our problem. I can't say anything over the phone. Walk outside and meet me in the bar across the street.'

'But the coroner is about to arrive.'

'Exactly. I must see you before you talk to him. Come immediately, it's a matter of life or death.'

Karamanlis went towards the window and looked across at the bar: there was a man standing at the phone wearing a homburg and a dark coat. 'I'm on my way,' he said, and hurried over.

Bogdanos was sitting at a table with a cup of Turkish coffee in front of him.

'This attempted bombing will get us out of a fix and provide us with two anonymous corpses to utilize as we like: the two occupants of the car were Claudio Setti and Heleni Kaloudis. She was a terrorist, and had convinced her young Italian lover to help her. Give this version to the press and our problems will be solved. The Italian embassy will open an investigation but they won't get anywhere.'

'Just one second, Admiral: I know the girl will never come back, but that boy was alive when I turned him over to you. Who's to tell me that he won't reappear after I've announced his death?'

Bogdanos's hat sat low over his eyes and he didn't even lift his head to look his interlocutor in the face: 'The boy won't turn up anywhere. After what he had seen we certainly couldn't let him go. But at least we got him to talk. You, with your disgraceful methods, you didn't learn a thing.'

'My methods may be disgraceful, but I use violence honestly, no tricks, just pure and simple violence: whoever is tougher wins. You deceived him: he thought you had come to save him. You're just bigger hypocrites.'

Bogdanos lifted his head slightly, revealing his clenched jaw: 'Deception is an intelligent human weapon, and is even compassionate at times. Violence is brutish. Do as I say. Do you have any of Heleni Kaloudis's personal effects, to prove her identity?'

'Her University ID.'

'Show it to the judge after you've burned it up a little with some gasoline. And add this.' He took a couple of little medals out of his pocket and handed them to Karamanlis. He turned one over: 'To Claudio, with love, Heleni', it said, in Greek. 'There won't be any follow-up. Both are actually dead, and the accomplices of whoever really was in that car certainly won't come forward.'

Karamanlis hesitated for a moment, then dropped the medal in his pocket and said: 'I think it's a good solution. I'll do as you say.' He looked towards the street. The coroner's car had arrived and one of his men was pointing at the bar. 'I have to go.'

'Karamanlis.'

'What?'

'What were you looking for last night in the basement storeroom at the National Museum?' Karamanlis thought he would faint; in just a few seconds his well-honed bloodhound's instinct sorted through dozens of possibilities, all of them absurd.

'A normal search. We'd had a report of . . .'

'Whatever you were looking for, forget it. Forget all about it. Do you understand me? Forget it if you want to save your skin. You won't be warned again.' He got up, left a coin on the table, and left.

Karamanlis followed him out and crossed the street as if drunk, greeting the official who had been charged with the investigation.

'Good morning.'

'Good morning, Captain. I'd say there's not much chance of identification.'

'I wouldn't say that, sir. We have some real proof of identity. When you're finished here, come into my office. I have something to show you.'

AN HOUR LATER, Claudio Setti, sitting in a bare, cold little room in the Piraeus port district, heard the news of his death and Heleni's.

He wept for Heleni's lost life, for the enormous outrage and the atrocious violation of her body, her soul and her memory, and he wept for his own life, lost as well. He would still be breathing the air of the living, for how long he didn't know. But he was certain that what awaited him was no longer life, not any more. His heart was already buried deep in an unknown ditch along with Heleni's profaned body.

That evening, the legal procedures completed, Professor Harvatis's funeral was held in the presence of a *papàs* and two grave-diggers. He was lowered into a hole dug by a mechanical digger and already partially flooded by the rain that had been falling heavily all day.

Ari had learned of the funeral from Kostas Tsountas when he had gone to work at the museum that morning, because the hospital – seeing that the dead man had no relatives – had notified the Antiquities and Fine Arts Service, which had sent out a bulletin to their main branches throughout the city.

He went to the funeral but remained far away from the coffin so he wouldn't be noticed. Hiding behind the column of a portico, he said the prayer of the dead for the soul of Periklis Harvatis so that God might greet him into his eternal light, but felt a weight on his heart that was not just pity for those hurried, unseemly funeral rites. He felt a dark presence, restless and uneasy, dominating that bleak landscape of crosses and mud. An unsolved mystery that was descending, for ever, into that tomb.

He looked around him, certain that the only person who knew whom or what Periklis Harvatis had died for would appear.

But the cemetery porticoes were deserted in whichever direction he turned to look.

The *papàs* and grave-diggers had already left. Ari dried his eyes and hurried towards the exit, because the custodian was closing the cemetery. He lingered at the gate for a moment, looking at the small mound scored by little rivulets of water. Reluctantly, he opened his umbrella and walked away in the driving rain.

6

Athens, 19 November, 6 p.m.

NORMAN SHIELDS READ the news about the deaths of Claudio Setti and Heleni Kaloudis in the evening edition of *Tà Nèa*. The story was on one of the inside pages and faced the sports page, with its eight-column story on the match of the year: Panathinaikos versus AEK. Norman had arrived at police headquarters that morning just after the explosion. He had realized that, given the circumstances, they would hardly be concerned with releasing his friends just then. Lying low in his car, he'd watched the comings and goings of the police and public officials, and had even seen Karamanlis at the bar across the street speaking with a stranger.

When he read the news in the newspaper, he was sure that he'd been played for a fool, yet he couldn't figure out why. He thought of going straight to the National Archaeological Museum, but it would be closed and Ari would have left hours ago. If he was on duty at all.

Maybe his father could help. He reached him at the British embassy and showed him the newspaper story of the bombing. How could Claudio and Heleni have been in that damned car if they were being held prisoner? He knew full well that they'd been arrested by the Greek police and dragged off down the streets of Plaka before the eyes of a special agent who had arrived too late.

'Norman . . . Norman, I'm afraid they've killed them,' said

his father in a low voice. 'They simulated a terrorist attack to get rid of the bodies. I'm sorry.'

Norman felt like dying. He turned towards the wall and burst out crying: 'But why?' he kept repeating. 'Why . . . why?'

'Norman, Heleni Kaloudis was considered one of the leaders of the students' movement at the Polytechnic. Maybe the police thought she had important information. Maybe they used a heavy hand to get her to talk . . . I'm just hypothesizing here, son. An interrogation can turn into a situation of no return where the sole solution is the physical elimination of all witnesses. I'm afraid this may have been the cause of your friends' deaths.'

'Okay, if that's how things went, we have proof that they were in the hands of the police and we can nail them with it. At least we can see justice done.'

'No. We can't. The only witness to their arrest was one of our secret service agents; we cannot create a scandal of this proportion in this situation and in this country. The consequences would be unforeseeable; it could destabilize our alliance. We're bound hand and foot. Unfortunately, you'll have to resign yourself to it. It's a very sad, very bitter experience for you . . . and for myself as well, son. Believe me. I did everything I could.'

'I know you did,' said Norman, completely giving up. 'Goodbye, father.'

'Where are you going?'

'Back to England. I can't stay in this country any longer. I'm leaving on the first flight out.'

'What about your studies?'

Norman didn't answer.

'Will you come to say goodbye?'

'I don't know. If I don't, don't feel badly. It's not you I blame, it's the whole world, myself. I just want to forget, although I know I never will. Goodbye, father.'

'Goodbye, son.'

James Shields walked his son to the door, and as he was

crossing the threshold he suddenly hugged him tightly. 'You'll forget these days,' he said. 'You're young.'

Norman freed himself from his father's embrace. 'Young? My God, there's nothing young left in me. I've lost everything.' He walked out on to the street and towards the bus stop.

His father watched him for a few minutes from the window of his study until he disappeared from sight. The elder Shields had never considered that his son might be affected by the consequences of his profession. He'd always kept him out of it, and he'd never opposed Norman's passion for archaeology, although he considered it an interest both costly and useless. Now, by a strange coincidence, their two lives had meshed dangerously and risked colliding. Looking at his mourning son, he felt suddenly close to the victims himself, unwillingly involved. They were no longer anonymous corpses like so many in his long career. The cynicism essential to a man who was used to considering reasons of state above all else was failing him. His son's tears made him feel close to the boy. It gave him reason to hope for a reconciliation after the exasperating conflicts of recent years; his son was a rebel, independent, scornful of the bond with authority that had been at the centre of his family tradition for generations. It was certainly a good idea, in any case, that he go back to England. Time would heal his wounds, and maybe he'd find a girl who would help him to forget about these unhappy days.

Norman closed himself into his little apartment in Kifissìa and packed up his personal things into a backpack. He counted up the money he had and realized it was insufficient to take a train, let alone an aeroplane.

He decided he'd hitch-hike, rather than ask his father for anything.

He fell into an agitated sleep, full of anguished dreams: the car packed with TNT exploding and disintegrating into thousands of bloody bits. He saw himself killing Karamanlis, plugging dozens of bullets into his body. He saw the cop's lifeless body jerking at every shot, his face mangled, his chest torn open, his impeccable uniform soaked in blood and excrement. He awoke again and again, drenched in a cold sweat.

. When morning finally arrived, he left the house, putting the keys and an envelope with the last month's rent under the landlady's door. It was still dark out, and the streets were empty and silent. He walked to the little bar at the corner that was just opening and sat down for a Turkish coffee and two sesame-seed bread rolls. They were always so good, these sesame rolls, so fresh and crisp. He'd eaten them countless times with his friends, around that very table. There was no one left but Michel now, but looking for him made no sense. Michel was hidden somewhere in France, wasting away with remorse and shame. What good would it do to ask him why he hadn't resisted, why he hadn't been stronger? Michel had a right to forget as well. Who knew, maybe one day the two of them would find the courage to meet up again somewhere. Maybe they'd meet by chance, and pretend that nothing had ever happened. They'd remember how it was at first, the day they met in Epirus, the evenings in the tavern, their studies, the girls . . .

He walked out on to the street, while a cold pale light sculpted the barren mound of Mount Hymettus against an ash-grey sky. He nudged the backpack up on to his shoulder and walked north. A truck transporting a herd of sheep to the pastures of Thessaly stopped to pick him up. He got into the rickety vehicle and curled up on the seat with his backpack between his legs. The bleating of the sheep, the chatter of the driver, the din of the old asthmatic engine and the unhinged side boards didn't even touch the abysmal silence of his soul, or alter the painful, stupefied look in his eyes.

He crossed Thessaly and Macedon, passed the border at Evzoni and travelled through Yugoslavia under torrential rain on a Bulgarian semi carrying a load of meat for Italy. He crossed Austria and Germany, sleeping in hostels or under the shelters at service stations. In three days and three nights he reached the Channel and landed at Dover, white with snow.

Athens seemed as distant then as a remote and desolate planet.

When he opened his passport at the border control station, a photo fell out: it was a polaroid he'd taken with Michel and Claudio next to the Deux-Chevaux on the mountains of Epirus. He didn't bend down to pick it up, allowing it to be trampled by the muddy boots of the truck drivers at the inspection counter.

And so he snuffed out the memories of the last years of his youth.

THE ITALIAN CONSULATE opened an investigation into the death of Claudio Setti, although he had no close relatives, as instructed by the Foreign Affairs Ministry. The version provided by the Greek police contrasted greatly with the information they were able to collect among his companions and professors at the Italian school of archaeology in Athens. Claudio was described as an easy-going, polite boy, with rather conservative political ideas, scrupulous in his studies. Not the picture of a dangerous terrorist, unless he had agreed to accompany his girlfriend that day without knowing what was in the car. In any case, no evidence for any involvement on his part ever turned up, and his death remained a mystery.

Captain Karamanlis, who had sought more information on Ari Malidis, ended up abandoning his efforts. The file he had asked for eventually came through, but bureaucratic red tape and the lack of eagerness on the part of the Fine Arts Service to collaborate with the political police led to considerable delays, and his request ended up fuelling suspicion on his account rather than providing any useful information. Moreover, Admiral Bogdanos's words had had a profound and long-lasting effect on him, hanging over his head like a permanent threat. Besides, normalization operations were taking up all of his time: inspections, interrogations, searches, arrests.

He had gone as far as Patras and Salonika to incriminate a number of professors who had declared their solidarity with the students during the Polytechnic revolt, and to arrest members of clandestine labour unions who had encouraged the students' demands for a general strike.

Throughout all these operations he was never able to uncover anything more than what everyone already knew: that there was widespread intolerance of and rebellion against the government. But he never had the least doubt that his convictions were absolutely on the ball: he was certain that the whole plot had been cooked up by outside organizers and that it was just through bad luck that only the little fish had got caught up in his nets.

Sometimes, late at night, he sat at his desk with a sandwich and a bottle of beer trying to trace the connections between the group of people who had given him so many headaches at this crucial moment of his life: Norman Shields, who had told him about the golden vase, was the son of James Henry Shields, the liaison between the Greek and American secret services, and was the friend of Claudio Setti, Michel Charrier and Heleni Kaloudis. Plus he knew Ari Malidis, who had brought a dying man to the hospital at Kifissìa in the middle of the night.

And this Admiral Bogdanos, who always knew everything and was everywhere. He'd even known about his unfortunate midnight excursion to the museum basement! Who could have informed him? The director of Antiquities? Improbable. The young Shields himself? But what connection could there be between a high-ranking secret service officer and a twenty-year-old student? The strangest thing was that there were no plausible connections between these people, apart from the group of friends, who were clearly all archaeology students. But there was one thing that they all had in common: the magnificent gold vase that he had held in his hands for a moment.

Was that the connection? The true centre of gravity? If only he could manage to find out where it was and what it meant – those figures engraved on the vase . . . so strange – then maybe he'd understand what it was that tied all those people together. But the vase had disappeared and he had no clue where he could find it. And something told him that it was too risky, business too big for someone like him. Bogdanos's order to stay away had nearly even made him forget about the blow a stranger had dealt him so unexpectedly that night in the National Museum.

For weeks and weeks he was also tortured by the thought that Bogdanos might screw him with that story about Claudio Setti. After all, he had no real proof that the kid had been rubbed out, and he cursed his hastiness that day. He'd let himself be drawn in like a novice. Maybe Bogdanos wanted to keep him on a leash with the threat of resurrecting a dead man and setting him on him. Okay, so what could be the worst possible scenario? He could always say he had acted in good faith, and refer to the personal objects, the ID card and medal that he'd shown to the coroner. When he'd nearly forgotten all about it – since nothing had happened in the meantime – one of the errand boys handed him an envelope. It contained a photograph showing Claudio Setti on the table of a morgue. If it had been anyone else, he would have turned it over to the technicians in the lab, but he thought it best to rely on cop's intuition this time. He burned the photo and banished it from his thoughts.

As time passed, the situation returned to normal; day after day, life was resuming its usual rhythms and at police head-quarters they went back to busying themselves with thieves and robbers, smugglers and swindlers. His opponents were in the cooler, meditating on their stupidity. This should have set his mind at rest, put his soul in peace. And yet . . . he was tense and nervous. Even at home, where he'd always managed to keep out work-day worries, he was irritable and bad-tempered and his wife did nothing but repeat 'What's wrong with you?' At times, getting out for a walk and a bit of fresh air, he even had the sensation he was being followed: a shadow that he could almost see out of the corner of his eye, but which vanished as soon as he turned his head. Him, followed! That was a laugh. He was the bloodhound, capable of hunting down his prey for weeks on end, for months. He must really be worn out.

One day he picked up the phone and called a friend at the Ministry of Defence: 'Do you have an officer named Bogdanos on the navy list?'

'Why do you want to know?'

'Nothing in particular. Just . . . curious.'

'Bogdanos, you said? Wait, I'll check. Certainly, Anastasios Bogdanos. I'll call you back when I've taken a look at his file. It'll be a fine opportunity to see you! You never come round any more. You never think of an old friend unless there's something you need, huh?'

'You're right, I should be ashamed of myself. Thanks for your trouble.'

They met a few days later at a tavern in the Plaka.

'He's a war hero. Did time on the submarine *Velos*, much decorated, gold medal, former commander of the navy academy, currently assigned to special duties with the staff office, of which he is a member.'

'Is it too much to ask what these special duties are?'

'You said it. Let him go, my friend, don't bite off more than you can chew.'

'Is he so powerful?'

'He's an honest man. No one has anything on him. In our current situation, that makes him a man to be feared, because he knows everything about everyone, but no one can accuse him of anything.'

'Would you say he can be trusted?'

'I don't think he's ever fallen back on his word. If you've collaborated with him in some operation, you're safe on all sides. He's a man who, when he has to, pays off his debts in person. And punishes . . . in person, if necessary.'

'Where is he now?'

'There's nothing more I can tell you, even if I wanted to. I hope I've been of some help to you, my friend.'

'Oh, you certainly have. Of great help. Thank you.'

His friend changed the subject, chatting about the soccer championship and the music festival at Salonika. But the sound of a bouzouki wafted in from a nearby house, with the words from a song by Theodorakis: *'In his cell they tortured Andreas, And tomorrow they'll take him to die . . .'*

'Listen to that garbage! They should be arrested and taken to trial. They should all be arrested.'

Karamanlis fingered his *komboloi*, passing the yellow plastic beads from one hand to the other.

'Right.'

'Good. Well then, I'll say goodbye. Come by some time. You only show up when you need something, dammit!'

It was getting dark and Karamanlis walked to his car. He stopped at a street vendor's to buy a packet of roasted chestnuts for the kids: they loved them.

TEN YEARS LATER

7

THE MAN AT the reception desk was obviously annoyed at having to take his eyes off the Formula One grand prix on his little portable TV. He turned to the client who had just walked in.

'There are no vacancies,' he said. 'Unless you have a reservation.'

'I do have a reservation,' said the stranger, resting his suitcase on the floor.

The clerk took the register, turning the TV set so he could still see it out of the corner of his eye.

'What's the name?'

'Kouras, Stàvros Kouras.'

The clerk ran his finger down the guest list.

'Kouras with a K, right? . . . Okay,' he said, 'here we are. Suite 45, second floor. Could you please give me an ID, and then you can go right up.'

The stranger placed his passport on the counter. 'Excuse me,' he said, 'I need some information.'

'Yes?' replied the clerk, increasingly torn between his job and the object of his true interest.

'I'm looking for a man named Dino Ferretti. He lives here in Tarquinia and he's a tour guide.'

'Ferretti? Sure, he often takes our guests around. Matter of fact, if you hurry you'll probably find him with the last group of tourists at the necropolis of Monterozzi. Do you know how to get there?'

95

'No, but I'll find someone who can tell me,' replied the stranger.

'Oh, sure,' said the clerk, turning the volume on his set back up.

The stranger asked a boy to take up his suitcase and walked out of the door, leaving the deafening roar of Niki Lauda's McLaren behind him. He went to his car and drove past the city limits to the entrance of the necropolis. It was nearly closing time and the custodian had already put away the tickets and pulled down the shutter. He stood beside the gate, waiting for the last tour group to leave. They trickled out a few at a time, strolling towards the bus that was waiting for them. The guide, a young man of about thirty-five with a tour agency badge in the buttonhole of his jacket, was among the last to arrive. He lingered, answering the questions of the two or three people most interested in the tour. They were elderly American ladies in leisure suits and hats, still piqued by the sex scene in the Tomb of the Bulls and asking for embarrassing elucidation.

When they were all in the bus, the guide stepped up on to the footboard, checking outside to make sure there were no laggers, when his eye fell on the black Mercedes with Athens plates parked at the end of the lot. He suddenly scowled, staring at the indistinct shape behind the windscreen. The bus's pneumatic door slid shut, and he sat down next to the driver, eyeing the rear-view mirror. The Mercedes pulled out behind the bus and followed it at a distance of a couple of hundred metres. The tourists got out in front of the Rasenna hotel as the guide waved goodbye and set off on foot towards the high part of town. The Mercedes had disappeared.

He stopped in a grocery store to buy some cheese and cold cuts and pick up a magazine at the news-stand. He walked off, paging through it, headed towards a small building not far from the cathedral square. He stopped and looked around, trying to shake the sensation that he was being followed, then went into the main door and took the stairs up to the top floor.

He stood at the window and let his gaze wander over the

spread of red roof tiles and the flower-filled countryside beyond smelling of freshly cut grass. A cloud of starlings wavered uncertainly in the sky, looking for shelter as night began to fall.

A knock sounded at the door: a dry, hard sound. He sensed the same presence behind the door as behind the shiny surface of the windscreen up at the necropolis. Far off, over the fields, the clouds of starlings scattered, the dark shadow of a kite splitting them apart. He went to open the door.

'Good evening, son.'

'Admiral Bogdanos . . . you?'

'You weren't expecting me? Maybe I should have called first.'

The young man lowered his gaze and stepped aside. 'Come in, please.'

The man entered the room, walking across it with a slow stride and stopping next to the window. 'Quite a beautiful place,' he said. 'An enchanting view. And so this is where Dino Ferretti lives.'

'Yes, it is. And it is here that he will die, very soon. I've decided to recover my original identity.'

Bogdanos turned towards him and Claudio Setti thought he saw, for the first time since he'd met him, an expression of dismay, nearly panic – if it hadn't been for the unchanging strength in his eyes. He felt ashamed at what he had said.

'I owe you so much, Commander. My life, the tranquillity of this place, my shelter in a storm. But I feel it's useless to keep up this facade. I'll never be able to lead a normal life this way.'

Bogdanos flared up: 'Normal? You want a normal life? I understand. You want your name back, a woman, most likely, and children and a house with a garden and summer vacations. Is that what you want? Tell me, is this what you want? Tell me, dammit, so I'll know that all I've done has been in vain and that the person who I met and saved no longer exists.'

Claudio dropped to a chair, covering his face with his hands: 'Time changes many things, Commander. Even the most horrible wound scars over. You can die right away, of anger and of pain, but if you survive, it means that an unknown force is pushing you towards life. You can't blame me for this, Commander.'

'I understand. Now that the political situation in Greece has changed so radically and you feel you are no longer threatened, you think it's time to take up your true identity again. The newspapers will love it: a dead man lives . . .'

'You think I'm an ingrate and a coward. You're wrong. I've lived for years in the dimension that you assigned to me, waiting for the moment at which I could take revenge. I've followed all your instructions to the letter, but now I feel that it's all been useless. Human wickedness will remain, no matter what I do.'

Bogdanos nodded and fell silent for a few moments, then took his hat and walked towards the door.

Claudio seemed suddenly to shake off his mood. 'Commander.' Bogdanos turned towards him, the door handle already in his hand. 'Why did you come here today?'

'It no longer has any importance.'

'No. I want to know.'

'I'm sorry to have found you in this state of mind. I came to open your wound up again, to make it bleed . . . against your will, I'm afraid. Son, I have the proof which will nail those responsible for Heleni's death as well as their accomplices. I have devised a plan to destroy them. Every last one.'

Claudio paled. 'Why don't you turn this proof over to the law?'

Bogdanos looked appalled, as though Claudio were a complete stranger, speaking nonsense, but his voice betrayed no emotion.

'All the crimes committed during that time have fallen under the statute of limitations or have been covered by amnesty. They are, in any case, outside the jurisdiction of the law. They would never be punished. I know where they disposed of Heleni's body: they threw it into the dam at Tournaras, after having taken off her clothes. They were afraid that some strip of clothing might have floated to the surface and given them away. A cold tomb . . .'

Claudio felt tears rise to his eyes and stream down his cheeks, but he couldn't say a word. Bogdanos looked at him in silence and then started down the stairs. Claudio ran to the railing on the landing: 'Commander!' he yelled, his voice breaking. Bogdanos stopped and slowly turned his head upwards. 'Why? Why are you still seeking . . .'

The door to the street opened and a woman came in with a shopping bag. Bogdanos waited until she disappeared behind the door of an apartment on the ground floor. 'I've always punished unwarranted violence. Mercilessly.' He continued down the stairs, in the dark.

Claudio shouted again, through his tears: 'Why did you choose me? Why didn't you let me die?'

Bogdanos was already at the bottom of the last ramp of stairs and was about to open the outside door. He turned again, and his voice echoed darkly, like a wolf snarling from the depths of his lair. 'I didn't choose you, fate chose you. You can't escape the consequences of what has happened. Why don't I take care of it? I can't expose myself. Not here, not now. I've been fighting a hostile destiny, for ever, it seems . . . And I have to go back to my hotel. I'm tired. I've been investigating for years, understand? I'm tired . . .'

'Which hotel?'

'The Rasenna.'

'In what name? If I . . . if I were to look for you, what name are you registered under?'

'Kouras, Stàvros Kouras. Goodnight, my son.'

He disappeared down the street and the door closed behind him with a bang. Claudio rested his head on the railing and remained in that position, mentally counting Admiral Bogdanos's steps as he walked away, and imagined Heleni's white body in the black water as she vanished, swallowed up in its depths. 'Goodnight, Commander,' he murmured.

8

France, University of Grenoble, 10 June, 9 a.m.

'GOOD MORNING, PROFESSOR.'

'Good morning, Jacques. What's new?'

'Just the usual, Professor. Oh, I wanted to remind you that there's a faculty board meeting this afternoon.'

'Right. Trouble in the air?'

'Looks like it. Madame Fournier is furious because your department has made off with two of her graduate scholarships, and the students are planning to present a motion for exam reform beginning the next academic year.'

'Got it. We'll try to weather the storm and survive. Don't pass me any calls for the next ten minutes; I have to open my mail and look over my notes for the lesson.'

Michel Charrier hung his jacket on a coat hook and sat down at his desk. The telephone rang not a minute later.

'Jacques, I thought I said ten minutes.'

'I couldn't say no: it's Senator Laroche, from Paris.'

'Oh right, thank you, Jacques. Hello? Hello? Is that you, Georges? To what do I owe this pleasure?'

'Yes, it's me, Michel. And I have good news. The executive committee at the party secretary's office have decided to support your candidacy for the coming parliamentary elections. Not bad, eh? Well? Cat got your tongue?'

'Good God, Georges . . . what can I say? I . . . good heavens, I don't know what to say. I never expected anything like this . . .

well . . . I'm happy, very happy. Please, could you thank them all on my behalf . . . I'm literally . . . speechless!'

'Someone like you, speechless! Don't make me laugh. You'll have to find the words, you know. Meetings, assemblies, conferences . . . You'll have to find a wealth of words!'

'But, Georges, what about the University?'

'Yes, that's important. See, we're preparing everything so far in advance because we want to be ready when the moment comes. And so we were thinking it would be good if you could be tenured before the next electoral campaign begins. An element of prestige like that would be just the thing. We're planning on pushing this image hard: the excellent intellectual level of our candidates. The time when we were putting labourers up for parliament is long gone. The competition is setting such sharks into the arena that we can't make too many concessions to ideology.'

'Tenure! As if that were nothing at all! It's no joke, you know. I don't think the department intends to even ask for a chair for this subject.'

'Oh, that's nothing that can't be fixed. We may be the minority, but we're pretty strong in this neck of the woods, and we've got the right friends.'

'Georges, I'm afraid that's not enough. What I need is more . . . direct support.'

'We'll try to find that as well, but you have to get moving: produce something important, something that will get people talking even outside the academic world, maybe even abroad . . .'

'I understand. I'll . . . see what I can do. You have to give me time. Just off the top of my head . . . well, there is some research I've been working on, but I'm afraid it's not very sensational. I'll have to think about it.'

'That's fine, nothing to worry about, Michel. We'll see each other and think of something together, with the help of other friends, if need be. What's important is that you feel up to the challenge.'

'Well, of course I do.'

'Great, that's what I like to hear. We'll worry about the rest. Have to run now; I'll call you back next week. Is next week okay?'

'Oh, certainly. And thank you, thanks again.'

Michel hung up, leaned back in his chair and took a long breath. My God: Michel Charrier, tenured professor and member of parliament in one fell swoop! Not bad, not bad at all. One of the youngest and most brilliant intellectuals of France, one of the youngest deputies . . . that's what the papers would be saying. If everything went as planned.

He stretched out his hand to reach for a frame with the photo of a beautiful blonde girl with the sun in her hair.

Mireille, a brilliant career at the same university, associate professor of art history. One of the most illustrious families in the city, the Saint-Cyrs; also one of the most disagreeable and haughty. If all this went well, they'd no longer have a reason for keeping him away from their daughter. They'd have to recognize him for what he was and stop hindering their relationship. Maybe they'd even get married.

He realized that he should be ashamed of such plotting. The classic story: he loves her, she loves him, but 'they' are against it. And then the enterprising young man of modest working-class origins climbs up the ivory tower of the oldest aristocracy of the city, without losing his progressive ideals, naturally . . . *merde!* A *feuilleton*, that's what he was. A shameless social climber. He felt totally ridiculous.

What the hell. You only live once, he thought, and sometimes life was made of clichés; so what? He really did love her, and they were very happy together. It was authentic love. Everyone else could go get screwed.

He tried to control his exhilaration, the heady delirium that grabbed him whenever the wheel of fortune spun his way and spurred him to jump right into the fray. He realized that he had to consider the whole thing carefully, unhurriedly. The party was willing to set their sights on him as a brilliant, successful intellectual, faithful to his political and ideological principles: this was the image they wanted to create for him, how they wanted the electors to see him. The senator had been polite and encouraging, but it was evident that he himself, Michel Charrier, had to pull out the winning hand.

He put Mireille's photograph back down on the table and picked up the notebook in which he'd written the outline of his latest study: 'The propagandistic value of Roman-age agora constructions in Ephesus.' Less than awe-inspiring. Rigorous, original, deftly argued, but . . . a little dry. Okay to add to the bunch in a tenure evaluation, but not impressive enough to win him the chair. Nor to get people talking inside the University and out. What he was being asked to do was to exploit his research and to pretend, on top of it, that this wasn't a contradiction in terms in itself; that politics and science could join in a chaste union – without politics fucking science, put simply.

Dial up the senator and tell him to go to hell, or try to reconcile the two with the least amount of damage? He could attempt to come up with something. If nothing interesting occurred to him, he'd withdraw, declaring nobly that intellectual honesty allowed no compromise. The fox and the grapes. Shit.

Michel took the pack of unopened mail that was sitting on his desk and began to look through it. He just couldn't concentrate; he'd been invaded by a craving to take the bull by the horns, to get started on this new challenge, a challenge which was arousing all his energies. Energies which were flying every which way, like flies trapped in a bottle.

'Steady, now,' he chastised himself. 'The moment has not arrived; no means nor methods yet, just intent. And not even certain intention. Better to open the mail and think about the lesson.'

Catalogues, subscriptions, an invitation to a convention, a bill from a bookstore. Abstracts: 'Obscene language in military life in the Imperial age'; 'The importance of the asyndeton in Sallustian prose'; 'The composition of cement mortar in Sillan age constructions'; 'Hypothesis on the necromantic rite in the *Odyssey*, Book XI'; 'Internal road networks and Hadrian's Wall'; 'Phallic metaphors in slingshot projectile inscriptions'. It didn't look like his colleagues scattered throughout the world were coming up with many sparkling ideas either.

The caretaker knocked on the door: 'Professor, it's time for your lesson. Your students are waiting.'

He picked up his bag, his books and his notes and went along to the classroom, but his concentration was close to zero. He dragged laboriously through the lesson; there was an idea taking shape in the back of his head, but he needed a connection that just wasn't forthcoming. It fluttered around aimlessly without its meaning becoming clear. But it was a good idea, he could feel it, an important idea. Something that could solve the problem. What the devil . . . He suddenly realized that he hadn't finished his sentence and the students were looking at him in surprised silence. 'Oh, I'm sorry,' he apologized. 'I'm afraid I'm a bit distracted this morning. What was it I was saying?'

'You were saying that a fragment of Heraclid Ponticus reveals Alexander the Great's intention to dominate the West,' prompted a girl sitting in the first row, always present and always attentive, the type who would do postgraduate work and stay on for life in the department.

'Thank you, mademoiselle. In fact, as I was saying, although Heraclid Ponticus doesn't directly mention Alexander's bellicose intentions, he talks about the god Dionysus subjugating India and Etruria; that is, the easternmost and westernmost regions of the known world. Now, we know that, in keeping with his mother Olympia's religious convictions, Alexander was brought up to think of himself as an imitator of Dionysus. Thus we may reasonably presume that after having conquered India he would have planned to conquer Etruria, as Dionysus did. Etruria – in other words, Italy and the West. The stuff of myths was often transformed, in antiquity, into a very real force, with concrete consequences. Well. That's all for today. And . . . sorry about losing track earlier, I guess I'm a bit tired.'

The students filed out one after another, while the girl who had brought the conclusive words of the lesson to mind lagged behind, giving him a look – over a pair of elegant gold-framed glasses – of maternal comprehension and more-than-scholarly admiration.

Michel smiled distractedly and remained in the classroom after they had all gone. All right, now he could concentrate on collecting his wandering thoughts and getting a handle on this evasive idea. The idea seemed to be accompanied by the strains of a song, something rare, an old folk song, perhaps, an intense, sad melody . . .

The idea had something to do with the title of one of those abstracts . . .

A hypothesis, yes . . .

Hypothesis on the necromantic rite in the *Odyssey*, Book XI.

That was the key! An incredible exploit that would make him famous and attract the attention of the whole world. The prophecy of Tiresias! The raising of the dead . . .

The idea struck like lightning, releasing an image that had been held prisoner, sealed and scarred over at the back of his brain, for many years. The idea sprang out, razor-sharp, and penetrated his soul with cruel force before he realized what was happening. It exploded like a spring long compressed: the image of a warrior with an oar on his shoulder, being questioned by a man in Scythian garb. An altar behind him, with a bull, a boar and a ram. The golden vase . . . it represented the last voyage of Odysseus, the prophecy of Tiresias. Along with other, unknown, adventures of the hero, stories the world had never heard. The vase of Tiresias revealed the continuation of the *Odyssey*!

But from that vase, as if it were Pandora's box, flowed hallucinations he had long banished – unacknowledged blame, forgotten deaths, the salt of ancient tears. The blue pallor in Heleni's eyes, Claudio Setti's last glance, veiled with death . . . and that strange melody. It was a song that Claudio used to sing or play on his flute when he was alone . . . sitting on the seashore, far from the jokes and laughter of his friends . . .

Michel waited for his heart to absorb the impact, for the mad beating to quieten down. When the whirlwind had subsided, and only the soft notes of Claudio's song remained at the bottom of his soul, his eyes returned to the table, to the notebook open in front of him. He took a pencil and sketched out a drawing freehand: a nearly perfect reproduction of the vase he had seen ten years earlier in the basement of the National Museum, the night of the Polytechnic massacre.

It suddenly seemed as if just a few moments had passed: the vase rotated in space in his mind's eye, revealing its storied bands, its sequence of scenes. His hand raced over the paper, the pencil etching out the contours, the light and the dark. He stopped for a moment to give his memory time to assemble and recreate the forms as his newly tormented conscience shook with emotion. Unknown beasts and monsters, heraldic animals rearing up on the hero's unsheathed sword, mountains and valleys, birds immobile on that golden sky, wings wide.

His shirt was drenched with sweat and his hair plastered to his forehead; he had no idea how much time had passed when the caretaker stuck his head in the door.

'Professor, what are you doing here? I've been looking for you everywhere. The faculty meeting ended half an hour ago!'

Michel raised his eyes and the caretaker looked at him with a mixture of surprise and apprehension.

'What's happened, Professor? Is something wrong?'

Michel hurriedly gathered the sheets spread all over the desk and stuffed them into his briefcase. He took a handkerchief out of his pocket and dried his forehead: 'What time is it?'

'It's seven-thirty. I was just making my rounds before closing up the place. If I hadn't looked in this classroom, I would have locked you in! I always say, better to check everything, you never know.'

'Seven-thirty. It's late . . . it really is late, isn't it? I'm sorry, Jacques. I felt . . . faint, so I waited for it to pass, I didn't want to alarm anyone. It's nothing at all, it's just that lately I've been laying it on too thick with my work, I'm afraid. Monday I'll be fine. You'll see, I'll be fine . . .'

'Do you want me to call you a cab?'

'No thanks, my car is outside. I'll be all right.'

'Well then, have a nice weekend, Professor.'

'Just a minute, Jacques.'

'Yes?'

'Could you come with me for just a minute? There's something I have to show you.'

'Of course.'

Michel went to his study, took the envelope with the *Odyssey* abstract from the rest of his mail, and showed it to the caretaker.

'Jacques, all of these abstracts are addressed to the department, and you always leave them for me, because I'm the one who takes care of them. But on this envelope there's just my first and last name, no sender, no university stamp. Could you find out if we have contacts with this publisher, and if there are other publications from the same house here at the University?'

'Monday I'll check, and I'll let you know if you leave the envelope with me. But to tell you the truth, I've never noticed that name before. If you don't know who sent it to you, I may not be of much help.'

'Check our files, if you will, Jacques, and see if we have any other publications by the same author, and make me up a report. I'll be out until Wednesday.'

'All right, Professor. When you come back, I'll let you know what I've found.'

'Thanks. I'll take the abstract, then.'

He put it in his jacket pocket and walked out. The square was still warm with the late afternoon sun and a towering cloud in the middle of the sky was rimmed with its blond light. Michel went to the café on the other side of the square, sat down and ordered a cognac: he needed something to whip him back into shape. It was as if he had walked for miles: his back ached, and his legs felt like they would give way. When the waiter brought his drink, he took a long swallow and pulled the abstract out of his pocket. He read the name of the author and the title and looked for the publisher's name. He'd never heard of them: Perièghesis, 17 Dionysìou Street, Athens.

Athens . . . Would he see Athens again?

Grenoble, 13 July, 8 p.m.

Mireille Catherine Genevieve de Saint-Cyr had been waiting for ages, dressed in jeans and a fringed jacket, for her theatre-bistro date with Michel and two other couples. She couldn't understand why he hadn't at least phoned to tell her he'd be late.

She decided to call him herself, because she hated to make other people wait. The phone rang and rang, but there was no answer. Michel had surely left home already and was on his way: even calculating that he was just getting into the car, even calculating the decrepit Deux-Chevaux he was driving – twelve years old or more, incredible even by his intellectual *gauchiste* standards – and even calculating Saturday night traffic, he should have been able to get there in half an hour at the very most. She called her friends, apologizing for the delay and waffling a plausible excuse that she would work out with Michel, but half an hour passed, then an hour, without him showing up. She called her friends back and told them to go on ahead, then tried Michel again. Still no answer. She was starting to get worried. Michel had been acting a little strangely recently, but she couldn't imagine why he hadn't come to pick her up.

She went down to the garage and sped in her car over to Michel's place on rue des Orfèvres. The Deux-Chevaux was parked in front, full of papers and dust. She looked up: the light in his apartment was on. But if he was home, why wasn't he answering the phone? Maybe he was ill, or maybe he'd been robbed, attacked?

She ran up the stairs lightly, reached Michel's apartment and knocked on the door. At first there was no answer, then a hesitant voice asked: 'Who's there?'

It was not Michel's voice. It was a voice she'd never heard

before, with a foreign accent. The light on the stairs was timer-set and went off, and Mireille fumbled along the wall to switch it back on, but hit the doorbell instead. The same voice said: 'It's open, come in.' She turned around, frightened, and was about to go back down the stairs when the door opened and a dark, still shape loomed up behind it. She screamed.

'Mireille, calm down. It's me.'

'Michel? But what's wrong, why didn't you call me? There's someone in there – who is it?'

'It's . . . a friend. He arrived unexpectedly. It's about something very important.'

'But we had a date. You could have phoned me at least. I've been calling and calling.'

'I'm sorry, Mireille, please don't be angry.' His voice was hoarse and husky, as though he'd been talking for hours. 'Something happened. I've been out.'

'Something serious? Is someone hurt?'

'No, honey. No one's hurt. But please go now. I'll call you tomorrow. I'll explain everything.'

He turned on the light and Mireille could at last see him: he was pale, but his eyes were bright. 'Are you sure you're okay? Don't you want me to stay?'

'I'm fine. Please go.'

She walked away unhappily and Michel stood with his hand on the light switch, listening to her receding footsteps.

'Your girlfriend?' asked the voice behind him.

'Yeah. I'd forgotten about her. She was worried.'

'I'm sorry. I've ruined your evening.'

'It doesn't matter, Norman. I don't think I would have felt like going out, anyway. Come on, I'll make some coffee.'

Michel put the coffee pot on and got two cups ready. 'Why me?' he asked without turning.

'We're friends, aren't we?'

'Yes, of course.'

'You're an expert in your field. One of the best.'

'There's better.'

'Maybe. But you see, what's happened to me in just a few days is too much for anyone to face alone: my father killed under such absurd circumstances, and the golden vase reappearing suddenly in a little town in the Peloponnesus. After ten years. It all goes back to those days we've tried to forget.'

'But why me?'

'My father was killed by an arrow that split his heart. With a double-pulleyed Pearson bow, an incredibly lethal weapon. And he was blindfolded and gagged after his death. What's more, I've been told, unofficially you understand, that a message was found on his body. Weird words in archaic Greek, I think, that no one's been able to interpret. Like a ... signal of some sort, a macabre warning. I don't know why, but my mind went straight back to that day I left Athens to go back to London. My father told me that he thought Claudio and Heleni had been murdered by the police, but that there was nothing he could do about it; reasons of state prevented him from speaking out. You see, Michel? Everything points back to those days and only you can help me, because you know ... you're the only one who knows ...'

'Yeah. What went on behind the scenes, shall we say.'

'That's right. I can't imagine attempting to do this with anyone else. And even if I had tried to do it on my own, and hadn't told you anything ... well, if I had succeeded, you would have hated me for not telling you anything.'

'Maybe I should hate you for having come looking for me.'

Norman lowered his gaze: 'You've never let go ...'

'Why, you have?'

'We were kids, Michel. We did what we could.'

'You, maybe.' His voice trembled. 'I ... I ...' He couldn't go on.

'You were just the unlucky one. You were the one who got caught, Michel.'

'They were the unlucky ones. They died.'

Norman didn't know what to say. He looked at his friend, his face all wrinkled up like an old man's, his mouth twisting into a grimace, the tears leaking from his closed lids. He put a hand on his shoulder: 'We were so young. My God, Michel, we were just kids.'

Michel dried his eyes. 'Oh Christ, the coffee, it's boiling over.' He turned off the flame and noisily blew his nose, then poured the boiling coffee into two unmatching cups. 'I had some nice ones somewhere, but I can't find them any more.'

'Don't worry about it. You've always been a shambles. But you're getting worse as you get older! Got a smoke?'

'Gauloises,' said Michel, taking a pack from his pocket.

Norman took the cigarette and lit up: 'My God, still smoking this same shit. It's like old times, Michel. This coffee's not bad, but I wouldn't mind a nice cup of the Turkish stuff: it's been ages.'

'Listen, let's get on with it,' said Michel, lighting up a cigarette as well. 'Let's not waste any more time with preliminaries. Tell me exactly what's happening. And what you're thinking of doing.'

'I want to find out who killed my father and why.'

'The Greek police and British Intelligence are at work on it. Not enough for you?'

'We know more than they do, if my intuition is right.'

'And then?'

'Recover that golden vase.' Michel's coffee cup remained in mid-air. 'Drink, it'll get cold.'

'What are you saying, Norman?'

'It's reappeared, as I said. In a little town in the Peloponnesus, Skardamoula. And it's for sale.'

'How much?'

'Half a million dollars.'

'Who knows about it, besides you?'

'No one, I think. Besides the sellers. I was informed about it directly. Three days ago. I work for a newspaper, the *Tribune*. But I've also been working as a consultant at a prominent auction house for four years, and I'm in charge of investigating archaeological pieces, even the clandestine stuff.'

'Stolen.'

'Right, sometimes the pieces are stolen,' replied Norman with no apparent embarrassment.

'How can you be sure it's that vase and not something else?'

Norman took a photograph from his briefcase and handed it to Michel. 'It's ours. Without a doubt.'

'You're right. Without a doubt. Who gave you this photo?'

'I don't know. A voice on the phone told me I'd find it under my windscreen wiper. It was a man's voice, with a foreign accent. Greek, I'd say, almost certainly Greek.'

'And he told you where the vase is?'

'Yes. And he also told me how to get there.'

'But . . . what good can I do? You can easily do it all on your own. Bring it back to England and sell it.'

'You know I can't buy it at the price they're asking. Michel, that vase might take us to Pavlos Karamanlis . . . and help us find out the truth about Claudio and Heleni.'

Michel put his cup down on the table, stood up and walked to the window. He remained there, still and silent. Out on the street, Saturday-night life was in full swing.

'You shouldn't have come,' he said abruptly. 'Norman, you shouldn't have come.'

'But I'm here, Michel, and I'm waiting for an answer.'

Michel returned to the table and picked up the abstract he'd found in his mail at the University. 'It's strange,' he said.

'What?'

'You got that photo. And I got a sign as well. Both leading directly to that vase.'

'Are you afraid of something?'

'Yes, but I couldn't tell you what.'

'Well, what's your decision?'

'I'll go with you. Just let me finish this exam session at the University.'

'What was that sign you were talking about?'

'This abstract.'

'Have you read it?'

'I've been studying it for weeks. It is a hypothesis regarding the rite for raising the dead described in the eleventh book of the *Odyssey*. And the hypothesis is closely connected to the scene represented on that vase. You know, for twenty-five centuries, Odysseus's end has remained an unsolved mystery. Oh, I'm sorry, Norman, I wasn't thinking ... your father died such a short time ago.'

'No. Please, go on.'

'The key is in the second part of the prophecy of Tiresias. You remember the story: Odysseus is stranded on Circe's island, and he asks her to foretell his destiny, but she's not able to. Only the prophet Tiresias can reveal his fate, but Tiresias is dead. And so Odysseus is told he must cross the sea, reach the ocean and find a rock which marks the point at which the Acheron, the Cocytus and the Piriphlegeton – the three rivers of hell – flow together. There he will sacrifice a black ram and collect its blood in a sacred pit dug with his sword. The blood of the ram will attract the souls of the dead from Hades, Tiresias among them. Odysseus will be able to question him, after allowing him to drink the blood.'

Norman walked to a shelf containing the Greek classics, and took out a version of the *Odyssey*.

'The prophecy begins at line 119,' said Michel.

Norman looked for the passage and began to read, slowly:

> After you have dealt out death – in open
> combat or by stealth – to all the suitors,
> go overland on foot, and take an oar,
> until one day you come where men have lived
> with meat unsalted, never known the sea,
> nor seen seagoing ships, with crimson bows
> and oars that fledge light hulls for dipping flight.
> The spot will soon be plain to you, and I
> can tell you how: some passerby will say,
> 'What winnowing fan is that upon your shoulder?'
> Halt, and implant your smooth oar in the turf
> and make fair sacrifice to Lord Poseidon:

a ram, a bull, a great buck boar; turn back,
and carry out pure hecatombs at home
to all wide heaven's lords, the undying gods,
to each in order. Then a seaborne death
soft as this hand of mist will come upon you
when you are wearied out with old age,
your country folk in blessed peace around you.
And this shall be just as I foretell.

' "*Thànatos èx halòs*",' repeated Michel. ' "Death from the sea."
Ever since ancient times, it has been thought that these three
words meant that Odysseus died at sea. Dante Alighieri –
although he didn't know the original Greek – imagined that
Odysseus dared the ocean beyond the Pillars of Hercules, sinking
to its depths with his ship before the mountain of Purgatory.
Tennyson has him die in the middle of the Atlantic, sailing
towards the New World. But the original expression in Greek
can also be interpreted in a different way: not as "from", but as
"away from", meaning that Odysseus would die far away from
his natural element.'

'The prophecy does talk about a journey inland.'

'Exactly, towards a land where men live so far from the sea
that they have never seen a ship and mistake an oar for a
winnowing fan, a blade used to toss the threshed grain up into
the air to separate it from the chaff.'

'An odyssey over land, then, of which no trace has ever been
found, is that what you're saying?' Norman looked for the notes
at the end of the chapter. 'This commentary says that the second
part of the prophecy of Tiresias is the device used by the poet to
patch up the hostility between Odysseus and the god Poseidon,
whose son, the Cyclops, had been blinded by Odysseus. Homer
could not conceive that a man would continue to challenge a
god to the bitter end.'

'You know, many scholars have considered the eleventh
book of the *Odyssey* to be an afterthought, that is, added on at a
later date, but now we have proof that this isn't so: this vase
is irrefutable evidence that this second *Odyssey* did exist, and

that it is at least four hundred years older than the first written version of the poem. See what I mean? This is a Mycenaean vase, without a doubt, dating back to the twelfth century BC.'

He opened a drawer, pulled out the drawings he'd made at the University and spread them out on the table, one by one. Norman was astonished: 'Who did these drawings? My God, these are perfect, where did they come from?'

'I did them. A while ago. The image of the vase sprang into my mind, so clear and well-defined that I drew it as if I had it in front of me.'

'So you would have gone looking for it even without me.'

'I don't know. Maybe. I've been overwrought for weeks.'

'Michel, I can tell that your mind is made up. Just what do you hope to achieve? A journey always has a purpose and a goal, remember? That's what we always used to tell each other.'

'I'm not sure. My goal has been constantly changing. My God, Norman, it's like . . . I can't even control my own emotions any more. First, it was pure ambition. I wanted to make the greatest discovery of the century – the last days of Odysseus – and to join my name to this incredible endeavour. But now . . . I don't know. Maybe I want to find Karamanlis as well. I'm thirty-five; he'll be nearly sixty. Time always gives you a second chance, if you are patient. Time has made me stronger, but it has pushed him closer to the edge – the natural turn of events, no? What about you, Norman? Is it just the truth that you're seeking? Or is it the treasure hunt that entices you? If we go together, we have to be honest with one another. Time has passed and we have changed . . . we have to turn our cards up if we want to take off together.'

'Okay. It's not only about my father's death. What happened back then has healed over inside me and I never thought I'd think about it again. But that photograph woke up a part of me that I thought was dead . . . the hate that I'd buried, the sadness, the dreams. Michel, I want to go back because I lost a part of myself ten years ago: I want to know who took it and why. And what's left to me. There's nothing that can stop me now.'

Michel put the *Odyssey* back up on the shelf, carried the coffee cups to the sink and rinsed them out. 'If we're going back,' he said, 'and if it's Pavlos Karamanlis who you want to see again, maybe I should tell you everything that happened to me that night . . . if you're not too tired.'

'No,' Norman said. 'That coffee you made was pretty strong. We've got the whole night ahead of us. And there are some things that I have to tell you as well.'

MIREILLE WAS CURLED up in the seat of her car, watching Michel's window. She could see him walking around the room, a dark shape against the light. His gestures were sharp, nervous; now it looked like he was bringing his hands to his face, back bent as if oppressed by pain or bitter memory.

A young man wearing a studded leather jacket over his nude chest stopped near the car and tapped his knuckles against the window: 'Hey, give me a ride, baby?'

'Go get fucked,' she said, turning the key in the ignition. She put the car into gear and stepped hard on the accelerator. The car flew through the carefree city, through the warm, sweetly scented countryside and towards the horizon, loaded with black clouds and streaked with lightning.

NORMAN AND MICHEL talked at length and then fell silent, unmoving on their chairs, nearly catatonic, looking without seeing each other. Only thus could their long-dormant feelings return to the surface. And when Michel had said the last word and had got up to leave the room, Norman stopped him.

'Michel.'

'We're tired. We have to go to bed.'

'What is that vase? What do those figures mean?'

'It's the dark side of the Odyssey, the unknown voyage that we all have to make. The route goes up, at first, towards dreams and adventures, towards the flaming horizon. But then it descends towards dark mist and icy solitude, towards the shores of the final ocean, its cold waters black and still.'

Norman pulled up the collar of his jacket as if a cold wind were suddenly breathing down his neck. 'No, it's just a vase, Michel,' he said. 'A stupendous Mycenaean vase of embossed gold. And we'll find it.'

9

Parthenion, Arcadia, 15 July, 9.30 p.m.

RETIRED POLICE OFFICER Petros Roussos was pedalling down the country road leading to his village, and the bicycle's headlight cast a wide glow over the dusty sides of the road. Olive groves stretched out right and left; the century-old trunks were twisted and gnarled and their silvery foliage sparkled under the rays of the full moon. A hare froze for an instant on the lane, blinded by the headlight, then leapt aside lightly, disappearing into the maze of shadows streaking across the ground.

He rode past a spring which flowed crystal clear from a little moss-covered cave, and crossed himself in front of the shrine of the Virgin Mary. Thousands of fireflies quivered like stars over a field of oats, a remnant of the heavens amidst the bushes.

It was what he had always wanted: to retire to his hometown in Arcadia, far away from the confusion of the city, the noise, the suffocating grey air. To breathe in the fragrance of lemon and cedar blossoms and the scent of wild rosemary, to enjoy the simple cuisine of the shepherds and farmers, to care for the fields and the pastures that his old folks had left him before they passed on so long ago.

And to forget all about the dirty work he had done for years. Everyone needed to make a living somehow, and certain jobs needed doing. There wasn't much choice for a poor country boy if he didn't want to starve. But, God willing, it was all over with. He'd been back for just six months, but he almost felt as though he had never left – except that so many friends of his childhood

and youth were no longer around. Some had emigrated to
America, some were dead, may their souls rest in peace, others
had gone to the city. Thank goodness some had remained, like
Yannis Kottàs. As boys they had brought the master's flocks to
pasture together for years, until they were called into the army.
They had been stationed together as well, at Alexandroupolis,
near the Turkish border. It had been wonderful to see him again,
to look under the wrinkles and grey hair for traces of the boy
he'd left so long ago, and to talk about old times. They saw each
other often, every Thursday evening for a game of cards and a
bottle of retsina.

He crossed the provincial road, ringing his bell loudly, and
continued along the lane, on a slight upgrade now, headed
towards the other side of town. A few houses, lit by a couple of
lamp-posts, and the church of Haghios Dimitrios on the hill,
then he was there. Yannis Kottàs worked as a nightwatchman in
the area's only factory, which made blocks of ice for the isolated
houses which didn't have electrical power. He leaned his bike
against the wall of the building and rang the bell twice so his
friend would know it was him. He peered through the office
window; the light was on but Yannis wasn't there. He must be
doing his rounds. The door was open and he walked in.

'Yannis? Yannis, it's me, Petros. Have you put our bottle on
ice? It's my turn to win tonight!'

There was no answer. He went into the warehouse and
called again loudly so his voice could be heard over the hum of
the compressors. He looked all around, but there was no one to
be seen.

'Yannis, you in the john?'

The lights went out suddenly, but the compressors continued to hum: 'Yannis, what kind of a joke is this? You trying
to scare me? Come on, turn the lights back on, stop fooling
around.'

Then the compressors went out as well, and the building was
plunged into silence. The only sound to be heard was the odd
car driving down the provincial road. One thing was sure – it

wasn't Yannis playing this trick on him; Yannis would never turn off the compressors. Roussos backed up towards the wall so no one could surprise him from behind and took the ice hook hanging from a rack. 'Come and get me, smart guy,' he said to himself, 'I'll teach you to play tricks.'

'Petros! Petros Roussos!' The voice boomed under the metal ceiling beams, sounding like thunder from the sky.

'Okay,' thought Roussos, 'now we'll see who's talking.' And in his mind he ran through all those episodes in which as a policeman he had created mortal enemies. Arrests, beatings, you name it. It must be one of them, someone with a grudge who had waited patiently until now. Who else?

'Who are you?' he shouted. 'What do you want?'

'Where did you put the girl, Roussos? Heleni Kaloudis, where did you put her?'

That's what it was. So the joke was on him. Something that had happened ten years ago! Just now that he'd come home to enjoy his retirement.

He flattened himself against the wall and gripped the ice hook in his hand. He realized that he might have only a few minutes to live. The voice resounded again, hard and cold, fractured into countless echoes by the cement walls. 'Aren't you the boatman of death? Roussos!'

'Who are you?' he asked again. 'Her father? Her brother? I'm a father, too . . . I can explain . . .' His voice was cracking: his throat was dry and he was soaked with sweat.

'I'm the one who's come to settle up, Roussos!'

The voice was coming from another direction, but no noise had been heard.

'Then come and get me; I'm waiting. I'll send you to hell!' He advanced cautiously towards the voice, brandishing the ice hook, but a loud crash very close by paralysed him completely. All the lights switched back on abruptly, blinding him. A block of ice had fallen from above, exploding into a thousand splinters that glittered on the floor like diamonds. He heard a sharp metallic click and then a roar of thunder: an avalanche of ice fell towards him, sweeping away everything it encountered. He turned, trying desperately to hide behind a pillar, but a block of ice hit him full force, hurling him against the wall and breaking his legs. In a last glimmer of consciousness he heard the rhythmic puff of the compressors as they were started up again, saw a shadow looming before him in the glare of the lights, and realized that his day of judgement had come.

YANNIS KOTTÀS HAD gone into town to buy a couple of bottles at the tavern; he didn't want his friend Petros to find him high and dry! He was walking back up towards the factory at a good pace. He was sure that there had been at least half a dozen bottles left, but he'd found the crate empty. Must have been the workers sampling his stuff, those sons of bitches. From now on, he'd put his stash under lock and key.

He saw his friend's bicycle leaning against the wall and called him: 'Hey, Petros, you there? Have you been here long? I just ran over to the tavern, I was out of wine . . .'

He took out his keys but saw the door standing ajar. He smelled a rat; he was sure he'd locked the door before leaving. Who could have opened it? Maybe they'd forced the lock. But where was Petros? He called him again, but got no answer.

He went to his guard station and took a gun out of the table drawer. He made sure it was loaded and walked towards the compressor area. He opened the door and was nearly blinded: all the lights were on and illuminating a catastrophe. Blocks of ice everywhere, shelves overturned, drums of ammonia scattered here and there on the floor. A bloodstain in the corner had left a trail leading towards one of the deep-freeze chests. The wall of the container was stained with blood as well. He lifted the lid to look in and his knees buckled as he began to shiver uncontrollably. The gun fell from his hand as the lid banged back into place. He staggered backwards, eyes as wild as if he'd seen the devil in flesh and blood. 'Oh, Mother of God,' he muttered, 'Oh, Holy Mother . . .'

THE POLICE INSPECTOR didn't arrive from the nearest station until around midnight, riding a scooter. Nearly all the men in town had already gathered around the ice factory. He found Petros Roussos's corpse completely naked, encased in a block of ice. His heel was still caught in the ice hook used to drag him there, like a butchered animal.

Inside the lid of the ice chest, someone had written some words with a piece of chalk. It sounded like some sick joke:

She's naked. She's cold.

He didn't touch a thing. Once the coroner and medical examiner had arrived and thoroughly investigated the scene of the crime, he was curious to know what the coroner thought of that message with the feminine pronoun.

The coroner shrugged and shook his head: no way could he figure it out. Roussos had no enemies in town; he was respected and well liked for his open, outgoing personality. The inspector didn't even consider calling the city police station to organize a roadblock; the killer was certainly far away by that time. He would have had all the time he needed to take off on the provincial road, by car or motorcycle. Or perhaps he'd taken one of the many mountain paths that went through the forest.

When he learned that Petros Roussos was a retired policeman, he thought of investigating a possible vendetta; some ex-con who was getting his revenge for being arrested and put away. At two in the morning, after having inspected the crime scene and taken the necessary photographs, he had to conclude that there was no direct evidence besides that strange, meaningless message. He asked the onlookers whether they could remember seeing anyone suspicious around town lately. When no one could come up with anything, he got back on his scooter and went home to bed.

The crowd broke up into little groups, discussing the events animatedly and coming up with the most outlandish hypotheses. Little by little, they ran out of steam and started to head back home, still chattering.

The next day, the coroner met with the medical examiner, who had his report ready: Petros Roussos had drowned after both his legs had been broken by a blunt instrument, almost certainly one of the many blocks of ice that had been released from the hopper at the far end of the warehouse. The murderer had then dragged the body towards one of the deep-freeze chests and thrown him in. When Yannis Kottàs had arrived, Roussos had probably only just died; in the two hours before the investigator arrived, the compressors had frozen the water around his body.

The coroner closed himself in his office to contemplate an apparently absurd case: such a ferocious crime in a quiet little town in the quietest region of Greece. He looked at the files and discovered that there had been only four murders in all of Arcadia in the previous twenty-five years. The solution had to come from outside. He called the local police station and had them give him Roussos's service record: prior to his retirement, the officer had been working with the Patras harbour police for two years. Before that, he had been with the political police in Athens for fifteen. It was there, he was convinced, that they should start looking.

POLICE SERGEANT YORGO Karagheorghis was in his last year of regular duty in a sleepy town of the southern Peloponnesus called Areopolis, in the Kalamata district. It was a pleasant place which attracted plenty of tourists in the summer, who sunned at the beach and visited the nearby Dirou caves at the tip of the peninsula near Cape Tenaros. His son usually came down to spend the summer holidays there as well, with his wife and little son. Every evening after his shift, Karagheorghis changed into civilian clothes and went for a long bicycle ride with his grandson along the seashore. Sometimes they took a fishing rod and sat out on the rocks. He cast his line, lit up a cigar and watched the little boy running up and down the beach gathering shells or teasing the crabs hiding in the sand with a stick. If he was lucky he caught a couple of mullets, which they grilled for dinner under the trellis of the little house they'd rented outside the town.

Sometimes the boy came to the police station and asked: 'Grandpa, can I see your gun?'

Karagheorghis would smile: 'Stay away from guns, Panos, don't touch. You should never play with a gun. If it goes off by mistake that means big trouble. You know we have to keep our weapons loaded?'

'Gramps, have you ever killed a bandit?' insisted the boy.

'Oh, a few here and there, but only in self-defence.' And then he'd tell him about all the dangerous operations he'd taken part in, miming all the chases, the shoot-outs, 'Boom-boom-boom!'

For a few days he'd been noticing someone he didn't know, a young man of about thirty, with brown hair that was a little grey at the temples, who'd sit for hours near the sea, just a couple of hundred metres from where he stopped to fish. He sat with his chin on his knees, watching the waves come in until it got dark, then he'd get up and take off southward on foot, towards Cape Tenaros. There was nothing down that way: the rugged crags of the mountain sloped towards the sea, where white- and blue-tipped waves broke on the jagged rocks. A few times he'd been tempted to follow him, out of pure curiosity, but he'd always held back. It was none of his business, after all, there were lots of strange people in this world.

One evening, when he'd finished his shift, he decided to take a spin with the squad car to get a better look. There he was, at the usual place, sitting on a rock and gazing out to sea. But as soon as he heard the engine and saw the patrol car at a distance, he jumped up and ran off in the opposite direction, disappearing behind a bend in the road. Karagheorghis accelerated, and after the curve, the youth got into a car parked alongside the road and took off in a southerly direction at full speed. The policeman refrained from stepping on the gas; he didn't want to lose the guy from sight, but it would be unwise to take risks on such a narrow, curving road. You could easily end up in the sea. The man couldn't get very far anyway; the road ended at the southernmost point of the peninsula.

He switched on the radio and called his fellow officer at the town police station: 'Andreas? It's me, Yorgo. I'm following a suspect. He's headed towards Dirou and he's driving like a maniac; as soon as he saw my car he took off like a shot. Try to reach me with the other car if you can; this guy might be a wacko, and he may be armed.'

The other policeman left immediately, speeding off south. Karagheorghis pulled his pistol from its holster and lay it on the seat next to him, locked and loaded. It was just a little over a kilometre to the promontory. The setting sun inflamed the entire bay of Messenia to his right. In a few minutes he was at the entrance to the caves of Dirou, where he found the car he'd been chasing, parked with its left door open. He grabbed his gun and approached: the car was empty and the radio was on. The mountain all around was steep and rocky and practically inaccessible; the only way the guy could have gone was over the enclosure fence and into the caves.

He climbed over the fence himself and went in, stopping at the entrance.

'Come out!' he yelled, and his voice was swallowed up in the underground labyrinth, turning into a low bellow. He looked back to see if his back-up had arrived; he didn't want to go into the belly of the cave alone. If this guy were dangerous he could take him out whenever he liked, just by hiding behind one of the craggy formations in the cave. He calculated how long it would take his buddy to get there: it was just a few kilometres, dammit, just a ten-minute drive. Why the hell was it taking him so long?

BUT ANDREAS WOULD certainly not be able to be there any time soon: he had met up with a huge truck proceeding in the opposite direction, loaded down with lumber and taking up the entire road.

'Move over, dammit, I have to get by!'

The driver leaned out of the window: 'Where do you want me to go? I can't fly! Both of us can't get by at once.'

'Then back up. There has to be some place you can pull over.'

'No, sir. You're the one that has to back up. There are no turning places for miles back and there's no way I can back up for a couple of miles with this baby; I'll end up down in the gulley.'

The policeman had no choice but to put the car in reverse and begin backing down the winding road, his head out the window to make sure that no one was going to ram him from behind.

KARAGHEORGHIS REALIZED THAT something must have happened and decided to go in on his own. He couldn't leave that guy down in the caves; tomorrow there would be a whole load of tourists and Lord only knew what he might try. And the police were always stuck with the blame. To hell with it. He went back to the car and switched on the radio: 'Will you move your ass? That nutcase has gone into the Katafigi caves; we've got to get him out of there right now.'

'Listen, there's a truck here taking up the whole road. I can't get by him and I'm backing up to the first turning place.'

'A truck? Who is it?'

'Listen, I don't know, but I think he's from Hierolimin.'

'Write him up a hefty fine, at least; he can't use this road with any kind of load. Then get the devil down here. I'm going in, in the meantime.'

'All right. I'll get there as soon as I can.'

Karagheorghis entered the cave and realized that the lighting system had been activated. So the guy had the keys, or at least he knew where to find them. He cocked the trigger on his gun and walked quickly along the first stretch. The tunnel soon widened and the passage was transformed into a vast clearing studded by a forest of diaphanous white stalagmites. He strained to hear, but all he could make out was the soft concert of drops falling from the ceiling of the cavern. All at once he heard a slight gurgling: the lake! The man had entered from the underground river; perhaps he'd stolen one of the boats used to ferry tourists.

He dashed over to the shore of the lake buried so deep beneath the surface of the earth. He had never seen a body of water look this way before: the absence of every living thing, the silence, the vast aperture of the cave, the eerie play of lights in the dark pool, the astonishing colours of the rocks. It gave him a sense of nearly religious wonder. Why had that man come all the way down here, at this time of day; what was he looking for? And where was he now?

He walked down the little path that circled the lake for a couple of hundred metres. The surface of the water was shiny and as black as a sheet of polished steel, without the tiniest ripple. Any dark thought could have taken shape and strength under that inky sheen. He picked up a stone and tossed it into the water, as if to break a spell or banish a nightmare. It was swallowed up without a sound. Yorgo Karagheorghis could hear nothing but his own breath, nothing but the beating of his own heart, which had suddenly quickened.

He thought that it would be best to turn back and wait for his buddy to show up. They could stake out the entrance, wait for the guy there; he'd have to get out somehow. He started to turn back, but a voice rumbled across the lake, ran down the walls of the cavern and splintered against the forest of stalagmites that rose from the ground and from the water.

'Yorgo Karagheorghis!'

His blood rushed, icy cold with fear, to his heart. He gripped his gun, which had become slippery in his numb, sweaty hand. All he could see was that pale forest of white pillars, streaked with green tears, without soul or life.

'How do you know my name?' he shouted. And his voice dashed up against the ceiling, thick with stalactites, and rained back down on his head, shivery and shattered.

'You threw the girl in the lake, Yorgo Karagheorghis. Did you not throw her naked into the lake?'

The voice seemed to be coming from behind him now . . . how was it possible? . . .

'Now I'm coming to get you. Don't you know that this is the mouth of hell?'

Karagheorghis flattened himself against a wall, still and silent. He drew a long breath. 'So it's me or you, then,' he thought, and he began to slip towards the darkest and most hidden corner of the cave. He raised his head and saw what looked like the wide open jaws of a monstrous dog – two pointy stalactites streaked with red like bloody fangs. Bad sign.

The silence was suddenly broken by a slight splash, and he dropped his eyes, astonished, towards the surface of the lake. On the opposite shore, a boat was emerging out of the gloom. A cloaked, hooded figure was standing at the stern, pushing himself along with an oar.

Karagheorghis smirked: 'Takes more than a trick like this to make me shit in my pants, my friend.' He swiftly calculated the distance that separated him from his target. When the boat was in range, he jumped out of his hiding place and pointed the pistol at the figure with both hands.

'Why did you do it?' shouted the voice, sounding vulnerable this time, touched with pain.

'I had no choice,' Karagheorghis shouted back. 'I had no choice, dammit!' But as he pulled the trigger, the lights abruptly went out. The shot exploded, tearing through the still atmosphere of the cavern. The roar reverberated into the cave's most secret recesses and flooded back out, multiplied a thousandfold, fractured and distorted, transformed into a chorus of screams, into a pounding howl.

When the fracas had died down, Karagheorghis, surrounded by total darkness, had lost all sense of time and space. He could only hear the furious beating of his heart.

Then he heard the splashing again: the boat was still advancing towards him, inexorably. He lost control and began to shoot out wildly. As soon as he had discharged the final shot, a flame tore through the darkness at his left. He didn't understand, couldn't think: an explosion and then a high-pitched whistle. Then two, three atrocious stabs of pain lacerated his body and his mind.

A small beam of light shone on him, and footsteps resounded on the gravel path. The cold hands of that ghost fell to work on his tormented body, leaving him naked and trembling. Then the little beam of light moved away, the sound of footsteps faded into the distance and he was left to die, alone, in the damp warmth of his own blood soaking the earth.

OFFICER ANDREAS PENDELENI reached the entrance of the Katafigi caverns and saw Karagheorghis's patrol car, parked, with the radio still on. He climbed over the fence and went in. The lights were on and the visitors' trail was well lit. The policeman advanced cautiously, holding on tight to the Beretta calibre 9, his finger on the trigger. He called out: 'Yorgo! Yorgo, are you in there? If you're in there, answer me.'.

He heard what sounded like a death rattle, and he ran in the direction it was coming from. He reached the shore of the lake and saw the naked, bloody body of Sergeant Karagheorghis gleaming, half-immersed in the water.

He had been run through by three stalactites, sharp and deadly as spears. One between the neck and collarbone, another in his stomach and the third in his groin.

He put a hand under his head: 'Who was it, Yorgo? What happened?'

Karagheorghis raised his eyes towards the ceiling of the cave and Andreas could see the broken stumps of the cluster of stalactites which had pierced him through. Certainly no natural phenomenon.

'Who was it?' asked Andreas. 'Did you see who it was?'

Karagheorghis opened his mouth, trying to utter a sound, and his companion put his ear to his lips, hoping he'd say the murderer's name, but all he heard was his last gasp as his body collapsed lifelessly. Andreas closed his friend's eyes, then took off his own jacket and tried to cover him up as best he could. As he was going back towards the entrance, he happened to glance at a rock along the edge of the trail. Someone had used the dead man's blood to write the words:

She's naked. She's cold.

He hurried back to his car. He switched on the radio and called headquarters at Kalamata.

'This is Officer Pendeleni. Something terrible has happened. No, a crime. Sergeant Karagheorghis has been murdered, at the Dirou caves. Send a team to investigate and inform the coroner right away. I'll wait here.'

The sun had dipped below the horizon and a pale golden reflection lapped at the grey towers of Hierolimin in the distance.

10

THE POLICE COMMISSIONER of the Kalamata district immediately ordered roadblocks on all the streets of the peninsula: they would trap the murderer at the end of the promontory. He had got there by car; when he tried to turn back he'd be caught in their net. The coastguard was put on alert to stop any suspicious boats trying to set sail from Hierolimin or Cape Tenaros. A helicopter patrolled all the cave exits from above.

When general headquarters in Athens was informed, the case was immediately connected to the murder of retired officer Petros Roussos at Parthenion in Arcadia. The message left by the killer was the same – apparently absurd and meaningless. Athens promised to send someone to work with the commissioner at Kalamata. In the meantime, it was essential that the criminal who had killed Karagheorghis be captured; it was surely the same person who had murdered Roussos. Same deranged mind, same sadistic imagination.

Officer Pendeleni, who had discovered his partner dying in the cave at Katafigi, participated actively in the investigation along with his colleagues. They searched the caves thoroughly with the aid of local guides; speleologists from the University of Patras who had been conducting research on the site were also called in, all to no avail. The police worked all night, in shifts, exploring every nook of every gallery. Divers sounded the waters of the underground lakes but never found a thing.

Pendeleni managed to locate the truck driver who had blocked off the road as he was trying to get to the caves, and arranged to meet with him that evening at a tavern in Hierolimin. The man was absolutely above and beyond suspicion; he had been working in the area for over thirty years. It was his load that seemed questionable; the boat that picked up the lumber he unloaded at the pier at his destination in Gythion seemed to be the same one that had delivered it earlier.

'And that didn't seem strange to you?' asked the officer.

'Oh, it seemed strange all right.'

'And it didn't occur to you to ask the guys on the boat why they were giving you the runaround?'

'They had paid me in advance: why should I stick my nose in other people's business? They asked me to pick up a load in one place and deliver it to another place. Fine with me, as long as the money's there.'

'And who placed the order? Can you remember?'

The truck driver nodded. 'You don't forget a face like that.'

'Is it someone from around here?'

'No. I've never seen him around here, but he sure knew the place.'

'What do you mean by that?'

'Well, a strong meltemi wind was blowing yesterday morning when he got there with the boat, and I can tell you that he was handling it as though he'd always navigated in these waters. I couldn't believe it.'

'Can you describe him?'

'Medium height, strong build, about fifty, I'd say. His eyes were blue . . . light blue, like the water near the rocks. A face of stone . . . a sailor, no doubt about it. And a good one.'

'And he was aboard the boat when you unloaded at Gythion?'

'No. There was no one on the boat. I unloaded the lumber at the pier and I got someone from the dock workers' cooperative to sign. May still be there for all I know.'

DEEP WITHIN THE bowels of the cramped, dark cave, the passage
finally started to widen. A slight, barely perceptible luminescence
lit up a bend ahead.

'It won't be long now, just a few more metres and we can
rest. Don't give up, just keep moving. Look . . .'

The passage widened and splayed open under an immense
vault curved over a vast surface. A slight but very distinct glow,
in contrast to the inky darkness preceding it, allowed them to
make out the boundaries of the chamber.

'Good God, Commander, what is this light?'

'It's the natural phosphorescence of the rocks, which are
somewhat radioactive here: that's why you're wearing that
plastic cape. Pull up the hood. We're going to be here for hours;
no sense taking unnecessary risks.'

'I don't understand. How did you know about this under-
water passage and how did you know that that horrible shaft
would lead to this underground cathedral?'

'There's far more here, my son. Soon the sea that covers
the bottom of this cave will ebb enough to let the reflection
of the moon filter through, and you'll see more wonders.'

'You haven't answered my question. You almost never
answer my questions.'

'You're wrong. I've always answered all of your questions.
The real ones. You wanted justice to be done and I've prepared
the day of judgement for those who have destroyed your life
and Heleni's. What does the rest matter?'

At that moment, the distant mouth of the cave started to
tremble and to glitter softly, and the vault was illuminated by a
wondrous light, fluid and shivering, animated by silent, ever-
changing waves: the light of the moon reflected by the rocky
surface of the sea. The rocks seemed alive with iridescence and
they could hear the sea breathing, a long powerful noise like that
of a sleeping giant. An acutely salty odour pervaded the atmosphere, which was vibrating with innumerable reflections.

'Come on,' said Admiral Bogdanos. 'It will take us nearly an
hour to reach the sea. We have to move before the water level

gets too high.' He began walking and the sound of his steps on the gravel mixed with the distant waves of the Aegean and the rustling of the wind. Claudio started after him but soon stopped dead in his tracks, immobilized by wonder: the light was flowing across the bottom of the cave as well, revealing every minimal detail.

The immense stretch was studded with countless burial mounds – thousands, tens of thousands of them, many with markers of limestone or selenite or quartzite. Others still were marked by weapons, corroded by the salt water, lying alongside the tomb or plunged into the ground. Rivulets of water had penetrated their way into some of the tombs, uncovering the bodies buried within. Incrustations of carbonate had coated the skeletons, their weapons and belongings, creating spectral compositions.

'What is this? Commander, what is this place, this endless necropolis? It's incredible. A place like this . . . cannot exist.'

Bogdanos continued walking without turning: 'This is Hades. The home of the dead. Legend has it that the cave of Dirou is the entrance to Avernus, to the underworld. This is Lake Avernus.'

'But that's nothing but a myth!'

'Myths, my son, are nothing but reality deformed by time, like objects sunk in deep water. This cave was used as a necropolis for three thousand years. Here sleep the Minians, the Pelasgians, mythical lords of the sea, the Achaeans of the shining greaves, destroyers of Troy. Here, for millennia, they have listened to the song of the sea every night, waiting for the light of Hecate, the moon, to caress their bare bones. Here lie youths mowed down before their time by the Chaera, maidens who had never known man, children torn from their mothers' breasts, warriors at the height of their virility, young boys with but the first hairs of their beards. They dominated the seas on agile ships and the land on fiery steeds, on gleaming chariots with blazing wheels . . . They sleep in the clean sand, among these sharp rocks, under this solemn dome, in this uncontaminated air. Their rest is sacred and inaccessible.'

He turned his head slowly: his pupils were fixed and dilated as if staring into the deepest darkness. Claudio looked at him, amazed: 'You speak as though you envied them, Commander. But why? Why are you so tired of life?'

Bogdanos lowered his head, his eyes hidden in the shadow of his hood. 'We have to continue walking,' he said.

OFFICER ANDREAS PENDELENI unlatched the belt with his regulation handgun and hung it on a coat hook. The police commissioner who had come from Kalamata raised his eyes with a questioning expression: 'Nothing?'

Pendeleni shook his head: 'Nothing. Nothing at all. The caves have been searched inch by inch, the lakes dragged for evidence: not a trace. Not a clue.'

The police commissioner had been up all night listening to his service radio: his eyes were puffy and his voice hoarse with all the cigarettes he had smoked. The ashtray on the table was overflowing with butts and the air was blue. Officer Pendeleni opened the window: 'Mind if I change the air?'

'Sure, go ahead. You must be as tired as I am. Go to bed. It's morning, dammit.'

'And we've failed.'

'Not a single clue? No leads at all?'

'I think the whole thing was carefully planned: when poor Karagheorghis called me over the radio to come and give him a hand, I took off immediately. But there was that truck full of lumber blocking my way – I wasted more than half an hour. Just the amount of time the killer needed to massacre the poor bastard. To think he was just a few months short of retiring.'

'Yeah. He died like those soldiers who die the last day of the war. Why didn't you arrest the truck driver?'

'Wouldn't have made any difference. He's not to blame. He was just carrying out someone else's carefully laid plans. The loaded truck started up the road just as Karagheorghis entered the Katafigi cave.'

'So the killer had an accomplice. That's a possible lead.'

'I've tried to follow up on it, but no one knows the man described by the truck driver. And even if we found him, how could we get him to talk? If he is the accomplice, that is. There's no law forbidding the transport of wood from one place to another . . .' He took a little slip of paper from the inside jacket of his pocket and placed it on the table. 'Here's the description of the man who commissioned the shipment from Hierolimin to Gythion.' He stood up to close the window. 'And the roadblocks? The helicopter? The coastguard?'

The commissioner shook his head, letting it drop down between his shoulders. 'Nothing. As if he had vanished. All we have is that stupid, absurd message.'

' "She's naked. She's cold." Like he's making fun of us. And the corpse, stripped of all his clothes. It must have been a maniac. A damned psychopathic son of a bitch.' Just then, a waiter from the bar around the corner came in with a tray.

'You must be hungry. I've sent out for coffee and sandwiches. Eat something.' The officer took a cup of steaming coffee. 'If you don't want to go back home to bed right away, they're sending someone over from Athens who should be here any minute. A supercop from headquarters. The kind who can figure their way out of anything.'

Pendeleni took his belt from the coat hanger: 'No, thanks. You give him my regards. I've had it and I'm going to bed. If you need me you know where I am.'

As he was leaving, a car pulled up in front of the police station. The officer who got out strode into the station without knocking. The commissioner walked towards him, holding out his hand. The officer gave him a quick salute and then shook his hand vigorously.

'Captain Karamanlis, Athens police. Don't get up, Commissioner.' He glanced over at the tray. 'I see you were just having breakfast. I didn't mean to disturb you.'

'Oh no, not at all. I was just grabbing a bite. We've been up all night here. Why don't you join me?'

Karamanlis took a seat: 'Don't mind if I do, commissioner. I've been up all night as well, I wanted to get here as quickly as I could. Please brief me on everything that's been going on. I'm sure you'll agree with me that we're dealing with a maniac here. Five weeks ago at Parthenion, in Arcadia, another colleague was found murdered – butchered, I should say. A retired officer, Petros Roussos.'

'Did you know him?'

'Personally. We had worked together for fifteen years. An excellent man. Capable, courageous, trustworthy.'

'What about Yorgo Karagheorghis. Did you know him?'

Karamanlis nodded. 'He was a direct collaborator of mine for many years. What's more, he fought at my side for months and months during the civil war, against the Communists in the mountains. Let me tell you, he had guts. Wasn't even afraid of the devil.'

The commissioner looked at him with a mixture of fear and astonishment: 'Karamanlis. But then you are Pavlos Karamanlis, better known by the battle name *O Tàvros* during the civil war. My God, Captain, I come from near Kastritza . . . they still talk about you around my parts. You're quite a legend.'

Karamanlis flashed a tired smile. 'So much time has gone by. But I'm pleased that someone still remembers "the Bull".'

The commissioner did not dare add why the people of Kastritza still remembered *O Tàvros*, letting Karamanlis think what he liked. 'But captain,' he added, 'if Roussos and Karagheorghis worked so closely with you for so many years, you must have more information to give us than we can give you. I spoke last night with the coroner who is investigating the death of Roussos at Parthenion. He also believes that the motive for this homicide involves the fact that the two victims worked for the political police in Athens. With you, that is.'

'There's certainly something that links these two crimes.

There is a suspicion arising in my mind, but it seems impossible, really. Absurd. I need more elements.'

'What about that message? I was told that they found the same words at Parthenion, near Roussos's body.'

'Right. The element that the two killings have in common. The assassin's signature. And his challenge, as well.'

'Could it be a sign?'

'Yes, of course, a sign. Or a trap. I have to find out. Now please tell me everything that's happened here.'

The commissioner took the last sip from his coffee, cleaned his lips with a napkin and lit up a Papastratos. 'Do you smoke?' he asked, offering the pack to Karamanlis.

'I quit a year ago.'

'Lucky man. Well, there's really not much to say. Our investigation has not uncovered much of anything. I think we're faced with an exceptionally intelligent criminal whose ferocity knows no bounds. The only lead we have, I'd say, is the unknown man who commissioned a shipment of lumber two days ago to be taken from the port of Hierolimin to Gythion, without any apparent reason.'

Karamanlis listened carefully while the commissioner repeated all the details. When he had finished, he read and reread the slip of paper that Officer Pendeleni had left with the description of the man who had ordered the wood shipment.

'Does it remind you of someone?' asked the commissioner.

'In a certain sense . . . it does. In any case, I mean to get to the bottom of this. Find the truck driver for me: I want an identikit. And don't let up – that bastard can't have disappeared into thin air.'

'Of course not, Captain. My deputy will be taking over from me shortly and he'll continue to coordinate the search efforts. This evening we should also have the autopsy report for you.'

'Thank you, commissioner. If you need me I'll be at Hotel Xenia.'

He put the slip of paper in his pocket and went out to the car. The sun was high and the day promised to be beautiful.

Karamanlis went to his hotel to take a shower and stretch out on the bed for a couple of hours before starting the hunt.

As the water poured down on him, relaxing the fatigue in his muscles after the long car ride on rough country roads, his mind returned to a call he'd got three days before in Athens. He had returned home late at night after an exhausting day and was sitting in his study taking a look at the newspaper. The telephone had begun to ring. In his mind he could hear the tone of voice perfectly, those slow, distinct words.

'Captain Karamanlis?'

'Who's speaking?'

'Do you remember the golden vase which disappeared ten years ago from the basement of the National Museum?'

'Who is this?'

'Someone who knows where it is.'

'Fine. Keep it and don't break my balls over it.'

'Don't say that. Listen to me for a moment. There are others who know, friends of yours from the good old days: Mr Charrier and Mr Shields. They just got off the boat at Patras this morning and they're headed south. They want the vase.'

'Let them take it.'

'But they may be here to open up an old wound, I'm afraid. The death of two of their friends under mysterious circumstances the night of the Polytechnic massacre. Claudio Setti and Heleni Kaloudis. Do those names mean anything to you, Captain?'

Karamanlis had hung up, but he hadn't been able to get his mind off the call. Shields and Charrier. What in the hell had they come back to do after such a long time? And together, on top of it. The pelting water calmed his nerves; he curled up on the floor and leant his head against the wall: God, he would like to dissolve into that water. And yet he'd soon have to get on his feet and unravel the most complicated mess of his lifetime. All the ghosts of that distant night seemed to have arranged a meeting in that lonely corner of the Peloponnesus, but one of them was striking out ferociously. Who would it be next time?

Him? And what did that absurd message mean? The trail of blood was marking out an answer. Maybe another dead man would make it clear . . . or would put an end to the questions – for ever.

The water turned tepid, then cold, and the captain jumped to his feet as if whiplashed. He dried off and lay on the bed. He was used to sleeping under the worst possible conditions, but he felt threatened from all sides. And didn't know which way to turn first.

MICHEL CHARRIER ENTERED the city of Skardamoula at a snail's pace. It was dusk, and he parked his car in the central square. He had left Norman at Kalamata that morning so he could meet with an old clerk from the British consulate who seemed to have news about his father's death.

It was the town's patron saint's day. A procession advanced through the streets of the centre, directed towards the church, which was strung with hundreds of coloured lights. Market stalls had been set up for the occasion; stands with fried fish and roasted *souvlaki* spread an inviting aroma through the air. He started pacing back and forth, checking his watch every few minutes. A hand slapped him on the shoulder.

'What do you say, Michel, shall we stop to eat here?' asked Norman, pointing at one of the stands.

'Ah, you're here,' answered Michel, turning towards his friend. 'Well? What did you find out?'

Norman shook his head: 'Practically nothing. The Yugoslav police are in the dark. My father was killed in the middle of a forest in the high valley of the Strimon in Macedonia, just a few kilometres from the Greek border. Someone laid a trap for him and shot him dead. With an arrow, just one, straight to the heart. The bow was the kind used for big game, very powerful, a Pearson, maybe, or a Kastert. The only other certain thing is that his mouth and his eyes were covered after he was already dead.'

'What was he doing in such a godforsaken place?'

'He was hunting. He liked going hunting all alone, for days at a time, sleeping in the open.'

'So he was armed as well.'

'He was. Didn't help him, though. Not a shot had been fired from his rifle. Why don't we find a place to sit down so we can talk? How about this place here? Smells good.'

'Yeah, fine with me,' answered Michel.

They sat at a little table and ordered fish, bread, wine and Greek salad with feta cheese. The man running the stand set out a sheet of newspaper as a tablecloth and put out dishes and silverware to keep it from blowing away, joined by a loaf of bread and a jug of retsina. He then brought two crisp mullets and a plate of salad. Norman poured a glass of wine for his friend and himself, and downed his in a single gulp, seemingly anxious to drive away his troubled thoughts. 'Only way to drink retsina. Right down your throat, the only way. God, these flavours, these smells, I feel like I've never left. Come on, drink up.'

Michel took a long sip, half closing his eyes as if he were swallowing an elixir: 'You're right, Norman, by God, you're right. It's as if we were kids again.'

'Remember the first time we met at Parga, when you gave us a lift in that Deux-Chevaux?'

'Yeah, and we went to that tavern, Tàssos's it was, right? And I got drunk for the first time in my life.'

'On this wine.'

'On retsina. And swore I'd never take another sip.'

'That's what they all say.'

'Yeah, right.'

Norman raised his glass: 'To those days, my friend.'

'To those days,' said Michel, raising his own. Then he lowered his head wordlessly, and Norman fell silent as well.

'Did you love your father?' asked Michel suddenly.

'We never had much of a relationship. After I went back to England, I only saw him once or twice a year. At Christmas, you know? But that doesn't mean anything . . .'

'No, no, it doesn't mean a thing . . .'

'The only time I thought we might really get close was that time in Athens, when he offered to help me save Claudio and Heleni.' Michel dropped his head. 'What? Now you're not going to get depressed on me, are you? We're here on a treasure hunt, not to cry over the past. A big treasure hunt – you understand me, Michel? Come on, have another, for God's sake.' He filled his glass again.

Michel raised his head, eyes suddenly full of consternation and bewilderment. He pointed his finger at the table: 'I know this guy, Norman! I know this man. I saw him, that night, in Athens, when they arrested me, when they got Claudio and Heleni . . .' His voice quavered and his eyes shone with anger and emotion.

'Michel, Michel, what are you saying? You never could hold a drink . . .'

Michel pushed his plate, glass and silverware over to Norman's side, then lifted the newspaper on his side of the table and turned it towards his friend: 'Look! Do you recognize him?' Norman saw a photograph of what appeared to be a cadaver, eyes staring blindly. His bare chest was covered with blood and he had a sharp object stuck between his neck and collarbone. The headline said: 'MYSTERIOUS CRIME AT THE DIROU CAVES: AREOPOLIS POLICE SERGEANT KARAGHEORGHIS KILLED BY MANIAC'.

Norman shook his head: 'I've never seen him. Are you sure you know him?'

'As God is my witness. He's older, his hair is thinner and his moustache is grey, but I'm telling you it's him. I saw him that night. It was him, along with another cop, who brought me to that cell for the interrogation, after they'd tortured me with the *falanga*.'

'Well, that's strange.'

'Wait, let me read what it says.' Michel rapidly skimmed the article, then let the newspaper drop on to the table and downed another glass of wine.

'Hey, cut that out. You can't hold that stuff.'

Michel leaned forward and took both of Norman's hands into his own. Forehead to forehead, his eyes wide, he blurted out: 'Claudio could still be alive.'

'You're drunk.'

'No, I'm not. Look at this: five weeks ago at Parthenion in Arcadia another policeman was killed, Petros Roussos. He was Karagheorghis's colleague for fifteen years at central police headquarters in Athens. In other words, working directly with Karamanlis. And guess who they've sent to coordinate the investigation: Pavlos Karamanlis himself. He's probably already in Areopolis; it's just a few kilometres from here. They're all tied in to that night at the Polytechnic.'

'But what does Claudio have to do with it? I don't understand about Claudio.'

A little girl with a tray of sweets approached them: 'Mister, want to buy some *loukoumia*?'

'No, sweetheart. Michel, listen to me. Claudio is dead. My father told me so when the story came out in the papers. He also told me that the business about them getting blown up was probably something the police made up to get rid of the two inopportune corpses without leaving a trace. Accept it.'

Michel continued to scan the newspaper. 'Maybe it's just a hunch, or maybe it's something more. But I bet we'll find out soon.'

'Maybe.'

'They found the same words next to the dead bodies of both Roussos and Karagheorghis: "She's naked. She's cold." It's a message, get it? It has to be a message, and if we can manage to figure it out we'll know who the murderer is and why he killed them with such deliberate cruelty.'

Norman frowned: 'A message . . . just like my father. But then it could be the same person. You think that Claudio has come back to kill his jailers, don't you?'

'You're thinking that I'm still trying after all these years to rid myself of the guilt of having turned him in, don't you? Say so! Go ahead and say so.'

'But what you're saying is crazy, can't you understand? If there were a connection between these three crimes, what does my father have to do with it? My father tried to save them. He sent one of his men, a car . . . I was there, he tried to save them, I'm telling you.'

The owner of the stand craned to get a look at them, as did the people sitting at the tables nearby. Norman lowered his head and finished eating in silence, while Michel bit his lower lip, forcing back the tears springing to his eyes.

'Your nerves are shot to hell,' he said to Michel. 'Eat. Fried fish tastes terrible cold.'

11

MICHEL KNOCKED ON Norman's door: 'I'm going down to get the car out. I'll wait for you downstairs.'

'All right,' said Norman. 'I'll be down in ten minutes.'

Michel drove the car out of the hotel's garage and on to the street, parking under a street light. He switched off the engine. He took the abstract by Periklis Harvatis – 'Hypothesis on the necromantic rite in the *Odyssey*, Book XI' – out of his briefcase and started to read.

Harvatis's hypothesis: Michel knew it by heart, having read it time and time again. The author held that the necromantic rite for raising the dead described in the eleventh book of the *Odyssey* – which Homer set at the ends of the earth on the shores of the Ocean – was the same rite used in Ephira for consulting the Oracle of the Dead. Ephira was in Epirus, right opposite the Ionian islands . . . opposite Ithaca, the homeland of Odysseus. Actual excavations had shown that the oracle had been active since as early as the Mycenaean age, from the time of the Homeric heroes.

It had been a magical, dreadful site for centuries. The Acheron flowed into Ephira after having been joined by the Cocytus and the Piriphlegeton. The Stygian swamp was found in Ephira, and in the villages on the surrounding mountains the dead were still buried with a twenty-drachma silver coin in their mouths – the obol demanded by Charon, who ferried the dead souls into the underworld. Raw fava beans were still eaten in commemoration of the dead – time seemed to have stood still in Ephira.

And the eeriest episode of all antiquity had taken place right opposite Ephira, near the island of Paxos. The commander of a ship headed for Italy at the time of emperor Tiberius had heard the cry: 'The great god Pan is dead!' He had heard it distinctly, more than once, and he had heard a mournful chorus of laments from the forests which covered the island. News spread, and Emperor Tiberius himself demanded to speak with the ship's commander to ask him about this mysterious event: the announcement that the pagan gods existed no more and that a new era had begun. It was the year, and perhaps the month and the day, of the death and resurrection of Christ . . . of Christ's return from the underworld.

Ephira knew.

And the anguish-laden voice of a dying world shouted to the sky and to the sea: 'The great god Pan is dead!'

Norman opened the passenger door and got in: 'You still reading that stuff? You must know that booklet by heart.'

'I do. And yet, you know, there's something I still can't understand. Harvatis's study is pretty naive, at times even superficial, and yet it led to the most incredible of discoveries: the vase of Tiresias, the proof of a second Odyssey. I'm starting to think that maybe this isn't the complete version of his studies. I think that something important – fundamental – is missing here.'

'It's possible. Maybe the conclusion was never published. Harvatis may never have had the time or the chance to gather all his notes and have them printed. Start the car – it'll take us nearly an hour to get to our appointment.'

Michel turned the key and started the engine. The car crossed the nearly empty town square and headed south towards Cape Tenaros. The sky was clear and full of stars, but there was no moon and the road was dark and narrow between the mountains and the sea.

'Norman.'

'Yes.'

'There's something there. At Ephira, I mean.'

Norman lit up a cigarette and took in a long draught of smoke. 'The door to the underworld. There was an Oracle of the Dead in ancient times, wasn't there?'

'You can laugh about it if you want, but there must have been something about that place that gave people the idea they could bridge the gap with the other world. For nearly two thousand years.'

'Well, sure, in Delphi they thought they could hear the voice of Apollo predicting the future . . .'

'There's a reason for that, as well. Did you know that it was directly off the shore of Ephira, during the age of Emperor Tiberius, that the Paxos incident occurred? Norman, it's believed to have happened on the very day of Christ's resurrection. Understand? A voice announcing the end of paganism and all the pagan gods, symbolized by the god Pan. And that voice came from Ephira . . .'

'From the gates of hell. So what did I say?'

Michel seemed not to listen to the irony in Norman's words. 'And that vase, the vase of Tiresias, also comes from Ephira. That's where Professor Harvatis found it, where it had once been immersed in the blood of so many victims. And now it's reappeared near Dirou: and there's another entrance to Hades in Dirou.

'Norman, you remember that night at the Polytechnic? Ari Malidis told us that that vase had been discovered by Professor Harvatis, that he had died for that vase. He said he would explain later. Just what did Periklis Harvatis die of? I never saw Malidis again. The next morning they put me on a plane to France. I never saw him again.'

'I know.'

'Maybe we'll find Malidis waiting for us today.'

'Or Pavlos Karamanlis.'

'Why?'

'I was the one who told Karamanlis where the vase was.'

Michel jerked suddenly towards Norman. 'Watch the road! You're driving off the road! Look, that town down at the bottom of the gulf is Oitylos. We go straight from there to Pirgos Dirou, then we turn left towards the mountain.'

At the Oitylos exit there was a police roadblock. The officer leaned down towards the window and shone a torch inside. Michel felt his blood run cold: for a moment he was that boy in his Deux-Chevaux, scared to death, trying to explain to the police why he was speeding through Athens before dawn that morning, and why the back seat was stained with blood.

'Your documents, please,' said the policeman.

Norman realized how frightened Michel was. He squeezed his friend's shoulder hard with his left hand and leaned over towards the police: 'Right away,' he said in Greek and handed over the car registration while Michel took out his licence. 'Is there a problem?'

'There was a crime the other night at the Dirou caves and we're checking everyone and everything. Where are you headed?'

Norman hesitated.

'Kharoudha,' said Michel. 'We have a boat down there and we've taken a couple of weeks off to go fishing. We wanted to see the caves, too, but they must be closed, after what's happened.'

'Oh no,' said the policeman. 'They'll be opening again tomorrow. You can see them, no problem.'

'Can we go now?'

'Yes, certainly. But be careful – the criminal who committed this murder may still be in the area.'

'Thanks for warning us, Officer,' said Norman. 'We'll be careful.'

'We said we were putting all our cards on the table,' said Michel after they'd driven off. 'Why didn't you tell me about Karamanlis?'

'I wanted to force him into making a bargain: the vase for

freeing Claudio and Heleni. I didn't tell you because I didn't want you to feel—'

'Even more humiliated.'

'I didn't think I should. But now, thinking about it, since we don't know who we'll be meeting, I thought that you . . . that we . . . should be ready for any possibility.'

'Then these signs – the abstract delivered to the University, the photo on your windscreen – could be a trap set by Karamanlis. We are the only two witnesses who know that Claudio and Heleni were his prisoners.'

'And that the terrorist story was invented by the police to cover up their deaths.'

'But why now, after so many years?'

'I don't know. Maybe someone else found out about it. Maybe he's been threatened, blackmailed. Or even, even . . .' A startling thought wrinkled his forehead. 'No, maybe we're worrying about nothing. We'll probably just meet up with your run-of-the-mill fence who'll want a lot of money from us.'

'No, all this is too much for a run-of-the-mill fence. Maybe it's even too much for Pavlos Karamanlis. Norman, listen, it's like we're working our way through some complicated maze. What I think is that everything is connected: the deaths of Roussos and Karagheorghis, the death of your father, the reappearance of the vase of Tiresias. Karamanlis being called into this and us too. It can't just be chance.'

Norman fell silent and kept his eyes on the narrow dirt-road full of twists and turns, squeezed between the walls of the rocky gorge that led to the pass. Michel broke the silence.

'Norman.'

'Yes.'

'No more secrets. If there's anything else that you know and haven't told me, even if it's going to hurt me, tell me now.'

'No, there's nothing else. Whatever else comes out of this, we'll face it together.'

They reached the pass and Michel took his foot off the

accelerator. For an instant, they could see the waters of the gulf of Messenia and the gulf of Laconia glittering to the east and the west. The whole promontory stretched out to the south, down to Cape Tenaros. The mountainous ridge, deeply eroded and worn away on the sides and crest, looked like the back of a dragon plunging into the sea.

'Why have us drive up this mule track when there's the low road that goes through Kotronas?' asked Michel.

'Obvious, my friend. Our man wanted us to admire this gorgeous panorama.'

'I'm glad you still feel like joking.'

'I'd say it's evident why he had us come this way. There's been a crime and the roads are crawling with police. This little affair of ours is hardly legal, and he's not asking for a small sum. I'm sure he doesn't want the police sniffing around half a million dollars.' He looked at his watch. 'It's one o'clock. The rendezvous is in half an hour, at an abandoned lighthouse six kilometres from the coastal road. We're to start measuring from the end of this road, heading south. We'll be told what to do there.'

Michel turned left and began the descent.

CAPTAIN KARAMANLIS TAPPED the shoulder of the officer driving the squad car: 'Stop at that roadblock,' he said. 'Let's see if there's anything new.' His driver pulled over and Karamanlis approached the policemen posted at the block. 'Anything to report?' he asked.

'Practically nothing.'

'That son of a bitch can't have vanished into thin air. Did you check all the outgoing vehicles?'

'All of them, sir.'

'No suspicious vehicles coming through?'

'I'd say not. Just a short time ago a car with English plates passed through with two tourists aboard, a Frenchman and an Englishman. They were going to Kharoudha to fish for a week.

They weren't new to the place, both of them spoke Greek very well.'

Karamanlis nodded then got back in the car and told the driver to proceed southward. A thought suddenly came to mind; he had the driver stop and got out again. 'What were their names?' he shouted towards the police. 'Do you remember their names?'

'The Frenchman was called Charrier, I think, Michel Charrier,' shouted back the policeman.

'What car were they driving?'

'A blue Rover.'

Karamanlis jumped back into the car. 'Get going,' he told the driver, 'and drive as fast as you can. To Kharoudha.'

AT THAT MOMENT Michel had just reached the Cape Tenaros provincial road. He turned right after checking his milometer; after exactly six kilometres he pulled over, leaving only his parking lights on.

'We're here,' said Norman. 'Now we just have to wait for the signal.'

'HOW ARE YOU feeling, son?'

'Weak. And very tired.'

'The sea is being watched too closely. We couldn't risk leaving by boat. We had to use this gallery. Others still have to pay their debt: you must not fail me.'

'But won't we be even more at risk on the ground, Commander?'

'On the ground there's someone waiting to take you away. To your next assignment. Now, stay where you are. Let me go ahead. I'll call you in a minute.'

Claudio heard a creaking, and a square of light opened above his head: a trapdoor, leading upwards. Admiral Bogdanos's figure stood out dark against the light. 'You can come up now. There's a stairway cut into the rock.'

Claudio made his way up the slippery steps and found himself in an empty, dusty chamber full of broken glass, with unhinged shutters on the single window. The swash of the undertow could be heard nearby. 'Where are we, Commander?'

'On the other side of the peninsula, on the eastern coast. This is the abandoned lighthouse of Kotronas, in disuse since the last war. Back then I used to use this passage to reach my submarine beneath the cliffs of Hierolimin.'

'Do you mean that we've crossed Cape Tenaros underground?'

'Exactly. And we've done it faster than the coastguard boats; they'll still be near Hierolimin, fighting the Meltemi and the rocks. As the poet says, "*Ephtes pezòs iòn è egò syn nei melàine*".'

'I understand ancient Greek: it's a line from the *Odyssey*. "You arrived sooner on foot than did I on the black ship",' said Claudio, without recalling the exact reference.

The older man nodded, and a fleeting melancholy crossed his blue eyes. 'They are words said to a friend who died before his time.'

Bogdanos neared the window: a dark vehicle was parked a hundred metres up the road with its parking lights on. 'Good, everything is working as planned. Come this way.' They walked into the next room, a kind of garage where a little truck was parked, a small Toyota pickup covered at the back by a tarp. Bogdanos lifted up a flap. 'Get in here. And stay put. This belongs to the fishing coop, and the police have seen it a thousand times. Someone will be bringing you north. There will be roadblocks up to Gythion. After you've passed the city, the truck will slow down at a certain point; you'll get out then and continue on foot. The person driving must not see you for any reason, understand? Bear up, at Aighia there's a truck stop that opens at six, you can get some fried eggs *ommatia* and stewed beans. A couple of hundred drachma, and you'll feel like a new man. We'll see each other as soon as possible, my son.'

Bogdanos lowered the tarp and returned to the lighthouse chamber. He lit a candle and passed it in front of the window three times. The car responded by flashing its headlights three times. A minute later two men left the car and walked towards the wall of the lighthouse, but Bogdanos retreated into the shadow of the window, his face hidden.

'There's been a setback,' he said. 'You'll have heard about the murder at Dirou; the police are sifting through every inch of the peninsula. I couldn't bring the vase – it was too dangerous.'

'I can see your point,' said Norman.

'When can we see it?' asked Michel.

'Soon,' replied Bogdanos. 'But you'll have to do what I say first. Leave me your car and take the truck you'll find in the garage. Drive through Gythion and then leave it at the Esso motel on your left just outside the city, five kilometres after the railroad crossing. You'll find your car back at your hotel tomorrow morning.'

'But why should we trust you? What's the reason for this switch?'

'Someone may have followed you or noticed your car. I don't want to run any risks.'

'Prove that you really have that vase,' said Michel.

'The vase was taken from the basement of the Archaeological Museum in Athens on the night between the eighteenth and nineteenth of November 1973, just before Captain Karamanlis of the Athens Police could get hold of it. Someone must have told him exactly where it was: in a bucket full of sawdust in a closet.'

'Okay, we believe you,' said Norman, astonished. 'We believe you . . . we'll do as you say.'

'Tell us your name,' said Michel, possessed by sudden anxiety. 'So we can reach you if we need to.'

'People like me have many names and no name at the same time. Go through that door, get into the truck and drive away. Now. Each of us will take his own road.'

A minute later Claudio heard the engine starting up and the old pickup began to gain speed. He looked out of the tailgate and saw the ruins of the old lighthouse standing out against the starry sky and the glittering waves. For a moment, he thought he saw the figure of Admiral Bogdanos raising his hand to say goodbye. As the truck drove steadily on, its irregular sway rocked him into the only dream which could keep him alive: the eyes of Heleni, her voice, her hands, her live, warm body, eternal. And the dream surrounded him like a tepid springtime wind that melts the ice and releases the waters to run clear through the ditches.

God, would the eternal winter of his existence ever end? Bogdanos knew, he had to know. He knew everything . . . he was not like other men . . . his mind took unknown, mysterious turns. He had pulled him back from the brink of his 'normal' life; he had opened up his old wounds, made him return to a past he had thought long-buried. And he had led him through hell. Could he ever make peace with the memory of Heleni? Maybe this was the bitter drink he had to swallow to its dregs in order to keep on living. But in the end, would he live, or would he die?

One thing was certain, Bogdanos was always right; he was right when he told him what awesome strength the sight of the guilty would unleash in him. How many more were there? How many times again would he be invaded by that force, that destructive frenzy that left him exhausted yet ominously at peace? But there was one of them, one in particular, whose ordeal he was patiently awaiting. The one on whom he would vent all the pent-up misery of the violence he had suffered. The one for whom he had already chosen the message of death.

CAPTAIN KARAMANLIS HAD dismissed his driver and driven himself down all the streets of Kharoudha, a sleepy, silent town. No trace of the blue Rover, as he had suspected. He imagined that Michel Charrier and Norman Shields – because he had no doubt that it was the two of them – must have turned west towards the eastern coast of the promontory. He meant to find them and have them followed. Discreetly, without them realizing it. He returned to the provincial road and at the fork turned right towards Kotronas. It was his lucky night; just a few kilometres later he saw a blue Rover with English plates leave a self-service petrol station and turn west. He did a fast U-turn and was behind him in a few minutes, keeping at a distance so as not to be noticed. The car reached the western provincial road and turned north towards Kalamata, until it had to pull over at the Oitylos roadblock. Karamanlis stopped as well, eager to continue the chase. He slowed down at the roadblock to allow himself to be recognized, but did not stop to speak with the officers who had changed shifts with the first patrol.

The Rover proceeded at a moderate speed to Skardamoula, where it parked in front of a small hotel. A man got out, closed the door, walked up to the front desk and then walked off shortly later on foot. Could he have been following the wrong car? How could there be two Rovers with British plates driving around these lonely streets so late at night? What if the man was the killer himself? Had it been a trick to get through the roadblock? Why hadn't the police stopped him? He got out of the car and entered the hotel.

'Police,' he announced to the night porter. 'Who was the man who walked in here a minute ago?'

'Don't know. I've never seen him before.'

'But he parked his car in the hotel lot.'

'That's right. Said he'd been instructed to by the owners, who are guests here.'

Karamanlis thanked him: 'Don't mention that I've been by. Just a mistake on my part. I wouldn't want the owner to become alarmed.'

'No problem,' answered the clerk, and turned back to his crossword puzzle.

Karamanlis got back into the car and set off in the same direction as the man who had walked away from the hotel: he had a few questions to ask him. He drove slowly, keeping his eye on the left side of the road until he saw him. The man was walking quickly, both hands in his pockets. He was wearing a pair of cotton trousers and a dark cotton jacket, with lightweight canvas shoes. Karamanlis accelerated, drove up to the first curve and turned the car around so he could shine his lights into the man's face. He recognized him immediately: same sharp gaze, same commanding expression, his face hard and deeply lined.

It was Anastasios Bogdanos.

Ten years had passed over his features like water over a basalt rock. He was about to step on the brake pedal, but he didn't. He drove a little further up the road and then got out so he could follow the man on foot. He saw him leave the street and walk up to the top of a small promontory facing the sea. He sat there, hands between his knees, perfectly still, contemplating the glittering expanse of waves.

FROM HIS VANTAGE point, Claudio Setti could see the curving road that led to Gythion. From the cab he heard an indistinct buzz of voices alternated with long silences and the sound of a radio. The pickup slowed down a couple of times at the roadblocks, but Claudio was not alarmed. He watched emotionless from the back of the truck as the police and their cars vanished in the dark.

They passed Gythion and took the road that led north. The roll of the truck made him drowsy. The low music on the radio reminded him of the tune which had comforted him during the most intense moments of his life, a popular ballad that his mother used to sing to him when he was a child. He had lost her when he was very young, and that song was the only thing he remembered about her.

Ten kilometres later the truck slowed down and stopped at a railway crossing, and Claudio shook himself awake. As it started to move forward again, Claudio jumped out. He lingered for a few minutes behind the line inspector's booth, then headed off on foot. Those strangers had helped him to slip through an impressive display of police force without even sensing they had a passenger.

He began to feel a little better, stronger and more confident, although he hadn't eaten for hours and hours. He walked at a brisk pace through the warm night, accompanied by the crowing of roosters and barking of dogs. As dawn was breaking, a tractor gave him a lift to the tavern at the gates of Aighia. The owner brought him fried eggs *ommatia* and stewed beans with fresh bread.

It all tasted good and only cost him two hundred drachmas.

12

CAPTAIN KARAMANLIS WAS woken up by the ringing of a telephone. It was one of his men from headquarters in Athens.

'Captain, I found an Interpol dispatch we had on file that I'm sure you'll be interested in: two months ago, an official of the British embassy in Belgrade was found murdered in Yugoslavia, a certain James Henry Shields. He was hunting in Macedonia along the Strimon valley. An arrow through the heart. And the corpse was found with his mouth and eyes closed up.'

Karamanlis was quiet for a minute, considering the news. 'Doesn't sound so strange, after all. He was a man with a dangerous job.'

'There's more: a slip of paper with a message in ancient Greek was found in his jacket pocket. That's why I thought you'd be interested; it made me think of the Roussos and Karagheorghis murders.'

'Do you know what the message said?'

'It apparently didn't make sense . . .'

'Read it to me, for Chrissake!'

'Yessir, captain. The Yugoslavian police report says: "You in your day have witnessed hundreds slaughtered, killed in single combat or killed in pitched battle, true, but if you'd laid eyes on this it would have wrenched your heart." '

Karamanlis fell back on the bed: the third crime that completed the picture. How couldn't they be connected to that night ten years ago? But what did the murderer want to say? What message was there in his words? The officer on the phone shook him from his thoughts: 'Captain, Captain, are you still there?'

'Yes, I'm listening.'

'Is there something more you want to know? Shall we ask for further clarification?'

'Vassilios Vlassos, Sergeant Vlassos: where is he right now?'

'I'll check for you right away, sir. Vlassos ... here it is, Vlassos is on leave, on holiday.'

'Where?'

'At Portolagos.'

'What kind of a shithole of a place is Portolagos? I've never heard of it.'

'It's a town in Thrace. Vlassos knows a woman there.'

'Contact him immediately and tell him to watch his ass. There's a good chance that there's someone who wants to knock him off in an imaginative way like Roussos, Karagheorghis and that other poor devil. Understand?'

'Yes, sir, of course. I'll do as you say immediately.'

'And let my colleague in Salonika know that I'll be getting in touch with him as soon as I arrive.'

'Will do, sir.'

Karamanlis hung up, took a notepad out of his pocket and jotted down the message found on Shields's body before he forgot the exact words. He washed and dressed quickly, stuffing his things into a little suitcase. Before leaving, he called police headquarters at Kalamata and instructed them to keep an eye on the blue Rover parked at the Plaja hotel and keep its occupants under surveillance without being noticed. He was in his car just a few minutes later.

There was a map in his glove compartment. He spread it over the steering wheel and pointed his finger at the rest and relaxation site chosen by Sergeant Vassilios Vlassos. It was a little town in eastern Thrace, not far from the Turkish border, halfway between Xanthi and Komotini. It looked like it was right in the middle of a swamp or a lagoon. Hard to tell. Not much of a vacation spot. He folded up the map and started off at a steady speed. No need to kill himself; he'd easily get there by tomorrow evening.

He also thought there was no need to worry about Bogdanos, at least not for the moment. His intuition told him that he'd be seeing him somewhere in the vicinity of Portolagos, and maybe the puzzle would start to unravel. He radioed headquarters and advised them to close down the roadblocks: the murderer had almost certainly got away. And they'd surely need more than a roadblock to stop him.

If he had figured it right, Vlassos would be next, then him. Yes, the murderer wanted to leave him until last, *dulcis in fundo*. Right, he thought, go ahead and save the best for last, you bastard, you son of a bitch, but I'll be there this time, waiting for you in that fucking swamp. I'll be there and I'll be ready for you.

When he passed Sparta it was late in the morning, and he stopped at Corinth to get something to eat for lunch. He also called his wife to tell her he'd be away for a few days.

'But when will you decide to retire?' asked the poor woman. 'You have enough years added up. With your retirement pay we could find a new house and get new furniture . . .'

'Irini, does this seem like the time to talk about this? Come on, don't be angry. I'll bring you some feta from Komotini.'

Retire . . . as if it were that easy. In his line of work, there was just one way to go out. When you'd settled all your accounts. Or when someone faster and smarter than you took you out of business once and for all. Poor Irini. She was a good woman, simple and so affectionate. He'd make her happy, he'd bring her some olives from Kalamata and some cheese from Komotini.

He drove past Athens, staying on the highway for Thermopylae and Lamia. Retire . . . why the hell not, after all. Irini was right – it was no good working until you were decrepit. You should retire when you could still enjoy life, take a trip or two, go to the sea, to the mountains. Their children had grown up – Dimitrios would soon be getting his degree in architecture in Florence, and Maria had begun to study medicine in Patras. She was so beautiful, it amazed him to think that he and his wife had managed to bring such a lovely child into the world, so sweet. All he had to do was lie in wait for the bastard and kill him like a dog: legitimate self-defence and that would be the end of that, party over. But who the hell could it be? Couldn't be the Englishman. But what about his French friend?

No. Only a madman would come back after so many years and risk his own skin. What did the Frenchman know anyway? Very little, when it came down to it. No. It had to be some relative of the girl, or of the boy. But how could they have found out about it? How could any of their relatives possibly know about James Henry Shields?

No. None of those hypotheses held water. One was crazier than the next. He realized that it frightened him to admit that there was only one solution to the mystery: Claudio Setti. Only Claudio Setti could know enough to want Roussos, Karagheorghis and Shields dead. If Setti weren't already dead . . . if he himself hadn't seen a photograph of the boy's corpse. Yeah . . . just a photograph, after all. Well, dammit, even if it were the devil himself he'd find him and kill him. He couldn't wait to have his chance.

He arrived in the evening at Salonika and stopped in a hotel near the sea. Before stretching out to sleep, he stuck his loaded long-barrelled Beretta calibre 9 under his pillow. He felt close to the front line.

Two weeks went by without a thing happening. Vlassos would get up late and go to the local café for breakfast. He'd stay there gossiping with some other slugs until nearly lunchtime. From their gestures they were talking about women and soccer. Every day, every blessed day. In the afternoon he slept until late, then usually took a boat into the middle of the fucking swamp and sat there like an idiot with a fishing pole in his hand for hours. He'd smoke, pull in the line and then smoke some more. He caught a fish every now and then, ugly, warty things. Karamanlis had begun to hate him.

Portolagos was the most horrible place you could imagine.

The mosquitoes bit even during the day and there were millions of them. He wondered how anyone in his right mind could live in a place where the mosquitoes bit all day long. He'd spread on the insect repellent every day, but after a while it made him break out in a rash, which was even worse. He got to the point where if someone felt like shooting Vassilios Vlassos in the back, they'd be doing him a favour.

The most unbearable part of it all was the surveillance after dark. Every night, or nearly, Vlassos went to visit his woman. She lived in a wretched house at the other end of the lagoon, near the bridge for Komotini, an old military bridge covered with wooden beams. Alongside the house was an ancient acacia tree surrounded by bushes whose branches held an unbelievable quantity of mosquitoes. There was no other place Karamanlis could hide. From there he could keep an eye on the territory all around, but to stay on the safe side, every once in a while he'd creep up to the window to see what was going on inside. They made love with the lights on and what he saw was more embarrassing each time.

The woman was a sort of fleshy giantess with enormous breasts and round, massive buttocks. The black, luxuriant hairiness under her arms stood out against her white skin, as did her pubic hair, which trailed down the inside of her thighs nearly to her knees. Vlassos dived into that sea of flesh with the ardour of a copulating boar, and he always succeeded in making that immense female tremble and sigh like a young girl in the arms of her one true love. When he lay back panting, she would kiss him and lick him all over like a cow with a newborn calf. Karamanlis, who had a delicate stomach for some things, often felt a wave of nausea overcoming him. But hell, from a certain point of view, Vlassos was admirable – a man his age who could still stay in the saddle for hours, dammit, and with a creature on whom any normal man wouldn't know where to start. Lord knew what he'd be capable of with a nice fresh young girl. Yeah, young and beautiful . . .

Karamanlis had nearly convinced himself that he'd been

wrong about the whole thing. Vlassos was a sitting duck while he was out there fishing on the swamp. Anyone could have killed him, a thousand times, easily. Roussos, Shields and Karagheorghis had all been murdered in solitary, hidden places. The killer certainly wouldn't want to wait until Vlassos was back on duty, armed and in similar company. Maybe he'd just dreamed the whole thing up? Well, just as well then, just as well. Although now he had no idea where to start looking.

On the last night of Vlassos's holiday, Karamanlis noticed that the sergeant hadn't gone out fishing as he usually did. He must have stayed at home to pack his bags. The captain decided to take some time off for dinner, and then go back to keep watch on the house until one or two in the morning. Then he'd return to the boarding house to sleep as he had every night, with his ears wide open, of course. Not that Vlassos needed him, really. He had been warned by the police, after all, and he surely kept a gun in the house. And probably wore a gun by day as well.

He reached a little town called Messemvria just east of Portolagos and sat down at the only tavern, in front of a panful of lamb chops and fried potatoes. The town *papàs* was sitting at the next table and lots of the people there spoke Turkish, the border being so close.

The tavern owner came to his table with a half litre of retsina. 'His treat,' he said with a backward jerk of his head, putting two clean glasses on the table. Karamanlis raised his head and his gaze – travelling past the hats and bald heads of the other taverngoers, above the blue fog of cigarette smoke – encountered the steady eyes of Admiral Bogdanos.

So the situation was finally starting to sort itself out. He gestured for the man to join him at his table, without showing particular surprise. Bogdanos got up, rising above the layer of smoke like a mountain peak over a stretch of clouds. He sat opposite Karamanlis as he poured some wine into the glasses.

'You don't seem surprised to see me after so many years,' said Bogdanos.

'I'm not. I saw you around Dirou a couple of weeks ago and in my heart I knew I'd see you again.'

'Really? And what made you think that?'

'Because this is where police sergeant Vassilios Vlassos from headquarters in Athens is spending his holidays. And something could happen to him, like those poor devils Karagheorghis and Roussos, or like Mr James Henry Shields.'

'It seems that you've already drawn some pretty firm conclusions from this chain of crimes.'

'It sounds like you have too, if I'm not mistaken.'

'You're not mistaken. So you really shouldn't be here just now – you've left Vlassos all alone, and the killer might have been waiting for just this moment to strike, safe and undisturbed.'

Karamanlis brought his fist down on the table, jingling the silverware on his plate and rolling the wine in his glass. 'You've got guts to come here and preach to me – it's thanks to you that we have a crazy nut getting his kicks out of butchering my men, and Lord only knows when we'll see the end of this story. And I want you to know that as far as I'm concerned there's only one answer to this: Claudio Setti did not die, as you had assured me. He's alive and kicking and having fun chopping us into pieces one by one. And making fools out of us with his idiotic messages.'

Bogdanos seemed to back down: 'I must honestly admit that everything does seem to lead to this conclusion . . .'

'Fine. I'm glad that my hypothesis meets with your approval. And just how do you justify this pretty mess? I'd say you didn't keep up your end of the deal.'

'I'm no butcher. You can't imagine that I would have physically eliminated a prisoner myself. I simply gave an order and I have no reason to believe that it wasn't carried out.'

'Right,' said Karamanlis. 'You keep your hands clean. You leave the dirty work to someone else. Anyway, it's us now in the sights of that bastard. I don't give a shit about your gentlemanly demeanour. Suppose you tell me what you know about what happened to Claudio Setti, and what the hell you were doing in Dirou and what the bloody hell you're doing here.'

Bogdanos drew back: 'Careful of what you say, Karamanlis. You are in no position to give me orders or make any demands. I'm here to look for an explanation for these crimes. To find the killer, and eliminate him, if possible. We won't be sure until we do . . . and then we'll be able to call the game. I can guarantee that you will never see me again. But time is growing short. They're starting to ask questions at the Ministry, starting to link a number of coincidences . . . we have to finish this game off. Now.'

'You sent me a photograph of his corpse . . .'

'It was sent to you by the person who carried out my orders. A trustworthy person. What did you expect in such a case? An official autopsy report? I had no reason to doubt the elimination of the . . . subject in question. But now it seems to me that we're wasting time needlessly. Where is Vlassos at this moment?'

'At his house, I think.'

'You think. Dammit, Karamanlis, I wonder how a man of your experience . . . Let's go now, before it's too late.'

They walked out on to the square of Messemvria, lit by a single bulb hanging on the front of the parish church. They both got into Karamanlis's Fiat 131, because Bogdanos had no means of transport. As if he'd dropped out of the sky. They raced down the low road that led to the provincial highway in a cloud of dust, turning left for Portolagos. It wasn't even ten o'clock when Karamanlis stopped his car near Vlassos's house. The kitchen light was on. He was home, thank God. Karamanlis approached the window and looked in: there was an open suitcase on the table with some clothing in it, and a pot boiling on the gas stove. Some milk, maybe. He knocked on the window, several times, and then called out. No answer.

'He's gone out, dammit,' said Bogdanos behind him. 'See if you can get in and look around the house.'

Karamanlis went to the front door. It was open. He made a

rapid round of inspection. Everything seemed to be in order, but it was obvious that Vlassos had left in a hurry – he'd left the flame burning in the kitchen, the suitcase open, the light on. Karamanlis turned everything off and walked out into the courtyard: 'Something or someone made him leave suddenly: he didn't even switch off the light and there was a pot of milk boiling on the stove.'

'Where could he have gone?' asked Bogdanos.

'The only person who can fire up his ass like that is his woman. Maybe she called him.'

'Or maybe someone used her to lure him out, God damn it.'

'Don't curse, damn you. If you had done your job right we wouldn't be here chasing after this animal in this shithole of a town.'

Bogdanos looked at his watch. 'Where is this woman's house?'

'Not far from the military bridge.'

'Let's get moving then. We may already be too late.'

They got back into the car and headed towards the bridge; in just a few minutes they were in front of the woman's house. The door was open here as well. The lights were on and the radio was blaring a Hadjidakis concert. The room was in a great mess, furniture was overturned and dishes broken: the lady had obviously tried to defend herself. Bogdanos frowned: 'Just as I feared. They've kidnapped the woman and used her to set a trap for Vlassos.'

'But where have they taken her?'

'The swamp. That's where we have to look for them.' A gust of cool air rippled the surface of the water.

'Damn. Now even the weather's turning on us,' mumbled Karamanlis.

'Looks like it,' replied Bogdanos. 'That's what they were predicting, anyway. No doubt our man already knew.'

They decided to separate so one could search the western bank while the other searched the eastern side, but Bogdanos held Karamanlis back: 'Stop. Over there.'

'I don't see anything.'

'A light. I saw a light for a second. What is there in that direction?'

'A little island with a church dedicated to Haghios Spiridion. There's a procession on the saint's day, the fifteenth of July, but it's closed for the rest of the year. On one side it's connected to the eastern shore by a pier about fifty metres long. Vlassos sometimes goes there to fish.'

'How far is it from here?'

'A kilometre and a half, more or less.'

'Which side is the entrance on?'

'The west shore.'

'Let's try approaching it from two sides. I'll go along the shore and head towards the pier, you take a boat and approach from the south. The murderer might try to escape on the water.'

They separated. Karamanlis took a flat-bottomed boat with a little outboard motor and began to row silently towards the island. Bogdanos checked his watch again, then set off on foot along the shore, heading towards the pier. The weather was getting worse. Stronger gusts of wind lashed the surface of the lagoon, raising spray and puffs of foam. The northern horizon flashed with lightning, and thunder rumbled from the mountain peaks, muffled by the waves of the Aegean. The tolling of the church bell of Portolagos sounded, nearly extinguished by the gusty wind. It was half past ten.

VASSILIOS VLASSOS STOPPED, panting, in front of the door to the little Haghios Spiridion church. He couldn't hear a sound, except for the creaking of the wave-beaten wooden pier and the shrill whistle of the wind. A slight glow emanated from the window, like that of a flickering candle burning in front of a sacred image.

Vlassos pulled out his Beretta and approached the window, but couldn't see a thing except for the pews inside the church, reverberating with the uncertain lamplight. He decided to go in the right way, by the door: he kicked it open and dived in, rolling sideways on to the floor behind one of the pews, gun tight in fist.

What he saw knocked the breath out of him: his woman was tied, nearly naked, to a column in the iconostasis like a grotesque and blasphemous Saint Sebastian. She was gagged and in front of her, on the floor, a candle wrapped in red paper was burning brightly.

A sharp, clear voice rose from behind the iconostasis. The close space made it sound very near, strangely intimate: 'Welcome, Sergeant Vlassos! You've come to get your woman, haven't you?'

Vlassos boiled with impotent rage: 'Let her go. I'll do anything you want. Let her go, you—'

'You care very much about your little turtle dove, don't you? Good. If you really do care, throw your gun over here, towards the altar.' Vlassos hesitated. 'You can't even imagine what it means to see your woman tortured to death, to witness her agony and her death, can you Vlassos?!' Vlassos tossed the gun to the ground and it skidded over to the balustrade. The woman shuddered at the noise and whimpered for help.

'Don't be afraid,' said Vlassos. 'Don't be afraid. I won't let him touch you. I know who you are,' he said, raising his voice. 'You're the one who slaughtered Roussos and Karagheorghis. But she doesn't have anything to do with it, dammit. Let her go and the two of us can work it out. Listen, I'll tell you everything. It wasn't our fault, it was Karamanlis. He was the one who told us—'

'There's nothing that you can tell me, Vlassos. I already know everything. I'm the one who has something to tell you. Come forward. Slowly.'

Vlassos got up and walked down the little nave towards the iconostasis. He already had a plan worked out: he would pretend to comply, then rush forwards towards the woman and stamp out that damn little candle. In the dark they'd manage to get away. He took another short step towards the halo of light.

A blinding flash of lightning, accompanied by a deafening clap of thunder, lit up the inside of the church suddenly, shone on the pale flesh of the prisoner and revealed an unreal figure at the top of the iconostasis: a hooded man gripping a bow. The arrow shot out with a clean whistle and ran through his groin. Vlassos screamed and fell to the floor while another arrow pierced his arm and yet another stuck in his thigh.

The wind died away and the rain began to pelt down. Vlassos twisted on the blood-soaked ground, crying, waiting for the *coup de grâce*. Nothing happened. He heard the sound of breaking glass shattering on to the floor, and then a low, pressing voice saying something like, 'You have to get out immediately. They are here already, they were waiting for you. Go. Now. Go, right away.' Scuttling, two, three gunshots, shouts, then nothing.

KARAMANLIS, SOAKED WITH the rain and holding a torch in his hand, set aground at that instant. Bogdanos walked towards him, smoking gun in hand: 'One minute. Just one minute sooner and we would have got him.'

'Doesn't matter,' said Karamanlis with a strange smile. 'This time I'm ready.' He took a walkie-talkie from an inside pocket. 'All units,' he said. 'Captain Pavlos Karamanlis here. Attempted homicide at the church of Haghios Spiridion in the lagoon of Portolagos. Suspect escaped on foot two minutes ago. Converge on this site. Block all exits, keep the entire perimeter of the lagoon under surveillance. You're all dead if he gets away this time.' Then, turning to Bogdanos: 'Which way did he go?'

'That way,' he said, pointing towards the mountains. 'I think I've wounded him. You'd better take care of your man in there – what a mess.'

They transferred Vlassos on to the boat along with the woman, covering them as best they could. Karamanlis started up the motor: 'Aren't you coming?'

'No. I want to take another look around.'

'As you wish,' said Karamanlis. 'My men will be surrounding the area – as you can see, this time I wasn't caught unawares.'

He sped off towards Portolagos, watching Bogdanos's profile for a moment against the lightning-lit sky under the pouring rain. Then nothing. His men were waiting for him with an ambulance. Vlassos was still alive, although he had lost a great deal of blood.

The fury of the storm was lessening and Karamanlis ran towards his car with a plastic bag on his head to protect himself from the last bursts of rain. He thought he heard gunshots towards the mountains. Had Bogdanos succeeded in killing that bastard? A crescent moon appeared amidst the black thunder-clouds torn by the meltemi wind, and a few stars glittered diamond light in the clearing sky. Echoes of gunshots? Or of thunder? Could Bogdanos control the elements as well?

He called an officer over and asked him to point out where all the patrols and roadblocks had been positioned. He closely examined the geological features of the area: no gorges, no caves, very little vegetation. The only access to the sea was being constantly flooded with searchlights. The perfect trap. All he had to do was wait. He warned his men not to let up for a moment, then took off for the hospital, where he was brought directly to the operating room.

The patient's blood pressure had been stabilized thanks to a transfusion, but the surgeon had managed to extract only one of the three arrows, the most life-threatening, the one that had run through his large intestine, made a neat exit just beneath the hip bone and cleanly amputated one of his testicles.

The surgeon stopped for a moment to wipe the sweat from his forehead as his assistants were stitching the wound up. 'Good God,' he said to Karamanlis. 'What reason can there be for such awful cruelty?'

Karamanlis glanced at the arrow they'd just extracted, still bloody. Words had been carved into the shaft. 'The reason?' he asked, putting on his glasses and scanning the letters. 'Here's the reason for you.'

The surgeon turned the shaft between his fingers. The phrase that had been carved there, by someone with a steady hand, was as mysterious and disturbing as a curse.

'You put the bread into a cold oven.'

13

Portolagos, Thrace, 9 September, 11.30 p.m.

THE DAMP, DARK night was shot through with cries and shouts, pierced by the beams of torches, rent by the insistent barking of dogs. Flattened against the wall inside the old farmhouse, Claudio trembled with tension and anxiety, still foaming with rage at not having been able to finish off the most hated of his enemies. He was appalled at the unexpected turn that events had taken. He had assumed that the events set into motion would take their inexorable toll, as all the other times the commander had planned and prepared his work for him.

He felt like a hunted animal, a scorpion trapped in a ring of fire. In his hands he clutched the deadly Pearson steel-plated bow with which he had riddled Vlassos's body, gripping it spasmodically. He was prepared to fight to the death. He'd let himself be ripped apart by the dogs rather than surrender. The suspicion that Bogdanos had delivered him to his enemies began to worm its way into his mind, as the shouting of men and the barking of dogs grew closer and closer.

He heard a sound like snapping branches. He opened the door slightly and glanced towards the unbroken stretch of scrub and bushes that extended in the direction of the swamp. He could barely make out the shape of a man on the path, still at quite a distance, amidst the mist rising from the swamp on the rain-laden summer night. It could be none other than Admiral Bogdanos. Claudio couldn't believe how – in that situation, at that time of night, with everything that had happened – his step could be so tranquil, so light and sure. Powerful yet unheeding at the same time.

When Bogdanos walked in, he nearly attacked him: 'Why didn't you let me slaughter that pig? And why did you make me come here? We're surrounded. They'll find us any minute.'

'Let's move to a safe place, son, and then I'll explain everything. This old farmhouse was once a monastery and the well is connected to an ancient Roman cistern the monks used to store fresh water. Follow me, we don't have much time.'

They walked out into the rear courtyard towards a well which seemed long abandoned.

'I'll lower you down with the chain. About halfway, you'll find the entrance to the passage that leads to the cistern. Swing back on the chain and slide in, then wait for me there. I'll lower the other end so I can drop down as you pull it taut. Take this torch. Leave me the bow – I'll bring it down myself.'

'All right,' said Claudio. 'But we've got to hurry: listen to those dogs barking. Damn, it's like they were waiting for us this time.'

'In a certain sense, they were. Our adversary is not only ruthless and brutal, he's also quite intelligent. But he doesn't know that it's our game he's playing. There you are, son: if I remember well, you're at the right depth. You should have the opening right in front of you.'

'I can see it, Commander.'

The torch beam wavered at the bottom of the well, its halo shining on the walls before disappearing suddenly, as if swallowed up into nothing. Claudio's voice sounded suffocated: 'You can drop down now, Commander, but first give me a length of chain. I need enough to pull it tight.' Bogdanos dropped down another couple of metres of the chain. With Claudio holding it taut, he began to lower himself, the bow over his shoulder. The barking of the dogs was very close. Once he reached the opening, Bogdanos handed the bow to Claudio and let himself be pulled into the passage, taking care to collect the chain and not allow it to fall to the bottom of the well.

'Why didn't you drop it? It's not like we can hoist ourselves out.'

'You'll understand soon,' said Bogdanos. 'Turn off that torch now.'

A group of police arrived just a few minutes later with the dogs. The hounds pawed the door of the farmhouse, then ran to the well, back and forth, whining and yelping.

'They're on to something,' said one of the men.

'You search the farmhouse,' said their commanding officer. 'I'll check the well.' He leaned over the side and flashed down a powerful beam of light. 'There's nothing here,' he reported, after having carefully inspected it. He turned towards the house, waiting for his men to finish their search.

'See,' said Bogdanos, 'if we had left the chain, that policeman would have seen the ripples on the water at the bottom and would have understood that someone had thrown or dropped something into the well. He would have become suspicious, perhaps even dropped down to inspect it. And a chain is always useful.'

They walked along the passage, lined with large clusters of maidenhair fern, lighting up their way with the torch. After about half an hour they reached the huge cistern, the *castellum aquarum* of the ancient Roman aqueduct.

'Ingenious, isn't it?' observed Bogdanos. 'When it rained enough or when the snow melted and the water level in the wells rose, they'd channel the water towards this cistern. The sediments deposited, and then the water could be used to feed other wells in areas which were dryer or had been contaminated by salt water.' He walked all around the cistern and started down one of the passages which branched off from it. 'There must have been much more water back then; the level's very low now, as you can see.' Claudio followed him in silence, gripping the big bow in his right hand. The ferns got smaller, then disappeared entirely and were replaced by lichen, as the tunnel evidently led them away from the damp area of the swamp.

'We're almost out,' said Bogdanos, turning back. A few

minutes later he stopped in front of a dark opening and gestured for Claudio to come closer: 'Come along, son. This is the well we'll use to get out. It's crumbling; you can use your hands and feet to climb up.'

Claudio went up first and Bogdanos soon joined him. They found themselves in the middle of a patch of brambles not far from the sea, just a couple of dozen metres from the state road for Komotini. They went on until they reached the sea shore. Lights twinkled on the beach, perhaps a small drink stand, and they could hear the notes of a song mixing with the roll of the tide. Bogdanos sat on the sand.

'How do you feel? Sit down, come on, sit down here.'

'Commander,' he said, dropping to the sand, 'why did we fail this time?'

Bogdanos lowered his head. 'The risk we took was great, my boy, although we came out well. But now, you see, we'll have to suspend our work for some time. The entire Greek police force will be looking for us, because we've plunged the stick right into the hornets' nest. Vlassos will be protected around the clock, and Karamanlis is no fool. He won't let himself be taken by surprise. Our goal has been accomplished: the third message has been delivered. You'll see, it won't be long before it starts to take effect.'

'I don't know how you can be so sure. I keep thinking about the two of them getting away. I haven't been a human being for a long, long time, Commander, and maybe I never will be again, and they are to blame. Only them. At this point, I want the game to end, understand? With you or without you, I have to finish this game. I'll never have any kind of life until I do.'

Low on the horizon, misty with clouds and vapours, the large red moon was setting, projecting long, bloody wakes on to the sea. Bogdanos turned suddenly towards him: 'You have to wait until it's time, my boy. You must wait – do you understand me? There is no other way. I stopped you from killing Vlassos because just one more minute would have led Karamanlis straight to you. What we did was well done. Your arrows struck their mark; I helped Karamanlis put him on the boat. He was bleeding like a stuck pig.' He reached out to stroke the grip on the Pearson bow. 'This is always the best weapon,' he said. 'Precise, silent. Modern technology has built jewels of such perfection ... once a bow had to be greased, heated over a fire ...'

'I want him dead.'

'You'll have him.'

'When?'

'Not now.'

'When?'

'And not here.'

'Well then?'

'First we have to gather them all together. All three, including Vlassos, if he lives. We have to lead them far away from here. Very far from here, where they can count on no one's help, and they will be at our mercy. Trust me. At the right moment, each one of them – without knowing why – will follow the trail that will lead to their deaths, all together. On the same day. At your hand. But the days will be very short ones, the sun will be low and pale on the horizon. Just like the days of the massacre, the days in which they spilled the blood and the tears of an innocent creature, trampling her body and her soul.'

Claudio didn't answer, watching the rim of the moon as it sank into the liquid boundaries of the horizon. The tears which flowed from his eyes were more bitter than the waves coming to die at his feet.

'Commander.'

'Yes, son.'

'Who was the man I killed in Macedon?'

'You recognized him, didn't you? It was the man speaking English who collaborated with Karamanlis that night.'

'Yes, I recognized him. But who was he?'

'Do you really want to know?'

'Yes.'

'It was James Henry Shields.'

'Shields? You don't mean . . .'

'Yes. He was Norman's father.'

He lowered his head, burying it between his knees. 'It was Norman, then . . . who betrayed me?'

'No. It was Michel.'

Claudio twisted his back as if whiplashed, then bent over again and wept silently.

Bogdanos stretched out a hand towards his shoulder, but didn't dare touch him. He stood up. 'I must go, I can't make Karamanlis suspicious. I have to give him proof that he can trust me.' He took a handkerchief from his pocket and wiped the blood from a small wound on Claudio's arm, cut by the brushwood.

'We won't see each other for many days,' said Bogdanos. 'On the night of the eleventh of November, be at the Cimmerian promontory in Ephira. It will be nearly the anniversary of the battle of the Polytechnic. Until then, watch yourself and make no errors. Before the year is out, justice will be done, but we still have a long way to go. It will all happen far from here. Very far from here.'

Claudio lifted his head and looked at him: 'Commander, if something should happen to me . . . If I should fall into their trap, be killed . . . would you finish this task?'

Bogdanos shot him a fiery look: 'Do not even say such a thing. You will strike, when the time is right. You will strike with a steady hand, for Heleni, for yourself and . . . for me. Farewell, my son.'

'Goodbye, Commander.'

He stepped into the shadows and Claudio was left alone with the waves on the beach and the ravaged clouds in the sky. He dragged himself under a rocky spur that had kept the sand dry during the rain. Fatigue overwhelmed him, and he fell asleep. He dreamed that the sun was rising and that Heleni was emerging nude from the waves and was running towards him as bright as the morning star.

Captain Karamanlis sat at the wheel of his squad car, so agitated that he was just about to light up a cigarette from the pack he always carried in his pocket even after he had quit smoking. He restrained himself; the last word had not yet been said. Not all of the patrols had reported in: there was still hope, after all. He turned on the light in the car and scanned a topographical map of the zone, marking all the areas his men had already sifted through. There wasn't much left, unfortunately. When he raised his head, he saw standing before him, in the brief, blinding beam of his headlights, none other than Admiral Bogdanos. He started involuntarily. He took a toothpick from his pocket and, chewing it in place of the cigarette, got out of the car: 'Where did you come from?'

'Did you get him?'

'No, we didn't get him. At least not yet. But just how did you get here?'

'I'd say they haven't a chance. If I managed to get out, so will he.'

'You're trying to tell me that you slipped out of the encirclement unnoticed? I can't believe that.'

'Don't. Ask your patrols whether anyone saw me. You won't get an answer.'

'So what you're saying is that a man – who we're presuming is wounded on top of everything else – has managed to give a dozen patrols and sixty men the slip?'

'Don't ask me, Karamanlis. He's already shown that he's uncommonly clever. Maybe he was helped by the rain, the darkness . . . maybe your men made a mistake. Lots of things could have happened. I did find something.' He handed him the bloody handkerchief. 'As you can see, I wasn't mistaken when I said he was wounded. It was near a grove of willows on the north-east part of the lagoon. If you get it analysed we'll learn his blood type. And if I'm not mistaken you still have a medal with Claudio Setti's blood type. If you haven't kept it, I hope you've written the type down somewhere. If they coincide, I'd say that gives us some solid proof. At least we'll know who we're looking for.'

Karamanlis gave him a strange smile: 'Thank you. I will certainly make every effort. But, as usual, I won't know where to look for you to inform you of the outcome of our investigation.'

'Don't worry. I'll find you. Haven't I always found you?'

'You have.'

'Goodbye.'

'Goodbye, Admiral.'

Karamanlis got back into the car and called in all the patrols, one by one, without much conviction. Something told him all the reports would be negative.

When his assumption was disappointedly confirmed, he switched off the radio and went back to the hospital. It was nearly morning and Vassilios Vlassos had already been moved to the ward after an operation of nearly four hours. He had needed another transfusion and had not yet fully regained consciousness.

'He suffered an incredible trauma,' the surgeon told Karamanlis. 'Anyone else's heart would have given out, but he seems to be doing well. He'll be feeling better in a few days. We're going to have to keep him on a drip until the sutures in his intestine have healed completely. He has lost a testicle, unfortunately; one of the arrows crushed it completely.'

'Thank you, doctor, for everything you've done.'

'No need for that,' said the doctor. 'Let me call the nurse; she has the arrows we extracted. I assume they will be used as material evidence.'

'You're right. Thanks once again, doctor.' Karamanlis waited a few more minutes for the nurse, who handed him a plastic bag closed with a rubber band. He opened it and examined the arrows, all three of which bore that strange phrase. As he twirled them between his fingers, Vassilios Vlassos opened his eyes.

'Steady now, Vlassos, you're all right. You were badly wounded, though – look at what they took out,' he said, showing him the arrows. 'One of these went through your gut and tore apart your testicle, but the doctor says there's nothing to worry about. You've still got one left, old boy. For a guy like you that's more than enough, isn't it?'

Vlassos moved his lips as if he wanted to say something, but no sound came out.

'Don't strain,' repeated Karamanlis. 'You can tell me everything when you're better.'

Vlassos motioned for him to come forward; his voice was little more than a whisper: 'I'll kill that bastard son of a bitch, Captain, I'll tear his balls out . . . I . . . I . . .'

'I know you will. But stay calm now, try to get some rest.'

Vlassos tried to push up on his elbows. 'Captain, you have to promise me . . . that you'll let me kill him with my own hands.'

'Lie down, you stubborn dunce. You're all stitched up inside and out. If one of the sutures splits you'll bleed to death for real this time.'

'Promise me . . .'

Karamanlis nodded. 'Yes. I promise. When we've caught him I'll leave him in your hands. You can do what you like with him.'

'Thanks, Captain. What about my lady friend?'

'She's fine. We brought her home. Scared the willies out of her, but she's all right now. I'll let her know the operation went well so she can come to visit.'

Vlassos dropped back on to the pillow, mouth in a foolish, ferocious smile. Karamanlis put a hand on his shoulder: 'We'll get him, old man. You can be sure of it. Sooner or later we'll catch him.' As he left the hospital, the sun was rising and the streets were coming to life with the confused buzz of traffic.

CLAUDIO WAS AWAKENED by the first rays of the sun and by the jingling bells of a flock of sheep. He sat up, rearranged his clothes and tried to look like a tourist who had stopped to enjoy the dawn during a morning stroll on the beach.

'Who are you?' asked a young voice behind him. Claudio turned and found the flock's shepherd: a boy of no more than thirteen.

'An Italian tourist. I wanted to see the sun rising. And what's your name?'

'Stelio. Do you know what place this is?'

'I think we're near Messemvria.'

'This is Ismaros, the city of the Cicones. This is where Odysseus landed when he returned from Troy. Here he got the wine that he used to make the Cyclops drunk. But how come a tourist like you doesn't know these things?'

Claudio smiled: 'Well, I do know about these things, but I didn't know this was the exact spot. How do you know?'

'My teacher told me. Want to meet him? He lives over there,' he said, pointing at a little white house on a small promontory.

'Sorry, but I can't now. I'd like to another time, if I'm passing by here again.'

'All right,' said the boy. 'You'll know where to find me. I always bring my sheep here in the morning.'

Claudio got up, waving goodbye to the boy, and headed towards the state road. He walked for a while along the edge of the road with his thumb out until a truck headed for Turkey stopped and let him in. An hour later, the big semi-trailer stopped at customs and the driver passed two passports to the police, one Turkish, issued to Tamer Unloglu, resident of Urfa, and one Italian, issued to Dino Ferretti, resident of Tarquinia.

'Hey, Italian!' called the policeman, in a good mood. 'Spaghetti, macaroni!'

Claudio waited until he had handed him back his passport and waved at him: 'That's right, buddy, spaghetti, macaroni and . . . all the rest.'

The truck started up again, crossed the Evros bridge and stopped a few minutes later at Turkish customs. Claudio filled out a form to request an entry visa, and exchanged a little money while he waited for the driver. They passed Ipsala and Kesan, where the driver turned south to Canakkale. Claudio got out at the turn-off to Istanbul. A few minutes later, another truck picked him up and took him all the way to the great bazaar by evening. Claudio waved goodbye and immediately disappeared into the multicoloured crowd swarming down the streets of the immense market.

CAPTAIN KARAMANLIS DECIDED to keep the message engraved on the arrows to himself this time. He asked the surgeon to keep quiet about it as well, explaining that this preliminary investigation demanded complete secrecy. He could not avoid reporting back to his superiors in Athens about his stay in Thrace and the attempted homicide of his subordinate while he was on holiday at Portolagos. This put him in a difficult position, because over the last ten years all the top-level security police positions had changed due to the new political situation and he could no longer count on the cover he had once enjoyed.

'Captain,' said the chief of police, 'you were sent to Dirou to coordinate the search and the investigation and you didn't accomplish a damn thing. At Portolagos, even worse luck: either we're chasing a ghost, which I have my doubts about, or you're proving to be quite incompetent. We've been able to keep the press out of this until now, but it won't be long before they catch wind of it.'

Karamanlis grimaced: 'Unfortunately, I must admit my failure. But please allow me to say, sir, that as far as I'm concerned the game is not over and the next hand will be mine.'

'Would you mind telling me then what cards you're holding?'

'I think I'm close to identifying the murderer. I also am quite sure that I'm on his list, and that makes me the person most suited to carrying on this investigation. I am both the predator and the prey.'

The police chief looked quite confused: 'It's very generous of you to offer to act as bait. But won't you tell me then why the assassin has included you – and your men – on his hit list?'

'I have not as yet drawn any definitive conclusions, and I shall certainly communicate them when I have. But it's hardly difficult to imagine why: our work involves turning over the worst scum of society to the law. When someone manages to escape, or to be pardoned for ... political reasons, then this someone will be out looking for revenge. Consider in any case that the killer was not allowed to succeed in his intent: sergeant Vlassos was saved, at the brink of death, by our operation.'

'This is also true. Then you want the case to stay in your hands?'

'If possible, I would like that, yes.'

'All right, Captain. I will give you one more opportunity, but don't count on a second.'

'That will not be necessary, sir,' said Karamanlis, and left the office.

That evening he went to headquarters to check on the identikit sent by the Kalamata police of the man who had hired the truck at Hierolimin used to transport the wood to Gythion. It was the same man who had brought the wood to Hierolimin by sea: almost certainly the face of Admiral Anastasios Bogdanos.

14

Skardamoula, 13 September, 9 a.m.

AFTER HAVING ABANDONED the fishing cooperative's truck at the gas station as they had been told, Norman and Michel took a bus back to their hotel, where they found the blue Rover in perfect running order and their keys at the Plaja reception desk. They waited days in vain for further contact. Michel had thought long and hard about the meaning of the phrase found next to the corpses of Petros Roussos and Yorgo Karagheorghis, without getting anywhere. They decided finally to take matters into their own hands, and to cast their thoughts back to the moment when they'd stumbled upon the golden vase in the basement of the National Archaeological Museum of Athens. They would return to the capital and try to contact Aristotelis Malidis. He had been with Periklis Harvatis during his last hours, and he had been the last caretaker of the vase of Tiresias. Perhaps he had some sort of connection with the mysterious person who had failed to take them to the vase.

Norman wanted to go first to Macedonia, to the place where his father had been found dead, to see if he could learn anything more than the bare facts Scotland Yard had provided. They decided to split up and to call each other every couple of days, meeting up in Athens ten days or so later to exchange information. It seemed like a good plan to both.

Norman drove up the Strimon valley one fine day in mid-September, finding the place so gorgeous that it nearly made him forget the reason for his mission. The river meandered in wide turns through woody groves and beautiful meadows. The slow-running waters were covered with pond lilies; big old plane and beech trees heavy with foliage bent to touch the water, where flocks of sheep came to drink during the hottest hours of the day. This was the ancestral homeland of Orpheus and Zalmoxis, the mythical land of centaurs and chimeras.

He spent the night in a clean, freshly whitewashed little room in a private home near a town called Sidirokastro. The stars had never seemed nearer: the galaxy curved over the ridge of Mount Pindus like the veil of a goddess fluttering in the dark, and the stars were so close to the ground that they seemed as bright and sweetly scented as mountain orchids.

That night at a tavern he asked around for a guide who was well acquainted with both sides of the border and who spoke Vlachì, the mountain dialect used on the Yugoslavian side of Macedonia as well as here on the Greek side. The generous fifty dollars a day Norman was offering attracted no shortage of takers. The next day, at dusk, a hunter of about forty named Haralambos Hackiris showed up: he had been born in the area and was familiar with every inch of the woods and river banks for a twenty-kilometre stretch, even on the Yugoslavian side, where he knew plenty of people. He was definitely a smuggler, and admitted as much to Norman, but on the whole seemed to be honest and trustworthy.

Norman told him why he had come to the mountains and asked him what he knew or had heard about an English gentleman, a hunter, who had been killed by an arrow and found gagged and blindfolded.

'I did hear about it,' said Hackiris. 'And I can tell you that whoever killed him was not from around here, otherwise we'd know who it was and why he'd done it. We know everything that goes on up here. There are still some poachers who hunt with a bow and arrow so the game wardens won't hear them, but there are very few of them, old men who wouldn't kill a person for all the gold in the world. There are others who carry

Turkish drugs over the border, but they certainly don't use bows and arrows.'

'I'll offer you an extra bonus of three hundred dollars,' said Norman, 'if you bring me news about who could have killed him and the circumstances of his death. But if you try to trick me, I won't even pay you for your services as a guide.'

The next day they left by car and crossed the Yugoslavian border. They parked the car in a garage near the state road and started on foot up to the ridge of the mountain and then up even further towards the high Strimon valley.

'If there's anyone who knows something, that's where we'll find him,' said Hackiris, pointing at a village halfway up the hillside beyond the river. They waded across the river and entered the town at around three in the afternoon. It seemed practically deserted. An old lady dressed in black carrying a bundle of grass or a jug of water on her head would pass every now and then. There were no law enforcement facilities to speak of, although they did find a local policeman who lived in a private residence. Hackiris explained why they had come and chatted with him for a few minutes in Vlachì.

'Do you have twenty dollars?' he asked Norman. Norman passed him a couple of bank notes.

'Well?'

'A few things you'll find interesting. He was the first one to examine the corpse. Said he only seemed to have been dead a couple of hours.'

'And what did he find?'

'There was a message sticking out of the dead man's jacket pocket. He had a friend of his who knows Greek copy it out before they turned him over to the Belgrade police.'

'For what reason?'

'Doesn't twenty dollars sound like a good reason? He thought that sooner or later it would be worth something.'

'Well, can I have it, then?'

'Certainly.'

The policeman took a vase from a shelf, stuck in his hand and took out a little notebook in which a couple of lines had been scribbled. Norman scanned it quickly:

You in your day have witnessed hundreds slaughtered,
killed in single combat or killed in pitched battle, true,
but if you'd laid eyes on this it would have wrenched your heart.

Hackiris saw his expression: 'Was it worth twenty dollars?' he asked.

'It was worth much more,' murmured Norman. 'It was worth a man's life . . .'

Hackiris chattered on in Vlachì with the man; neither of them seemed bothered in the least by Norman's words.

'There's something else,' he said. 'But this will cost you twice as much. Forty dollars.'

'All right,' said Norman, putting his hand back on his wallet. The policeman walked into another room and came back with a newspaper-wrapped bundle that he placed on the table. Norman opened it: it contained an arrow. 'He found it stuck in a trunk at a height of about two metres,' translated Hackiris, 'at a short distance from where your father's body was found. He dug out the head with his hunting knife and took it home. Obviously the weapon of a foreigner.'

'He failed his first shot,' Norman muttered to himself. 'His hand can tremble, then . . .' Turning to his guide, he said, 'Ask him to tell you where he found the body, and take me there.'

The policeman led them out of the house and took them to the outskirts of the village. With ample hand gestures indicating the bottom of the valley, he explained how they could get to the scene of the crime.

Norman followed his guide through a damp, wooded ravine where gigantic beech trees with multiple trunks sprouted from large masses of sandstone covered with dripping moss. He raised his eyes to the sun filtering through the foliage, and then lowered his gaze to a huge tree trunk. A spring of crystalline water gushed alongside.

'I think it happened there,' said the guide, pointing at a kind of niche between two enormous roots.

Norman sat on a stone and passed his hand over the rough bark of the tree to which his father had been nailed by the lethal dart. Eyes welling with tears, he listened for a while to the rustling of the leaves and the gurgling of the spring, the low voices of the forest in the deep peace of midday. 'It was a good place to die,' he said. 'Goodbye, Father.'

ATHENS AWOKE VIOLENT emotions in Michel: the Acropolis, the Polytechnic, the French School of Archaeology, the National Museum. It was as if the clock of his life had been turned back, taking him back to the moment in which, unable to stand on his feet, tortured in body and soul, he was led out of police headquarters and put on a plane.

He settled into the hotel in the Plaka where he had told Norman he could be reached, then walked out on to the street without a precise destination in mind. He passed near the Olimpieion, and then Syntagmatos Square, where the tourists were waiting to take pictures of the evzoni at the changing of the guard. He ended up at a bar on the corner of Stadiou Street where he had spent many an evening with friends. He sat down at a table and ordered a Fix beer.

'They don't make it any more, sir,' said the waiter.

'An Alfa then.'

'Not that one either. You must have been away from Greece for a long time, sir. Now we have export beer.'

'Yeah, I've been away for a long time. I don't want any beer then. Bring me a coffee. Turkish.'

The waiter brought the coffee and Michel sat watching a group of young people joking and laughing at a nearby table. Time had flattened out so entirely in his mind that he felt like joining them, as if he were as young as they were, as if nothing had ever happened. He suddenly caught a glimpse of himself reflected in the glass of the window: a little grey at the temples, with wrinkles at the sides of his eyes. He was sitting all alone and surrounded by ghosts, only darkness and emptiness around him. Michel took off with a knot in his throat, pushing through the crowds swarming from the offices and shops on their way home. He burst into a run without knowing where he was going, walking fast and then running again until, as if in a dream, he suddenly found himself at the start of Dionysìou Street, long and oddly deserted.

He stopped and began to walk slowly down the right-hand pavement, observing the odd street numbers across the way. It was getting dark, and the grey sky of Athens was turning a hazy light red. A boy on a bicycle rode by. A child ran out on to a balcony after a ball and drew up short, watching him in silence. An aeroplane passed in the distance, scoring the sky with a white wake of smoke.

17 Dionysìou Street.

The faded sign of an old printer's shop, paint peeling. A dusty shutter pulled all the way down, closed with a rusty padlock just as dusty. It looked like the shutter hadn't been opened in years. Michel stood silently in front of the abandoned, unlikely shop, losing track of time. Then he noticed a bar further on down the road, where a lighted 'Milos's Bar' sign was just being switched on. He went in and sat near the door, so he could have a view of the street nearly the whole way down. He ordered an ouzo with water and ice. When the waiter brought it, he asked, pointing to the shutter at number 17, 'Is that printer still in business, as far as you know?'

The waiter leaned over and then shook his head: 'It's always been closed up like that. Since I've been here, anyway.'

'And how long have you worked here?'

'Seven years.'

'And you go by there every morning?'

'Every blessed morning.'

'And you've never seen anyone go in or out?'

'Never. Can I ask why you want to know?'

'I collect a magazine that was once printed there and I'm looking for some back issues.'

'I see.'

'Do you know if that building has a doorman?'

'No, I wouldn't say so, sir. You only find doormen in those big modern buildings on Patission Street or Stadiou Street or in Omonia Square. These houses are all very old – they've been here since before the war against the Turks.'

'Thanks,' Michel said, leaving him a good tip. He left and walked away. He wanted to get back to the hotel, in case Norman called.

The waiter cleared off the table, pocketing the tip, then walked out to put sheets of plastic on the outdoor tables. He glanced over to the other side of the street. It had become dark, and he could see a thin stream of light coming from under the shutter at number 17.

'Sir!' he shouted towards Michel, who had reached the end of the street. 'Sir, wait!' But Michel didn't hear him over the sound of the traffic on the main street he was approaching, and he turned the corner. The waiter went back to work, but as he waited on his customers that evening, he continued to check the other side of the street. When he got off work at 2 a.m. there was still a little light seeping out from under the shutter.

NORMAN CALLED AT nine that evening.

'Where are you?' asked Michel.

'In a garage not far from the border. I'll be staying at Sidirokastro tonight and then tomorrow I'll drive down.'

'That was quick. What did you find out?'

'The information I'd been given was correct: Scotland Yard had kept a detail of my father's death hidden. There was a message found on the corpse.'

'What did it say?'

'"*You in your day have witnessed hundreds slaughtered, killed in single combat or killed in pitched battle, true, but if you'd laid eyes on this it would have wrenched your heart.*" What is it, Michel? What does it mean?'

'Wait, I know, I've heard it before, I'm sure. Give me ten minutes and I'll tell you. I'm sure I've heard it before.'

Norman hung up and Michel opened his suitcase and took out his copy of the *Odyssey*, which he had brought with him. He had marked several passages which had struck him. Here – *Odyssey* XI, Agamemnon speaking to Odysseus in the Kingdom of the Dead.

When Norman called back, he was ready with the book in his hands. 'It's from the Nekya, Norman, Book eleven of the *Odyssey*. Odysseus has raised Agamemnon's shade from the dead, and the Great Atreid tells of how he, his comrades and Cassandra were murdered upon their return from the Trojan war, in his own house . . . those words express his horror at the massacre of his comrades and of a helpless girl . . .' Silence on the other end of the line as the international phone call counter ticked away. 'Norman, are you there?'

Norman's voice sounded tired and detached. Every word was costing him great effort. 'Yes, I am. This links my father's death to Roussos and Karagheorghis.'

'That seems possible.'

'There's no other explanation.'

'I don't know, Norman. It's not simple. Come to Athens and we'll talk about it. I'll try to find out what the other messages mean. An idea has come to me.'

'All right,' said Norman. 'I'll come.'

'Norman?'

'Yes.'

'Don't lose heart. We've got to see this thing through to the end.'

'Don't worry about me. Think about your idea. I'll be bringing you something.'

'What is it?'

'An arrow. Identical to the one that killed my father.'

Michel went and sat at the little table in his room, took out a cigarette, and began to look at the *Odyssey*. He compared Norman's message with the original wording and scanned the poem page by page to search for the words found on the bodies of Roussos and Karagheorghis. They sounded as if they might be from passages in the *Odyssey*, but his efforts proved fruitless.

He lay down on the bed and tried to relax, but his thoughts would not let him rest. He and Norman certainly hadn't had much success. Their hunt for the vase of Tiresias had run up a dead end, and they hadn't heard a thing from the man they'd met at Kotronas. And now James Shields's death seemed somehow connected to the murders of Roussos and Karagheorghis, but how? And why? And who the hell had printed Periklis Harvatis's little book, if the print shop at 17 Dionysìou Street had been closed for so long?

The next day he would ask for an appointment with the director of the National Museum and attempt to get in touch with Aristotelis Malidis. It was the only possible way out of a blind alley.

The phone rang again; it was the front desk with an international call.

'Michel? It's Mireille. I've finally found you!'

'I'm sorry. I didn't have time to call and tell you I'd got to the hotel here in Athens.'

'Doesn't matter. I managed to find you anyway, didn't I? How's it going?'

'This research is hairier than I'd imagined. We're running into all sorts of obstacles.'

'But I want to see you!'

'So do I, very much.'

'I'm off work next week. I want to come to Athens to be with you.'

'Mireille, this isn't just academic research. I'm helping my friend Norman to investigate his father's death. There may even be some danger involved.'

'That's why I want to be with you.'

'Believe me, it's what I want most right now. I dream about you every night, but I'm afraid you being here could create problems ... especially for Norman. I'm sure he wants some things to remain just between the two of us. You can understand, can't you?'

'Yeah. You don't want me in the way, right?'

'Mireille, just give me a few days. If there's a break, I'll call you immediately.'

'All right. But remember, the longer the abstinence you're forcing on me, the greater the penance you'll have to pay.'

Michel smiled: 'Ready and willing for any penance you have in mind, my lady.'

'I miss you.'

'Me too.'

'Michel, are you hiding something from me?'

'Mireille, there is something, but I can't tell you now. I don't know how to tell you. Please keep loving me, even ... afterwards. You're the most important thing in my life.'

NORMAN STOPPED THE car at the Greek border at Sidirokastro and paid the guide the amount they had agreed upon. Hackiris thanked him, showed the police his border pass and went on his way. Norman pulled out his own passport. The official looked at the photograph and then at him, but did not hand back the passport. 'Mr Shields, would you follow me, please?'

'What's wrong?'

'Just ordinary procedure. Please follow me, it will take just a few minutes. Routine inspection. Leave your keys in the car, I'll have one of my men park it.'

Norman obeyed and followed the man into the police station. He was taken into a small office lit by a single lamp on the table. In the darkness, he could barely make out the shape of a person sitting on the other side of the table.

'Good evening, Mr Shields. Sit down, please.'

'Listen, it's midnight, I'm dead tired and I'd like to go to bed. If this is just a routine border check, could we please ...'

'I'm surprised, Mr Shields, that you don't remember me. Can't you spare a few minutes for an old acquaintance?'

Norman sat down and scrutinized the man sitting at the

table. His face wasn't new to him, and his voice sounded kind of familiar, and he suddenly realized with dismay just who it was.

'Pavlos Karamanlis!'

'Exactly, Mr Shields.'

'What is this farce about a customs inspection – what do you want from me?'

'Fine. I see you've got straight to the meat of the matter, and I'll be glad to tell you just what I want. I want to know what you've come to do in Greece, you and your friend Michel Charrier. I want to know what you were doing in Dirou when my man Karagheorghis was killed at the Katafigi caves. I want to know who you met on the evening of August the twenty-fourth on the western coast of the Laconian peninsula, and who you turned your car over to.'

Norman stood his ground: 'It's not the frightened boy of ten years ago you have in front of you now, Karamanlis. I couldn't give a shit about you, or about your questions. You have no right to detain me here and I'm leaving.'

Karamanlis stood up: 'I'd advise you against that. My boys have had just enough time to plant a good quantity of snow under the seats in your Rover. More than enough to send you straight to prison.'

'You're bluffing, Karamanlis.'

'And I also want to know what you were doing in Yugoslavia with that mountain guide.'

Norman shook his head and pushed his chair back.

'Listen, this is no joke, Shields, you know I don't fool around. Even if you manage to prove your innocence in the long run, you'll be in jail for months, interrogations, the trial. I can still ruin you.'

Norman got to his feet.

'Wait. Let's say I don't want to get you in trouble, but I do want to know who's practising target shooting with my men: Roussos, Karagheorghis. And your father, Shields. What about your father?'

Norman suddenly felt faint: his suspicions were confirmed,

then. He leaned back against the chair again. 'What does my father have to do with it?' he asked, head low.

'Your father was the link between the American Secret Service and our political police force at the time of the Polytechnic battle. He died for the same reasons Roussos and Karagheorghis died, for the same reasons that another officer of mine, Vassilios Vlassos, nearly lost his life.'

Norman lifted his head, his features taut: 'What happened to him?'

'Vlassos had more holes in him than a soup strainer. One of his balls shot clean off. Nearly bought it.'

'When did it happen, where?'

'Wait a minute, Shields. I'm asking the questions.'

'Listen, Karamanlis, I detest you, and God only knows what it's costing me to be in the same room with you, even for just a few minutes. I realize you have information that I'm interested in, and I can repay you with the things you want to know. But we're still enemies, clear?'

'I didn't take that vase.'

'I don't care. You are responsible for the deaths of Claudio Setti and Heleni Kaloudis.'

Karamanlis did not seem perturbed: 'All I want to know from you is what I asked you.'

'I'll talk, but I have questions to ask as well.'

Karamanlis stood up. 'I'll have to search you,' he said. 'You could be wearing a tape recorder.'

Norman let him pat him down, then took a seat again.

'First of all,' he said, 'I want to know exactly how my father figures in this whole thing.'

Karamanlis stared at him for a long minute. 'As you wish,' he said.

As they spoke, Norman lit cigarette after cigarette, trying to gather his thoughts and put together the pieces of the mosaic that was slowly forming. At the end, he asked: 'Did you see the arrows shot at Vlassos?'

'I have them with me,' replied Karamanlis.

'Get them. I'll be right back.' He got up, went out to the car and took the newspaper bundle with the arrow he'd paid forty dollars for in Yugoslavia. When he entered Karamanlis's office, there were three arrows lined up on the table, and he set his down alongside. They were identical, and quite particular. Wooden Easton Eagles with steel tips.

IT WAS TWO in the morning when the phone rang in Michel's room.

'Michel Charrier. Who is it?'

'Michel, they've tried to kill another one of Karamanlis's men, his name's Vassilios Vlassos, with a bow and arrow . . . Just like my father.'

'Is that you, Norman?' Michel's voice sounded sleepy. 'Are you sure?'

'There was a phrase carved on the shaft: "You put the bread in a cold oven."'

'Another enigma. When are you coming to Athens?'

Norman didn't answer at first. His voice cracked. 'Michel,' he said, 'Michel, I think you're right.'

'What do you mean?'

'Claudio . . . Claudio's alive . . . and he's killing them one by one.'

15

Athens, 28 September, 3 a.m.

MICHEL COULDN'T GET back to sleep: could it really be Claudio? Had his old friend turned into this cruel executioner? Ten years . . . was it possible? Ten years in shadows and silence, his hate smouldering? Ten years planning revenge, ten years refining a single deadly skill? Was a man capable of all that? Was Claudio capable of it?

He tried to recall other episodes from their life together before it had all happened: cracking jokes, talking, fooling around. Was there anything, a single, miserable clue, that connected that boy with this man? As hard as he tried to comb his memory, he could find nothing. He thought of that phrase that Norman had told him over the phone – *You put the bread in a cold oven* – but still nothing suggested itself. He was about to take a sleeping pill and lie down again when suddenly an idea came to him. Why hadn't it occurred to him sooner? If the phrase on Shields's body came from the *Odyssey*, maybe the other phrases came from another classic. But how could he sift through such an immense body of literature if the phrases meant nothing to him? Maybe they were from a passage he should know about; something simple, from some obvious source. But this phrase was so strange he couldn't imagine any context. He had never fully realized how vast the body of writings that remained of the ancients actually was – too vast for a single person, alone, to hope to find a word, an anonymous expression.

Wait! A person, right. A person alone couldn't do it – but a computer could: Icarus!

Icarus could find any association of at least two words in the entire corpus of Greek and Latin literature from Homer to Isidore of Seville: fifteen centuries of human thought enclosed in an optical disk of five million kilobytes. But could he get access to it? Was the program ready, and had all the texts been scanned? As far as he knew, British Informatics had already announced it in their catalogue, and they'd been working on the databank for years – but had any of the research institutes actually been hooked up with it?

Mireille! Her parents had stocks in the company, they were even on the board of directors. She could get through. If she got authorization she could go to the company headquarters and test out the program: two words like 'cold oven' or 'she's naked' would be sufficient to find the passages. So even if the transcription wasn't exact, the computer would be able to find the original expression.

He finally lay down on the bed and took a couple of Valium, so he could get some sleep and shut down the agitation in his head that would otherwise have kept him up all night.

As SOON AS Michel woke up the next morning, he called Mireille. He was lucky: despite the time difference, she hadn't left the house yet.

'Mireille, I need your help. You can solve a problem for me; I'll never get to the bottom of it without you.'

'What? In just a few hours you've completely changed your mind? First you don't want me and now I can save your life?' said the girl, seemingly quite amused.

'Mireille, it's not a joke. It is really a question of life or death, understand? Now, British Informatics has a program called Icarus that we mere mortals don't have access to. I need you to get into the databank and do some research for me.'

Mireille fell silent in surprise, then said: 'I would have to ask my father . . .'

'Tell him it's for your own research. He won't say no.'

'That's not the point. You know what our relationship is like . . .'

'Mireille, you've got to believe me when I say it's a matter of life or death.'

'All right. I'll do it.'

'Thank you.'

'And I'll bring the outcome to Athens myself.'

'Blackmail, I see.'

'Take it or leave it.'

'You got it. Get some paper and a pen, and I'll dictate all the possible combinations. It's a message in modern Greek that I think has been translated from an original in ancient Greek, okay?'

'Right. And you want to know the passage and the author.'

'If you can manage it. And if my hunch is correct.'

Michel dictated all the possible variations in ancient Greek of the phrases to feed into Icarus. 'Did you get it all down?' he asked.

'Yes,' answered Mireille. 'Strange words, very odd. Don't know why but they give me the creeps.'

IF PAVLOS KARAMANLIS had any doubts, his conversation with Norman Shields swept them away: a single person had killed James Shields, Petros Roussos, Yorgo Karagheorghis and had tried to kill Vassilios Vlassos. That same person was saving him, police Captain Karamanlis, for last. He was watching him make his moves, playing with him as a cat does with a mouse. That person was, in all probability, Claudio Setti. There had never been certain proof of his death. The only other possibility was that it was someone trying to make him believe, for some unknown reason, that he was Claudio Setti.

He was reasonably sure, in any case, that the killer would be trying again with Vlassos, and this gave him an advantage. He would prepare another trap, and this time he would not fail.

He left the Sidirokastro police station at eight in the morning and walked into town to buy some feta cheese for his wife. He got a nice piece in a grocery store that the sergeant had recommended, along with some sausages, fresh ricotta, bread and a bottle of retsina, tapped from the barrel. He was back in his car by eight thirty and headed south towards the Salonika highway.

What he couldn't manage to explain was the role that Bogdanos was playing in all this; the story that Shields had fed him about their meeting at Kotronas didn't convince him in the least.

He still had a suspicion – or perhaps just a sensation – that Bogdanos had something to do with the murders. But then why had he stuck his neck out to save Vlassos's life, and what was his real reason for meeting Shields and Charrier?

It was absolutely necessary to understand what game Bogdanos was playing and what the stakes were. He entered the highway and set off at a good speed. If he got to Athens at a decent hour he'd look up that old friend of his at the Ministry of Defence and ask him a few questions. If he hadn't retired. He ate a sandwich in the car at lunchtime and afterwards drove straight through to the centre of Athens. He phoned his friend from a little square near the Ministry, but the man's answer left him speechless.

'Anastasios Bogdanos is dead, my friend.'

'Dead? That's not possible. I spoke to him just a couple of weeks ago.'

'It just happened. The funeral was in Volos. That's where he was from.'

'Can you tell me exactly when it happened?'

'Hold on a minute,' said the functionary. 'I have to find the papers. Here . . . the funeral was last Tuesday.'

'Last Tuesday . . . and what did he die of?' asked Karamanlis.

'As far as I know he'd been ill a long time. His heart, I think. Guess there was nothing to be done. Anything else you wanted to know?' asked his friend.

'Nothing. Nothing . . . for now. I'll call you again if I need you.'

Karamanlis looked at his pocket calendar: last Tuesday . . . so Bogdanos died just ten days after he'd seen him at Portolagos . . . strange. Very strange indeed. A bad heart. He thought of how quick, how agile he had been that night at Skardamoula. He hadn't acted like a man with a bad heart. He picked up the phone again and called his wife: 'Irini, it's me. I'm sorry, but I'll be back very late tonight, if I come back at all. I'm not sure.'

'But why? You told me you'd be back early! That nice fresh ricotta from Sidirokastro will go bad.'

'Irini, for God's sake, what do you think I care about the damned ricotta . . . I'm sorry, I didn't want to hurt your feelings, but you know how my work is. Okay? Goodbye, honey, maybe I'll see you later tonight . . . who knows.'

He jumped back in the car and turned back towards the highway, sounding the siren so he could make his way more quickly through the chaotic city traffic. He stepped on the gas, squeezing every last drop of energy from the car's old engine. He reached Volos in two and a half hours and started looking for the cemetery. It was closed, naturally, and he had to call the town hall to get the name and number of the custodian who could let him in. When the caretaker turned the key in the padlock on the gate, the sun was low on the horizon and it was near dusk. The cemetery was on a little hill, and he could see the whole bay of Volos reddening with the rays of the dying sun. Towards the east a star already glittered over the peak of Mount Pelium.

'Could you tell me where Admiral Bogdanos was buried?'

The custodian shut the gate again after letting him in and pointed towards a corner of the cemetery. 'Down there,' he said, 'in that white marble building. It's the family tomb.'

Karamanlis hurried towards the spot, and entered: he could immediately pick out the slab which had just been added because it was very shiny, and the flowers in front of it were fresh.

Someone must have put them there that very day. The tomb-stone reported only the man's first and last name, and his dates of birth and death, in large bronze letters.

Karamanlis put on his glasses and got closer to look at the photograph: the man had a minute face, a thin, drooping moustache and small dark eyes. A lock of thinning hair attempted to provide some cover for an otherwise bald scalp. Karamanlis fell silent in shock: that man was not Admiral Bogdanos! Or rather, the man who he had always thought was Bogdanos.

He walked back towards the gate where the custodian was waiting for him.

'Were you relatives?' he asked.

'Relatives? No . . . we were in the war together.'

'I see,' said the custodian, snapping shut the lock.

Karamanlis drove straight back to the city police headquarters and had an identikit of the impostor issued to all the other stations in the country, requesting identification and indicating that the man might be in possession of information which could provide a direct lead to the deaths of Roussos and Karagheorghis. He also had it sent to Scotland Yard, adding that the man might have information regarding the murder of James Henry Shields as well. He asked headquarters in Athens to inform him immediately of any development, no matter what time of day or night.

He realized that he'd been played for a fool: when that man had taken Claudio Setti away ten years ago he was still alive, and he had surely saved the boy. He'd been wangled all right, like a stupid greenhorn. But at least now he'd managed to blow the fake's cover, and he wouldn't be tricked again. What he had to do now was find a name for that man who had hidden behind the identity of Admiral Anastasios Bogdanos for the last ten years. All he had was a face, but maybe that would be enough. He'd be getting news from someplace in Greece soon, or maybe even from England. He'd contact Interpol if he had to. The game had got serious – it had become a question of life or death.

He got home just before ten.

His wife opened the door. He stood on the landing, package of feta in one hand and bottle of retsina in the other.

'You look awful,' she said. 'What happened to you?'

MIREILLE HAD NOT asked her father for a personal favour for at least two years, since she had started going out with Michel. It wasn't easy or pleasant thinking up a plausible reason why her father, Guy François de Saint-Cyr, should arrange for her to access Icarus. But she would have done anything to be back with Michel and to find her way into his life again. He'd excluded her for so long . . . for months and months now. The memory of that night at rue des Orfèvres in Grenoble was still very vivid and it gave her a sense of apprehension and uneasiness that the strange words he'd asked her to look up only served to increase.

'I'm interested in a certain type of technical terminology in ancient literature,' she told him. 'It's for a publication; Icarus can save me months and months of work. But I don't want to create any problems . . . if it's inconvenient just forget about it. I'll go to the US where there are a couple of universities with partial collections: Stanford, I think, or UCLA.'

The mere thought that Mireille would head out towards those wild Californian schools full of queers and drug addicts was enough for Saint-Cyr to promise all his support. He was surprised and secretly delighted that his daughter had asked for his help as she used to do in the past.

Mireille had to wait a few days for approval to arrive from London and in the meantime she called Michel whenever she could. He didn't want to waste time, and had already started looking in the National Library in Athens, going through all the books that he thought might contain such phrases. But the best he could do was guess: the Old Testament, Athenaeus, Apollodorus, Dionysius Areopagitas, the Fathers of the Church, Lucianus. He'd also gone to the land registry office to see if he could find out who the building at 17 Dionysìou Street belonged to, but had been told that it would take some time. He'd tried slipping the clerk a tip, but it hadn't helped much, because anyone who needed anything from the office had obviously done the same. So it was back to square one.

Mireille didn't manage to get access to Icarus until mid-October, when she received a formal appointment from the company. She arrived fresh off the plane from Paris, emanating the elegance and style of her social rank and her personal beauty, and was taken directly to the office of the director, who was reluctant to hand her over to Dr Jones, the technician who was to help her in her research. He was a shy, young, freckle-faced man with red hair who had certainly never had to deal with a woman so intelligent that she wanted to interrogate Icarus, and so beautiful as to make his legs tremble and muddle his thoughts. His attempts at small talk were wholly inadequate, his compliments awkward and inopportune, but Mireille smiled regardless as he led her along the long hall and accompanied her down to the sterile, uniformly lit basement room where the company devised its computer strategies. And where all the knowledge salvaged from the shipwrecked ancient world was saved on a disk a few centimetres wide.

Mireille did not want her father to regret having obtained this privilege for her, and so for a good hour she entered a series of questions in which she had absolutely no interest but which fitted in with her alibi, were it ever to be checked. But she couldn't wait to type in those phrases that she'd copied in her notebook.

'Dr Jones,' she said, when she felt ready, 'I don't know how to thank you: Icarus is a dream come true – it's saved me months and months of work and research.'

'Oh, I've done nothing. And I've enjoyed your company immensely. You see, it's not every day that I get to assist such a lovely girl. These thinking machines have an advantage over us – they're completely insensitive to female beauty and can work quickly and rationally, while any human being would be hopelessly confused by . . . well, anyone like me, anyway . . .'

'How sweet of you to say such a thing, Dr Jones.'

Jones gulped. 'Are you sure there isn't anything else you'd like to ask our program?'

'Now that you ask, there are a couple of odd phrases that I copied down from a book a long time ago, and I would be curious to know where they come from. But I don't want to inconvenience you. It's really not important.'

'No, no, I wouldn't mind in the least, believe me. What exactly are you looking for?'

'You know ancient Greek, obviously.'

'Of course, I've been one of the main contributors to the Icarus program.'

'It's something that a friend of mine transcribed into modern Greek from the ancient Greek. I'd like to identify the original source. It's just a couple of phrases . . .'

She showed him the transcriptions in her notebook: 'She's naked, she's cold,' and 'You put the bread into a cold oven.'

'Weird stuff,' said Jones.

'You're right.'

'Okay. Let's try.'

The technician typed in the first phrase, then hit the search key. The numbers of the files being scanned flew over the display while the following message appeared:

Estimated search time: eight minutes

Eight minutes! The machine could go through the entire body of classical literature in just eight minutes!

'Found it,' said the technician suddenly. 'Look, he's found it.' A blue blinking light at the top right of the screen signalled that the search was over, and the exact source of the quotation appeared at the centre of the display:

Oracles of the Dead, in Herodot, V. 92, 2

Jones turned to the girl with a vaguely dismayed look on his face. 'It's an Oracle of the Dead, miss, reported by Herodotus.'

Herodotus! Lord knew what obscure sources Michel was

looking through that very minute. Why was it that one tried the most difficult things first? Herodotus of all things!

'Let's see who it refers to,' added Jones, as he typed in another query. Icarus responded instantly:

See Melissa

and then again

Periander's dead wife

'The phrase refers to Melissa, the dead wife of Periander, tyrant of Corinth, if I'm not mistaken.'

Correct

Icarus answered at his request for confirmation.

'Let's look at the second phrase now,' said Jones, and entered the first of the versions Mireille had written down.

Not found

replied Icarus after a few minutes, adding:

Searching for a similar expression

Several more minutes passed. A window on the screen was analysing all the possible grammatical and stylistic variations that the program's endless philological memory could assemble. Mireille was fascinated: 'Incredible,' she murmured, her eyes glued to the screen. 'Fantastic.' A message finally appeared:

Sentence not available in direct speech

'Let's try it this way,' suggested Jones, entering:

Try indirect speech

Icarus promptly started searching again, and, after just a few seconds, provided the answer, together with the phrase in ancient Greek:

Original sentence found:
Óti epí psychrón tón ipnòn toús ártous epébale

It concluded with the text source:

Oracles of the Dead, in Herodot, V. 92, 3

'Strange,' said Mireille. 'Could it be the same passage?'

'Not quite, miss. It's in the following paragraph. Look, I can call up the entire chapter.'

It took just a few seconds for chapter 92 of Book V of Herodotus to show up on the display. Both read it in silence, then Jones said with a naughty tone: 'Quite some story, miss.'

'Yeah,' replied Mireille, a bit embarrassed. 'I wonder what it could have meant in the context I found it in . . .'

'Icarus is printing all the operations we've requested. If you need more than one copy, we have to specify that.'

'Two. Two would be fine, thank you.'

'Of everything?'

'Yes, everything. Please.'

Jones took the sheets coming off the printer, slipped them into a folder and handed it to Mireille, who thanked him warmly.

'You're not going straight back to France, I hope,' Jones found the courage to ask in a small voice.

Mireille looked at her watch. 'If I hurry I'll be able to catch the five-thirty plane from Heathrow. I just don't know how to thank you, Dr Jones. You'll say goodbye to the director for me, won't you?'

'Oh, yes, certainly,' stammered Jones, disappointed. They got into the elevator, and in that brief moment of forced intimacy he wanted to make another attempt, but before he got his courage up, the elevator had already arrived at its destination and the door was opening.

'Thanks so much again,' said Mireille, hurrying down the corridor that led to the exit.

Jones stood watching the soft roll of her hips under her white linen skirt, and blushed at the thoughts running through his mind.

He shouted after her: 'Come back any time you like!'

Mireille turned with a smile and waved, then reached the

exit. She tried Michel's number from the first booth she found and then again at the airport, but got no answer. Michel at that moment was futilely pouring over his books at the National Library. She found him after midnight, calling from a restaurant along the highway:

'Mission accomplished, Professor.'

'Mireille, you've really succeeded?'

'Icarus is great, It didn't take longer than fifteen minutes. Both phrases are from Herodotus.'

'Herodotus? Good God, I can't believe it.'

'Right, Herodotus, Book V, chapter 92, paragraphs 2 and 3. Both Oracles of the Dead. Messages from the underworld.'

PAVLOS KARAMANLIS ARRIVED at police headquarters eager to see whether the identikit he'd sent around the country had found a match, but he was immediately disappointed. Lots of answers on the table: all negative. No one seemed to remember having seen that face. Except for Skardamoula and Hierolimin, but he hadn't even bothered sending it to them.

He asked his friend at the Ministry of Defence for an appointment and met him for dinner in a tavern.

'Listen,' he said. 'Has there ever been a mix-up in your files? Like, a mistaken identity for instance?'

'Absolutely not. Why do you ask?'

He took a copy of the identikit out of his pocket: 'Have you ever seen this man?' His friend shook his head. 'Look at him carefully,' insisted Karamanlis, 'it's very important. Are you certain you've never seen him?'

'Absolutely certain. It's not the type of face you forget easily.'

'Well, I've been dealing with this man over the last ten years as if he were Admiral Anastasios Bogdanos. That's how he introduced himself ten years ago, and that's who I believed he was.'

'Oh no, Admiral Bogdanos looked absolutely nothing like that. My God, how could a man like you let that happen? Didn't you get information on him?'

'It was you who gave me all the information I needed. I just never thought of asking you what he looked like. The thing is, he was always so perfectly informed about everything, so determined, so damned right at the right time and in the right place that it never occurred to me that he could be anyone else.'

'And you said that you'd seen him recently?'

'That's right. It was thanks to him that one of my men, sergeant Vlassos, made it out of a murder attempt alive.'

'That Portolagos business?'

'Yeah. We've tried to keep the press out of it, but it looks like the same hand that struck Roussos and Karagheorghis.'

'That's possible.'

'I've got to find him, understand? If I can't get the upper hand here, I'm screwed. I've got the authorities on one side – they're getting suspicious and have probably started their own investigation – and I've got this murderous lunatic on the other . . .'

'Out looking for you?'

'I'm absolutely certain of it.'

'What does this con man know about you?'

'A lot. Too much.'

'And you? What do you know about him?'

'Nothing. Not even his name.'

'No clue?'

Karamanlis shook his head. 'My only lead is a golden vase that disappeared ten years ago from the National Museum during the assault of the Polytechnic. It was important to him.'

'Where is it now?'

'Don't know. Maybe he has it, maybe he's sold it or given it away . . .'

'That's it?'

'Yeah, that's it. Nearly, anyway.'

They'd finished eating and the waiter had brought their coffee. A group at the next table had begun singing; between one song and the next they ate pistachio nuts and drank wine, loudly arguing about the soccer season.

'Practically nothing. That's strange, very strange. There seems to be something underneath it all which is beyond our under-standing. I don't know what it is, but I can feel it. When did you learn that that man was an impostor?'

'When you told me he was dead. It seemed impossible to me, so I went directly to Volos, to the cemetery. I saw his photo.'

'Listen, I have a suggestion for you. You've got so little to go on, it probably can't hurt. There are people who, just by looking at a photograph of someone, or a sketch even, can perceive where that person might be, like a radar beam localizing a shape in the sky or in the sea . . .'

Karamanlis smiled: 'Is that how badly off I seem? Let's get a crystal-gazer over here to look at our coffee grounds!'

The other man seemed offended. 'The person I'm talking about is no crystal-gazer. This person is exceptionally gifted. They say that members of the government, and even the President himself, have consulted him in critical situations. He lives completely isolated in a hovel on Mount Peristeri, living on what game he can catch and on milk from the sheep and goats that share his house with him. No one knows how old he is, no one even knows his name. Go to him and show him that sketch, describe the vase to him, the one that disappeared. He'll get a complete picture of it in his head. He goes where he wants to go, in any moment, no matter how far. He's . . . he is . . . a *kallikàntharos*.'

Very few people were still lingering in the tavern. An old man, probably a drunk, was slumped over a corner table, sleeping. Karamanlis got up and put on his jacket.

'I don't know,' he said. 'It's not the kind of thing you do every day. I'll have to think about it.'

16

NORMAN ORDERED A Metaxa brandy for himself, and a glass of Roditis for Michel. 'I feel like ordering something for that cop over there in the car.'

'You really think he's watching us?'

'What else is he doing? He's been on me since Sidirokastro. Well, we'll just let him stew in his own juices. So, tell me how it feels to be back in this café after all these years.'

'I was here a few weeks ago, just ran into it by chance. It made me feel terrible. Really awful. All of this has been hard on me.'

'You said that you'd discovered the meaning of those messages, didn't you?'

'Well, I found the context, and that's something. Mireille went to London, to the central headquarters of British Informatics, to consult Icarus, a program that can analyse any aspect of classical literature, including literary criticism over the last ten years. The author is Herodotus, very well known.'

'And we'd imagined some obscure source.'

'Yeah, right. So, there are two phrases: the first – "She's naked, she's cold" – was left on the corpses of both Roussos and Karagheorghis. The phrase comes from an Oracle of the Dead, and it's the response that Periander, the tyrant of Corinth, receives from the oracle by calling up the ghost of his dead wife Melissa at Ephira. Periander had consulted the oracle to find out where a certain treasure had been buried, but the oracle shamed him with its answer: Periander was so miserly that he had refused to burn Melissa's bridal gown on her funeral pyre because it was too precious, leaving his wife naked and cold in her grave.

'In an attempt to exculpate himself, Periander gathered all the most illustrious ladies of the city and had them remove their clothing so it could be burned in honour of his dead wife. He queried the oracle once again, and this time he got the second response. The phrase that was carved on the arrow which ran through Vlassos, if you can trust Karamanlis on this one: "You put the bread in a cold oven."

'The phrase was a crude reminder that Periander had coupled with his wife after her death. Melissa, through the oracle, was accusing him of raping and desecrating her corpse. We'd consider him some kind of psycho, but for the ancients his crime was even worse. It was considered a heartless monstrosity, deserving of the most horrible punishment.'

'Good God. But what do you suppose it can possibly mean here and now?'

'I've thought and thought about it. The most logical deduction – if we can call any of this logical – is that the messages reveal the reason these men were condemned to death. Since the first message was identical for Roussos and Karagheorghis, we have to assume that they committed the same crime, although I have no idea of what it could have been. The second message, on the other hand, is very explicit . . .'

The juke box, which had been mute up to that moment, suddenly started playing a song and Michel started. 'Norman,' he said, 'this song – do you remember this song?' Norman shook his head, puzzled. 'Claudio used to play this song when we first met him at Parga. He used to play it on his flute . . .' He jumped up and ran over to the juke box. He looked at the man who had chosen it: dark skin, black eyes, a thick moustache. Lebanese, maybe, or a Cypriot, there were lots of them in Athens. He sat down again, shaking and bewildered.

Norman looked into his eyes: 'Michel, Michel . . . Claudio's song was an old Italian folk song. How could it be in that juke box? You're hearing things.'

Michel lowered his head and fell silent, choked up with the hopelessness of his memories. When he lifted his head again his eyes were gleaming: 'I can't think of anything else. Heleni must have . . .' he faltered.

'Come on,' said Norman, 'you've got to get it out.'

'Heleni must have suffered the same . . . outrage . . . as Melissa. Her dead body . . . Oh God, oh my God!' He raised his hand to his forehead to cover his tears, uncontrollable now.

Norman was upset as well. 'I think you've hit on the truth – that arrow hit Vlassos through his groin. I think it was deliberate.'

'If what we think is true, can you imagine how much they suffered, the two of them? If Claudio survived, he has become poisoned by hate and the desire for revenge. A death machine. Not a man any more, Norman, he's no longer a man. Think of what he had to go through. It was my fault, Norman . . .'

Norman passed him his full glass of brandy: 'Drink this, it's a lot stronger. Swallow it, I said.' He put a hand on Michel's shoulder: 'Every person in this world can only resist for so long. You were just a kid, and you were incapable of withstanding the torture they were subjecting you to. Maybe even Claudio wouldn't have held up at that point. Or me, for that matter. You mustn't be ashamed, Michel. You mustn't take the blame. Listen, right now we have to do everything we can to get in touch with him, if he's alive. We have to talk to him and force him out of the crazy isolation he must have been living in all these years. We have to stop him from committing more crimes. Tell him what's happened, make him understand what he's doing. We have got to find him. Karamanlis believes that he's going to go for the kill with Vlassos and that then it will be his turn.'

Michel still couldn't talk: he seemed to be watching the people pass by on the pavement, but he wasn't really looking at anything. His eyes were filled with ghosts.

'Maybe I'm on the list too. I've never thought about it. I always loved him – I never thought he'd want to kill me.'

'Me too. I could be just as blameworthy in his eyes. I was supposed to meet him that night in the Plaka, with a doctor for Heleni. Claudio may think I betrayed him. Think of my father. The message on his body implies that he took part in that crime, even though Karamanlis told me that wasn't true when I talked to him in Sidirokastro. We have no choice, Michel. We have to find him and tell him the truth. He'll believe us – for Christ's sake, he has to believe us. But if we want to find him we have to ask for Karamanlis's collaboration. We have to meet with him and . . .'

Michel wheeled around: 'No! You'd have to kill me first! That man is the cause of everything. He's the one who had me tortured. He's the one who had Heleni killed and who has turned Claudio into a machine without a soul, if it's true that he survived.' There was a cold light in his eyes. 'If I see Karamanlis it'll be to pay up my bill.'

Norman grabbed him by the shoulders: 'Don't be an idiot! We have to meet with him, understand? We have no choice. When we talked at Sidirokastro, I don't think he told me the whole story. I'm sure he didn't. He was just trying to get information from me. Now we've managed to decipher those messages while he's still groping around in the dark. We'll tell him what we know if he agrees to give us the full picture. That's the only way we can be sure about the messages and . . . decide how to respond.'

Michel lit up a cigarette and smoked it in silence. 'Norman, I don't know if I can stand the sight of him. Put yourself in my shoes.'

'Michel, you were there that night at police headquarters. Things might come back to you if you see him. You were there, Michel.'

Michel sucked in a deep breath and balled up his fists between his knees, as if he was trying to gather up all his strength. 'All right,' he said. 'When?'

'Now. Right now.'

Norman got up and walked straight towards the car parked on the other side of the road. The man behind the wheel tried to start it up, but Norman got there quicker. 'Hey, you,' he said. 'Yeah, I'm talking to you. Call the captain and tell him we have to talk to him, my French friend and me. Now. We'll wait for him inside the bar.'

After his initial embarrassment, the policeman started up the car and drove off. He radioed Captain Karamanlis shortly thereafter and told him about the invitation he had received. Karamanlis had been interrogating an ex-convict; he turned him over to his deputy and took off towards the café on Odòs Stadiou. The sun was setting over the port of Piraeus, sinking into the thick smog in a sulphurous haze.

MICHEL AND NORMAN walked to one of the bar's inside rooms and took a table near the window, looking out on the street.

'Michel,' said Norman, 'what do you think of the message that was found on my father's body?'

'I'm not sure, but I think it means something like, "You're a man used to seeing death and violence but even you couldn't have stood the sight of this." Whoever wrote it probably knew about your father's past as an operative or his role in the war, but he also wanted to reproach him for the girl's death.'

'Heleni as Cassandra?'

'Maybe. In any case, all these messages have something in common.'

'What?'

'They are all words pronounced by the dead. And that in itself is a message.'

'Hold on,' said Norman suddenly, watching the street. 'He's coming.'

Michel paled but stayed composed. When Karamanlis sat down opposite him, he looked him straight in the eye and without a tremor in his voice said: 'Those whom death does not part are destined to meet again. A drink, Captain Karamanlis?'

But it was Norman who began to talk, to explain how they'd managed to find the sources for the death messages, and Karamanlis realized he'd have to turn up new cards if he wanted to find out what they had in their hand. None of them noticed a black Mercedes with dark windows parked along the pavement in front of the bar. And none of them saw the camera behind the windscreen that captured them talking and drinking together.

By the time they had finished talking, Norman – who had been told only partial truths in Sidirokastro – knew exactly why his father had been killed. And the meaning of the death messages had become clear to them all. Karamanlis told them what was behind the first message, identical for Roussos and Karagheorghis, and Michel spelt out what the message carved on Vlassos's arrow meant. Taking the captain's embarrassed silence as an admission of guilt, he continued, seething with hate and indignation: 'You allowed Sergeant Vlassos to commit such a monstrous act! You are an abomination. You should be locked up in an asylum for the criminally insane for the rest of your life, and never be allowed to see the light of day again. I'd like to see you smashed dead like a toad . . .'

Norman interrupted, afraid that he would go too far. 'Michel, please. This is not what we're here for.'

Karamanlis seemed shaken. 'I didn't want it to turn out that way,' he said with an uncertain voice. 'The situation degenerated before I could do anything about it.'

'That's none of our concern,' said Norman. 'The only reason we asked to meet you was to fully understand the meaning of the death messages. You were the only person who had the necessary information. We could have avoided such a disagreeable meeting had you told me everything at Sidirokastro.' A deep, tense silence fell between them. The waiter passed and asked if he could bring them something, but the three pale, distracted men, motionless as mannequins, though sitting around the same table, seemed as distant as planets in the icy immensity of space. He got no reply, and slipped away unnoticed and a little cowed.

'You said that my father was against what happened,' Norman began again. 'That he tried to oppose it. I don't want your pity, and he's dead already. But at least make sure you're telling me the fucking truth.'

'It is the truth. Your father was so angry he would have killed me. The only thing I can imagine is that Setti saw him standing behind me when he was brought to the cell, and connected him to what was happening. What I cannot understand, and I think about it day and night, is how Setti could have found out who he was and killed him ten years later in a forest in Yugoslavian Macedonia. I don't know what to think: it's almost like someone else has orchestrated the whole thing to cast the blame on a man who died ten years ago.'

'You tried to make me believe at Sidirokastro that you weren't responsible for Claudio Setti's death,' said Norman.

'That's right,' said Karamanlis. 'The last time I saw him he was still alive. Later I was informed by the secret services that Claudio Setti was dead. But I'm still at a loss as to who else could be behind this.'

Michel seemed to awaken from his apparent torpor. 'Don't be deceived. All of those messages come from a single place and they are all pronounced by a dead soul: Agamemnon's ghost talking to Odysseus in Hades, Melissa's spirit called up by the Oracle of the Dead. That's the meaning behind the words: they come from a dead man, speaking from the other world, where you thought you had buried him. Claudio's sending the messages and he wants us on the banks of the Acheron. There we'll find out what death he has in mind for us.'

Karamanlis stood up. 'Well, he's not scaring me,' he said. 'I've been in situations much worse than this. My men were not butchered by a ghost. A man who kills can be killed – he's not invulnerable. If there's anything more you know and haven't told me, you'd better come clean now, otherwise you go down your road and I'll take mine. I don't know what you're planning on doing, but it doesn't concern me. If you want my advice,

leave. Go home. Who's dead is dead and there's no bringing
them back to life. What's done is done. Leave and let me solve
this my way. It'll be better all around. If what you say is true,
you're no safer than I am. You were the only ones who knew
where he was that day with the girl, and he knows that. By now
he knows that for sure.'

He tapped his index finger on the table peremptorily.

'Leave Athens and Greece now, while you're still in time,' he
said. Then he turned his back on them and left.

THREE DAYS LATER, in Istanbul, Claudio Setti was approached
by a young boy as he sat drinking a cup of tea in a *çayone* at
Galata bridge. 'The commander said to bring you these,' he said,
handing him an envelope and disappearing without waiting for a
tip or a reply. Claudio opened the envelope and found a black
and white photograph depicting Michel sitting at a table in a bar
talking to Karamanlis. He felt a sharp pain in his chest and tears
rose to his eyes. He stood up and walked towards the railing:
below him the water of the Golden Horn twinkled with a myriad
reflections as great ships sailed past. Storms of seagulls dived in,
fighting with shrill cries over the garbage thrown in by the little
restaurants and stands facing the water between the spans of the
bridge. In the distance, he could see the endless Asian shoreline.
He threw the picture in and watched it until it sank.

'*Güle güle, arkadash,*' he murmured in Turkish. 'Goodbye, my
friend.'

He returned to his table and went back to sipping his tea. His
gaze was even now, his eyes clear and dry, staring at a fixed
point in the sky, just like those of the emaciated barefooted
old man sitting on the ground next to him, exhausted by age,
covered with rags.

MIREILLE DECIDED TO join Michel in Greece, because none of
the reasons he gave for staying away from his own country for
so long convinced her. Those words that Icarus had found for
her had disturbed her deeply: what could Michel want with such

a macabre story? And what was he hiding from her? When she had suggested again that she come to Athens with the results of her research, he had firmly refused and told her in no uncertain terms to stay put.

When her father realized that she was leaving for Greece to join Michel, he decided it was time to tell her straight out what the family thought of their relationship: not only was Michel's family not up to the standards of Saint-Cyr, it wasn't his family to start with. The Charriers had adopted him from an orphanage in Château Mouton: Michel was in reality a 'mouton', or lost sheep, as the foundlings were derisively called. Mireille had to understand that such a background would never do for the family, especially if it became public knowledge. Unknown parents could mean anything: Michel might even be the son of a prostitute. Count Saint-Cyr was neither insolent nor condescending, but very effective in pointing out the insurmountable problems Michel would cause for the family.

Mireille in turn was neither insolent nor condescending. She let her father know in clear terms that she would not give up Michel for any reason in the world. If he would have her, she would marry him even if he didn't have a cent, because he was brilliant, successful and intelligent, and she had her own work as an assistant professor with a decent salary. There was nothing that the family could do to keep them apart. And that was the end of that.

At this point the Count, in order to prevent his daughter from making a decision she would some day regret, pulled out his trump card, which he imagined would resolve the situation once and for all.

'Please don't misjudge my intentions, dear,' he began. 'I've done this for your own good. I used my influence to see the papers which accompanied the child when he was left at the orphanage—'

Mireille, who had been admirably controlling her temper, burst into a fit of rage: 'And you call yourself a gentleman? Oh my God, I can't believe how low you've stooped to break us up.

Whatever you've found, let me tell you that Michel should be ashamed to marry into a family like ours!'

'Mireille, I will not allow you—'

'Fine, father. Now that I've told you what I think, tell me what you've found. I'm curious to know just what kind of original sin has made my man unworthy of the Saint-Cyrs.'

'Well, since you asked, your man, as you call him, was born from the union of an Arab woman and an Italian soldier imprisoned by the English during the war. He managed to escape and found shelter with a Bedouin tribe at the Siwa oasis. That's where the child was born. Then the mother died of typhus and the soldier went to Algiers, where he enrolled in the foreign legion. The child was brought to France and admitted to the orphanage. Now you know . . .'

Mireille shook her head. 'Half Italian and half Bedouin. The worst you can imagine, right, Daddy? Well now that you've told me, I hope you're satisfied, and I hope you'll be interested to know that I couldn't give a damn. Actually, now I understand just where he got his fabulous virility from.'

The Count became furious at this provocation and raised his hand to slap her, but Mireille continued to gaze impassively into his eyes. 'Just try to touch me and you'll never see me again,' she said. 'I'm serious.' She spoke with such determination that her father's hand dropped and he lowered his head, defeated if not resigned.

'Well, I'm leaving,' announced Mireille after a moment or two. 'Try to get over your hypocrisy in the meantime, if you can.'

Her family's vileness made her feel even closer to Michel, and the misfortunes of his childhood made her love him even more deeply. She felt a strong desire to embrace him, to smell the dry fragrance of his skin which reminded her of the forests at the beach in Sète and the wind-beaten bushes in the Camargue where they had so often gone horse riding or driven around in his absurd Deux-Chevaux. But at that moment she had no idea even where to look for him. He had left at the University the phone number of a hotel in Parga, a little city in Epirus, near the archaeological site of Ephira, where he planned to be at the beginning of November.

Mireille went up to her room and took the keys of Michel's apartment on rue des Orfèvres. She would spend the night there so she could at least dream of being held in his arms. She wanted to be close to his things, listen to his music, leaf through his books, take a bath in his tub.

She had a sandwich and a glass of Beaujolais nouveau at a bar in the centre of town, then went to Michel's apartment. The door to the bedroom was slightly ajar: she couldn't help but think how he was always a little shy about getting undressed in front of her, and how he always forgot to take off his socks before his trousers.

She went into the kitchen, twisted the gas valve and put on a pot of coffee, then went into his study. Everything was in perfect order except for his work desk, crowded, as always, with an infinite heap of papers, books, sketches, notes, maps, answered and unanswered letters, articles, rulers, pencils and markers.

She took a look at the mess and realized that somehow there was meaning in the madness. It all seemed to revolve around a central point, and that point seemed to be a sheet of tracing paper on which a single straight line was drawn, marked off by letters of the alphabet: a D on top, a T a little further down and an S at the end. Between the first two letters a cross marked the word 'Ephira', and there was a heading at the top of the page: 'The axis of Harvatis'. Ephira. She'd just heard that name, hadn't she? Wasn't that the place Michel was supposed to be at in a short time? That's right, the hotel he'd left the phone number for.

She could hear the coffee percolating on the flame and went to pour herself a cup of excellent Italian espresso. Now that she knew that Michel was half Italian, she thought that his taste for espresso coffee must be genetic. Otherwise he was so French! She went back into the study and sat down to sip the coffee, still staring at the line.

She lifted her head and noticed a map of ancient Greece and the eastern Mediterranean – *Graecia Antiqua Cum Oris Maris Agei* – hanging on the wall. Was the line traced over that map? She got closer and clearly saw Ephira on the coast facing the Ionian islands, north of the gulf of Ambracia. Ephira . . . that was it! The Oracle of the Dead was at Ephira, where Periander had evoked the ghost of his wife Melissa! That's where she'd heard it. She still had a copy of the passage from Herodotus in her purse. What was Michel going to do there?

She swallowed the last sip of coffee, walked over to the desk, freed the tracing paper from all the other things lying around it, then placed it over the map on the wall. She lined up the little cross marked Ephira with the same name on the map, then patiently started turning the sheet until all the letters matched up with places on the map. 'D' was for Dodona, the prophetic sanctuary of Zeus, the most ancient oracle of the Greek world; 'T' stood for Tainaron, the central promontory of the Peloponnesus, Cape Tenaros; and at the end, much further south, in the north African desert, 'S' lined up with Siwa, the oasis of the oracle of Ammon. This was Harvatis's axis? What could it possibly mean? What on earth could unite such far-flung places?

She returned to the table and started exploring, taking care to put each thing back in its exact place in the general mess. She found a notebook with a bibliographic reference written in it: 'Periklis Harvatis, "Hypothesis on the necromantic rite in the *Odyssey*, Book XI".' Okay, something about this Harvatis, a good start. She started to skim what Michel had written: a kind of outline, she supposed, of what was in the article.

She became fascinated: Harvatis's theory was that the rite for calling up the spirits of the dead as described in the eleventh book of the *Odyssey* was the same rite used in the Necromantion of Ephira as early as the Mycenaean age. In other words, the rite set on the shores of the Ocean in Homer's poem – when Odysseus seeks to learn his destiny by calling up the Shades of the Dead – could actually have taken place in Epirus, at the mouth of the Acheron. The 'city of the Cimmerians' mentioned by the poet could be identified as the Cimmerian promontory, just a mile from Ephira.

Michel had written a couple of notes alongside, under the heading 'The prophecy of Tiresias':

The three animals that Odysseus was told to sacrifice – a bull, a boar and a ram – could refer to astrological signs. There is much evidence that the ancients applied the map of the constellations to the sites of their ancestral cults on the ground for magical or divinatory purposes. The axis of the zodiac which, transferred upon the earth, connects Siwa in Egypt with Dodona in Epirus also passes through the entrance to Hades at Cape Tenaros (the caves at Dirou) and the entrance to Hades at Ephira. What's more, the great sanctuaries aligned by the axis, including Olympia, the great temple of Panhellenic Zeus, are linked to symbols of the zodiac (N.B. The boar is a water sign identifiable with Pisces and is linked to the sanctuary of Zeus in Dodona).

Note: Harvatis's hypothesis regarding the notion that an axis of the zodiac joins all the main sanctuaries of the ancient Mediterranean is not wholly original. It is nonetheless not often taken into account by scholars because it has never been demonstrated that the ancients were capable of calculating latitude and longitude, much less of tracing the loxodromic curves between such distant points (like Siwa and Ephira, or Dodona).

Mireille copied out the notes page by page, as well as the sketch of the line that Michel had called the 'axis of Harvatis'. When she was about to put the notebook back where she'd found it, she discovered another couple of pages scribbled in Michel's writing, starting from the back cover.

The first said: 'Problem: Cults have arisen at every point in the Mediterranean where Odysseus's ship is said to have landed, or one of his companions died, or another Homeric hero was present (Diomedes in Apulia, Teucer in Cyprus, Antenor in Veneto, Aeneas in Latium); such events have typically been commemorated with sanctuaries, statues, etc. In Ithaca, the homeland of Odysseus, there has never been a cult dedicated to the hero. Why? No man is a prophet in his own land? No, too banal. There has to be a deeper reason. But what could it be?'

The second page was headed by the word 'KELKEA' in capital letters. Underneath it said: 'See Scholium Homer XI, 112. The term "Kelkea" (associated in some texts with "Bouneima") is perhaps the only remaining trace of a lost poem. The sequel to the *Odyssey*? Kelkea was the place in which Odysseus was supposed to conclude his adventure for all time, celebrating the sacrifice of the bull, the boar and the ram. Where was Kelkea?'

How odd, thought Mireille. Everything he'd written seemed to revolve around the *Odyssey*. She'd never known Michel was so interested in the subject. Perhaps some research he was considering to obtain that promotion at the University?

There was more. Another note at the bottom of the page read: 'Look for Harvatis's publisher at 17 Dionysìou St., Athens. How will I ever find the heart to see Athens again?'

Mireille stayed up late copying notes, reading, following the thoughts that the sight of those sheets and of Michel's nervous, fragmentary writing called up in her mind. She finally undressed and crawled into Michel's bed. She thought of the last time they'd made love in that bed, of Michel's lean boyish body, his long legs, his flat, muscular stomach, his black eyelashes, his eyes as moist and deep as a thoroughbred's. She wanted him then, terribly.

17

Athens, Glifada airport, 2 November, 9.30 a.m.

MIREILLE LANDED AT Glifada airport in Athens on a hazy day and took a cab directly to the small residential hotel she'd booked near the Plaka. At home she had left a message on the answering machine in case Michel called: she didn't want him to know she was in Greece, not right away. There was so much that Michel had kept hidden from her; she needed to check out a few things first.

As soon as she arrived, she took a shower to rinse away the smoggy air of Athens, then lay on the bed in her bathrobe to look at the notes she'd taken from Michel's papers in his study on rue des Orfèvres. What had struck her most was: 'Look for Harvatis's publisher at 17 Dionysìou St., Athens. How will I ever find the heart to see Athens again?' Something awful must have happened in Athens, something he wanted to forget. She took a map of the city and found Dionysìou Street. It was located in the centre near the old city . . . but why look for the publisher? Why not try to find the author first?

She took the phone book and looked up the name Periklis Harvatis, but found nothing. She thought she'd try the city registry. She dressed well and had a taxi take her to the City Hall, where she found the registry office tucked away in the basement. The clerk was quite distinctive-looking. Closer to sixty than fifty, short and impeccably dressed in a light-coloured suit with a carnation in his buttonhole, he sat behind a table smoking an elegant oval Macedonia and taking little sips of his

Turkish coffee. She made up the first story that came into her head: 'I worked with Professor Harvatis many years ago, and I'd like to look him up while I'm here in Athens but I've lost his address.'

'He may not be in Athens at all. If you didn't find his name in the phone book, I doubt that he still lives here. Wait . . .' He opened the drawer of a file cabinet and began to look. 'Here it is,' he said, just a few minutes later. 'Harvatis, Periklis. Born in Ioannina on 4 April 1901 and deceased in Athens on 17 November 1973.'

'Deceased?'

'I'm afraid so, miss. The professor passed away some ten years ago. Yes, that's right – in two weeks' time it will be exactly ten years.'

'Couldn't you at least look up his last address? Perhaps some of his family members are still alive. Please help me, I'd really like to contact them. Would you mind if I took a sheet of paper to make a few notes?'

Anyone could see that the clerk would have gone through fire for her. He handed her a sheet of City Hall *dimos athinon* letterhead, with the seal of the owl.

'Sorry, his records say that he lived in the Neapolis district. Alone apparently; there are no other names listed. I am sorry, miss.'

Mireille wanted to offer the clerk a tip for his help, but he refused courteously. She was about to go when she thought of another possibility. 'Could you do something else for me?' she asked, with just a hint of flirtatiousness. There was no need: an aura of femininity surrounded her, enveloping even the steel cabinets. The gentleman nodded, eager to do anything that would make her happy.

'Do you think you could find his death certificate and the name of the doctor who signed it?'

'Certainly. That can be done.'

'Do you think that in a couple of hours . . .'

'A couple of hours? I'll need more time than that. I won't

have time during my working hours, but if you'd like to come by my house tonight . . .'

Mireille was expecting such a proposal, and had her own counterproposal ready. 'I'll come by at two and we can have lunch together. Is that all right, Mr . . .'

'Zolotas, Andreas Zolotas, but please call me Andreas. That would be fine. I'll try to have the information ready.'

Mireille thanked him with a smile and left the basement, where the slow movement of a single fan could not clear the damp air of a gloomy day.

17 Dionysìou Street. It wouldn't take long to walk over from City Hall. When she saw nothing but a lowered shutter at the address, she went to sit at the bar across the street and ordered an ouzo with ice, nearly as good as her favourite, Pernod.

'Doesn't anyone live at number seventeen?' she asked the waiter serving her. The waiter told her that she wasn't the first to want to know. Another foreigner had asked him the same question, a man about so tall, hair like so, and he'd told him no, that he'd never seen anyone. But then that very night he had seen a light filtering from under the shutter, and he'd seen it again since then, always late at night. But the man had never come back, so he'd never been able to tell him.

Mireille realized from the waiter's description that the man asking about the occupant of number 17 could be none other than Michel. She gave the waiter a thousand-drachma note as a tip and left her hotel phone number, asking him to call her if he should ever see that light under the shutter again. The waiter thanked her and assured her that he would.

She still had some time before her appointment with Mr Zolotas, and she walked back towards Odòs Stadiou, glancing over at the dusty, closed shutter at number 17. If someone was working there, they must have got in some other way. That shutter looked like it had been closed for years.

Andreas Zolotas had been very efficient, and was quite proud of himself as he pointed out to Mireille that he'd succeeded in getting quite a lot of difficult-to-access information in such a short time.

'I could tell right away,' said Mireille, 'that you're a man with important responsibilities here at City Hall.'

'Professor Harvatis died of a heart attack at three a.m. on Saturday the seventeenth of November 1973. It was the night of the assault on the Polytechnic. A terrible night, indeed. You see, miss, I've always sympathized with the left. I'm against dictator-ships—'

'I'm sure,' said Mireille, although Zolotas looked very much like a conservative lower middle-class government worker nurs-ing his job at City Hall.

'The act of death was signed by Dr Psarros at the Kifissìa hospital. I've called: he still works there. And he lives at Odòs Spetses, number twenty-eight.'

'Goodness, I'm amazed by such efficiency, Mr Zolotas. How can I ever thank you?'

'There's no need. When I found out the circumstances of Professor Harvatis's death, and the cause, I realized that your curiosity, miss, probably went beyond the reasons you gave me. Many students died that night, and a number of professors – the ones who were on their side – were targeted by the police as well.'

'Mr Zolotas, I . . . I don't know whether . . .'

'Don't say another word, miss. I had a son at the Polytechnic that night: they carried him back home over the rooftops. He was wounded, covered with blood, ruined for the rest of his life. Today he still doesn't have a job; maybe he's a thief. Maybe he takes drugs. He was a good boy, miss. Good-looking, tall, much taller than me . . .'

He prevented her firmly from giving him a tip. He took a fresh carnation from the table to replace the wilted one in his buttonhole, kissed her hand with a light, elegant gesture and walked away.

Mireille felt ashamed for imagining that she would have had

to fight off the unwanted attentions of a middle-aged lech. She looked at her watch: she'd been in Athens for just a few hours, and yet she felt like a fast current was pulling her under. A whirlpool. She didn't know how much faster it could get, or what the point of no return was, and she didn't want to think about it.

SHE WAS WAITING for Dr Psarros in front of his home on Odòs Spetses when he finished his work shift at five-thirty.

'Why are you interested in Professor Harvatis?'

'It has to do with some research I'm working on. Harvatis was writing an article of enormous importance to my work when he died, and it was never completed. If I knew something about the last days of his life, it might help me to understand certain aspects of his study.'

'We can go up to my house,' he said, rummaging through his pockets for his keys. 'Or if you'd rather, there's a tavern around the corner where we could sit down and have a drink.'

'Oh, I'd love that,' said Mireille. 'A glass of retsina would be perfect.'

'Fine, then. I have to tell you, first of all,' he said as they walked down the street, 'that when you called me an hour ago I was really surprised. I'd nearly forgotten all about that episode; it's been ten years, not just a couple of days.'

'Right. Exactly ten years ago. Two weeks from now is the anniversary of the Polytechnic battle.'

Psarros grimaced: 'Battle? Please, miss, that's hardly the word. It was a normal police operation for restoring order at the University. A handful of ruffians were preventing a public service from being carried on properly. The media made a big thing of it, talking about dozens of deaths, hundreds of wounded. A few bruises, a few heads bashed in, nothing more than that. Look what this country is reduced to now! They wanted democracy? I hope they're happy now. Just look,' he said, opening a copy of *To Vradi* that had been left on the table. 'Look at this – double-digit inflation, national debt out of control, corruption, drugs. Believe me, when the army was in charge these things just didn't happen. Young people cut their hair and dressed decently . . .'

'Well, it's true that democracy has its drawbacks . . . You Greeks are the ones who invented it. You Athenians, if I'm not mistaken,' offered Mireille. 'But please tell me about Harvatis.'

'Oh, yes, Harvatis. Well, there's not much to say. I dug up his old hospital file, and a few notes that I wrote in my own diary. Harvatis was brought to the hospital at about two a.m. by a certain Aristotelis Malidis, who worked with him, a custodian, I believe, employed at the National Archaeological Museum. The professor was in a critical condition. He seemed to be in shock and was practically unconscious. His heart was in fibrillation and · his overall physical condition was quite poor. Although his chances for recovery were slight, we put him under intensive therapy. Without success. He died an hour later. The man who'd brought him, Malidis, had disappeared. I notified the police, a certain Captain Karamanlis, Pavlos Karamanlis, if I remember correctly, because his death seemed suspicious, but I was never told the results of their investigation. I have no idea if there was an investigation, actually.'

'Do you know where Professor Harvatis was buried?'

'No. Why do you want to know?'

'I don't know. I'd like to know what he looked like. Maybe there's a photograph on his tomb.'

'That's possible. You could try the Kifissìa city cemetery. Do you know where it is?' He took a pen from his pocket and began to sketch out directions on a paper napkin. 'We're here. Go back to the main road and follow it all the way down, then turn right here. At the third traffic light, turn left . . .' he finished his little map, folded the napkin and handed it to her.

'Doctor Psarros, was an autopsy done on his body?'

'I did request an autopsy. It wasn't done immediately; things were very busy just then. But the autopsy was done. I remember it perfectly.'

'What was found?'

'It was strange, actually. We thought he'd had a devastating heart attack.'

'And?'

'Nothing. There was no damage to the heart muscle.'.

'But what was the cause of death?'

'Cardiac arrest.'

'That doesn't mean much, does it?'

'Exactly. Practically nothing.'

'What do you think?'

'Who knows. Some kind of a shock. There's not much you can say in a case like this. Maybe the man who brought him, that Malidis, could have told us what had happened, but I never saw him again. Perhaps Captain Karamanlis interrogated him. I have no idea.'

'Thank you, Doctor.'

'Not at all. If you discover something, let me know.'

Mireille got into her rented Peugeot and thought of driving out to the cemetery, but it was nearly six o'clock. It was surely closed by now, but perhaps if she found the custodian, she could give him a tip and have him open it.

'For one thousand drachmas, I'll even dig him up for you, miss,' said the custodian, who had been about to go home when Mireille slipped him the bill.

'But you have to come with me,' said the girl. 'It's getting dark and I'm a little afraid of walking around here by myself.'

He smiled and followed her in: 'There's no need to be afraid of the dead, miss. It's the living who are sons of bitches, if you'll pardon the expression. Like my brother-in-law – I gave him some money to open a shop five years ago, and I've never seen a penny of it . . .' The custodian turned to the right and pointed to a tomb. 'There he is,' he said. 'Mr Periklis Harvatis. I know all my boys, each and every one.'

Mireille looked at the small oval photograph which showed an old man with thin, snow-white hair. A gaunt but very dignified face. The inscription had only his first and last name, date of birth and date of death, but there was a fresh bunch of flowers, and the area was well taken care of. 'Do you put the flowers here?' asked Mireille. The custodian raised his head and closed his eyes. Negative. Mireille smiled to herself, thinking what an odd way all the inhabitants of the south-east Mediterranean – from Sicily to Lebanon – had of saying no. He led her to the exit and pointed to a flower shop: not the one on the right, the second on the left. The lady from the flower shop came by every so often.

'How often?' wondered Mireille. He shrugged; too much to ask. Mireille thanked him again, shaking his hand warmly, then crossed the street and walked into the flower shop.

THE WAITER MADE himself a sandwich with feta cheese, olives and tomatoes and poured himself a glass of wine. His usual snack before going home. He sat down, finally, after serving so many people, and relaxed, paging through the newspaper. The wind was coming from the south and the weather was still warm, but you could feel that it was about to change. The sports pages were the most crumpled, but still legible, and there was nothing he liked better than checking the results of the horse races to see if he had won. He'd lost.

He closed up the paper, calculating how much money he'd thrown away over his lifetime betting on the horses every Sunday and always losing, when suddenly he noticed a black Mercedes moving slowly up the street and stopping in front of number 17. He waited to see who would get out. The engine was turned off, as were the headlights, but no one left the car. Strange.

A few minutes later, when he was walking towards home on the other side of the street, he glanced into the car: it was empty. Instinctively he looked towards the shutter and saw a stream of light filtering out from under the bottom. He pressed his ear against the shutter, but could hear very little: receding footsteps, barely perceptible, as if someone was walking down a long hall. He remembered the one thousand-drachma bill he'd been given that morning and walked over to the nearest phone booth. Mireille was in her hotel room.

'Miss? The lights are on at seventeen Dionysìou Street.' Mireille had been sleeping for a couple of hours and she had trouble understanding what was going on. 'Miss, did you hear me? It's me, the waiter from Bar Milos. You gave me one thousand drachmas, remember?'

'Oh yes, of course. Thanks, my friend.'

'There's more. There's a black Mercedes parked in front, but no one has got out.'

'Are you sure?' asked Mireille.

'Yes, sir,' answered the waiter, forgetting he was talking to a woman.

'Okay, thank you.'

'Goodnight,' said the waiter and started walking back home, like he did every night.

Mireille looked at her watch and was about to sink back into a deep sleep, tired after the trip and all the various events of that very long day, but then it hit her that this was possibly a one-off opportunity that she couldn't afford to miss. She got up, and even put on a little make-up, in spite of the time and the situation. She dressed quickly, went down and started up her car, and headed towards Dionysìou Street on the nearly deserted roads of Athens.

She passed slowly in front of number 17. The light was on, all right, but the shutter was still locked. How had they got in? And that black Mercedes? It was still parked out in front, and it was empty. The main door to the building was closed as well. Mireille could not seem to piece together the puzzle, no matter how hard she tried. This was supposedly the press which had printed Professor Harvatis's article, and someone was in there at one-thirty in the morning. She turned around at the end of the road, beyond the bar, and parked so she could see the Mercedes clearly. And the car's owner, when he decided to come out.

The street was poorly lit and Mireille was a little afraid. She curled up so her head didn't show above the seat, while keeping her eyes trained on that thin stream of light filtering from under the shutter, as well as on the black car parked alongside the pavement. She kept the radio on low for a while to keep her company, but all she could tune into were those damned Greek folk songs, so she switched it off. She tried smoking to stay awake, but every so often her head would drop and she'd fall asleep for a few minutes, then shake herself awake to force her tired eyes back to that yellow light, that black mass. It all seemed ridiculous. Just a few hours ago she was in her own nice, comfortable room, and now she was freezing to death and couldn't keep her eyes open in this damned rented car, guarding a locked shutter.

Just before six in the morning, sleep overcame her and she nodded off, her head resting on the seat for a few minutes. She was awakened by the soft sound of an engine starting up. She started, realized where she was and looked towards the shutter: the light was off. The Mercedes's parking lights were just coming on and the car was pulling off, slow and silent, headed towards Stadiou Street. Mireille started up her own car and, without turning on her lights, followed the Mercedes at a distance. It was easier on Stadiou Street: there was already a little traffic, so her car blended in with the others.

At a red light she managed to pull up alongside the car on the left and stole a glance at the man behind the wheel: about fifty, tanned face with black hair and a beard streaked with some white. He was wearing a light-coloured crew-necked sweater and a blue blazer. His hands on the steering wheel were large and strong and aristocratic. The hands of a nobleman. When the light turned green, Mireille slipped back into position behind him.

The sky was beginning to lighten, but large dark clouds were skimming rapidly from west to east. The Mercedes turned off towards Faliron, and then Cape Sounion. Mireille checked a map and realized that this was the only road going inland, ending up at the temple of Poseidon; she decided to drop back so she wouldn't look suspicious. It took nearly an hour to get to Sounion, and the sun was just coming up over the horizon, piercing through the dense clouds forming over the sea. One of the long rays of light suddenly struck the Doric temple at the top of the promontory and it shone as white as a lily, vivid and glorious against the waves of the sea and the clouds in the sky. The wind which always swept the cliff bent the broom bushes, creating waves shorter and more ruffled than the slow, solemn roll of the sea.

The Mercedes had stopped alongside a fleshy euphorbia bush and the man, who was now wearing a raincoat, stood motionless atop a boulder in front of the temple, which had turned as grey as the threatening sky. Mireille stopped before the last curve, just past the Poseidon hotel, turned off the engine and sat watching him, unseen. The man stood there for at least ten minutes, and his small, dark, erect figure seemed unevenly matched against the colossal white columns which supported the sanctuary archi-trave. He then turned and went towards the cliff that towered over the sea. A gust of cold wind puffed up his raincoat, and from this distance he looked like a bird about to take flight over the dark expanse of the Aegean. Far off, white foam seethed all around the island of Patroclos, as black and shiny as the back of a whale.

When the Mercedes took off again, distancing itself from the sea and heading north inland towards Attica, Mireille continued to follow at a distance for another hour. She hadn't had a moment for breakfast and was tired and hungry. All this strange wandering seemed pointless and futile. She had almost decided to stop following him when she saw the Mercedes leave the main road and head up a trail which rose towards a solitary house at the edge of a forest of oak saplings. She got out of the car and walked up on foot, concealed behind a ridge.

She saw him knock on the door, which was opened by an old man who then shut it behind him. There didn't seem to be any dogs around, and Mireille sneaked up to the window that looked out on to the forest: she could hide behind the bushes if need be. The room was a couple of metres wide, illuminated by two windows: an artist's studio.

In one corner, a bucket of fresh clay was covered with a sheet of plastic. A tripod on the other side of the room held a relief panel, still damp, representing a fishing scene: lean-armed men throwing a net from a boat, the sun shining above, while tunas and dolphins splashed inside and outside the net. The man who had got out of the Mercedes had taken off his raincoat and was sitting on a stool on the far side of the room; she could see his profile. The old man sat with his back to her and she saw only the back of his head: a tumble of white locks falling over the collar of a cotton smock. Listening hard, Mireille could make out what they were saying.

'I'm happy to see you, Commander. Have you come to finish the work?' asked the old man.

'I have, maestro. I'm happy to see you as well. How are you feeling?'

'The way you feel when you've reached the end.'

'Why say that?'

'I've lived too much. How long could I possibly have left?'

'Does that distress you?'

'I'm losing my sight. Night is coming.'

'Has there ever been a night not followed by the dawn?'

'It's a thought that does not console me. I can't bear to lose the vision of nature . . . for ever.'

A gust of wind rustled up the forest and Mireille could no longer hear the men. She could only see the eyes of the stranger, such a deep blue, gleaming like the only thing alive in the grey atmosphere of the room. He spoke, then listened. He remained seated on the stool, his hands joined around his knee. The artist approached him now and then, touching his face with his long bony fingers as if to capture his features and infuse them into the clay. He was creating his likeness.

Mireille kept turning around, fearful that someone might turn up, but the area was quite deserted and the wind was now whistling through the forest. She could no longer hear their words, but lingered close to the window until the old sculptor had finished. She saw him take off his smock and go to wash his hands. As he moved away from the window, she could see what he had been working on: a bas relief portraying only the face of the man who was posing. Only his face, with his eyes closed in sleep . . . or in death?

The face had lost the hard tension and domineering intensity of the man's gaze, and looked mysteriously tranquil. The grave, solemn majesty of a king at rest.

The sculptor accompanied him to the door and Mireille, concealed behind the corner of the house, could hear what they were saying.

'My work is finished. The clay will be fired in the kiln before evening.'

'All that's missing is the gold.'

'Bring it soon. This could be my last work. I want it to be perfect . . . but I also want you to tell me why you have had me make it.'

'You have depicted my face, you have touched my soul with your fingers. What can I tell you that you don't already know in the bottom of your heart? As far as the gold is concerned, there's something I must tell you. It won't be just a bar of metal. You'll have to destroy . . . no, refashion an object that perhaps you yourself crafted very very long ago. You, or someone like you. Thus I'll be able to close the circle and put an end to something that no man, no matter how patient, would have been able to bear. Will you do it for me?'

The old man nodded: 'For you, Commander.'

'I knew you would not refuse me. Farewell, maestro.'

The old man stood on the threshold, watching him as he got into the car and drove off down the little dusty road, towards the provincial highway. Mireille took her camera, and before the artist returned to his modest studio, took several pictures of the clay mask through the slightly misted glass of the window. It reminded her of something she'd already seen.

MIREILLE WOKE UP at two that afternoon and tried to contact Michel at the hotel in Ephira that he'd left the number for, but the receptionist said that although he had a reservation, he hadn't arrived yet. She went downstairs and got something to eat at the bar, then asked the hotel manager to call the Antiquities and Fine Arts Service to see if a certain Aristotelis Malidis still worked at the National Archaeological Museum.

They answered that Malidis had retired and that they knew nothing more about him. Perhaps he had returned to Parga, his home town. She should look for him there. Mireille thanked them. Parga . . . Parga was the town nearest Ephira: had Michel gone there to meet Malidis?

She walked out on to the street, over to the photo lab where she had left her roll of film from that morning at Cape Sounion. She'd asked for large black and white prints: they'd come out rather well, even if they were a little out of focus. She bought some tracing paper and pencils and went back to her hotel room. She placed the paper over the photograph and traced the face, changing it here and there so that it resembled the model more closely. When she lifted the paper, she thought that the likeness was really rather good. She'd captured his deep, intense gaze and his strong features. She put the drawing into her purse, got into the car and headed out towards the cemetery at Kifissìa. The flower shop was open and Mireille entered, showing her sketch to the owner: 'Is this the man who orders the flowers for the tomb of Periklis Harvatis?'

The woman stared at the drawing in surprise, looked up at Mireille and back at the drawing. She nodded her head excitedly: 'Né, né, aftòs ine.' It was him, precisely him.

The same evening she showed the drawing to Dr Psarros. 'This man is tied in some way to Periklis Harvatis,' she said. 'I don't know how, but I'm certain of it. Have you ever seen him?'

Psarros shook his head: 'Never. Who is he?'

'I'd like to know. This man embodies more mysteries than the Holy Trinity. I don't know anything about him. All I have is the licence number of his car. A black Mercedes.'

Psarros thought for a while in silence: 'Why don't you go to the captain of police, Pavlos Karamanlis? I think he's still in service. Maybe he can help you. Maybe he did carry out some kind of investigation back then . . . who knows.'

'That's a good idea,' said Mireille. 'Thank you, Doctor Psarros.'

Towards midnight, when Karamanlis phoned in to the station to see what was new, the officer on duty told him that there was something new, for a change.

'Captain, do you remember that identikit that you had distributed to Interpol?'

'Of course I remember. I'm the one who had it done.'

'Today a foreign girl came in with a drawing that looked just like him. Well, kind of. She asked if we knew anything about him. She wanted to talk with you.'

'What do you mean, with me?'

'With you, in person. She said "I want to talk to Captain Karamanlis".'

'What was her name?'

'Mireille de Saint-Cyr. Must be an aristocrat.'

'Saint-Cyr? Never heard of her.'

'She said she followed this guy and that she has his plates, but she wouldn't give me the number.'

Karamanlis started: 'Don't let her get away if you want to save your ass.'

'Should I arrest her?'

'No, you imbecile. Just keep an eye on her. I absolutely have to talk to her. I'll be there tomorrow.'

'Where are you now, Captain?'

'It's my own fucking business where I am now. I said I'd be there tomorrow.'

18

PAVLOS KARAMANLIS HAD not believed that his admonition would be enough to make Norman Shields and Michel Charrier leave Greece. He knew that they had left Athens and were headed west towards Missolungi: the road for Parga. The road that led to the Oracle of the Dead at Ephira, if he was guessing right. Idiots: they were walking into the trap, reeled in by those messages. The angel of death wouldn't stop to listen to explanations; the two of them might very well be on the list themselves.

Was it there that Claudio Setti was waiting for them? For the day of reckoning? Well, Karamanlis would be there as well when the roll was called, but he had to get a couple of things out of the way first. He wanted to set up a credible line of defence if Claudio Setti came to settle up, and he wanted to get some information from the man who called himself Admiral Bogdanos; he would know where Claudio Setti was, if he truly was still alive.

And if Setti was alive and determined to exterminate all those who remained – at least Vlassos and himself – nothing would stop him, if all these years of police work had taught Karamanlis anything about human nature.

Ephira could wait. He'd asked his colleagues in Parga to keep an eye on Charrier and Shields as soon as they registered at a hotel. Karamanlis set off for Kalabaka and for Kozani. He'd got an idea. The Kaloudis family had recently moved to Drepano, a village near Kozani. They had sold their property in Thrace after Heleni's death and bought a woodworking factory there.

The Kaloudises still had a daughter, Heleni's younger sister. She must be about twenty now, the age Heleni was when she died. Karamanlis wanted to see her.

And when he spotted her walking home from town with a shopping bag in hand, his face lit up: she was the living likeness of her sister!

He had a picture of Heleni in his office which his men had taken at the time of the Polytechnic incident. Every now and then he would look at it without a reason. He couldn't explain to himself why he was drawn to that old photograph; but since he had the girl's face in his mind's eye, he was sure that her younger sister resembled her in an extraordinary way.

He stayed at Kozani that night, and the next day took several pictures of her with a good telephoto lens. Riding her bike into town. Coming out of a shop. Talking with a girlfriend. Laughing at a couple of boys.

He had them printed, and they came out so well he decided he would leave. If the worst came to the worst, these photographs might mean his salvation. Or could be the lure for a good trap, a trap he'd had in mind since he'd seen Vlassos run through like Saint Sebastian. A trap he could set up if the circumstances were right. He just had to find out where that son of a bitch was hiding. When he'd called headquarters and had learned that there was a girl on the trail of the mysterious Admiral Bogdanos, his mood soared. Destiny was giving him a good hand to play. Finally.

The next day he headed south towards Athens, but instead of taking the direct Larissa route, he choose the Grevena-Kalabaka provincial road. When he got to the turn-off for Kalabaka, he realized that he wasn't far from a place he'd been thinking about a lot over the last few days, a place which intrigued him and made him strangely uncomfortable.

Did people with mystic powers really exist? People capable of penetrating the dark curtain?

He stopped for a few minutes at the crossroads and then turned right, instead of left, towards Metsovon.

MOUNT PERISTERI WAS a striking, solitary mountain, swept by the wind most of the year. It rose, barren and harsh, at the centre of the Pindus ridge, halfway between Metsovon and Kalabaka. These towns were briefly populated for a couple of months a year when Metsovon enjoyed a little local tourism: people from Athens – mostly small-businessmen or government employees – would come up for an escape from the stifling heat in the summer. But as early as September, the area was practically deserted again, home only to a few shepherds who brought their flocks to graze on the meadows at the foot of the great mountain.

Pavlos Karamanlis left his car in a parking area at the side of the provincial road and headed on foot up a narrow trail which cut into the mountainside. The identikit of the man who for years he had thought was Admiral Bogdanos was in his pocket – the sketch which had not turned up a single lead from the police or Interpol. Unless that foreign girl who had turned up at headquarters knew something. It had been an impulsive decision to take that walk up the mountains of Epirus – because he figured he had nothing to lose. At worst, he'd have to listen to the ravings of a *kallikàntharos*. But if his friend was right, perhaps that hermit could really see into the other world, and would set him on the right path.

His friend had told him that the secret police often used mediums and psychics to solve intricate, unsolvable cases. Not only in Greece, but in many other countries as well. He had claimed that in Italy, when statesman Aldo Moro was kidnapped and imprisoned by the Red Brigades, a psychic had told the police the exact name of the street where they could find him. The only reason they hadn't been able to save him was that there happened to be a town of the same name which they'd mistakenly raided instead.

Karamanlis knew that the seer lived in an old shack next to a cave which opened on to the southern slope of Mount Peristeri, not far from a spring. He found a shepherd who knew enough to provide him with reasonable directions to the place.

He quickened his pace, because it was already three in the afternoon and the days were getting shorter. It would take him another hour to get up there and just as long to get back down, and he didn't want to be stuck up there when darkness fell.

He was soon struggling and drenched with sweat, dressed as he was in a brown suit, shirt and tie, with shoes that were absolutely unsuitable for such a hike. He slipped several times, falling to his knees and covering his trousers with dust and burrs. When he was finally close enough to see the shack, the weather started to turn. Clouds cloaked the sun which had begun to set over the Ionian Sea in the direction of Metsovon.

Just a few dozen metres away was a drystone-wall cabin, its roof covered with schist slabs like all the old houses in the area. All around were pens with sheep, goats, pigs, a couple of donkeys, chickens and turkeys, geese. But he could hear the cries of other animals as well: monkeys, or parrots, it sounded like. That discordant chorus of beastly voices created a sinister atmosphere in the place, which seemed devoid of any human presence.

Karamanlis was about to turn back, because the clouds were gathering rapidly and the idea of remaining in that place longer than necessary gave him the creeps, but stopped when the door suddenly swung open. He thought he would see the owner come out, but nothing happened: the door had opened on to a black, empty space inside.

Karamanlis walked slowly towards the house. 'Anyone home?' he asked, 'May I come in?' He was given no answer.

All at once, he realized that his men had been killed after being lured into a solitary, out-of-the-way place. Just like this. Stupid. What an idiot. Had he come on his own legs to meet his butcher? His friend at the Ministry hadn't given him much information, after all. Perhaps he knew more about Bogdanos than he'd let on. After all, their 'friendship' had always been greased by sums of money Karamanlis had appropriated from funds destined for informers and spies.

He took his gun from its holster and hid it in his pocket, so he'd be ready to fire at the slightest provocation.

He then heard a voice from inside.

'You won't need your weapons. There is no danger for you here. The danger is elsewhere . . .'

Karamanlis started and paused at the threshold, looking in. There was a man sitting next to the hearth, although the fire was out. His back was to the door. To his left a bird was perched on a stand: a hawk, or a kite. A large grey-haired dog lay at his feet, absolutely immobile.

'I'm—'

'You are O Tàvros. Chief of many men, yet you fear remaining alone, do you not?'

'I see someone has spoken to you about me,' said Karamanlis, putting the gun back in its holster under his armpit.

The man turned towards him: his hair was dark and curly, his skin swarthy. He had long, nervous hands and strong arms. He was wearing the traditional costume of the area: a pleated fustanella and a puff-sleeved shirt under a black wool vest. Karamanlis was disconcerted.

'You called me O Tàvros. That was my battle name during the civil war. Someone must have told you about me . . .'

'In a certain sense. What do you want from me?'

The light outside was fading quickly and the dog whined softly.

'I'm looking for a man who I knew under a false identity for many years. I cannot understand his behaviour for the life of me. Each one of his actions contradicts another, and I cannot explain them, as hard as I try. His appearance is always accompanied by death, either just before or just after I have seen him . . .' He was amazed at how he was talking to the shepherd, as if he could really provide a response. 'I know only his face. It's a face that is difficult to forget because it seems unchangeable. As if time never passes for him.'

'There are people who wear their years well,' said the man.

'Do you know who I am speaking about?'

'No.'

Karamanlis reproved himself for being so gullible. He'd come to this godforsaken place for nothing.

'But I feel him looming over you,' the man continued. 'Can you describe him?'

'More than that,' said Karamanlis. 'I can show you a very good likeness of him.' He took the identikit from his pocket and handed it to him.

The man took the sketch but didn't seem even to look at it. He put it on a stool in front of him and placed his open hand over it. His voice suddenly became deep and hoarse, distorted. 'What do you want from me?' he asked.

'My life is threatened,' said Karamanlis. 'What must I do?'

'Your life is threatened by this man. I know.'

'By this man? Not by another man? This man saved one of my officers . . .'

'It is he who administers death. Where are you going now?'

'To Athens.'

'This is not the road to Athens.'

'I know.'

'What is your next destination?'

'Ephira. I'll be going to Ephira, sooner or later.'

'Where the Acheron flows. The swamp of the dead is there. Did you know that?' His voice seemed full of pain, as though each word were costing him a dear sacrifice.

'I know. That's what I've been told, but all the leads I have point there. I'm a bloodhound, and I have to follow the trail, even if it takes me to the mouth of hell. I don't want you to tell me if I'm going to die there. I wouldn't give up the chase now, even if that were the case.'

'The danger . . . is . . . not there.' His lips were white with dried spit; the hand he held over the likeness was beaded with sweat. The animals outside were silent, but he could hear their hooves scuttling on the stony ground as if they were running frantically back and forth in their pens. The *kallikàntharos* began to speak again: 'Your soul is hard . . . but every man must fight to survive. Avoid . . . if you can . . . stay away from the vertex of the great triangle. And beware the pyramid at the vertex of the triangle. There where east and west touch, shoulder to shoulder. It is there that the bull, the ram, and . . .' Karamanlis drew closer to the man, until their brows nearly touched. The man's features were taut, his forehead covered with perspiration and his face carved by deep wrinkles. He seemed to have aged ten years.

'Tell me who he is, and where he is, now!' he implored.

The man's head jerked forward as if a fist as heavy as a maul had slammed against his back. The dog suddenly got up on its back legs and sniffed the air, turning towards the door with a fearful yelp.

'He is—'

'Who is he?' shouted Karamanlis, seizing him by his vest. 'Tell me who the bastard who's been screwing me for the last ten years is!'

The man lifted his head with supreme effort. His hand still hovered over the drawing, still and solid, while the rest of his body trembled uncontrollably: 'He is . . . here!'

Karamanlis jumped: 'Here? What are you saying?' He looked wildly around the room and pointed his gun at the door, as if a nightmare figure might appear there. When he turned again towards the *kallikàntharos*, the man was unrecognizable. His breathing sounded like a weak hiss. He slowly removed his hand from the sheet with a great effort and turned to speak. When the sound of his words formed in his mouth, Karamanlis shuddered with horror: it was no longer the voice of the man sitting in front of him, but of the man who for years and years he had thought was Admiral Bogdanos.

'What are you doing here, Captain Karamanlis?'

Karamanlis staggered backwards; a gust of wind hit him from behind through the open door, dishevelling his hair and pasting his jacket collar to the nape of his neck: '*Who are you?*' he cried. '*Who are you?*'

He stumbled back until he found himself outside. The wind slammed the door shut, banging it two or three times, loudly. The top of the mountain was no longer visible, completely hidden by huge black clouds. Karamanlis took off at a run as the rain started to pelt down. There was not a single shelter from there to his car, and he ran with every last bit of energy he could gather, panting, falling, wheeling around at every peal of thunder and bolt of lightning until he reached it. His heart was bursting, he was soaked and tattered. He switched on the engine and the heat and stripped down. He sat naked and still, sheltered from the pouring rain, trembling with fear and chilled to the bone. A car finally drove by on the road, then a truck and a camper full of foreign tourists: he was back in the world made up of people, noise and real voices. He would never again leave it of his own will. Never.

AFTER TALKING TO the police, Mireille returned to Odòs Diony-sìou to check with the waiter at Milos's Bar. She gave him another tip to make sure that he'd promise to call her hotel again if he saw the light under the shutter of number 17 or if he saw a black Mercedes parked anywhere nearby. The waiter assured her that if she wasn't in her room, he would leave a message with the front desk. Then Mireille called Mr Zolotas, asking him to meet her in a bar in Omonia Square. He showed up in a dark blue suit with a polka-dotted pocket handkerchief and a gardenia in his buttonhole. Given his job, his apparel was incredibly elegant, albeit slightly démodé.

'Well, miss, how is your little investigation proceeding?' he asked as soon as he saw her.

'Better than I'd hoped, but unfortunately all the information I've gathered isn't leading me to any solution. I need to know more. I even went to the police, but the person I was looking for was out. He'll be back today, they said.'

'Can I ask who you were looking for, miss, if I'm not being indiscreet?'

'An officer who was involved somehow in the events that

followed the death of Professor Harvatis – his name is captain Pavlos Karamanlis.' Zolotas paled. 'Do you know him?' asked Mireille.

'I do. Unfortunately. He is a dangerous man. During the dictatorship he was one of the mastiffs of the repression. He never rested the night of the Polytechnic, and those he got his hands on still carry the signs, I can assure you. Be careful. Careful of what you say, and say as little as you can.'

'Thank you for warning me. You have given me precious help, Mr Zolotas.'

'What kind of information do you still need?'

'Land registry. Can you consult those records?'

'Not personally, but I know a person who can. What do you need to know?'

'Who the printer's shop on 17 Dionysìou Street belongs to. If there's someone who pays the rent. If it has other entrances besides the front shutter, which has been closed for seven years, if not more.'

Zolotas took notes on a little pad with a slim pencil. He looked up at her when he had finished writing: he certainly wasn't a good-looking man. His light-coloured eyes were protruding, his nose aquiline and his cheeks a bit jowly, but his hair was carefully combed and he reminded Mireille of one of those Hellenistic busts in the National Museum portraying a stoic philosopher or a late-generation academic. She was becoming quite fond of him.

'What did you want to ask Captain Karamanlis?'

'I wanted to show him a sketch I've made of a man to see if he knows him. I even have his licence plate number.'

'I wouldn't give Karamanlis that number if I were you.'

'Why?' asked Mireille with a disappointed tone, since she had already told the police she had it.

'Let him look for the man, if he's interested. Why should you help him?'

'Because I'm interested as well.'

'Do you trust me, miss?'

'Yes.'

'Give me that number. I'll go to the automobile registry. My Greek is better than yours.'

'I'm making progress, though,' said the girl.

'That's true. In a month or two, it'll be perfect.'

'I've come here often on vacation, and I went to a classical lyceum for high school. Modern Greek's not that hard, once you get used to your strange pronunciation.'

Zolotas arched his eyebrows: 'Strange? But we are the Greeks here, aren't we, miss?'

'That's true too.' Mireille gave him her phone number at the hotel. 'This is where you'll find me if you need me. I'm going to the police tonight.'

'Be careful, miss. Please promise me you'll be careful.'

'I will be careful, Mr Zolotas. You don't possibly think I could be in danger?'

'Not if you drop everything now and go back to wait for your boyfriend in France. But if these things have remained hidden for all these years, there must be a reason. And it might well be a serious reason. Farewell, miss.'

'Goodbye, Mr Zolotas.'

CAPTAIN KARAMANLIS DIDN'T get to headquarters until five the following afternoon, and went directly to his office without saying hello to anyone. He sat at his desk and used a key to open the bottom drawer. He pulled out the file with Heleni's photographs, chose one and placed it on his desk. He then took one of the photos he had taken of her sister from his bag and placed it alongside. He had been right: they looked like two pictures of the same person. A little bit of laboratory retouching would make the illusion perfect, or nearly so.

He put back the negatives and started to read his mail. The officer on guard soon called him.

'Captain, that girl is here for you. And hey, Captain, she's really a nice piece of—'

Karamanlis was not in the mood for lewd remarks. 'Take

your comments and stick them up your ass. Show her in immediately.'

'Yes, sir, Captain. Right away, Captain.'

Karamanlis did his best to seem open, honest and cordial with Mireille, and most of all not like an inquisitor.

'You came with a likeness of a man,' he said, 'to see if we know anything about him.'

'That's right.'

'Can I see it?'

Mireille took the drawing she had made from her bag and showed it to him. Karamanlis could barely hide his amazement.

'You drew this, miss?'

'Yes.'

'It's perfect. And I know, because I've seen this man many times. What is it you want to know?'

'I'm looking for information about an archaeologist who died ten years ago here in Athens. His name was Periklis Harvatis. He left a very important study incomplete, and it is essential that I find his writings. As far as I know, the people who may have been in contact with him before his death are a man who worked for the Antiquities and Fine Arts Service, a certain Aristotelis Malidis, and –' she pointed her finger at the drawing on the table – 'this man here.'

Karamanlis continued to stare at the drawing, and felt, despite himself, that the man's gaze was looking right through him, watching his every move, like the eye of God.

'Someone told you to contact me personally, isn't that right?' he asked.

'Yes, that's right.'

'May I ask who it was?'

'A doctor. Doctor Psarros at the Kifissìa hospital.'

'Psarros . . . yes, I remember now, I remember. He phoned me the night Periklis Harvatis died, or maybe the night after, reporting the strange conditions of the patient who had been brought in on the brink of death. I investigated Malidis: he was his excavation foreman.'

'On what dig?'

'I don't know. The Service did provide a list of all the excavations in progress, but I was told I'd have to contact every single branch office for complete information. I got nowhere.'

'Well, I got somewhere. I went to the National Library before coming here and consulted the excavation journals. On 16 November 1973, Periklis Harvatis was exploring the *adyton* of the Oracle of the Dead at Ephira. The dig was published by his successor, Professor Makaris.'

Karamanlis felt caught unawares by this girl, apparently such a doll and in reality so quick-witted. Too quick, maybe. Ephira . . . so that was where the golden vase came from. Who else could have come to Athens that night with a piece from an archaeological dig? And maybe the vase was now back. Maybe that was why Charrier and Shields were returning to Ephira, defying death there?

'You're better at this than I am, miss,' he said with a grudging smile. 'In any case, absolutely nothing against Malidis ever emerged. I had my suspicions, but I never found anything I could use against him.'

'What about this man here? What was his relationship to Professor Harvatis?' asked Mireille, pointing to the drawing on the table.

Karamanlis wasn't sure how to proceed. There were a lot of things he wanted to know from the girl, but he realized he wouldn't get them for free. He had to come up with something feasible without implicating himself.

'Miss,' he said, 'this man has been a real headache for me. But I'm beginning to see through him, and I believe that with your help we'll manage to find out everything we need to know. You told my men you had a licence plate number.'

'Captain,' said Mireille, 'I'm sure that we'll become good friends. When that happens you'll do me a favour, I'll give you a hand . . . but for now, let's do things my way: I tell you something, you tell me something. Okay?'

'Absolutely,' muttered Karamanlis. 'Well then, I'll start. I've known this man for years under what has proven to be a false name. He knew about the existence of an archaeological find, very precious, which in all probability was brought to Athens by Malidis or Harvatis himself on the night between the sixteenth and seventeenth of November 1973. From Ephira, I must presume.'

'You've inferred this from my investigation in the excavation journals, correct?'

'Well, yes.'

'Okay, so now we're even. If I hadn't told you that Harvatis was digging at Ephira, you wouldn't have been able to connect that object with Harvatis, Malidis and – let's say – our Mister X.'

'You're terrible. You know that here people are used to collaborating with the police without expecting something in return.'

'Naturally, my collaboration is free of charge, but I want to understand exactly what we're talking about. Seems legitimate to me. So this man is connected with this archaeological object. In what way? And what kind of object is it?'

'Look, I'm the one who asks questions in this office.'

'If that's how it is . . .' Mireille started to get up.

'Sit down, please. We need to identify this man. People's lives are at risk. And he . . . he is the only lead we have which could enable us to avert this threat.'

'I see. Then tell me what the object was. I teach history of art, perhaps I can offer an interpretation.'

'Your turn first.'

'My turn? All right, I've found a flower shop in town that has been paid to put fresh flowers every week on Harvatis's grave, by . . . this man,' she said, again pointing to the pencil sketch on Karamanlis's desk.

'How on earth did you manage . . .'

'Your turn to tell me what the object was. It could be very important.'

'A vase. A very ancient vase. In gold.'

'Did you see it?'

'Yes I did.'

'Where?'

'In the basement of the National Archaeological Museum.'

'Where, obviously, it no longer is?'

'Obviously.'

'Who has it?

'I think he has it,' said Karamanlis, nodding towards the drawing. 'He may be trying to sell it to two foreigners.'

'Can you remember what the vase is like? Can you describe it?'

Karamanlis made an effort to picture the vase, although he'd only seen it for a few moments ten years earlier.

'. . . and at the centre there was a man with something on his shoulder, a shovel or a club, something like that. And behind him a bull, a ram and a pig . . . or a boar, I guess. Then someone hit me over the head, and when I came to, the vase had disappeared. I'm convinced that he, this man here, had it stolen.'

'Maybe it was his. Or maybe it was for him.'

'Miss, how did you come to sketch out this likeness, and what is the licence plate number?'

'Okay. On the night between the sixteenth and seventeenth of November 1973, at least two people arrive in Athens from Ephira: Professor Harvatis, let's say, and his dig foreman, Aristotelis Malidis. Harvatis is dying, but when Doctor Psarros later examines the autopsy results, he is unable to establish the cause of death. His symptoms seemed to indicate a massive heart attack, but there are no traces of heart damage whatsoever. The vase is certainly brought into the museum basement by Malidis: he works for the Antiquities and Fine Arts Service and has easy access to the museum. But it's just a temporary storage place; it soon disappears, into the hands of our mysterious friend, we can presume . . .'

'You're good,' said Karamanlis, annoyed at not having pulled things together himself throughout all these years. 'But you think I've never reflected on all this myself? And what then? Well? What then? See, you see? All of this leads nowhere, if we don't

understand who this man is and what he wants. And you know
something you're not telling me.'

'You were there that night at the assault of the Polytechnic,
weren't you, Captain Karamanlis? Weren't you?' She recalled the
note scribbled at the bottom of Michel's notebook page: 'Athens
. . . how will I ever find the heart to see Athens again?'

'That's right. What of it?'

'Nothing. It has nothing to do with the rest.'

'Then are you going to tell me how you made that sketch?
Trust me: there are human lives at stake.'

Mireille took out one of the photographs she had taken of
the bas-relief that day near Cape Sounion, and handed it to him:
'I traced it from this.'

Karamanlis took it and examined it, astounded.

'Can you give this to me? You must have the negative.'

'I'm sorry, I'm afraid I don't. It's the only copy I've got and I
can't give it to you.'

'Let me get a copy made, at least.'

Mireille nodded.

'It won't take more than five minutes,' said Karamanlis. 'I'll
bring it right back for you.'

He left the office and went to the photo lab. As soon as he
had closed the door after him, Mireille noticed a bag on the floor
next to his seat. She couldn't resist the temptation to look inside,
but there was nothing of interest. Some legal papers, documents,
an appointment book earmarked at yesterday's date. There was
a phrase written in pencil at the centre of the page that seemed
strange. She copied it as best she could and put the book back in
its place. Karamanlis entered shortly afterwards, the photograph
in his hand.

'Where did you take this photograph? What's behind this
sculpture?'

'I took it in the studio of the artist who crafted it. That's all I
can tell you for now.'

'But what is it, in your opinion?'

'I've studied it at length, and thought about it a lot. There's only one explanation, in my eyes. It's a mask. I'd say a . . . funeral mask.' She fell silent for an instant, then added: 'You've seen the golden masks from the Royal Tomb of Mycenae at the National Museum, haven't you?'

19

'I WANT TO KNOW where she's staying and I want a car on her constantly, beginning this instant.'

The officer consulted the main computer of the *astynomia*: 'She's been at the Neon Hermis in the Plaka for three or four days.'

'Who do we have in the area?'

'Manoulis and Papanikolaou.'

'Are they on the ball?'

'They're good, Captain.'

'I want them to search her room. I want that licence plate number.'

'Yes, sir, Captain.'

'Wait a minute: tell them to go lightly. I don't want her to notice a thing.'

'Okay. The velvet touch.'

'And I want her telephone under surveillance. Right away.'

'But it's a hotel extension, sir.'

'I couldn't care less. Bug the whole hotel if you have to.'

'As you wish, Captain.'

Karamanlis went back to his office and took out the two photographs again: Heleni and Angheliki Kaloudis, Kiki to her friends. Like two drops of water. He looked at his appointment book, trying to make sense of the gibberish pronounced by the seer, words he'd rather forget: 'Stay away from the vertex of the great triangle. And beware the pyramid at the vertex of the triangle.' Pure idiocy. Geometrical bunk. Didn't make any sense at all. Just about anyone could make up something that stupid, even if he weren't a psychic. There was a knock at the door.

'Captain: got a weird one for you.'

'What is it?'

'We've got a lead on that identikit.'

'From where?'

'Corsica.'

Karamanlis stood up and followed his subordinate into the fax room.

'Here, take a look at this.'

He was handed a faxed photo showing a platoon of the Foreign Legion in an African oasis: the head of one of the officers was circled.

'A warrant officer from Sûreté of San Clemente says he recognizes the man in the identikit: he was his commander in the Legion when they were backing the British between Sidi el-Barrani and Alexandria. This photo was taken at the Siwa oasis on 14 April 1943.'

Karamanlis took a magnifying lens and inspected the photo carefully. 'Looks a hell of a lot like him,' he said, 'but it can't be him. This man would be at least eighty years old now. The man we're looking for is no more than fifty. Keep at it. Something may still come in.'

NORMAN AND MICHEL had discussed at length what their next move should be after their meeting with Karamanlis. They added up everything they knew, or thought they knew, about the event that had affected their lives so profoundly, but still had no clue about what might happen next. They realized that they'd completely lost track of the vase of Tiresias, the object that could have linked them up with that night so long ago and led them to the others who had played a role in the tragedy. At least, those who had survived. One thing was certain: since all the messages had come from Ephira – and the Oracle of the Dead had started spouting predictions again – that was where they had to go, sooner or later. Michel still knew people at the National Museum through his academic contacts, and he managed to get some precise information about Aristotelis Malidis without raising suspicions: he'd retired two years ago and had gone back to Parga, where he had a little house. Michel contacted the State Treasury Department and had them give him the address where his retirement cheque was sent.

'He's got to know more than we do,' Michel said to Norman. 'He was here for years after you and I left.'

'Maybe he even knows where the vase is. He was the last person to see it and probably the only one. Maybe he was behind the person who contacted us at Dirou . . .'

'Could be.'

They left their hotel in Athens and headed west towards Missolungi. From there they went north to Ephira. When they reached the town it was nearly dusk: the days were getting shorter and shorter. Norman stopped the car in a little square and got out to stretch his legs. Michel joined him, leaning against the car's bumper, and lit a cigarette.

'My God, it's so beautiful here. I've never forgotten these places. Look, up there on the hillside: the little town where we saw Claudio for the first time and gave him a lift to Parga.'

'The beginning of a great friendship.'

'Yeah. Beautiful. And short. It was here that it all started. Look, the sun setting over the sea of Paxos. A cry rises from the dark recesses of the island's caves: "The great god Pan is dead!"'

'Right. And night falls on the black firs of Parga.'

'And on the cold banks of the Acheron . . .'

'My God, Michel, what a dreamer you are! Look around you. Just look. There's a pizza parlour right over there. And check out the discotech that's going up. The cold banks of the Acheron will be rocking soon. Michel, there are certain situations that you live too intensely. This is a place just like any other, and why we're here is to put an end to all that we've suffered over these years. To find a lost friend, if we can, and to prevent another tragedy, if we can. To find an incredibly old and beautiful object, if possible, and to discover what it means. But this is a place just like any other place, understand?'

Michel threw the butt of his Gauloise on to the asphalt. 'There's no need for you to play things down. I feel perfectly calm and I'm not about to go off the deep end. And right, this is a place like lots of others: down there is the cliff of Laucade, from which human victims were hurled into the sea for centuries. Ithaca, over there, is the birthplace of the most astounding and profound legend of all humankind. And here's the island of Paxos, from which a mysterious voice announced the end of the ancient world. That lagoon we just drove through was where the fate of the world was decided, when Octavianus and Agrippa defeated Mark Antony and Cleopatra. The Peloponnesian Wars began in this sea; they led to the end of the civilization of Athens. And here, at our feet, the Acheron poured into the Stygian swamp. Beyond those mountains in front of us, the Pelasgian oracle of Dodona – the oldest in Europe – spoke for over two thousand years through the rustling leaves of a gigantic oak tree. You're absolutely right, Norman, this is exactly a place just like any other place.'

Norman grumbled, 'Can't we get something to eat? I'm starving,' and got back into the car. Michel followed.

'Want to bet that Tassos's tavern in Parga is still open?'

'That would be great. I'd love to stop there. Do you think he'll recognize us?'

'Well, we never used to stay very long, but we did go often.'

Tassos had lost a lot of hair and put on a belly, but his memory was still good: 'Welcome back, boys,' he said when he saw them. 'How are you?'

'Pretty well, Tassos, and we're happy to see you,' said Norman. 'We thought we'd get a bite to eat before going to our hotel.' They sat down outside, under a canopy.

'Sure!' said Tassos as he poured them some wine and gestured to the waiter to bring out some food. 'Are you sure you don't want to come inside? It'll start getting cold soon.'

'No thanks,' said Michel. 'We're dressed well, and we've been sitting inside the car all day.'

'Your choice,' said their host, and started reminiscing about the time when he'd first met them, still students, roaming the hills of Epirus in their search for antiquities. 'And your Italian friend?'

'Ahh, Claudio has left us, Tassos. He got mixed up in the Polytechnic affair ten years ago. He's dead.'

'Dead?' said the host, and his voice revealed surprise mixed with incredulity.

'That's what we were told,' said Norman. 'You never heard otherwise, did you?'

Tassos poured himself a glass of wine and lifted it in a toast: 'To your health!' The others lifted their glasses as well, smiling with a melancholy air. 'Isn't that a sin! It would have been beautiful to have a toast together, like in the good old times. You say he died at the Polytechnic?'

'Not that night. A couple of days later. That's what we read in the papers,' said Norman again.

There was no one along the road and Tassos's tavern was half empty. A dog on a chain started to bark suddenly, and others from all the nearby houses started howling as well, filling the valley with fragile echoes. The host kicked the dog, who yelped in pain and lay down quietly. The other dogs quieted down as well, one by one. The distant sea was a slab of slate, but a cold, grey wind started to rise and invade the valley. The waiter brought their dinner and Tassos poured himself another glass.

'I don't know, I could have sworn I'd seen your friend around, but I couldn't say when. Maybe I'm wrong. It will be the anniversary of the Polytechnic battle in a few days . . .'

'Right,' said Michel. 'And I'll have to go back to Grenoble soon. The school year will be starting.'

'Do you know Aristotelis Malidis?' asked Norman.

'Old Ari? You bet.'

'Where does he live?'

'He has an apartment in Parga, but I think he's renting it. He's the custodian of the archaeological site at Ephira. You know, the Oracle of the Dead. He lives in the guest house and takes a few visitors around during the tourist season.'

When it was completely dark and starting to get quite cold, Norman and Michel paid for the meal and left for their hotel.

'Did you hear what Tassos said about Claudio?' asked Norman.

'Yes, I did. And I can't stand this uncertainty. I just can't stand it any more.'

10 *November, 8 p.m.*

'Michel. It's Mireille, I've finally found you.'

'Darling! It's wonderful to hear your voice. I would have called you later this evening.'

'It's safer for me to call you.'

'Where are you?'

'At home. Senator Laroche has called several times; he says he hasn't heard from you.'

'That's true. Tell him I'm very busy with this important research I'm doing and that I'll call him as soon as I can. That should hold him off for a while, I hope.'

'When are you coming back?'

'Soon, I think.'

'There's so much I want to say, Michel, but I don't like making love over the telephone. I've never been away from you for so long. I can't understand what's important enough to keep you away from me all this time.'

'It's been awful for me. I'm living in this strange dimension which I can't even explain to myself. I think you'll understand when I come back and tell you everything.'

'What's happening there right now?'

'Nothing. Nothing's happening. Everything is strangely

motionless in this place: the birds don't sing and they don't fly. The sea itself is absolutely still.'

'Come back to me. Now.'

'Mireille, Mireille, I feel so close to you.'

'So do I. That makes it worse.'

'Don't say that. I have to finish this research.'

'Michel. Tell me what you're looking for. It's important. Maybe I can help, you know.'

'It's difficult . . . hard to say. I'm looking for a piece of my life and I'm looking for a lost friend. I'm looking—'

'Who is this friend?'

'His name was Claudio.'

'An Italian? Why are you looking for him there?'

'It seems that someone has seen him around here. There's still hope . . .'

'Michel, I'm not at home. I'm in Greece.'

'You're in Greece? Where?'

'Wherever I can find an answer to my questions. Whatever you're looking for concerns me as well, have you forgotten? I have to know too. I love you.'

'Mireille. Please, go home.'

'Why?'

'Because you can't follow me down this road. It's too dangerous.'

'What about your friend Norman?'

'He was there when it all started. Go back home, Mireille, darling, do it for me.'

'Silly. If you found me naked in your bed . . .'

'Go home. Please. I'm . . . I'm about to consult the Oracle of the Dead and I don't know . . . what the answer will be.'

'No. I'm going to find you and pull you out of this.'

'Mireille, I want you with me, but I'm at a point of no return. I can feel that something's about to happen. Please go away.'

'I don't want to.'

'Mireille. There's a stain in my past, and I have to work my way out of it. Alone. Even if it's the last thing I do. It's something that causes me deep pain. And incredible shame. Something I have the right to keep to myself.' Mireille fell silent, humiliated. 'I'm sorry,' said Michel. 'I didn't want to hurt you. When I can explain it all, you'll understand.'

'Michel, strange things are happening on 17 Dionysìou Street. I think I've found the man who printed that study of Harvatis's that you're interested in.'

Michel was speechless: 'How could you know . . .'

'I read some notes you left on your desk in Grenoble, and I'm following a good lead here in Athens. Are you still sure you don't want to see me?'

'Mireille, you are playing with fire. But if you want to come, come.'

'I will, as soon as I've solved a little problem. I'll call you soon. In the meantime, don't worry about me. I know how to take care of myself. You're the one I'm worried about. If something should happen to you, it wouldn't be easy to find a stand-in . . . in my heart, Michel, in my mind, in my eyes . . . in my bed.'

Mireille hung up without imagining that her conversation with Michel would be relayed to Captain Karamanlis in a few minutes' time, right down to the smallest detail. She went to sit at her desk and started looking at the notes she'd taken from Michel's papers in his study in Grenoble, piecing them together with the information she'd got in Athens. She realized that there were many odd elements in Norman and Michel's trip to Greece, but she still couldn't manage to get at the heart of the whole thing. If only she could get behind that shutter on Dionysìou Street . . .

The doorman buzzed up: 'A visitor for you in the lobby, miss.' It was Mr Zòlotas.

'I'm so happy to see you!' said Mireille.

'So am I, miss.'

'Any news?'

'No, unfortunately. I looked up that licence plate. It's regis-

tered to a leasing company whose general headquarters are in
Beirut. They have a branch here in Athens, on Odòs Dimokritou,
but that licence plate number comes out of Beirut. Here in
Athens they have no idea who the car dealer or leaseholder is.
As for the property registry, I hope to have an answer for you
tomorrow.'

'Thank you, Mr Zolotas. You've been wonderful. Can I offer
you something to drink?'

'Coffee would be good. They make excellent espresso here.'

Mireille ordered coffee for her guest and a glass of water for
herself.

'How did it go with Karamanlis?' asked Zolotas.

'He really wants that licence plate number, but I didn't give
it to him. I did find out that, most probably, Professor Harvatis
was carrying a very precious find with him that night, an ancient
gold vase from Ephira. Karamanlis himself told me that it
disappeared that same night without leaving a trace. I somehow
have the impression that it was connected with Professor Harvatis's death.'

'That could be,' nodded Zolotas. 'That was an unfortunate
night for many of us. Well, it's a bit late, my dear. I think I'll be
going to bed. If you need me again, please call. I'd be delighted
to help you.'

'I will,' promised Mireille. 'Goodnight, Mr Zolotas.'

Mireille went back to her room, turned on the radio, and
sifted through all the papers she had on her desk. She'd put a
photo of Michel on the mirror and she lifted her eyes to look
at him. He felt like her guardian angel. The phone rang again:
'Miss, I'm the waiter from Milos's Bar: the black Mercedes is
parked on Dionysìou Street.'

'Thank you,' said Mireille. 'I'll be right there. Please don't let
him out of your sight!'

'Don't worry,' said the waiter. 'I'll be here for at least a
couple more hours.'

Mireille looked out of the window: the sky was black and
there wasn't a star to be seen. It was windy and looked like rain.

She pulled on the only heavy sweater she'd brought with her, threw her leather jacket over her shoulders and left.

A minute later Pavlos Karamanlis learned from headquarters that Mireille was heading towards Dionysìou Street because someone had told her that a black Mercedes was parked there, probably the same one he was looking for. 'Post two undercover cars at the beginning and end of the street to keep an eye on the vehicle without being seen. I'll be there in ten minutes.'

The waiter had cleared off the last two tables and served a couple of coffees when he went back to the window to check out the car. There was still someone sitting in the driver's seat, he could make him out against the light. What was he doing in there all alone at eleven o'clock at night? The waiter noticed a big antenna on the roof and saw that the man was holding something to his ear. Could he be making a phone call?

CLAUDIO SETTI'S VOICE crackled, distorted by electrical discharges over the line: a strong storm was brewing up somewhere. 'Commander, it's Claudio, can you hear me?'

'I hear you. Where are you, son?'

'Metsovon. I'll be going to Preveza. Is our appointment at the Cimmerian promontory still on?'

'It is. Although I can't move from here yet.'

'But I need to see you. Where are you now?'

'I'm in Athens. I'm calling from the car phone. Listen, you have to go see Ari in Ephira. Tell him he has to take the vase to the place we've agreed upon. He'll get the usual signal by phone. Tell him that I thank him for everything he's done for me. This is the last thing I will ever ask him. The last. And you be careful: there are people around who know you. Do you understand what I'm saying? Only go out at night, and after you've made sure there's no one around.'

'But Commander, why did you have me come here?'

'I told you. People are gathering. You have to lure them away. Away to a place where there's no one and nothing they can count on. Where no one will look for you afterwards. Are you up to it?'

'Will you be here?'

'I'll be there, and everything will go fine. This is important, son, and it's the last thing I'll be asking of you. We'll settle up with Karamanlis and the others, at the right place and time. I'll explain everything to you once . . .' his voice faded off.

'Commander? Commander, I can't hear you any longer. Are you still there?'

'Yes, son, but I have to leave you. There's something suspicious going on here, I'm afraid . . .'

'Are you in danger?'

'It's not easy to trap me, but someone's trying. Please, do as I've asked.'

'I will, but be careful. Are you sure you don't need me? I can be in Athens in just three hours . . .'

'No, I'll get out of this one myself. Ari will give you the next appointment. I have to go now, I've got myself to worry about.'

'As you wish. Let me know what happens.'

MIREILLE DECIDED TO park at a distance so she wouldn't be seen. She walked down the shadowy, tree-lined road which led to Dionysìou Street. Before crossing the intersection she stopped, having noticed a car which was just pulling over. A man got out and walked past the street corner, craning his neck towards the black Mercedes parked a couple of hundred metres further up the street. Other men materialized from the darkness to join him; he seemed to be giving them instructions.

Mireille got closer, and as he turned his head she recognized him: it was Captain Karamanlis. She saw him take a radio receiver from his car and continue to give instructions: was he setting a trap for the man in the Mercedes?

Mireille turned back, ran around the block to reach another side street that led into Dionysìou Street and found herself practically straight across the road from where the Mercedes was parked. She leaned forward and looked both to her right and to her left: she could see the men taking position; or at least, that's what they seemed to be doing. She raised her eyes and could even see someone poised up on the roof.

She thought of the man who had posed for that disturbing mask. His proud features and high forehead. She thought of Karamanlis's hypocritical voice and cold hands, and her instinct told her which side she had to take. She'd run towards the Mercedes and drag him over to the side street she was on; there were a lot of low houses with terraces he could use to easily escape over the rooftops of the city. But as she was gathering her courage to do so, she saw two cars roar up on either side of the street, blocking it off completely. They screeched to a stop, and the men who vaulted out surrounded the Mercedes in no time. Mireille flattened herself against the shadowy wall.

Karamanlis approached the driver's side with a torch in hand and put out his hand to open the door, but pulled back angrily. There was no one in the car. It was completely empty. 'That's not possible,' he said. 'I saw him, you all saw him!'

'You're right, Captain,' agreed one of the men, drawing closer. 'We saw him too.'

Karamanlis stepped away; he could practically hear that taunting voice from the shack up at Mount Peristeri: 'What are you doing here, Captain Karamanlis?' He was furious. 'There must be some kind of trapdoor in this thing. Inspect the bottom, quickly.'

One of the men stretched out on the ground under the car. 'Right again, Captain,' he said shortly. 'There's a slide-out panel on the floor of the passenger's side, and there's a manhole cover right underneath.'

'Pull it off!' ordered Karamanlis. They pushed the car a few metres up the road and the captain dropped down into the sewer hole, followed by a couple of his men. Mireille was watching everything, checking behind her every now and then to make sure no one was sneaking up on her. She could hear Karamanlis's suffocated voice crying out: 'Follow me, hurry! I can hear the sound of his footsteps!'

It was cold and her hands were numb, yet her armpits and breasts were moist with perspiration. She tried to imagine what was happening underground, where the owner of the black Mercedes might be at that moment. Maybe his pursuers were already on his heels. Maybe he was wandering, out of breath and disoriented, under low, dripping vaults, putrid water and disgusting rats at his feet.

'Check all the other manholes in the area!' ordered the officer who had stayed behind with the car. 'He won't have any way out.'

ARI HAD JUST finished his tour of inspection and was watching television. The evening news was commemorating the events that he had been a part of ten years earlier, showing the scenes of the assault on the Polytechnic. The smoke bombs, the screeching tanks, the shouted threats, an *astynomia* officer shooting at close range. But the commentator's voice soothed over the old tragedy, filed it away, defused it so it seemed like so much ancient history.

Old Ari felt inexplicably nervous, agitated. He got up often to go to the window. It was pitch-black outside and raining; the windows reflected the wavering images of the TV. The doorbell rang and Ari went to answer it:

'Who's there?'

'It's me, Ari, it's Michel Charrier. Do you remember me?'

Ari backed up in confusion. 'Oh, yes,' he said after a moment of bewilderment. 'Oh yes, I remember, my boy. Come in, don't stand there at the doorway, come in and sit down.' He turned off the television and went to a cabinet, from which he took a bottle and a couple of glasses. Michel was wearing a raincoat and his hair was wet and tousled. He sat down and combed it through with nervous fingers.

'Do you like Metaxa?'

'You aren't surprised to see me.'

'At my age nothing surprises me.'

'You're not so old. You're not even seventy.'

'It feels more like a hundred. I'm tired, my boy, tired. But tell me then, to what do I owe the pleasure of your visit?'

Michel appeared confused, ashamed. 'Ari, it's hard for me to find the words. We've never seen each other since . . . that awful night.'

'No. Not since then.'

'And don't you want to know why?'

'From the tone of your voice it must be a sad story, or one that is difficult to tell. You don't owe me any explanation, my boy, I'm only an old custodian. I've retired to this quiet little corner to end my days. You don't owe me any explanation at all.'

He looked at Michel with clear, tranquil eyes. Michel fell silent, sipping his brandy, while the old man fingered a *komboloi* of fake amber, clicking the beads together in his hands.

'I was taken away by the police, Ari . . .'

'Please, I don't want—'

'They forced me to talk.'

'What does it matter? It's all finished now, part of the past . . .'

'No. That's not true. Claudio Setti is still alive, I'm certain of it. You must know something. I've been told that he's been seen around here. Is that true, Ari?'

Ari stood up and walked to the window. The soft sound of a flute and singing could be heard coming from town. He looked out into the darkness. 'Someone is playing the flute at Tassos's place . . . it's a beautiful song, can you hear it? The music is lovely.' The singing could be heard more clearly now, a melody without words, and Ari started singing it to himself, following the distant notes.

Michel started: 'It's his song! It's him singing somewhere in the night. This agony is going to kill me.' He jumped up, went to the door and threw it open. 'Where are you?' he yelled. 'You don't want to sing with me any more? Where are you!'

Ari put a hand on his shoulder: 'It's raining. You're getting all wet, come back inside.'

Michel swallowed the tears rising to his eyes and turned towards the old man. 'Ari, in the name of God, listen to me. Norman and I have come back to Greece after all these years, after we'd nearly succeeded in forgetting everything, because someone spoke to us about that golden vase. Remember it? The golden vase you brought to Athens that night. That's what's lured us back here after so long. The vase disappeared that night. Only you could have taken it, so you must know why we've been called back here. First to the Peloponnesus and now to Epirus, through a series of messages, of clues ... You are our only contact with that damned vase. You brought it to Athens and you took it away. Ari, it's Claudio who wants us here, isn't it? Ari, you were with us, you knew we were just kids – why were we touched by such a terrible destiny that night? Why us?'

The old man looked at him with resigned compassion: 'We are all touched by destiny, my boy. It's difficult to pull back when our moment comes.'

'Ari, for the love of God, if Claudio's alive, tell me how I can talk to him ... oh God, let me talk to him ...'

Ari had an absorbed expression and seemed to be listening to the distant music: 'Oh, my boy ... I don't know whether he is dead or alive, but certainly there is no language that you could speak in that he would understand ... Do you know what I mean? Do you?'

The music was confused now by the sound of the rain. More distant, yet even more beautiful and tormented, pushed and pulled by the gusts of the western wind.

'Ari. Help me find him. In the name of God, I beg of you.'

Ari slid the *komboloi* beads through his fingers. When he opened his mouth, his gaze was intense and penetrating: 'Go away, son. For heaven's sake, go home and forget everything. Go away ... far away. You're still in time.'

'I can't. Tell me where to look for him.'

The old man lifted his eyes to the ceiling as if to escape from

Michel's obsessive insistence. 'Your friend . . . Norman – his name is Norman, isn't it? Where is he now?'

'He's here in Ephira. He's looking for him too.'

The old man stared at him with eyes full of melancholy, shiny with emotion: 'This could have been a happy celebration. We could be here drinking a glass of retsina together and remembering old times . . .'

Michel took his hands and leaned closer until they were face to face, his expression troubled: 'Tell me . . . where . . . he is. Tell me now.'

'Look for the crossing between life and death . . . if death is what you want, you'll find him. At the pier at Canakkale, the day after tomorrow, just before midnight. Maybe you'll see him there.'

Michel's face lit up: 'I was right, then. Claudio is alive.'

'Alive? Oh, my son . . . there are places . . . times . . . and people for whom the words "alive" or "dead" no longer have the meaning we are familiar with.'

20

MIREILLE FELT FRUSTRATED and impotent and somehow to blame for what had happened: Karamanlis must have been there because of her. How else could he have known about it? Maybe it had been naive of her to trust Zolotas, or maybe the police were watching her. While she was pondering what could possibly have happened, she was startled to hear a barely perceptible creaking behind her, and the low yelping of a dog.

There was an enclosure wall just a few metres away, behind which she could see an external stair leading from a little door on the second floor of a modest building. A man wrapped in a dark coat, wearing a hat, was just coming out of that door. A big, dark-haired dog was greeting him joyfully and wagging his tail. The man closed the door, touched the rain gutter above with his right hand and bent down to pet the dog who was rubbing against him. He went down the stairs and disappeared from her sight, but Mireille thought she could hear him talking softly to the dog, who was whimpering in response to his owner's affectionate voice.

A minute later, the little door which opened on to the street from the courtyard opened and the man walked off in the opposite direction. Mireille, hidden behind the wall, watched him walk, neither quickly nor slowly, with long, even strides, his hands in his pockets. She suddenly had a keen sensation of having seen that walk before, that way of holding his head so erect: it was him! The man from the black Mercedes, the man who had posed for that mysterious sculpture, that stone face with its closed eyes.

How could that be? He had just dropped down into the sewers through a manhole – Karamanlis had heard his steps underground. And yet in her heart she felt sure it was him. She walked quickly around the block, passing just a few metres from Karamanlis's men, still crowded around the sewer hole. The shutter of number 17 was still locked, but light glowed faintly from the basement of the next door down. The sign above it said 'Artopoleion', and the delicious smell of warm bread meant that the baker had begun his long night's work.

She spotted the man opposite her, walking in her direction. She measured her pace so that they crossed paths under the street light, and she looked up into his face: it was him, without a doubt. She sniffed him in passing – if he'd been in the sewers she'd definitely be able to perceive the stench.

He smelled like bread. Fresh bread right out of the oven. She couldn't understand it. She stopped at the first intersection and turned around. He was about thirty metres away, and was entering a phone booth.

THE TELEPHONE BEGAN ringing in Ari's house, but he made no move to answer it.

'I don't understand what you're saying,' said Michel, starting at the noise, 'but if he's alive, I'll find him and I'll make him listen to me. He'll have to listen to me.'

The telephone rang five times, fell silent and then started up again. Michel looked at Ari expectantly, then looked back at the phone on the table. The ringing filled up the bare little room with an intolerable anxiety, until Ari suddenly put his hand down on the receiver. The ringing stopped and then started again. Four times.

The old man didn't say a word, as if he were listening intently, then said: 'There are places and times and even people for whom the words "life" or "death" do not have the meaning we are accustomed to . . . the final hour has come. I beg you, my son, leave. Go home. I shouldn't be the one who has to tell you, but I'm telling you. Go home while you're still in time to save yourself, please! Oh, Holy Mother of God, wouldn't it have been nice to get together for a glass of ouzo, a song . . . it would have been nice. Oh, Dear Mother of God. Leave now, my boy, go away.'

'The day after tomorrow at Canakkale . . . there's not much time.' Michel got up, opened the door and clutched his raincoat close as he was hit by a strong gust of rain. The sound of the flute had stopped, and the last light in Tassos's tavern had been turned off.

MIREILLE OBSERVED HIM carefully and had the impression that the man had not said a word into the telephone. Maybe there was no one there on the other side of the line. Or maybe he was sending some sort of signal. What could it be? And how could he have escaped their trap? He smelled like bread. The bakery! The light coming from the basement apartment next to number 17 – he must have gone through there and come up on the other side of the street. She remembered that little gesture, his hand rapidly passing over the gutter above the door. She went back to the house and approached the little door in the enclosure wall, but a sudden shuffling and a deep growl reminded her that there was a guard on duty.

She backed off to take a better look at the door the man had come out of, and noticed that the roof of the building was topped by a little attic that could easily by reached by climbing up a thick wisteria trunk in front of the next house over: the wisteria formed a trellis above the attic. The wind was even blowing in that direction; with any luck, the dog wouldn't smell her.

She was frightened and had a strong impulse to flee, to go back to the hotel and wait for Michel. But she was also keenly aware that she had to do this for him; nothing had ever been so necessary in her whole lifetime.

She scrambled up the trunk without much difficulty. Every

so often she'd feel a sparrow flitting away through her fingers; they'd chosen the boughs for their evening shelter. The beating of the small frightened wings vanished instantly into the dark.

She reached the attic, covered with dry leaves, and dropped to the rooftop of the neighbouring house, crawling over the tiles until she reached the door. She stretched her hand into the rain gutter and felt around until she came up with a Yale key. The key to enter the secret refuge of that enigmatic man. Maybe she'd be able to uncover the mystery of that mask, and of the light which filtered from under the closed shutter of number 17 Dionysìou Street late at night.

She had to figure out where the dog was. As soon as she dropped down on to the landing, she knew he would leap at her. She had to manage to open the door and close it again as quickly as possible. But where was the dog? She waited with an ever more rapidly beating heart, aching to hear him move so that she could calculate how far away from the door he was. Was he down in the garden, or already on the stairs? But not a sound was to be heard: he was absolutely still and hidden somewhere in the garden, ready to spring, no doubt.

She waited a bit longer: she had no intention of being torn to scraps just to satisfy her curiosity. She heard a low mewing and saw the dark shadow of a cat standing out on the top of the enclosure wall. Finally! He'd have to come out now. The cat continued its slow prowl, but nothing happened. It stopped and hesitated, wiggling its front paw into the emptiness, then jumped into the garden. Again, no response from the dog. It seemed that the guardian knew that the intruder was elsewhere, and was waiting for her, immobile, on the threshold.

Mireille decided that she had to try anyway. If she left without trying, she'd never be able to forgive herself. She considered how best to drop on to the landing without making any noise, keeping the key in her hand so she wouldn't have to fumble around in her pocket for it. She ardently hoped that she'd have enough time to slip it into the keyhole and turn it before the dog went wild. She took a deep breath and lowered herself, feeling for the landing with her toe. She dropped down without making a sound. She was in the doorway, lit by the lamp above the door. Anyone could see her, as she had seen the man when he stepped out.

She looked for the keyhole and feverishly tried to insert the key. It wouldn't go in. She reversed it and was finally able to turn it; with a sharp click, the door opened. Mireille stopped a second, straining for any sound in the darkness.

She was lucky: total silence. She pushed the door open slowly so it wouldn't creak, slipped into the opening and turned to close it behind her when a sudden furious barking froze her in terror. The dog had catapulted from the top of the stairs and was bent on keeping the door open with claws and teeth. Mireille pushed with all her might, but the dog had nearly got his head through the jamb and was struggling to get his body through as well. His frenzied barking echoed in the closed room with endless, overwhelming energy. Mireille had her back against the door and her feet propped firmly on the floor, but she realized that her strength could not hold out any longer than a few more seconds.

Amidst her confusion and terror, she remembered that she had a can of spray deodorant in her inside jacket pocket. She felt for it and found it. Keeping her feet firmly planted, she turned and sprayed its contents into the dog's face. Suddenly blinded, he pulled back and Mireille pushed the door shut. A moment later he began his attack again with even greater fury, hurling himself against the door so it felt like the whole wall was shaking. Mireille quickly ran down what seemed to be a dark hall, then crossed a room and started down some stairs. The dog's barking seemed slightly allayed, fading into a low, distant growling.

She found a switch and turned on the light. She was inside, finally, but inside what? She walked between two white, completely bare walls and found herself in front of another door. She figured that she must be at ground level and opened it on to another room, not very big but beautifully furnished. In the corner, on an easel, was an unfinished portrait of a woman: she appeared to be an actress dressed in a costume from a classical theatre piece. She was quite lovely, with an aristocratic, intense beauty, reminding her a bit of Irene Papas. On the wall was the photo of a bare-chested young man, no older than thirty, drawing a double-pulleyed bow. The youth was lean and muscular, with the sun at his shoulders illuminating his left arm. A diagonal beam struck his eye, concentrated on its target, creating a sinister flash. That dark glaring eye seemed to be intent on delivering implacable justice.

There were no windows in the room, nor were there any in the hall preceding it. She caught her breath in fright and tension. What would she do if the owner of this strange refuge suddenly appeared? She walked towards the door at the end of the room and was about to turn the handle when she pulled back her hand, her heart skipping a beat: agitated steps sounded in the next room.

She wheeled around, desperately seeking shelter, somewhere to hide. Nothing. She couldn't leave the way she came or the dog would tear her to shreds. There was no way out.

'THAT WAY, CAPTAIN, he went that way. I can hear his footsteps. We've got him now. Hurry, Captain!'

Karamanlis ran panting towards the beam of the torch which one of his men was using to illuminate the walkway alongside the sewer's trunk line.

'Did you see him?' he asked, leaning back against the dripping wall.

'No, Captain, but I could hear him.'

'I don't hear anything.'

'No, really, Captain . . .'

'He's duped us again. That son of a bitch has got away.' All at once he heard the sound of footsteps in the distance, accelerating into a run.

'You are right, dammit, it's coming from that way. Come on! Get moving and catch him for me, goddamn you, I'm out of breath.'

The policeman and his companion ran off in the direction of
the noise but soon came up short against a solid wall. They
looked each other in the face, astonished, and turned back in
the direction they'd come from. The silence was total under the
mould-encrusted vaults, but not a minute passed before they
heard the footsteps again, nice and slow this time, as if whoever
it was was perfectly at home in that stinking underground maze,
indifferently touring his realm.

MIREILLE WAS CROUCHING in the only concealed corner, behind
a couch, but her hiding place offered her no security. Once those
footsteps reached the threshold and the door was opened, how
long would she be able to remain hidden? A minute? Two? But
there was something strange in the pace of those steps. They
slowed down, stopped, quickened, but never got any closer.

Mireille plucked up her courage and went to the door. She
clutched the handle and opened it just a crack. On the other side
were a few descending steps and another rather small room,
faintly lit by a hanging bulb and by what seemed to be the
flashing lights of an electronic control panel. Suddenly she could
hear the steps again, but there was obviously no one in that
small space.

She opened the door wide and walked down the stairs. The
electronic console in front of her stretched along the far wall.
The display showed a glowing layout that looked like a network
of streets, or a railroad or subway. At a point at which a lateral
pathway cut away from the main trunk she could see a pulsating
red light moving along at the same rate as the footsteps she was
still hearing. A trick. A computerized illusion. But what was the
point?

There were some switches at the lower left. She impulsively
flipped the first one and a voice made her start with fright: 'Stop!
Stop, you imbeciles. Can't you see that we're running around
like idiots in this shit, in pursuit of no one at all!?'

'But Captain, you heard the footsteps yourself . . .'

'Yeah, and we're still hearing footsteps. And where are they coming from? From over there, where we just were. And the only way to over there is from over here. Did you see anyone pass by? It's a trick, dammit, a dirty, fucking trick.'

My God, it was Karamanlis! And his voice resounded as if he were standing under a vault. So he must still be in the sewers, and this machinery must be able to identify his position – perhaps from his voice or his own footsteps or those of his men – and program acoustic traps to lure them here and there down the sewer lines, in senseless pursuit of a ghost!

Mireille flipped the switch again and the voices ceased. Good God, what kind of mind could think up such a devilish defence? And how many more were there behind the closed shutter on Dionysìou Street?

She walked into the next room and found herself in another passageway intensely permeated with the smell of freshly baked bread. She raised her eyes to the ceiling and saw that there were air vents evidently somehow in communication with the oven of the basement bakery at number 15. So number 17 must be more or less directly above her. And that was where the booklet that had robbed Michel of his sleep had been printed: 'Hypothesis on the necromantic rite in the *Odyssey*, Book XI'.

There was a little wooden ladder at the end of the hall which gave access to a closed hatch in the ceiling. She approached and began to go up. As she got closer and closer to the hatch, she felt a distressful feeling of oppression and suffocation gripping her at the throat, as if she were entering the gates of hell.

CAPTAIN KARAMANLIS CONSIDERED the ladder leading back up to the surface and said to his men: 'If I'm not mistaken, that'll lead me right up to where my car is parked. You can go back to where we came in and get the hell out of here. Whoever is still on duty, go back to the station and resume your normal patrol. No reports and no talk about any of this, obviously.'

'Yes, sir, Captain.'

Karamanlis went up the slippery, rusty iron ladder to the manhole, holding a lit torch in his hand. He pushed open the cover and stuck his head out, then hoisted up his body. He closed up the manhole again and switched off his torch. He had always had an excellent sense of direction: his car was parked fifty metres down the street, on the left. He strode towards it and inserted his key in the lock. Right at that moment, his old policeman's sixth sense gave him the distinct impression that someone was behind him. A moment later, a voice that he would have never dreamed of hearing at that time and in that place confirmed that he hadn't been wrong.

'Hello, Captain Karamanlis.' Karamanlis spun around, pale with surprise and fatigue.

'So it's Admiral Bogdanos himself. Fine. And the game is over.' He was breathing hard. 'You'll follow me now to head-quarters. I have some questions for you. And I'd like to see an ID.'

'Don't be an idiot. I'm here to save your life. Claudio Setti is alive.'

'If that's all you have to tell me, you can follow me to the police station. We can talk much more comfortably there.'

'Claudio Setti is preparing to kill you and that awful beast that I've already saved once from sure death. He's also prepared a fully documented report regarding the murder of Heleni Kaloudis and will be sending it to the Attorney-General. In the best of all hypotheses, you'll spend the rest of your years rotting away in prison, and your friend will be quartered like a hog and hung up by the hocks. But he may well have the same fate in mind for you as well . . . the boy is unpredictable, you know.'

'I don't believe a word of what you're saying. You are an impostor.'

'Then look at this photograph. It was taken in Istanbul eight days ago. Take a look at the poster behind him advertising the Turkey–Spain game.' Karamanlis looked at the picture – it was undoubtedly Claudio Setti, on a city street in Turkey. 'Right now he's in Greece. Under a false name.'

'Where?'

'At Ephira.'

'Ephira.' Karamanlis suddenly remembered the hoarse, taunting voice that he'd heard coming from the mouth of the *kallikàntharos* on Mount Peristeri.

'That's where you want me, isn't it? Why? Why in that shithole of a place? Why can't we just get it all over with here in Athens? There are plenty of nice places here in Athens . . .'

'Stop this foolishness. Setti is in Ephira because he has a friend there, Aristotelis Malidis. I think he's been helping him and protecting Setti all these years. But he won't stay there long, if my information is correct. If we don't succeed in hooking him now, we never will. And if we lose him, you'll find him on your back. When you least expect it. He's capable of lying low for years and then of striking out when everyone's forgotten about him. Just think of Roussos and Karagheorghis. Of that night in Portolagos.'

Karamanlis seemed shaken, despite himself: 'But why would you do all this? You are not Admiral Bogdanos. Admiral Bogdanos lies in his family tomb in Volos. I don't even know who you are.'

'It's better that you continue not to know, for the time being at least. In any case, you may not know who is actually buried in that tomb in Volos.'

'You can't make me believe that the man buried in the cemetery in Volos is the real impostor.'

'I've given you all the information you need. I'm serving a man up into your very hands. Let's hope you don't let him get away again this time. And when this whole lamentable situation is over with, it won't matter who I am anyway. You have to neutralize that young man as fast as you can, and then you'll have all the explanations you want. These orders are coming from above, if the matter interests you.'

'Won't you sit in the car with me for a minute, Mr . . . I don't know what to call you. I'm exhausted.'

'According to the new documents my superiors have given me, I am now Commander Dimitrios Ritzos, Frigate Captain.' He handed Karamanlis a regular navy identity card, perfectly in order. 'A navy officer, once again. Why don't you just call me "Commander"? It's easier, less formal. I'm sorry, but I'd rather not get into the car. You stink, Karamanlis.'

'Yeah.'

'You see, Karamanlis, they used to call me "Commander" around Kastritza during the civil war, when I was fighting against General Tsolaglu's security men.'

'Kastritza. We were on opposite sides, then. "Commander", huh? Wait, I remember hearing about you . . .'

'Forget about it, Karamanlis. Water under the bridge. Now the good of our country demands that we cooperate. In any case, there's not much more to say. Take Vlassos with you. He's the perfect lure. Setti will lose control as soon as he sees him in circulation and he's bound to commit some error.'

Karamanlis sat down in the driver's seat of his car, leaving the door open. He stretched his hand into the glove compartment and took out an unopened pack of cigarettes that had been there for months. He took one out and lit it. 'To hell with it. They can't be any more dangerous than the trap I'm about to walk into.' He relished a long drag.

'One thing, Karamanlis. You'll have realized that I could have torn you to pieces at any time. I've played with you like a cat with a rat, just so that you know who sets the rules here. And now be good and do as I say.' He turned around and began walking towards Stadiou Street. Karamanlis leaned out of the car.

'Just one moment . . . Commander.' The man stopped. 'Were you ever on Mount Peristeri? I mean, did we ever meet somewhere around there?'

He turned suddenly towards Karamanlis and his teeth gleamed, in the dark, in a wolf's leer. 'There were times,' he said, 'during the civil war, but I don't remember if you were there with your battalion.'

'No. I wasn't,' said Karamanlis. He closed the door and watched the man as he walked off with his long, even stride, his jacket collar turned up and his hat down over his eyes. He was painfully reminded of the words of the *kallikàntharos* on the wind-beaten peak of Mount Peristeri: 'It is he who administers death'.

Fine, so the only thing left to do was keep this appointment. What the devil. *O Tàvros* had always knocked off all the toughest and craftiest of his enemies. Gored them at the last minute, when they distractedly thought they had the situation in hand. And after all . . . Setti had never got close enough to know what the old bull was capable of.

He switched on the radio and called headquarters: 'Karamanlis here. Tell Sergeant Vlassos to get ready to leave with me. Tomorrow morning at six.'

'With you, sir? Where to?'

'It's my own fucking business where to. You just tell him what I said.' When he lifted his head the commander, or whoever the hell he was, had disappeared around the corner. He started up the car and headed home.

The 'commander'. He had heard plenty of talk about him during the resistance. A strange figure, no one knew exactly whose side he was on; he had been known to destroy entire police battalions, but he'd also harshly punished any excess on the part of the partisans. The people considered him a hero, a legend, although no one knew who he really was. He certainly knew about the operations that he, Karamanlis, had carried out in the area of Kastritza and other regions of the north at the head of his police division. Back when he was known as *O Tàvros*. So now the game was drawing to a close, and in one way or another a number of things would come to light.

He parked in the usual place, walked slowly up the stairs and opened the door to his apartment. He took off his shoes and didn't turn on the light, but his wife heard him anyway and scurried in slippers down the hall: 'Is that you? Oh Holy Mother, do you know what time it is? And this smell? What is this smell?'

MIREILLE REACHED OUT to the hatch and pushed it up gently. It was counterweighted and opened easily, and there she was: in the printer's shop on 17 Dionysìou Street. Everything was in perfect order, as if work had just come to a stop for the night: the floor was clean and packs of paper were neatly stacked on the shelves. The press was in the corner. So this was where Periklis Harvatis's article had been printed.

She felt tired, exhausted by tension and lack of sleep. Her throat was dry and her heartbeat was irregular, making her feel as if she would suffocate.

She got to her feet. Where was Michel right now? She had the panicky sensation that there was a threat hovering over him, like a hail cloud over a field of wheat. She walked around the little room and scanned the shelves; there were all kinds of things: documents, certificates, papers, electronic components, books, records, an old bouzouki.

The room at the back of the shop was much bigger than the printing room itself and held the strangest assembly of objects that Mireille had ever seen. An old Lee-Enfield gun and an American revolver, an eighteenth-century manifesto of the Klephts against the Turks, the combat flag of a Byzantine dromond from the fourteenth century, a banner of the sacred battalion of Ypsilandis, old photographs, objets d'art of every type, antique weapons, paintings, prints, the oars and rudder of a boat, a fishing net, models of antique ships, a classical Attic red-figured cup, a late Mycenaean damascened blade, a game table . . .

In the corner, a stack of articles; hundreds of copies, rather, of the same article. It was what she was looking for, the work of Harvatis: 'Hypothesis on the necromantic rite in the *Odyssey*, Book XI'.

Alongside was a folder with a typescript by the same author entitled: 'Hypothesis on the position of the site called "Kelkea", or, in other works, "Bounima" or "Bouneima".'

Those were the same names she'd seen in Michel's notes in his apartment! She urged herself to remember the context: something about the final sacrifice of Odysseus.

Mireille was completely worn out, but sensed that she had to sit down and squeeze all the meaning she could out of those pages, even from the most unimportant-looking expressions. She didn't feel that she could take anything out of that room, which emanated a spirit of silent and intense sacredness; she wanted to leave no trace of her passage, and certainly didn't want the inhabitant of that unique refuge – so jealous of his own solitude – to have any clue of where to come looking for her.

She plunged into the manuscript, nervous and jittery, after having switched off the light in the printing shop. She looked at her watch: perhaps the waiter at the bar across the street was cleaning up and had noticed the light switching on and off for the second time that night and was wondering who to call. Wondering why the girl who had given him the thousand drachmas wasn't answering the phone in her hotel.

The article by Harvatis was obviously unfinished; actually, rather than a scholarly article, it was more of a collection of notes and observations:

Comments of the classic sources which mention this problem:

Aristarchus (Scholium H) mentions the name of the internal region of Epirus through which Odysseus must make his way: *éis Bouniman è éis Kelkean* (towards Bounima or towards Kelkea).

Eustatius: the ancients (that is, Aristarchus and his school) refer to the 'dark, barbarian sounds' of the names of the sites – Bounima or Kelkea – where Odysseus was supposed to stop and render honour to Poseidon.

Pausanias (I, 12) interprets the passage from Homer as if the men 'who lived with meat unsalted' were Epirotes in general, although those who lived on the coast must have been familiar with navigation. Scholia B and Q refer that in even the interior of Epirus, *hales oryktoi* (that is, rock-salt) did exist, but it is clear that the prophecy of Tiresias meant simply to refer to populations who lived so far from the sea that they had never been exposed to salt.

Hence, the localization of the place in which Odysseus

was to have offered sacrifice to Poseidon – in order to rid himself of the curse and deliver himself from the hostility of the gods – may be identifiable with Epirus, at least according to some scholars (Aristarchus and Pausanias). I believe this is questionable, for a number of reasons.

First of all, in the ancient sources there seems to be some confusion between 'Epirus' (the region) and '*épeiron*' (meaning continent), seeing that it was commonly held that Odysseus had to go deep into a continental area. Furthermore, according to Tiresias's prophecy, the oar which Odysseus would carry on his back would be mistaken by a wayfarer for a winnowing fan, which was used to separate the wheat from the chaff. Yet where could wheat possibly have been grown among the bare mountains of Epirus?

Moreover, there were certainly lakes in Epirus which were navigable, and thus boats and oars were perfectly familiar objects. And Epirus was the realm of the maternal grandfather of Odysseus, Autolicos, and thus quite familiar to him: why then would the theatre of the hero's last gestures be veiled with such mystery in the oracle of Tiresias?

The term Kelkea, which Pausanias relates to the cult of Artemis Brauronia, suggests an Asian location, perhaps in Phrygia. In any case, inland Asia. And the other term as well – Bouneima, which seems to mean 'pasture of the oxen' – could refer to the high plains of Anatolia. But the word may also derive from '*Bounòs*', or 'mountain' and simply indicate a mountain.

What's more, the 'dark, barbarian sounds' which Eustatius mentions would more likely refer to the inarticulate noises of some incomprehensible foreign language than to a recognizable Hellenic dialect like Epirote.

Mireille's head was spinning with all this puzzling information. She was convinced that it must mean something, something important, something connected to Michel. But what? She delved on. The pages which followed were covered with difficult-to-interpret sketches, isolated phrases, verses. And then again:

I am practically certain that the necromantic rite of the *Odyssey*, Book XI can be localized in Ephira, where we find the source of the Acheron, the Stygian swamp and the Cimmerian promontory: it is there that the solution to the problem must be sought. And perhaps even the clues needed to reconstruct the final journey of Odysseus.

Notes from his excavation journal followed with sketches, sections, stratigraphies and drawings of the objects found. Dense notes written in a neat, minute hand. She thought of the vase, the golden vase that Karamanlis had described to her. It had come from Ephira; Harvatis had almost certainly unearthed it himself. Why was there no mention of it?

Mireille looked at her watch: it was three-thirty in the morning. She certainly didn't want the owner of the place to surprise her there at this hour. She knew she couldn't hold up under the intensity of that gaze. Mireille listened carefully, but there was not a sound to be heard: the place seemed completely isolated or soundproofed, and it was quite warm inside.

She got to the end of the article without finding anything else that particularly attracted her attention. But right between the last page and the back cover was an envelope addressed in Harvatis's hand, although the writing was very different: wavering, weak, scribbled:

Kyrios Stàvros Kouras
Odòs Dionysìou 17
Athinai

The envelope had been opened hurriedly and the paper was torn. Mireille took out the sheet of paper it contained and began to read:

Ephira, 16 November 1973

My dear friend,

I fear that these are the last words I shall be allowed to say to you. For you I have defied the gate of the underworld. It is open now, and awaits the conclusion of this long,

terrible story. Unfortunately, the gelid breath of those recesses has numbed me and snuffed out what little vitality was
left in my veins. But at the same moment in which Erebus
rose to snatch me away, as I clutched between my hands the
vase of gold engraved with the images of the last adventure,
something illuminated me for a brief instant. Perhaps the
clairvoyance of he who knows he is abandoning life. The
figures engraved on the vase spoke to me.

The place at which it must all take place – the place
called 'Kelkea' by some and 'Bouneima' by others – has its
base where the black doves of Egyptian Thebes alighted on
land to give origin to the most ancient oracles of the earth:
Dodona and Siwa. The former is under the sign of the wild
boar that today astrologers call the sign of Pisces. The latter
is under the sign of the ram, Aries. Two of the victims who
are to be sacrificed must come from these two places.

Between those two points are two entrances to the other
world: at Ephira, the place from which I write, and at Cape
Tenaros. The distance which separates Ephira from Tenaros
and the distance which separates Tenaros from Siwa are
related in a magical, set numerical ratio. This ratio, which I
represent here with the last strength that remains to me,
expressed in a mathematical formula and in a graph, will
take you to the place where the story must be ended:

$$\frac{ET}{TS} = 0.37 = rho$$

$$\frac{alpha}{180} = rho \left| \frac{alpha}{180} = 0.37 \right.$$

The Bull is the third victim and he was born on the
slopes of Mount Cillene, the fulcrum on the earth of the
astrological sign of Taurus. At the foot of the mountain, in
the Stinphalis swamp, exists another entrance to Hades. All
three of the victims must cross the waters of the Acheron
before they are sacrificed.

Certainly, a divinity who loves you left this message in
the bowels of the earth, carved in gold, and willed me to

find it. This is my viaticum, and may fortune provide for the rest. Farewell, Commander, *chaire*! To you, to whom with immense admiration I have dedicated my whole life,
     Periklis Harvatis

She didn't understand, but her eyes filled up with tears. She sensed the great, limitless devotion behind those words. A man's life given for a friend, without any reward. She could feel the extreme, defenceless solitude of a fragile human being finding himself face to face with the gaping mouth of the icy, dismal mystery of death.

She hurriedly recopied the graph which incorporated the axis of Harvatis – the same she had seen on Michel's desk – into her notebook, along with the formulae which accompanied it. A sudden suspicion gave her a chill: Siwa! If her father had been telling the truth, Michel was born in Siwa and he was an Aries. No, what did that have to do with anything . . . There was no connection. The late hour, her emotional state and the suffocating atmosphere of that strange place were giving her hallucinations. She had to get out as soon as possible. How to deal with the dog, that was her next problem. Could she face that big black beast crouching in the garden, waiting to rip her throat out?

Her heart suddenly stopped short as she heard the sound of steps, muffled and far away, but definitely footsteps. She switched off the lights in both rooms and flattened herself behind some of the shelves. The steps were drawing nearer and nearer, she could hear them coming from under the floor. Then they stopped and she heard the creaking of the hinge that opened the trapdoor into the print shop. Someone had turned on the light and was walking around in the next room. Steps, papers being shuffled, the handle turning . . . and there he was, his figure standing out darkly in the open doorway.

He raised his hand to the light switch to turn on the bulb swinging from the ceiling, closing the door behind him. Mireille flattened herself even further against the wall, but realized that if he came just four, five more steps forward, he couldn't help but see her. The light suddenly quivered and went out: the light bulb must have blown. The man walked back to the door and let the light from the other room flood in. He then went over to the left wall and moved a pack of paper from a shelf, revealing a little safe.

He pressed out the combination on a little electronic keypad – Mireille could see the numbers out of the corner of her eye as they appeared on the display: 15 . . . 20 . . . 19 . . . 9 . . . 18. The safe opened and he put his hand inside, extracting a long black case with a couple of zippered closures, like a case for a musical instrument or a weapon. He turned off the light in the printer's shop, then walked through the second room again in the dark, passing just a few steps away from Mireille, who stood holding her breath. He took an item off one of the shelves, as confidently as if he could see perfectly, and disappeared behind the door. Mireille hadn't been able to see what he had taken.

She listened to the sound of his footsteps as they faded away, then returned to the safe and tried the combination again: 15, 20, 19, 9, 18. The safe swung open and Mireille lit up the inside with the little torch she kept on her key ring. There was a booklet with a strange charcoal drawing on its cover: the heads of a boar, a bull and a ram. As she started turning the pages, her features contracted and her eyes darkened until she got to the last page. An expression of pure terror transformed her face, and she burst out crying.

'No!' she cried out, throwing the little booklet back into the safe as if she had touched a red-hot iron. She slammed it shut and ran crying towards the rear door. Still in the dark, she stumbled down a little stair and found herself in a sort of basement. Her torch beam lead her to an old coal chute which led outside. She climbed through it and out, under the drowsy eyes of a stray dog who was rummaging in a nearby garbage can. She found herself on Odòs Pallenes and began running, her heart pounding madly, towards Omonia Square. She stopped at the first telephone booth she could find, and called Michel's hotel in Ephira. Norman answered.

'Mireille? What's wrong?'

'Norman, pass me Michel, please. Even if he's sleeping.' A brief silence followed. 'Norman, answer me! I have to talk to Michel.'

'Michel's not here, Mireille. He left this afternoon and I've been waiting for him since then. He went looking for Ari, but Ari's not here any more, and he never came back. I've told the police and they're looking for him. It seems that his car was seen heading towards Metsovon.'

'Metsovon? Oh my God, no . . .'

21

ARI DROVE PAST the great temple of Cape Sounion as a milky glow was just beginning to colour the horizon. How many sailors for how many thousands of years had seen its grey bulk disappearing in the distance along with the homeland they longed for as they were swiftly snatched off by the north wind?

He turned north, leaving the white spectres of the Doric columns behind him, and headed towards Marathon, until he found the little road that climbed up towards an isolated house at the edge of an oak forest.

He got out of the car with a bundle in his hands, then rang the doorbell and waited for someone to answer. There was no wind, and the sky was still and grey.

A few minutes later the door opened, and a man with long grey hair wearing a dark cotton robe came to the door.

'The commander has sent me,' said Ari.

'I know,' said the man. 'Come in.' And he led him past the small entryway, down a hall to the large unadorned room where he usually worked.

Ari placed the bundle he was carrying on a table and took off its wrapping: the magnificent embossed Mycenaean vase emerged. 'The commander said you are to use this gold for your work.'

'This? Oh my God, how can I . . .'

Ari watched without saying a word, arms crossed over his stomach as if waiting for a reply. The man contemplated the beautiful object at length, turning and touching it as if to impress every detail in his mind for ever.

Ari said: 'The commander doesn't want anything to remain . . . you must not dare make a copy.'

The sculptor turned towards the draped easel standing in the corner and uncovered the mask he had fashioned first in clay and then in white cement. 'But why destroy this miracle?'

'That's what the commander wants. The gold must come from this vase. The entire vase. If you are his friend, do as he says.'

The man nodded. 'All right. I'll do as he wishes. Come back in two days.'

'No. I'll wait until it's finished. It's time now.'

Ari went to sit in a corner and took out his pipe.

'Where will you bring it when it is finished?'

'To Ephira,' said Ari. 'It will all be over soon, very soon. The time has come.'

The sculptor lowered his head and began working.

THE COASTAL HIGHWAY to Patras was nearly empty at that time of morning and Sergeant Vlassos was driving fast, taking a bite of a sausage sandwich and a swig of beer every so often, sticking the bottle in the glove compartment between gulps. Captain Karamanlis sat next to him and paged through his notes.

'Why don't we get some help from our colleagues at Preveza, boss?' asked Vlassos between one mouthful and the next. 'We'll set up roadblocks all around the city and then more of them a little farther out. The fish will swim right into our net. And I'll take care of him afterwards. We'll get rid of the bastard once and for all. I'll tear the creep to pieces. He has to pay for what he did to me . . . for everything I've suffered. Damned son-of-a-bitch bastard.'

'And what did we do at Dirou and Portolagos? Roadblocks, encirclements that not even a mosquito could get through, but he got through, didn't he? He got through just fine. He's got the devil on his side, that bastard. Yeah, if I believed in the stories that priests tell, I'd say I'd met the devil himself, in person. In the flesh, just like you're sitting next to me now.' Vlassos's mouth, full of sausage, dropped open. 'Even if I couldn't tell you whose side he was really on. But we'll find out soon, very soon. I've tried everything, but there's only one sure way to get our man now: he wants me, but he wants you even more. At Portolagos he would have finished you off if we hadn't stopped him in time.'

'Then I'll be the lure for our fishy. Fine. Let him try. This time the hook will stick.'

'I'm glad you're in favour of all this. But be careful. This time we can't count on anyone else's help. It's too dangerous. I don't want any of the behind-the-scenes stuff coming out. You know what I mean. The more people we involve the messier it gets. We're going to do it by ourselves this time. The game is up, and it's two against one, right? Maybe even three against one. If the worst comes to the worst, two against two . . .'

'Who the hell is this other guy, and why don't we know whose side he's on?'

'He's the guy who saved your ass at Portolagos.'

'Then he's on our side.'

'No. Not on our side. But maybe not on the other side, either. I have a hunch that he's playing a game of his own, but I don't know his cards. Or the rules, for that matter. But it won't be long. It won't be much longer now . . .'

Vlassos swallowed. 'Captain,' he asked, 'we'll come out on top this time, won't we? You've got a plan, right? Something up your sleeve, I bet.'

Karamanlis continued to go through his notes until he came to the colour photo of a beautiful dark-haired girl: Kiki Kaloudis.

'Yeah,' he said, raising his head and watching the ribbon of asphalt unwind in front of him. 'Yeah, I've got something up my sleeve all right. But I'm not using it till all my other cards are played out. Hey, stop here a minute, I have to take a piss. This damned prostate . . . maybe Irini's right, maybe it's time I made up my mind to retire.'

Vlassos gulped down a little beer and wiped his mouth with the back of his hand. 'You'll retire all right, boss. When we've got this fixed. Now I'll stop so you can pee.'

MIREILLE HADN'T SLEPT at all. She drove back to the hotel, paid the night porter for her room with a credit card and started off immediately, after leaving a message for Mr Zolotas and a generous tip for the waiter at Milos's Bar.

She was heading down the same highway and had at least three hours' advantage over Karamanlis, but every once in a while she was forced to stop, overwhelmed by fatigue. She'd pull over and sleep five, ten minutes, then wipe her face with a wet towel and start off again.

She knew that she was caught in a race against time, and that Michel's very life depended on the outcome. She didn't have enough information on where she could find him, but she had to get there first. Before fate had its way; a fate that had every advantage over her and could strike at any time.

It was already daylight when she lined up at Rion behind a couple of cars and half a dozen trucks to take the ferry to the northern side of the Gulf of Corinth. She passed Missolungi and Arta without stopping, eating a few crackers and an apple, and arrived at Preveza in the early afternoon. The November sun was low and pale. Norman was waiting for her at the hotel.

'I've looked everywhere,' he told her, 'but this is all I found.' He handed her a slip of paper which said: 'I'll call you the day after tomorrow from Canakkale, I hope. Had no time. Michel.'

'The best thing to do is wait here until he calls, so we can find out why he had to leave in such a hurry. We have an old friend who lives here – his name's Aristotelis Malidis; he helped us back during the Polytechnic uprising. I think Michel might have gone to talk with him. I've looked for him too, but he seems to have disappeared.'

'He helped you? With what?'

'Michel never told you anything about what happened, did he?'

'No.'

'Well, I'm sorry, then, but I don't think I have the right . . .'

'Fine. In any case, I'm leaving.'

'Leaving? But you can't even stand up. You look awful.'

'Thanks,' said the girl, her feminine pride slightly offended.

'What I mean is that it looks like you haven't slept in a week.
Listen, take a shower and lie down until dinner time. Maybe
Michel will call early, and you'll be able to talk to him.'

'No. Michel's life is in danger. I absolutely have to find him.'

Norman's forehead wrinkled: 'His life is in danger? Why?'

'I don't have time to explain and you probably wouldn't
believe me anyway. If there's nothing else you can tell me, I'm
leaving.'

Norman took her arm. 'But you don't even know where to
look for him. Canakkale is no village.'

'I'll manage somehow. I have to go.' She was pale and
clammy. Norman could see that nothing would stop her.

'All right. If you've really got to go, I'm coming with you.
I'll drive, at least, so you can get some sleep. Rest a little. And
maybe I'll be able to spot Michel; he did leave with my car. Take
a shower while I put a few things together. I'll tell the receptionist to say when he calls that we're heading out that way, and to
let us know where we can find him. Then we'll call the hotel
along the way. How about that?'

Mireille lowered her head and dropped her bag on the floor:
'Sounds good to me. I'll be ready in ten minutes. My car is the
Hertz Peugeot parked in front.'

KARAMANLIS AND VLASSOS arrived at dusk. Karamanlis dropped
Vlassos off at the small motel on the road to Ephira that they
had booked for the night. He drove to the Preveza police
station, where he identified himself and asked for the guest lists
of all the hotels and boarding houses in the area in an attempt
to locate any foreigner whose description might fit that of
Claudio Setti. There wouldn't be many foreigners around so off-
season. He did learn that Norman Shields and Michel Charrier

had both been in the area and had left at a few days' distance from each other.

He went to the hotel they had been staying at, where he learned that Norman Shields had gone off that afternoon with a beautiful girl. From the porter's description, it sounded just like Mireille.

All here. They'd all passed through here. But why? And where had they gone to? He went back to the motel and picked up his key at the front desk. There was already a message waiting for him: 'He's meeting Ari Malidis at eleven o'clock tonight at the excavation site, at the guest house where Malidis lives. He has already spotted Vlassos in town and is out of his mind. Don't get it wrong this time.'

He went to knock at Vlassos's room, and the sergeant came to the door in his underwear. 'Thought I'd lie down for a few minutes, Captain. Something new?'

'Listen. I've found out that our man is going to be at the guest quarters of the archaeological site down by the river at eleven o'clock tonight. It's a good place, isolated. There's a little church right nearby; I'll be able to keep an eye on the place from there. I'll wait until he goes in; it's better that we do our business indoors. As soon as I'm ready to go in I'll signal you with my walkie-talkie and you come in through the back. Got it?'

'You bet. But why don't you let me go in first? You promised you'd let me have first crack at him. You promised, remember?'

'Of course I remember. And I want to take him alive, if I can. Before I send him off to hell I want to ask him a few things, and you're the best person I know to get someone to sing. There's an old abandoned sheep pen on the mountainside nearby. We'll take him there so we won't be disturbed.'

'That's the way I like it, Captain.' He took out the case with his gear and started to inspect and to test the long-barrelled Beretta calibre 9 and the sharpshooter's rifle with its infrared sights. He tossed it from one hand to the other, aimed to shoot, pretended to pull the trigger.

'And the old man? What are we going to do with him?'

'He's alone and there will be no witnesses. Still, it's best not to kill him if we can avoid it. We'll tell him that we're arresting Setti and have to interrogate him.'

Karamanlis began to check his gun as well, loading it with great care and precision.

'One more thing, Vlassos.'

'What?'

'You have to be ready for the unexpected. This might even be a trap, you know, to lure us to where they want us. Someone else might show up – the guy who gave me this tip, actually. He's about fifty, medium height. And he's tough. The last time I saw him he was wearing a black leather jacket and a light-coloured sweater. If you see him, watch out. He could take you out before you have the chance to bat an eyelid.'

'But didn't you say he was the guy who saved my skin at Portolagos?'

'He saved you, all right, but I don't think it makes a difference. We don't know anything about him. Not even his name. We can't trust him. Just watch out, I'm telling you. Maybe it'll all go smoothly, but you watch your ass.'

They left the motel separately, each with a walkie-talkie to stay in contact, Vlassos at ten, to stake himself out in a concealed spot from which he could keep an eye on the rear door of the guest house and the road from town, Karamanlis shortly after-wards, heading towards the deconsecrated church located on the hillside above the Oracle of the Dead. The entrance to the guest quarters was directly in front of him, at a short distance. Anyone who went in or out would be within range. It was chilly, but the breeze still carried the residual mildness of the late autumn day.

Suddenly, headlights illuminated the top of the little bell tower and Karamanlis saw a car descending alongside the church and stopping in front of the guest house. An elderly man got out: Aristotelis Malidis. Okay, so far so good. He looked at his watch: ten-thirty.

The old man held a wrapped bundle under his left arm, while he unlocked the door to the little house with his right and switched on the lights inside. He went through a second door and when he reappeared in the main room a few minutes later he was no longer carrying the bundle. He had a torch in his hand, which he switched off and put in a drawer. He sat down and turned on the TV.

Karamanlis didn't lose sight of him for a second through his binoculars, and called Vlassos every few minutes to check on the situation.

At just a few minutes before eleven, another light slashed through the darkness, and a second car approached the guest house. Vlassos had seen it as well. 'Is it him, boss? Is it him?' he hissed over the walkie-talkie.

'How the hell do I know if I can't see him? But I think it must be. You stay ready to come in through the back, but make sure first that there's no one anywhere around you.'

'All right. I'll wait for your signal.'

The car, a small Alfa Romeo with Italian plates, stopped with the driver's door practically touching the front entrance. A man got out and slipped into the house. Karamanlis couldn't even get a glimpse.

He put down his pistol and picked up the binoculars, looking through the window: he saw him for a second before the old man closed the blinds, and his inveterate policeman's heart skipped a beat: it was him! Claudio Setti!

He was wearing an army jacket, his hair was dishevelled and he had a couple of days' beard. It was him. The guy who had broken Roussos's bones, dragging him by his heel with an ice hook, the one who had riddled Karagheorghis with a rain of stalactites, who had nailed Vlassos to the ground and half castrated him. The guy who ten years ago had left the Athens police station nearly dead in the trunk of a car, stuck in there with his girlfriend's bloody, raped corpse. All these thoughts exploded in Captain Karamanlis's mind and convinced him that there was not enough room in the world for both of them after all that had happened. What good would it do to capture or interrogate him? He screwed the silencer on to his gun barrel.

He would kill him straight off, and the old guy too. He'd have plenty of time to get rid of their bodies.

'Vlassos,' he said softly into the walkie-talkie.

'I'm here, Captain.'

'He just walked in. It's him, no doubt about it. Check your watch. When I give you the go-ahead you'll have ten seconds to come through the back. I'll go in the front. Is there anyone around?'

'No, don't worry. Not a soul.'

'Good, no one on this side either. All right . . . Now!'

Karamanlis was up against the door in a few seconds; when his watch gave him the ten-seconds-up signal, he kicked the door wide open and burst in, gun levelled. He heard Vlassos smashing through the back door and yelling 'No one move!'

Ari jumped and backed up to the wall, raising his hands above his head.

'Where's the kid?' shouted Karamanlis. 'Vlassos, fast, search this shithole and watch out for the other guy I told you about. He's screwed us again, God damn him!'

Vlassos ran back through the door he'd come in, and a moment later they heard his agitated footsteps up the stairs, all over the second floor and then outside down at the archaeological site.

'Where is he?' insisted Karamanlis, pointing his pistol at the old man's throat.

'I don't know,' said Ari.

'I'll blow your brains out if you don't answer. You have two seconds.' He pulled the firing pin. 'One . . .'

The roar of the Alfa Romeo exploded in the courtyard. The window glass and the walls were machine-gunned with a hail of stones flung up by the wheels of the car which shot off like a bullet down the road to Preveza.

Karamanlis released Ari and ran out as Vlassos dashed around the corner of the house. Karamanlis shot repeatedly at the car, but he hadn't had time to take off the silencer and his range was not sufficient. When Vlassos started shooting with the rifle, the car was already behind a curve, and when it reappeared for a second slightly further on, he had no time even to take aim before it disappeared again.

'Shit, shit, shit!' howled Karamanlis, pounding his fist against the wall. Vlassos's glance fell to his pistol: 'Captain, why the silencer? You would have got him without the silencer.'

Karamanlis wheeled around in a rage: 'It's my fucking business why, all right! Shut the fuck up!'

They went back in and Vlassos lifted Ari up by the collar from the seat he'd fallen over on to: "This pretty boy will tell us where the kid went in his Alfa Romeo. Won't you, gramps?'

'Well?' demanded Karamanlis. Ari shook his head. Karamanlis gestured towards Vlassos, who struck the old man with a strong back-handed blow. Ari fell to the ground, his mouth full of blood.

'I'll tear your balls off, you ugly slobbering old fucker, if you don't tell me where he went,' Vlassos yelled. Ari replied with a groan. Karamanlis nodded again, and Vlassos started beating the old man, hitting his stomach, his face, his groin.

'That's enough, for now,' said Karamanlis. 'I want him to talk, not die.' Ari struggled to sit up, back to the wall. 'Well?'

'You'll never get him,' he muttered.

'That remains to be seen. You tell us where he's headed if you want us to stop.'

'Wouldn't help. By now he has a different car, different documents. He'll already have changed his clothes and the colour of his hair. You'll never catch him. But he will get you . . .'

Vlassos raised his fist, but Karamanlis stopped him this time.

'No, leave him alone. It won't help.'

'Let's kill him now. This old bastard knows too much.'

'He hasn't said a thing. Why should he talk now? Right, old man?'

'I haven't said a word,' said Ari, 'but not out of fear. I'm just waiting for the day you'll be punished. If there is any punishment that can match what you've done.'

'Where is Claudio Setti?' asked Karamanlis again.

'Tomorrow night he'll be in Turkey. Maybe by sea, maybe by land. See? You don't stand a chance. You'll never find him. But he will find you, when the time is right.'

'We'll see about that,' said Karamanlis. He then turned to Vlassos: 'Let's get out of here.' They left, slamming the door, and returned to their cars. Karamanlis was back in his motel room before midnight. He dropped on to the bed, his head aching. How could it have happened? He had watched him as he walked into the house and greeted the old man. A minute later he was no longer there. What had he come for? To get something? Or to leave something? Just to be seen? Or to fuck him over? Had someone warned him? And now how the hell would he find him? Blast it all! It was like having scabies and not being able to scratch.

'How did it go, Captain Karamanlis?' The voice sounded from the end of the room as the table lamp lit up, revealing the man sitting behind it.

Karamanlis started: 'How did you get in?'

'They let me in. Didn't you say at the front desk that your TV wasn't working?'

'My TV? Oh, God damn you.'

'Well?'

'It went badly. Very badly. He got away and we have no idea where he's headed. Turkey, maybe. And now if you would like to get the fuck out of here . . .'

'The information I gave you was exact.'

'The information you give me is always exact, but there always turns out to be some fuck-up.'

'Because you are incompetent.'

'Go to hell!'

'Fine. But let me inform you that you will be taken off the previous homicides and the attempted homicide at Portolagos, and someone else will be taking over the investigation. You will probably be investigated yourself. Almost certainly. Some explanation must be found for all this. And you, Captain, are the best explanation. Once your head has fallen, the case will be closed, and everyone will be happy.'

'I don't believe you. Nothing will happen. You don't count for anything.'

'Optimism is a good quality. I hope that everything goes as well as you hope. Goodbye, Karamanlis,' he said, walking towards the door.

'Wait.'

'I'm listening.'

'No one cares about an old mastiff who's lost his teeth, do they?'

'Unfortunately.'

'Even if he's always served faithfully, risked his life . . .'

'Isn't it a pity.'

'It's a fucking world.'

'It is.'

'What card do I have left to play?'

'Either kill Claudio Setti or turn yourself in and confess to everything.'

'Why don't you kill him, damn you?'

'You are a fool, Karamanlis. Consider me the explicit but informal expression of the powers that be. The collaboration I offer you is already a great sign of our appreciation that you do not seem to understand. I cannot act personally for the simple reason that you are the one who has committed such a serious transgression without succeeding in preventing or suffocating the consequences. A good policeman can get away with anything, but he must be able to cover it up.'

'Can I . . . can I still find him?'

'There is one hope.'

'What is it?'

'His friend Michel Charrier is looking for him, and we have reason to believe that he may know where he is. He's driving the blue Rover that you are familiar with, and he's somewhere between here and Alexandroupolis. It shouldn't be too difficult to locate him and follow him. Remember, even if you don't find Setti, he will surely find you. But the choice of the battlefield may be important. Decisive, even. Goodnight, Karamanlis.'

22

Parga, 11 November, midnight

CLAUDIO SETTI SAT waiting in silence at the wheel of his Alfa Romeo, watching the steely glitter of the sea under the pale glow of a hazy sky, listening to music on a cassette and glancing at his watch every now and then. A few minutes later the dark bulk of a Mercedes pulled up alongside his car. The driver's door opened, letting out the notes of some other music for a moment, different music, a Mahler symphony.

'Hello, my boy. How are you?'

'Hello, Commander. I'm well.'

'I hope it wasn't too risky for you.'

'I'm used to it. It was no worse than the other times. But Ari . . . they'll have hurt him. Couldn't that have been avoided?'

'No. There was no other way. Ari is a strong, courageous man. If they've hurt him, they'll pay for that as well. We are at the end. The last journey is about to begin: three days from now it will all be over. You'll understand then, I believe, that this was the only way.'

'And afterwards? What then, Commander?'

'You're young. You will close a sad chapter of your life, but an important one. Your flesh has known the most atrocious suffering, and your spirit has known the most extreme emotions. You know how it feels to inflict capital punishment, like God, like a king. With justice. For justice. You'll go back to being a man like other men.'

'And I won't see you again?'

The commander laid a hand on his shoulder and it seemed to Claudio that his eyes were moist: 'I would like to leave this . . . work that I've been doing for much too long, and I'd like to return . . . home. It depends on how this story ends, if your strength is sufficient and if fortune is on my side. Anyway, you see, I've been used to living alone for a long, long time. This adventure that we've lived through together has passed by so quickly, and I've become very fond of you . . . as if you were my son.'

'Don't you have a family, Commander?'

'I did. A woman who was beautiful and proud . . . she came from around here. And a boy, who'd be as old as you are. He was a lot like you. Quite a lot. But let's not talk about such sad things. We'll see each other tomorrow evening at Canakkale. There I will give you your last assignment . . .'

Claudio felt a knot tightening in his throat and lowered his head in silence. He had nothing more to ask.

MIREILLE DROPPED OFF as soon as her head touched the reclining passenger's seat of her car, and Norman drove on and on in silence, without even turning on the radio. He looked over at her every now and then and thought that Michel was very lucky to have such a beautiful and passionate girl in love with him. Mireille had fallen into a deep but troubled sleep. She moaned and let out a suffocated cry. She must really be worried about him.

Canakkale. What the devil could Michel have gone to Canakkale for? It sure wouldn't be easy to find him. Even if Michel learned from the hotel that he and Mireille had set off to look for him, he might not want to let them know where he was. Not right away, at least. And he might have no intention of even phoning the hotel, otherwise why would he have left in such a hurry without saying anything?

The first three hundred kilometres were the worst; Mireille had been right about leaving right away if they hoped to reach Canakkale in less than thirty-six hours. At Ioannina he stopped to get a couple of sandwiches at a bar and to call the hotel, but there had been no word from Michel. He started off again towards Metsovon. The road was very steep, full of hairpin turns. They had nearly reached the pass when Mireille awoke.

'You really slept a long time, you must have been exhausted. Would you like a sandwich?'

'Thank you, I'd love one,' said Mireille. 'I'm famished. What time is it?'

'One o'clock.'

'Want me to take over the driving?'

'Not yet, thanks. I'll drive for another hour at least. There's a can of Coke in the back too. Don't you want to tell me what kind of danger Michel is in? Why do you have to reach him?'

She turned to him with a fierce look: 'Michel could be killed at any time.'

'Then it's not true that you don't know anything about what happened in Athens ten years ago.'

Mireille lowered her head, not contradicting him.

'Well,' Norman said, 'we've got a long night ahead of us and nothing to do. Maybe I should let you know how things really went, in case you just got part of the story.' Norman began talking, recalling distant, anguish-filled hours, the story of three young men dragged into a whirlpool of horror and blood, as the flame of his cigarette burned between his lips, the only grim light in the darkness of the night and of his memories. Mireille still could not connect what she had seen in the basement of Dionysìou Street with what Norman was telling her. Her anxiety grew, as if the reasons for Michel being killed were multiplying out of control.

'Can you imagine the reason why Michel left for Canakkale so suddenly?' she asked Norman when he'd finished.

'I've been thinking hard about that. There seems to be a good chance that our Italian friend Claudio Setti is alive, despite what we were led to believe at the time. And that he is obsessed by a desire for revenge . . . he may have gone totally off the deep end. Michel is tormented by remorse and obsessed by the idea of somehow justifying what he did, of redeeming himself in his friend's eyes. While you were sleeping, I was thinking: it could be Claudio Setti who's waiting for Michel at Canakkale.'

'A trap?'

'I couldn't say. Maybe. All those who were involved in one way or another with the death of Heleni, Claudio's girlfriend, have died a horrible death or come close. But how did you find out the truth?'

'The truth? From what you just told me.'

'You were bluffing.'

'No. I know of another danger, just as lethal, hanging over his head. But the two roads to death may come together. We must find out where . . . and when. I don't want to lose him, Norman. I couldn't bear it.'

A long silence fell between them, and Norman switched on the radio to dispel the anguish that was suffocating them. Then, not far from Trikala, he pulled over. 'I'm really tired. Would you mind taking over?'

As Mireille was getting out to switch sides, a patrol car proceeding in the opposite direction stopped and one of the policemen got out to check their car.

'Any problems?' he asked, raising his hand to his cap.

'No, sir, thank you,' replied Norman. 'She's just going to drive for a while. I've been at the wheel for hours, and she's been resting.'

'I see,' said the policeman. 'Be careful, and if you want my advice, stop at a hotel at Trikala; you won't have problems finding a room. Better not to risk going on if you're tired.'

'Thank you, officer,' said Norman. 'But there's a place we have to get to.'

'You know your business,' said the man. 'Safe driving, then, and goodnight.'

As SOON AS they took off, the policeman got back into his car and switched on the radio. 'Headquarters? Officer Laridis here. I'm at kilometre 52 of state road E 87. We've just spotted the car that Preveza has requested localization of. There's a man of about thirty-five and a younger woman aboard.'

'Headquarters here,' replied a voice on the radio. 'Where are they headed?'

'East towards Larisa and probably further. They have no intention of stopping at Trikala and seem to be driving non-stop, taking turns at the wheel.'

The Trikala station promptly relayed the news to Preveza, but the officer on duty did not immediately communicate the information to his colleagues from Athens who were staying at the Cleopatra motel. He had been ordered to wake them only if he had news of a blue Rover with English plates driven by a single man, aged thirty. Which happened at six a.m.

'Captain Karamanlis,' said the officer as soon as he answered the phone, 'we've located both cars: the Hertz Peugeot and the blue Rover.'

Karamanlis sat up in bed and took a sip of water from the glass at his bedside. 'Good work. Do you have the times and positions?'

'The Peugeot was entering Trikala a little before two o'clock this morning, and the blue Rover has just been reported at Rendina, in Calcidica. Both are directed east. The Peugeot may be catching up; the two drivers are switching and proceeding non-stop.'

'Thank you. And now find us a quick passage to Thrace. I promise you'll have a bonus for distinctive merit if you do.'

'Thrace, Captain? Where in Thrace?'

'Anywhere, as close as possible to the Turkish border. See if you can find out whether they are headed for Kesan or Edirne. You never know.' Karamanlis dressed and woke Vlassos, dragging him into the hotel's front hall, where a sleepy bartender was just turning on the coffee machine.

'Rendina, the Frenchman is already at Rendina?' asked Vlassos. 'We'll never catch him, boss, if you don't have him stopped at the border.'

'No. We won't stop him. We have to follow him. We'll see who has the last word here. Get yourself something to eat.'

They asked for coffee, and Karamanlis dipped a couple of cookies in his, suddenly hungry. The chase always primed his appetite and made everything else fade away. When they'd finished breakfast, Karamanlis took the paper and sat down to read it in the lounge, under the amazed look of his companion, who was pacing back and forth, smoking one cigarette after another. Headquarters called half an hour later, at seven-thirty.

'Captain, we've found a flight. A small Esso Papas plane is taking off in half an hour from Aktion; it's headed for Piges, transporting some engineers who have to inspect a chemical plant. They'll give you a lift. A car will be by to pick you up in five minutes. Take the seven-forty-five ferry: the airport is on the other side of the gulf.'

'You're top-notch, my boy. Top-notch. You've earned your raise, let me tell you. Have an undercover car ready at the airport, with a full tank and some food. Goodbye.'

'But Captain, don't you want to know my name?'

'Oh, right. Of course, where is my head this morning. I was forgetting the most important thing. Your name, son?'

MICHEL'S TENSION AND exhaustion mounted the further east he got. His eyes were burning and his stomach was cramping up insufferably. He'd passed Kavala and Xanthi and was approaching Komotini. Canakkale was very close as the crow flies, but the road was still quite long. After the Turkish border, he'd have to continue east for a number of kilometres and then turn back west again, following the edge of the Gallipoli peninsula until he reached Eceabat at its tip, where he'd be able to catch the ferry for the Asian side.

It was dark already, and there was nothing but truck traffic on the road: big semis carrying goods all over the Middle East. He stopped at a petrol station to fill up the tank and grab something to eat, but his stomach was in knots and he couldn't swallow a thing. He knew that if he didn't find Claudio, the rest of his life would be hell. He'd never be able to forget, to bury the past.

He downed a glass of milk while a group of Hungarian truck drivers sat down in front of huge platters of steaming sausages and a pitcher of beer. He crawled back into the car to rest for a few minutes, just long enough to make sure he wouldn't end up crashing into the guard rail, but he fell instead into a deep sleep.

The blaring horn of a huge truck, as violent and as piercing as the trumpet of justice, jolted him awake. He'd slept much longer than he had meant to.

He gulped some coffee from a Thermos he'd put in the car, lit a cigarette and got back on the road, travelling as fast as he could. He made up pretty well for the lost time, but at the border at Ipsala, a customs guard made a long and thorough inspection of his suitcases and documents as he fumed helplessly, his eyes fixed on the huge electric clock in the window of the duty-free shop.

He finally took off at top speed for Gallipoli, but he missed the eleven o'clock ferry by a whisker. It was the only way he could have got to the pier at Canakkale before midnight.

He ran up and down the wharf, trying to find a private boat that would take him over. He was sweaty, panicky, overwhelmed with fatigue and sleeplessness, but the open-sea fishermen had already set off to cast their nets in the Marmara Sea and the tourist services had been closed for hours, given the season. He had no choice but to wait until the next ferry dropped its loading bridge on to the pier. When the ship docked on the Asian side at Canakkale it was ten minutes past midnight. He was the first to drive off as soon as the bridge touched the wharf. He parked in the first space he could find and jumped out, looking around in the glow of the lamplight. The cars coming off the ferry drove one by one towards their destinations, while the truck drivers sought a space big enough to stop, switch off their engines and pull the shades over their windscreens to curl up for a while in their bunks.

There was practically no one on foot. A boy walked up to him: 'Hotel? Hotel, sir? Three stars four stars five stars no problem good food no sheep good price ... nice girls if you like—'

'*Ahir, teshekur.*' He cut him short in Turkish to get rid of him. Just then, a dark corner of the square was lit up by the headlights of a crane manoeuvring at the wharf, and for a fraction of a second Michel saw him – a man standing next to the open door of a Toyota Land Cruiser, grey-green jacket, dark, unkempt beard, talking to an older man whose hand was on his shoulder. It was him! Claudio!

Michel opened his mouth to shout his name, but the younger man disappeared into the car and took off, tyres squealing. Michel took off at a run with every ounce of energy he had left, shouting: 'Claudio! Stop! Stop! Oh God, Claudio, stop!' He tripped and fell to his knees as the Toyota disappeared into the night. He stayed on his knees, pummelling his fists on his legs, drained of energy and will. A big semi-trailer coming from the opposite direction sounded its horn and flooded him with blinding light. He got up, moved to the side of the road and walked back, disheartened, towards the square. The customs building was still lit up and there seemed to be a bar inside. Michel went in.

As he was eating a sandwich with a glass of milk, he noticed that the car rental shop was still open. It might have been right there that Claudio had rented the Toyota he was driving.

He slipped a ten-dollar bill under the service window and said to the clerk: 'Excuse me, I need your help. A friend of mine just left here with a Toyota Land Cruiser that he rented from you. I absolutely have to reach him to give him a message from his family, but I lost sight of him and he must have driven off. Can you tell me where he's arranged to turn the car in?'

The clerk took up the bill with a slight movement of his

hand and it vanished into a little purse he held in his lap. He began to flip through the rental contracts he had on the table. 'What did you say your friend's name was?'

Michel was taken by surprise. He didn't know how to answer and tried to gain time: 'Well, my friend's Italian, he's . . .'

'Oh sure, the Italian we rented the Toyota to. Here he is: Dino Ferretti, resident of Tarquinia, Italy. That him?'

'Oh yes, of course, it's him. Thanks. Can you tell me where he'll be dropping off the car?'

'Here it is . . . Eski Kahta. Know where it is? No? It's near Adyaman. Pretty far, if you've got to reach him there.'

'I'll make it, even if it's all the way to hell,' said Michel. 'Teshekur ederim. Thanks a lot.'

He got into the blue Rover and set off for Smyrna. He thought he'd pull over when he found a rest stop so he could sleep for a few hours. Claudio had left alone, and, all told, he was flesh and blood too, wasn't he?

He drove twenty or thirty kilometres without finding any place to stop, until he noticed a turn-off on to a small road that led to the excavation site at Ilium. He drove down the road a little way until he reached the little car park in front of the entrance, where the Turks had set up a towering and quite horrible horse for the delight of tourists. It looked like a good place to stop; there was a custodian and a sentry box with a policeman on duty. Before he lay down on the back seat, he took a look around to see if anyone else had had the same idea. A black Mercedes was parked about one hundred metres further down. The driver was standing outside, leaning against the hood. His gaze seemed to scan the underlying plains, buried in fog and darkness, ears keened to the intermittent cries of the night birds of prey. The ember of his cigarette slightly illuminated his face now and then with its reflected light.

CAPTAIN KARAMANLIS FOUND an unmarked car waiting for him at the airport in Piges, along with the latest report on the Peugeot Norman and Mireille were driving: it had been spotted an hour earlier at Kavala. He'd most likely manage to intercept them before long on the state road leading to the border.

He was practically sure that Norman and Mireille were following Michel, and that this was his best lead.

He asked his colleagues to provide civilian documents for Vlassos and himself at the border in case they had to cross into Turkey, and they patiently lay in wait on the state road until they saw the Hertz Peugeot pass. It was nearly noon and Norman was at the wheel. The passenger seat was lowered completely; the girl must be sleeping.

At the border police station, Karamanlis pulled out an ID card made out for Sotiris Arnopoulos, businessman from Salonika, while Vlassos passed as Mr Konstantinos Tsulis, clerk.

They stayed on the car's tail without being noticed, and when it had passed Kesan and turned right down the road for Eceabat-Canakkale, Karamanlis decided to overtake the Peugeot while it stopped to get petrol. Vlassos drove straight to the port, where they took the first ferry for the Asian side. They'd wait there.

WHEN MIREILLE AND Norman got off the ship at four o'clock that afternoon, the sun was already low in the sky. They drove around town trying to spot Michel's Rover, unsuccessfully. The traffic policeman they contacted couldn't offer much help either.

'If you could at least tell me where your friend was headed, I could send word through my patrol cars; they'd stop him sooner or later and he'd get your message. But if you can't even give me the slightest indication . . . he may have gone south, or east, he may have decided to get back on the ferry. I'd have to search for him in all of Turkey, my friends, and Turkey is a very big country. You could try to have a message broadcast over the radio, but it may not work: most European tourists don't like oriental music, so they tune in to a foreign station or listen to their own tapes.'

He did take note of their request and promised that if the Rover was still in his area, he'd try to get their message through.

Karamanlis, who had been following their wanderings for a while, realized that they didn't have a clue as to where their friend was, and cursed himself as an idiot for having wasted time so stupidly.

'Yeah, they know less than we do, Captain,' said Vlassos. 'I say we go home; if these damned Turks find out we're a couple of plain-clothes Greek police, it won't be easy to save our asses.'

'Just drop everything after months of investigation? After we've been jerked around left and right?' Karamanlis would have done anything to get to the end of this loathsome business. 'Let's just give them a little more time,' he said, 'let's see what they're up to. You never know. It's clear that they're looking for him, and they may have more information than we do. The last word is not said . . .' He looked into Vlassos's little piggy eyes and put a hand on his shoulder. And then we've got you, my friend, he thought. Might just be that with a lure like you we'll get the fish to bite.

Norman and Mireille stopped at a restaurant and ordered something to eat. Norman was completely disheartened.

'I actually do have directions for a precise location,' Mireille burst out. 'I haven't said anything about it until now because you would have thought I was totally crazy. But we have no choice if we want to find Michel.'

'What do you mean by directions for a precise location?' asked Norman.

'Just what I said. The directions are precise. But I don't know how to decipher them. Listen carefully, because everything I'm about to tell you is absolutely true, even though the conclusions – I'll be the first to admit – sound like pure folly.'

'We'll see about that,' said Norman. 'Now tell me everything you know, without leaving out a single word.'

VLASSOS HAD BEEN ordered by Karamanlis not to lose sight of Norman and Mireille for any reason whatsoever as he left him alone and went to contact a friend of his in Istanbul. Vlassos had parked his car right across from the restaurant to keep an eye on the couple, while constantly checking his rear- and side-view mirrors as well. The night at Portolagos still burned in his memory, and waiting there like a sitting duck, practically unarmed, made his skin prickle.

In the window to the right of the entrance was a huge rotating meat kebab, dripping grease, and to the left was a sign with the restaurant's name. But right in between he could see the animated features of that beautiful girl. Some story she was telling, to judge from her gestures and facial expressions. The young man sitting across from her was completely absorbed in her tale, nothing moving but his eyes, in synch with the rapid movements of her hands. Every so often he'd write something on a piece of paper: numbers? signs? What the hell were they doing? He'd chop off his little finger to know what they were talking about. The young man seemed nervous, upset about something. He got up suddenly, rushed out to the car and got a map. Now what?

He ran back in and laid out the map on the table while the girl continued to talk, distressed. It looked like she had tears in her eyes.

Finally Karamanlis arrived, and he was even in a good mood. 'Got us some weapons. Finally. Felt like I was in my underwear.'

'Tell me about it, Captain. The idea that that bastard could use me for target practice without me being able to shoot back was giving me the creeps.'

'What's been happening here?'

Vlassos tried as best he could to explain what he'd seen through the window, including the steaming kebab, Norman's comings and goings, the map and all the rest.

It was dark enough for them to approach without being seen from inside, and Karamanlis inched up along the wall to the window: Mireille and Norman were using a small calculator and had the map spread out on the table. Karamanlis was considerably cheered: it looked like they were examining a route that might get them somewhere. The idea of wandering through Turkey flaunting Vlassos's ugly face in the vague hope that Claudio Setti would be watching hadn't exactly thrilled him.

THINGS WERE ACTUALLY not so simple. Norman felt close to the solution but understood that there was still something very important missing.

'Good God, Mireille, if you haven't dreamed all this up, maybe we can figure out where he's headed. As far as all the rest goes, it's ridiculous. Do you hear me? Absolutely impossible. If any part of it is true, even the tiniest part, it'll make a great story to tell one day. But let's not even think about it now.'

'Well then?'

'Look. See? What Michel calls the "axis of Harvatis" is a loxodromic line which joins Dodona with the oasis of Siwa in Egypt. Look, it passes through the source of the Acheron river, then Ephira, here, and then it goes right through Cape Tenaros . . .'

'The two doves who flew from Egyptian Thebes . . .'

'Mireille. Doves?'

'It's a story that Herodotus tells, explaining how the most ancient oracles of the world – Dodona and Siwa – were born. Two black doves took off simultaneously from Thebes of Egypt; one alighted on an oak in Dodona and the other on a palm tree at the oasis of Siwa. They were transformed into two priestesses who revealed oracles.'

'Oh. I see. Anyway, if you'd taken the original it would have all been much easier, but this formula seems clear enough: ET/TS = 0.37; it must refer to the ratio between the two distances: Ephira to Cape Tenaros, Tenaros to Siwa. Now, let's say that the Dodona-Siwa segment is the base; to identify this place called Kelkea or Bouneima, we need some sort of convergence. Let's say, for instance, a triangle with the axis of Harvatis at its base.'

'A triangle? That's possible, I hadn't thought of that.' Mireille bent over the map, and then over the sheet Norman was using to make his calculations.

'But there's still an unknown: alpha. How can we calculate the other angle?'

Norman lit a cigarette; his hands were trembling so badly he couldn't even hold the match up to the tip. 'One unknown. Dammit! Wait a minute – what if the triangle were isosceles?' He hit his forehead. 'That's it! How stupid, it has to be an isosceles triangle, so the two angles at the base are identical. All we have to do is calculate alpha.' He switched back on the little calculator. 'Let's multiply 180 times 0.37 . . . here it is: 66.6. If your Harvatis got it right, the point which Michel is headed towards is the vertex of an isosceles triangle with its base from Dodona to Siwa and a base angle of 66.6 degrees.'

'Norman.'

'What's wrong?'

'Six, six, six: isn't that an evil number, a curse? Isn't that the number of the apocalypse?'

'My God, Mireille, what does the apocalypse have to do with it? You're thinking of that American film The Omen with that little boy who's the antichrist with three sixcs tattooed on his forehead.'

'Exactly, the antichrist. The apocalypse.'

'Listen, Mireille, let's not get carried away; let's leave the apocalypse out of this, okay? As if we didn't have enough to worry about. Now we need a goniometer to measure the angles. Where the hell are we going to find a goniometer at this time of night . . .'

'It's not even eight o'clock. You'll find some place open; they're not strict about closing time here in Turkey.'

'I'll be right back,' said Norman, springing for the door. He flew out, but then stuck his head back in nearly immediately: 'Do you know how to say goniometer in Turkish?' Mireille shook her head. 'It doesn't matter, I'll use sign language. And you don't move from here. Don't you dare move.'

He jumped into the car.

'Shall we follow him, Captain?' asked Vlassos, putting his hand on the steering wheel.

'No, he's left the girl here, he'll be back.'

It took Norman more than half an hour to find a stationery shop, explain to the owner that he needed a goniometer which the store didn't stock, and go to the vegetable shop of the owner's friend whose son was a surveyor and would surely lend him a goniometer.

'Okay, let's see the map,' said Norman, sweaty and out of breath. He'd taken an aluminium section from the jack kit in his car and used it to draw in the base of the triangle. Then he placed the little clear plastic goniometer at the two angles of the base, measuring out 66.6 degrees. But when he tried to draw in the sides, he realized that the vertex of the triangle was far out of range of the mapped area.

'Damn,' complained Mireille. 'We need a map that includes Greece and the Middle East, or at least Greece and Turkey.'

'The bar down at the port!' exclaimed Norman. 'There's a Freytag & Berndt down at the port that covers the entire area. It's there for the truckers coming down from the Balkans. There's another one just like it at the Capitan Adreevo customs in Bulgaria. Let's go.'

Norman had remembered correctly: on the wall of the bar was a Freytag & Berndt with a scale of 1/800,000. Under the curious stares of the bar goers, Norman and Mireille traced out the axis of Harvatis on the wall map and joined up the two sides.

'My God,' said Mireille, backing up. 'My God, it's the Nemrut Dagi!'

23

THEY LEFT THE bar and got into the car.

'Nemrut Dagi . . .' said Norman, starting it up. 'What the hell is that?'

'You should know,' said Mireille. 'Didn't you study archaeology?'

'Yes I did, but it was just for two years, it was a long time ago, and what I studied was building techniques in the Roman Empire: streets and aqueducts. Then I left it. Archaeology made me think of Athens, of the friends I'd lost. I switched, found a new profession. Journalism – something different every day.'

'Nemrut Dagi is a solitary mountain of the eastern Tauern range which faces the Euphrates plain. It's completely barren and wind-beaten. Antiochos IV Epiphanes of Kommagene, a minor king allied with the Romans, had a monumental tomb built for himself in the first century AD at the very top. A pyramid of pebbles, sixty metres high, flanked by two terraces and guarded by fourteen colossal statues, each thirteen metres tall. In front . . . there's a sacrificial altar. From time immemorial, the mountain was said to be a magical place: an Islamic legend says that Abraham brought his son Isaac to be sacrificed there. The legendary Nemrod – the man who dared to defy God – went hunting there. There are even traces of Hittite civilization, magical astrological signs left by the Persians . . .'

'So this is the place called Kelkea or Bouneima?'

'I'm convinced of it. And I'm convinced that Michel is racing towards it . . . and that death awaits him there if we don't get there first.'

'Before who?'

'I don't know. I don't know. Before it happens. We don't have a moment to lose.'

'But how could Michel have figured out how to get to this place if you were alone when you broke into the basement of that house?'

'He does not know what the place is. He'll have been lured there somehow . . . I don't know how. Along with the others.'

'What do you mean the others?'

'He is . . . the ram.'

'Oh, Mireille!'

'Did you know that Michel was born at Siwa? That he's the son of an Italian soldier and a Bedouin woman? Michel was born on April the thirteenth, so that makes him an Aries, the sign of the ram. And Siwa is the site of Aries, the ram. He was brought up at an institute for orphans called Chateau Mouton, where the children were called "moutons" or lost sheep. He has been branded by that sign his whole life.'

'I don't believe in astrology or any of that other nonsense.'

'The other two are the bull and the boar.'

Norman shook his head: 'This is pure folly, you know that, don't you? I believe that there is a rational solution to everything, and I refuse to accept this madness. But I will follow you, Mireille. Because I want to find my friend Michel. And Claudio, who killed my father. I need to know whether I'll throw my arms around his neck or put a bullet through his forehead. Now you lie back and rest. I'm going to drive all night.'

Mireille lowered the seat back and closed her eyes while Norman sped off towards Smyrna. From there he would take the road that led inland through the high plain: Afyon . . . Konya . . . Kayseri . . . Malatia. Good God, it would be exhausting.

Norman reflected that if Michel were really headed towards the same place, he would have to take the same road; it was the only way to reach Nemrut Dagi. He hadn't lost hope of catching up with him – he'd have to sleep sooner or later, stop along the way. His car was much faster and more powerful than the Peugeot that Mireille had rented, and over such a long distance that could mean a lot. All at once, while Norman was thinking his own thoughts and calculating the times and distances of such a long journey, Mireille sat up.

'Beware the pyramid at the vertex of the great triangle . . .' she said.

'Mireille, are you dreaming?'

'No. I'm wide awake. A few days ago, at the Athens police station, I took a look at Captain Karamanlis's appointment book. A page was marked, and that phrase was written on the page.'

'So?'

'You don't get it? The pyramid at the vertex of the great triangle: it's the funeral mound at the peak of Nemrut Dagi, the vertex of the triangle that we calculated. So Karamanlis was warned against getting too close. My God, Karamanlis must be the boar . . . or the bull. But who was it that warned him? Who else knows about this?'

Norman had no idea how to answer. At the bottom of a hill, he downshifted and revved up the engine, pushing it as far as it would go with anger and frustration. He got to the top of the hill and raced down at full speed.

THE REAR LIGHTS grew fainter and fainter in the distance.

'They're driving like crazy,' said Karamanlis. 'Speed it up or we'll lose them.'

Vlassos accelerated: 'Don't worry, Captain, they won't get away. We're in better shape than they are; we slept all last night, while they were taking turns at the wheel of that junk heap.'

'Right,' agreed Karamanlis, 'but they're younger than we are.'

'You think they're headed to that place they marked on the map at the bar?'

'Yes. I do.'

'But why all that confusion, running here, running there, to scribble a few lines on a map hanging on a wall?'

Karamanlis seemed not to have heard his last question; he'd turned on the reading light and was going through his appointment book. By chance, he opened to the page dated 5 November where he'd written the words 'Beware the pyramid at the vertex of the great triangle', which immediately brought to mind the big triangle that Norman and Mireille had drawn on the map in that smoky bar at the port. Okay, so his destiny was waiting for him at some godforsaken place in the mountains of Anatolia. His day of reckoning? So it seemed, and he thought of the contorted face of the *kallikàntharos* on Mount Peristeri, that cruel, alien voice: 'What are you doing here Captain Karamanlis?'

A rush of adrenaline coursed through his veins and he pounded his fist on the open book.

'It's my own fucking business what I'm doing here!' he shouted.

Vlassos turned towards him, disconcerted: 'Hey, Captain, who are you yelling at? Are you sure you're feeling all right?'

Karamanlis closed the appointment book and leaned back as if he wanted to rest: 'Fine. Of course I'm fine, I've never felt better.'

Vlassos shut his mouth for a while, sneaking looks at his travel companion who was sitting with his arms crossed over his chest and his eyes half closed.

'Captain,' he said, 'what if there's more than one person waiting for us there? There's only two of us. What are we going to do? That one guy . . . you said he was so tough . . .'

'Afraid are you, Vlassos? No, you needn't be afraid. Don't you know I've got a lot of friends in this country? Back during the war in Cyprus, when there was the arms embargo against Turkey, I let a couple of shipments of spare parts get through . . . they remember their friends around here.'

'You made military shipments to the Turks? Captain . . .'

'Idiot, what do you know about international strategies? What's important is that at Adyaman we'll find a little group of Kurds armed to the teeth. They're going to help us – let's say – hunt down some drug traffickers, loaded with dope and with dollars. The traffickers are ours – dead, of course – the money is theirs. Not bad, huh? They thought they'd be luring us off into a strange land where we'd have no one to count on, but they were wrong, weren't they? A gentleman always has friends, remember that. Now let me sleep for a while. Wake me up when you can't keep your eyes open any more. Until then, race like the wind, Vlassos.'

Eski Kahta, eastern Anatolia, 16 November, 5 p.m.

Michel got out of the car and found himself leaning up against the wall of a nearby house, weak from fatigue. Over the last three days he hadn't slept more than a few hours, but he was tormented by the idea of not getting to Claudio in time. So much time had been wasted; he'd had to have the car repaired when it could no longer stand up to his gruelling demands, and he'd even turned down the wrong road a couple of times, exhausted as he was.

The cold night air whipped a bit of vitality into him, until he felt steady enough on his feet to go towards the agency which rented jeeps during the summer to tourists for a jaunt into the mountains. The office was closed, but a little boy assured him that it was not only in Smyrna, in Istanbul, in Adana that there were important tourist agencies. In fact, the local rent-a-car agent turned out to be easily located: the man, in his sixties, worked as a leather tanner in the off-season, and he greeted Michel in the midst of a flock of shorn sheep. He said that the Italian had indeed passed through, but that he hadn't left the car; he'd wanted to keep it for another twenty-four hours.

'Where was he going?' asked Michel. 'Did he say?'

The man shook his head: 'He's crazy, that one. He took the road that goes up the mountain. I told him about the bad weather that's been predicted, but he didn't even answer. Well, all the cars are fully insured, so if he's happy, I've got no problem with it.'

'What could he have gone to do on the mountain?'

The man widened his arms: 'To see the pyramid, why else? I've never seen so many people at this time of year, that's for sure.'

'Has someone else been by?'

'Two men, a couple of hours ago.'

'Did you see them?'

'One about sixty with a grey moustache and balding head, the other a little younger, about fifty, big man, well built. Both of them all tooled up.'

'Thanks,' said Michel. 'Listen, how far do you think I can get with that?' he asked, pointing to the dusty blue Rover.

'Almost up to the peak unless it starts to rain. Or worse, snow. I wouldn't want to be in your shoes if that happened.'

'Thanks for warning me,' said Michel.

He found a store open that sold everything from olive oil to climbing boots, and bought a pair of heavy shoes, a blanket and a sheepskin jacket. He got some bread and a bottle of water too, returned to the car, and sped in a cloud of dust through the little town of low houses surrounding a minaret. The mountain top towered before him now, silhouetted against the reddened sky.

Herds of sheep traversed the fields all around, being led towards winter pastures by their shepherds dressed in full-length fur capes and flanked by ferocious Cappadocian mastiffs with iron-spiked collars and ears clipped to the root. What could Claudio be doing on that mountain? For a moment he thought he'd made a crazy mistake, following a spectre he'd seen for a few seconds in a dusty truck-packed car park through the whole of Anatolia. But Claudio's image in his memory was solid and very real, turning towards him for an instance in the beam of full headlights, his eyes filled with pain just like that night in the courtyard of the *astynomia* in Athens. Had he recognized Michel? Was that why he had fled so quickly? Or was he too racing towards an appointment he couldn't miss?

He went as far as he could by car, then abandoned it at the

side of the road, shouldered his backpack with the blanket, bread and cigarettes and began the climb. The mountain peak got darker and darker, step by step, the black pinnacle standing out against the night sky. The tall grass, desiccated by the long dry season, bowed under sudden gusts of icy wind.

The fatigue brought on by climbing suddenly overwhelmed him, his legs buckled and he fell to his knees. He looked around in a panic: if the storm surprised him in this condition he'd surely die. There was a little cave just ahead, sheltered from the wind. He hobbled towards it. Some shepherd must have used it; there was some hay in the corner and a little straw. He curled up with the blanket around him and ate some bread from his pack, forcing down a few sips of water. He felt a little better but decided to wait until dawn to continue his climb towards the peak. Who would be crazy enough to venture out in such solitude? He pulled his jacket tighter around him and lit a cigarette. That small glow in such a deserted land shone like a beacon over a wide sea.

'CAPTAIN, CAPTAIN, DID you see that?'

Karamanlis was staring at the black pinnacle looming up at less than a kilometre's distance: the enormous mausoleum of Commagene. He turned towards Vlassos, annoyed: 'See what?'

'A light. Down there, look, now . . . see it?'

'So? A shepherd lighting up a stinking cigar. Calm down and get some rest. As soon as it's light, we'll go and see if there's anyone up there. And if so, what their intentions are. Our friends will be along soon; they're used to travelling in the dark, like cats.'

Vlassos tucked his gun close, checking that it was loaded, and stretched out in the sleeping bag. 'Well, if anyone gets close, shepherd or no shepherd, I'll do him a favour. To stay on the safe side. I don't like this place.'

The hiss of the wind died down and the distant grumbling of thunder quieted as well. But in the growing silence, an unnatural sound rained down from the summit. A flute: soft and sweet, achingly beautiful. It slipped down the rocky gorges, seeped into the dry grass, licked the bare branches of the trees.

Vlassos sat up: 'What the hell is that?'

Karamanlis strained to hear as well, not understanding at first, but as the music became louder and clearer he saw, as in a dream, that underground corridor in the *astynomia* ten years earlier, heard that desolate, proud song that had penetrated the massive walls of the cell. 'I know what it is,' he said. 'I've heard this melody before. It's a challenge: he wants us to know that he's here and he's waiting for us.'

'Christ, I'm going to go up there and . . .'

'Don't move yet. Let him play. We'll make him dance, and we'll set the tune when the rest of the orchestra gets here.'

THE REST OF the orchestra were making their way up on foot, up the western face of the mountain. They had instructions to circle the entire area around the peak, and to cut off all access roads.

There were five of them, armed with Kalashnikovs, dressed in dark clothing, with the puffed trousers and wide waistbands of the southern Kurds. They must have come from around Jezireh, close to the Iraqi border. They marched with the slow, untiring step of highlanders towards the place where they were to meet the two foreigners before dawn. On the other side of a rocky outcrop, the head of the party raised his hand to stop the others and pointed to something a few dozen metres in front of him.

It looked like a camp, but there was only a single man, sitting alone in front of the fire. The leader approached and looked more closely at him: his head was covered by a hood, but his hair and beard were black, his skin dark and his eyes blue, hard and penetrating. He was dressed like the peasants of the high plains and had a strange object in front of him, leaning against his knee.

'Isn't it too late in the season, farmer,' asked the Kurd, 'to be using that?' He turned towards the mountain. 'The wind is blowing hard, but I don't see any threshed grain to be aired with your winnow here.'

The man's eyes blazed: 'You're right, *peshmerga*. I'm here for another reason. Turn back with your men, turn back and go in peace. This is a bad night . . .' He raised his eyes, which glittered with the reflection of the flame. 'I'm not here to scatter the chaff from the grain with what you have taken for a winnowing fan. I'm here to scatter souls to the wind, if the gods so wish . . .' He lowered his head.

'Sorry, dad,' replied the Kurdish warrior. 'But we're expecting a good harvest on this mountain, and you'll have to let us by.' He put his hand on his gun.

MICHEL, CURLED UP in a shelter he'd found higher up on the mountain, heard a gunshot echo in the valley, then another and yet another, and then a furious volleying of shots, how many he couldn't say. The echoes multiplied wildly amidst the ravines and cliffs on the barren slopes of Nemrut Dagi.

Sergeant Vlassos sprang awake in his sleeping bag and grabbed his rifle: 'Christ! What the hell kind of music is that?'

Karamanlis didn't know what to think. 'Don't move. The mountain is crawling with smugglers; they might have met up with some army unit. Or it's a gunfight among shepherds robbing each other's sheep. Listen . . . See, it's all over.' The mountain had fallen back into a deep silence. 'This is a strange place, all right. Let's try to get some sleep now. Tomorrow we'll take care of this business and then we'll never think of it again. Saturday we'll be in the Plaka eating a nice bowl of bean soup with some new retsina.'

'Yeah,' said Vlassos, 'You're right. I hadn't thought about that. The retsina should be ready to drink by now.'

NORMAN AND MIREILLE got to Eski Kahta a little after midnight in a new car, a Ford Blazer which they'd traded for the Peugeot at a rental agency in Kayseri. It had started to rain and the dusty roads of Eski Kahta had turned into slimy streams. The loud-speakers on top of the minaret invited the faithful to the last prayer of the day, and the chanting of the muezzin spread like a wail in the downpour.

Norman and Mireille decided that they should both sleep for at least an hour, and set the alarm. When his electronic watch started to beep, Norman sat up, raised the seat to an upright position and started up the car, letting Mireille sleep a little longer. He looked over at her: even so worn out, with black circles under her eyes and an oversized sweater, she was incredibly beautiful.

The Ford Blazer started down the dirt road that crawled up the mountain, skidding at every curve on a thick layer of mud. Norman turned on the radio and tuned into the station of the US base at Diarbakir. Snow was forecast that night over three thousand feet.

CAPTAIN KARAMANLIS WOKE up stiff with cold. The wind was blowing hard and frozen sleet was falling like tiny balls of hail, piercing his hands and face. He looked at his watch: it was five o'clock and still dark, but the white sleet and the cloudy sky emanated a light glow, as if dawn – actually nowhere to be seen – were approaching. He glanced up towards the mountain peak and saw a quivering light. Yeah, there was something moving up there. A halo of flame became increasingly evident, casting a reddish glow on the colossal stone statues which sat motionless at the foot of the enormous mausoleum, looking like the spirits of darkness. There was a fire in the clearing, and again he could hear that flute, barely perceptible, soft and sorrowful as a sigh, then hard and cutting as the screech of an attacking hawk.

He woke Vlassos, who rubbed his eyes and pulled up his jacket collar: 'Let's get moving. He's up there waiting for us. Let's get this over with.'

'But Captain, weren't we supposed to get help?'

Karamanlis lowered his head. 'They should have been here hours ago. Men who had no fear of the mountain or of the

snow. I'm afraid those shots we heard . . .' Vlassos's eyes opened
wide in an expression of pathetic bewilderment. 'But then . . .
Captain . . . maybe it's better to turn back . . . I don't know if . . .'

'Shitting in your pants, are you? Fine, go to the devil, go
get fucked, go wherever you want to go. I'll go up alone, but get
the hell out of here at least, you sorry excuse for a man!'

Vlassos changed his expression: 'Hey, Captain, that's enough.
I'm not shitting in my pants. I'm better with one ball than you
and that bastard up there with both. I'll show you who's a sorry
excuse for a man.' He took the machine gun and jacked up the
magazine with the palm of his hand, heading up towards the top
of the mountain.

'Wait,' said Karamanlis. 'There are two of us, we can split
up. The pyramid up there is flanked by two terraces – one on
the east and one on the west. I'll go up the back, on the western
side, and it will take me a little longer. You go up this way. You
have an infrared sight on that piece you're carrying. You can see
that demon even if he's hiding. Don't give him time to take a
breath, lay him out as soon as you see him: he's too dangerous.
I'll be coming up the other side, so be careful not to shoot me.
Good luck.'

'You too, Captain. We'll drink up tonight and then get out of
this damned country with the first ship, the first plane, whatever.'
He moved off, lying low, dashing between the rocky outcrops
and dry tree trunks that covered the white mountain.

Fifteen minutes of silent advance brought Vlassos to the huge
landing on which the immense complex stood. In front of him
rose the colossal heads of the statues, wide-eyed as if surprised
by a monstrous axe which had chopped them off their trunks.
Behind them, nearly at the centre of the landing, crackled a fire
made of branches and twigs.

He scoured the disturbing space in front of him until his face
suddenly lit up: there he was, the bastard! Half hidden behind a
stone block, wearing the same damn grey-green jacket with an
American army emblem that he'd had on the last time he'd seen
him in the underground prison of the police station. He was

peering left and right to see around the post, checking his surroundings. Vlassos pointed his gun, and his infrared sight confirmed the body's natural heat. Not for long. He shot five times in rapid succession and saw the man crumble to the ground.

He ran forward shouting: 'Captain, I got him! I killed him dead, Captain!' But as soon as he reached his objective his heart stopped still: what he'd shot was a dummy lashed on to a stick frame over a handful of embers. The rising heat had permeated it and fooled the infrared sight on his M-16.

A voice he'd never forgotten sounded behind him: 'Here I am, *Chiros!*' And before he could turn round an arrow pierced his back between his shoulder blades and came out of the front of his chest. Vlassos spun around with enough strength still in him to want to empty out the rest of the magazine, but his executioner had a gun of his own and turned his hand to pulp with a series of shots.

Vlassos collapsed into his own blood, which flowed copiously on to the great altar, and before his eyes glazed over he recognized the young man who so many years before had suffered – at his own hand – the cruellest of tortures in an underground chamber of the police station in Athens. With a last burst of energy he raised his arm in an obscene gesture muttering: 'I fucked . . .' But the words never left his mouth. The final bullet pierced his throat, cutting the phrase in half, and Vassilios Vlassos, known as *O Chiros*, reclined his head, breathing his last into the gelid mountain wind.

The sound of the shots had reached Michel, who shook himself awake and left his shelter. They stopped Norman cold as well. He'd switched off the engine, unsure what he was hearing, but the next shots were as clear as could be, carried on the north wind blowing stronger and stronger in their direction. Mireille got out and could see the flash of gunfire near the top of the mountain. 'Oh my God, Michel!' she started to yell. 'Michel, turn back, it's me, turn back!' But Michel could not hear her because her shouts were carried away on the wind and because he was already crawling up the mountain in the direction of the shooting and the fire.

Captain Karamanlis had heard the first volley of shots just as he was arriving at the edge of the western platform. He'd heard Vlassos's voice calling him, but couldn't make out what he was saying as his feet noisily scrambled over the pebbles.

He had tried at first to climb up the pyramid, but the loose pebbles slid beneath him and he rolled back down to the base of the monument. He had decided to advance along the southern side of the mound, slipping between the huge slabs that once flanked the processional road.

He finally reached the side of the eastern landing, hammered by the wind and sleet, from where he could see the dying light of the fire. He crept alongside an open-jawed stone lion guarding the tomb of King Antioch. As it dawned on him that he was looking at Vlassos's rigid corpse, already covered by a veil of ice, a voice rang out from behind the statue, darker than the night and colder than the wind, deep and vibrant, as if it were coming from a throat of bronze.

'What are you doing here, Captain Karamanlis?'

And then the flash of eyes as blue as ice on a winter's morning, the glint of a wolf's smile. And he suddenly heard the warning of the *kallikàntharos* echoing in his head: *It is he who administers death.*

He jumped out, firing and shouting like a madman: 'You damned impostor, you've dragged me all the way here, but you'll come to hell with me!' But the man had disappeared just as quickly as he had appeared, and as he spun around, bewildered, he heard his name raining from above: 'Karamanlis!'

He turned and pointed his pistol to the sky and saw Claudio Setti standing on the knees of the headless statue of Zeus Dolichenus, already aiming at him. He felt paralysed and impotent, at the mercy of an implacable enemy. He shouted to save his life: 'No! Wait! Heleni is alive and I know where she is!' He had taken the photograph from his pocket and was waving it upwards: 'Look! Heleni is alive!' But the wind carried away his words and Claudio didn't hear him. He raised his gun and fired: one shot hit Karamanlis at the centre of his collarbone, and another flung him, lifeless, between the paws of the stone lion.

Claudio leapt to the ground and looked at his defeated enemies. He turned towards the stone lion: 'Vlassos and Karamanlis are dead, Commander!' he shouted.

At that moment Michel appeared on the landing: he was soaking wet, his clothes torn, his hands dirty and bloody.

'Your work is not yet over!' shouted the voice behind him. 'It is he who betrayed you! Give him his due and strike him down!'

Pale, Claudio raised his weapon against Michel, who stood absolutely still, his hands at his sides. 'I was deceived, Claudio. For the love of God, listen to me,' he shouted. 'Just listen to me for a moment and then kill me, if you want.' His face was lined with tears. 'Claudio, for the love of God, I'm Michel, I'm your friend.'

'His cowardice caused Heleni to be tortured and raped. He deserves to die!' thundered the voice that seemed to come from the lion's mouth.

Claudio raised the pistol again to aim, but just then Norman and Mireille appeared at the edge of the landing. Mireille cried out: 'No! Claudio, no! You are not serving justice! You are making a human sacrifice! You have been chosen to immolate the bull, the boar and the ram! Look behind you, at the top of the pyramid, look! And spare your friend, Claudio. Spare him, for the love of God!'

Norman had turned to stone and could neither move nor say a word.

'It is he who betrayed you. He came up here with Karamanlis!' The voice seemed to come from above, from the very top of the mound. Claudio pressed the trigger, but the hammer just clicked. The magazine was empty. He mechanically pulled the bow off his shoulder, nocked an arrow and aimed at Michel's chest, while Mireille shouted desperately, her eyes filled with tears: 'Look behind you, at the top of the hill!'

Michel came to. 'You've already killed me,' he said, staring deeply at Claudio. 'Now nothing matters any more. But I didn't come up here with your enemies. I've been searching for you for all this time to humble myself before you, to ask you to forgive me for my weakness, for not having given my life for Heleni's.'

The bow trembled in Claudio's hands, and he twisted his head back. In the swirling sleet he saw something implanted in the top of the mound: a boat's oar! He shouted: 'Commander!'

The voice was close to him now: 'I'm here, son.'

'Commander, must I kill an unarmed man asking for my forgiveness?'

He felt him at his side now: a powerful, dark presence. He turned to his right, and saw two glistening blue eyes veiled with tears: 'You must do what your heart tells you. There's no other way for humans . . . Farewell, my son.'

Claudio listened to his slow footsteps; he felt his strength dissipating into the distance. He dropped the bow; the quiver and arrows rolled away on the stone. 'Commander!' he shouted. 'I've always done what you asked of me. But this I couldn't do. I could not do it!'

He collapsed to his knees, and the wind died down as dawn rose over the boundless Mesopotamian plain, illuminating the top of the mountain with its pale light. He remained there as his friends hesitantly made their way towards him. They looked silently into each other's eyes, overwhelmed with emotion, incapable of speaking or making the smallest movement. Drenched by the sleet, they looked like statues of ice. In the end, seeing that Claudio had not reacted nor said a word, they left, one after another, returning to the valley.

Claudio remained alone on the great landing with the dead bodies of his enemies. He stood, picked up the bow and quiver and started down the western side. As he walked along the processional pathway, he remembered that Karamanlis had been waving something at him, yelling something before he died. He turned back and saw that his hand was still gripping a photograph. There was a date on the back, and the name of a place. Claudio looked at the girl's beautiful face, her raven hair, her moist red lips, and put the photograph in his inside jacket pocket. He then continued down his road.

24

Ephira, 17 November, 10 p.m.

ARI WAS SITTING at his work table after having cleared his dinner and washed the dishes. He was sorting out the ticket-office receipts for the excavation site and counting up the modest proceeds. He raised his glance to the window every now and then, listening to the sounds on the road and the distant rush of the river.

The telephone suddenly began ringing. Three times and it fell still. Then it rang again: six times, six times, six times. Then silence.

The old man was seized by a painful tremor. He curled forward and remained still for a long, long time. He finally got up, dried his eyes, noisily blew his nose and walked resolutely towards the Necromantion. He used a shovel to clear off a stone slab carved with the figure of a serpent, lifted it and descended into the underground chamber which so many years ago had accommodated the faltering step of Professor Harvatis. He switched on a torch and lit up a wooden chest in a corner of the chamber. He opened it and took out a superb mask of the purest gold: the solemn and majestic face of a dozing king. He brought it to the centre of the room and buried it, covering it with fine sand.

'The time has not yet come, Commander, for you to end your long journey,' he said in a low voice, his eyes moist. 'There is still no place in this world for a long, serene old age, there are no happy peoples over which you may reign ... Not yet. Another time, another year ... Who knows ...'

He returned to his apartment in the guest house, and as he walked up the stairs he thought he heard, behind him, the dull thud of a stone door closing. He put his things in order, closed the account books, placed them neatly in a drawer, turned off the light and left.

Athens, Milos's Bar, 18 November, 8 p.m.

'I'm telling you that behind those shutters is the proof of everything that I've told you. Norman, you just try to give me a logical explanation for what we saw and experienced on that mountain!' Mireille sprang up from the bar table and turned away from Norman and Michel to hide her disappointment.

'Mireille,' said Norman, 'we simply don't have enough evidence. An investigation would have to be made ...'

Mireille pointed at the newspaper page which reported the deaths of Vlassos and Karamanlis. 'Just look at this. Vlassos was born at Kalendzi, a few miles from Dodona, on March the fifteenth, 1938, so he's a Pisces; that is the sign of the boar, according to the ancient zodiac, the same sign that distinguishes the oracle of Dodona. Karamanlis was born in Gura near Mount Cillene, identified with the sign of the bull. And his battle name was *O Tàvros*, the bull. And all of this was explained in Harvatis's letter written ten years ago. I have the combination of the safe – do I have to be any clearer? I can take you in there, open the safe and show you that it's all true. Look.' She took a slip of paper from her wallet and laid it on the table: the numbers of the combination.

Michel picked it up and looked at it without speaking. Then he took out a notebook and copied down the numbers one after another, drawing symbols next to them.

'Oh my God, look!' said Mireille suddenly. Norman and Michel joined her at the window: a big moving company truck was parking in front of 17 Dionysìou Street. Two men got out, opened the shutter with a key and went in, closing it behind them.

'I'm not leaving here until I see what happens,' said Mireille. 'You two can do as you like.'

They waited together. Every so often, Michel said, as if talking to himself: 'Where could Claudio be? Will we ever see him again?'

'Of course we'll see him,' Norman finally said. 'In Italy, in France, maybe even here in Athens. He's hiding somewhere now, waiting for his wounds to heal. And ours. But he'll be back . . . I'm sure of it.'

'You know something?' said Michel. 'As I was approaching the eastern landing at Nemrut Dagi I thought I heard Karamanlis yelling: "Stop! Stop! Heleni isn't dead, Heleni's alive!" How could that be?'

Norman shook his head. 'It's hard for me to believe, but nothing seems impossible any more. One thing is certain, in any case: if Heleni is alive, or if some part of her has survived, Claudio will find her. Wherever she is.'

An hour later, the shutter at number 17 was opened again and the two men began to load the truck with a number of crates of varying sizes. When it was clear that they were about to close the shutter again and leave, Mireille ran out, followed by Norman and Michel.

'Excuse me, sorry to bother you,' she said. 'We're interested in renting this place. Can you tell us if the current lease is up?'

'I'm sorry, miss,' said the younger of the two, 'I know nothing about that at all. We were just told to move this stuff out.'

'Well, the former leaseholder could surely give us some information. Can you tell us where you're taking his things?'

'To the port of Piraeus, miss. We're loading it on to a yacht that's setting sail tonight.'

'Thanks anyway,' said Mireille.

The two men got into the truck and started to drive off.

Michel, who hadn't said a word until then, suddenly started running after the movers: 'Wait! Just a minute!'

The driver saw him running in his rear-view mirror and stopped. 'What is it, sir?' he asked.

'Listen, I . . . well, if you see the . . . the owner of these things that you're taking away, tell him that I . . . I . . .' He was biting his lower lip, incapable of finding the words. 'That's okay, it doesn't matter,' he finally said with a trembling voice. 'It doesn't matter . . .'

The truck started up again and soon disappeared at the end of Dionysìou Street. The three friends went back into Milos's Bar.

'Well,' said Norman. 'Now we'll never be able to find proof, Mireille. The truth is, all we'll ever know is what we've seen: too much on the one hand, too little on the other. A man decides to punish his enemies. To do so, he exploits another man's desire for revenge, using the rituals of ancient legend and myth to motivate or manipulate him. Ingenious, strange, even unique, but not incomprehensible: there's no limit to human imagination.'

'But there was no reason for him to want Michel to die,' protested Mireille. 'Except for the oracle inscribed on the vase of Tiresias.'

'The truth is that we know nothing about him and we'll never figure out his true motives,' concluded Norman.

'That's not true,' said Michel. 'We know his name. It's written in the combination for the safe.'

'Oh yeah?' asked Norman, as Mireille looked at him disconcerted.

'Look.' Michel showed them the notebook page where he had written the safe combination. 'In ancient Greek, numbers were written using the letters of the alphabet: alpha is one, beta is two, and so on. Look.'

Norman took the notebook from his friend's hand and looked at the transcription of the numbers in letters:

15   20   19   9   18
o   y   t   i   s

'Oytis,' he murmured, shaking his head. 'Nobody. His name is "nobody", then. What a strange coincidence.'

They paid their bill. The waiter was new; the old waiter had quit and didn't work there any more. They walked off in the rainy night, in silence. It was Mireille who spoke first.

'Michel, I read the notes I found on your desk in your study at Grenoble before I left.'

'You've told me that.'

'There's something that you wrote in the margin of one of the pages that just came to my mind. It said something like: "In the entire Mediterranean, wherever legend conserves the memory of the death of a Homeric hero, even a minor one, a cult has sprung up in his honour." Why has there never been a cult which honours Odysseus in Ithaca, in his own homeland?'

Michel seemed not to have heard the question. All at once he stopped, with a strange smile.

'Why? Because Odysseus has never died,' he replied. And he walked on, in silence.

AUTHOR'S NOTES

This story is a mixture – like the others I have written – of historical fact and reality and of imagination. Since, in this case, some of the 'real' elements are important parts of the story, both in the present and in the past, there are a few points I'd like to mention specifically.

The pages regarding the Athens Polytechnic Battle were scrupulously reconstructed on the basis of actual documents, personal experiences and eyewitness reports by people whom I consider trustworthy, but they can under no circumstances be considered a historical account, because emotions played a far larger role than facts. The characters of the story, and the accompanying events, are completely imaginary.

As far as references to antiquity are concerned, all of the historical sources quoted from are authentic (including the Oracles of the Dead),* as are the Homeric scholia regarding the mysterious and never identified sites of 'Kelkea' and 'Bouneima'. The identification of the Nemrut Dagi with 'Bouneima' is not a scientific certainty. I was merely intrigued by the fact that years ago, as I was doing research on another topic, I learned from local inhabitants that there was a place on the mountain whose name in Turkish meant 'pasture of the oxen', much like Bouneima, if we accept the etymological interpretation *bous* (oxen) plus *némo* (to put to pasture) as an alternative to (or alongside) the more commonly accepted *bounòs* (mountain). If we accept this identification as a

* A slight change was made in the original 'I'm naked, I'm cold' (rendered as 'She's naked. She's cold' in English) in order to maintain the feminine meaning expressed by the adjectives in the ancient Greek.

fictional hypothesis, the mathematical relationship between the segments of the 'axis of Harvatis' (inspired by Jean Richer's studies on astrological archaeology in his 1983 *Géographie Sacrée du Monde Grec*) is authentic, yet purely coincidental, as is the devil's number 66.6, which emerged through pure – although quite curious – chance.

As far as the epilogue to Odysseus's adventures is concerned, many hypotheses have emerged throughout the ages. According to the *Telegonia* – a poem written by Eugammon of Cyrene in the sixth century BC – Telegonus, son of Odysseus and the enchantress Circe, sailing in search of his father, actually kills him in a duel, without realizing it is him. Eugammon thus fulfils the prophecy of Tiresias: 'Death [will come to you] from the sea', although the poet is most likely unaware of the part which speaks of the hero's journey inland. Telegonus later marries Penelope, and Telemachus, Circe, on the Isle of the Blessed.

This version of the story does not seem as old as the *Odyssey*, but is probably crafted by Eugammon on the basis of Tiresias's prophecy as expressed in the eleventh book of the *Odyssey*. Much more ancient – and perhaps directly connected to the *Odyssey* – was the lost poem called Thesprotis, from which the place names 'Bouneima' and 'Kelkea' are perhaps the only existing fragments.

A scholium of Lykophron (Scheer, II, p. 253, l. 21), a Hellenistic poet, reports (perhaps on the basis of Theopompus, frgm. 354 Jacoby) two different hypotheses regarding the death of Odysseus. The first has the hero dying at Gortynia in Etruria and buried at Perge (Pyrgi), while according to the other tradition, Odysseus died in a city of Epirus called Eurytana (of which no trace remains). In reality, the hero's end is still shrouded in mystery.

As far as the topography of the places is concerned, it is largely accurate. I've taken some liberty in describing the caves of Dirou and their immediate surroundings. Portolagos is nowadays a town like any other; my description refers to the dank atmosphere of an overnight stay of mine under the stars, quite a few years ago, when the place was semi-deserted.

Icarus is inspired by the Hewlett-Packard program Ibicus, just in the making when this book was first written.

Dionysìou Street doesn't exist. Not under that name, anyway.

Translations of the passages from the *Odyssey*:

Robert Fitzgerald, Book Nine, lines 366–7, and Book Eleven, lines 14–20, 23–8, 122–41, Anchor Books, Doubleday & Company Inc., 1963;

Robert Fagles, Book Eleven, lines 471–3, Penguin Books, 1996.

OTHER PAN BOOKS
AVAILABLE FROM PAN MACMILLAN

VALERIO MASSIMO MANFREDI

ALEXANDER: CHILD OF A DREAM	0 330 39170 4	£7.99
ALEXANDER: THE SANDS OF AMMON	0 330 39171 2	£7.99
ALEXANDER: THE ENDS OF THE EARTH	0 330 39172 0	£7.99
SPARTAN	0 330 49102 4	£7.99
THE LAST LEGION	0 330 48975 5	£7.99
THE TALISMAN OF TROY	0 330 42653 2	£6.99

All Pan Macmillan titles can be ordered from our website, www.panmacmillan.com, or from your local bookshop and are also available by post from:

Bookpost, PO Box 29, Douglas, Isle of Man IM99 1BQ
Credit cards accepted. For details:
Telephone: +44 (0)1624 677237
Fax: +44 (0)1624 670923
E-mail: bookshop@enterprise.net
www.bookpost.co.uk

Free postage and packing in the United Kingdom

Prices shown above were correct at the time of going to press.
Pan Macmillan reserve the right to show new retail prices on covers
which may differ from those previously advertised in the text
or elsewhere.